THE *Cry* OF A *Broken* WOMAN

OSMOND CONSTANCE

PALMETTO
PUBLISHING

Charleston, SC
www.PalmettoPublishing.com

The Cry of a Broken Woman

First Edition

Hardcover ISBN: 979-8-8229-0574-0

Paperback ISBN: 979-8-8229-0583-2

eBook ISBN: 979-8-8229-0584-9

THE CRY OF A BROKEN WOMAN

Thank you, Deborah and Britney, for your support, also to my friend Beverly, thank you for the great help you provided.

Prologue

WE'RE ALL BROKEN IN one way or another.

Follow Cindy on her imperfect and human real-life journey, a journey of struggles and hardship.

Just like ours, Cindy's personal agenda will always pale in comparison to Gods plan for our life.

Cindy finally learned that Jesus' mercy and goodness follow us all the days of our lives and He doesn't condemn us when we choose to go our own way.

He waits patiently for us – He always has our back.

It takes courage to follow Jesus.

Chapter ONE

JASON AND KAREN WERE lovers from the eleventh grade; they broke up and made up on numerous, occasions.

After high school they moved to different states to attend college and upon graduation, they both moved back to Texas.

They became heavily involved again, and moved in together, and after three years of living together, they decided to get married.

The couple had three children within ten years of their marriage, two boys and one girl.

The relationship was good at the beginning, but as the years went by, the relationship soured, and there were many unpleasant situations.

There were lots of arguments and fighting, which eventually led to them getting divorced.

Jason left Karen with the three children, David was just beyond 8 years, while his brother Joshua was seven, and the only girl, Cindy was five.

They were still young and did not understand what was going on, except that their dad had left them, and was not coming back to live with them.

Jason visited his children quite regularly after his divorce from Karen, but as time went by, his visits became less and less, then eventually stopped altogether.

Chapter TWO

GROWING UP FOR CINDY was exceedingly difficult. The hardship started at an early age especially after her dad vanished from her life so early.

Cindy's mom was so angry at her ex-husband for walking away from her and the kids, that she harbored a great deal of hatred towards him.

Sometimes she channeled that hatred towards the children, especially Cindy, because she looked so much like him, and constantly reminded her of him.

Being a single parent was exceedingly difficult for Karen; she struggled to make life enjoyable for her and the children.

After a couple of years of struggling as a single lady, Karen made up her mind to venture out in the dating world to see what would come out of it.

Despite her need to have someone to accompany her through life's journey, she decided to be careful, and to be very meticulous.

She dated a few guys, but they did not meet her requirements.

But on that day at the grocery store, everything changed.

She went to pick up a few items that were needed for the week and while maneuvering her shopping cart through the aisles, (not paying attention to where she was going because she was looking at the items on the shelf) she ran right into this guy who was about to put his box of eggs into his basket which he was carrying. The eggs splattered on the floor, and instantly everyone turned around to the direction of the incident.

Embarrassed, she went up to him and said, "hi, I am so sorry, I should have been more careful, I am truly sorry."

While talking, she stooped down with a gesture to help, but the guy said to her, "it is okay, I will get the attention of an employee to come and clean it up", and then he said, "by the way, my name is Donald, and what is your name?"

"Oh, I am Karen, sorry we had to meet this way."

The two exchanged phone numbers and spoke for a while and promised to stay in touch.

Donald was in the same situation as Karen. He was divorced and was looking for someone to share his life with.

They called each other often, and not too long after they started dating which led them to being closer and eventually to a stable relationship.

After a year from their first meeting, Donald and Karen got married and joined their families into one big family.

Donald had a son and a daughter from his previous marriage, and he had custody of the children, and together with Karen and her children, they became a family of seven.

Lots of adjustments had to be made, especially for the children.

Cindy was not thrilled to have Shawn joining the rest of her brothers because she knew that her level of torment would go up a notch, plus she did not want to share her brothers with anyone else.

Cindy was content in not having a sister, and then, here comes Kellie.

Cindy was very bitter, she had so much on her little mind. She loved her dad, and when he and her mom divorced, it affected her very deeply.

She loved and hated her dad all at once. She loved him because he was the best person in the world yet she disliked him because he walked out of her life.

She remembered the few years he lived with them and the fun she had with him and now that was gone. She did not know all the circumstances, neither did she understand what caused him to abandon her.

Cindy developed a resentment towards her father and because of him, she disliked a father figure, so Donald's relationship with her was doomed from the beginning. She showed resistance towards Donald even when he tried to show love towards her. She hated him even more whenever he tried to discipline her, especially when the offence that she committed was petty.

Donald was trying his best to be a father to Karen's children because he cared for her and wanted to please her as much as possible, but her children were very reluctant towards him. They considered him a replacement for their dad, and they hated that.

Chapter *THREE*

FIRST DAY OF CINDY'S elementary school days started on a sour note. Her stepdad took her to school, and it did not go well when saying goodbye, he tried hugging her and attempted to kiss her on her cheeks. She pulled away from him, she did not want these kids seeing this man kissing her, especially when that man was not her father.

Cindy was extremely hot tempered, so making new friends was a challenge for her, especially when she wanted to make friends on her term and benefit.

Cindy spent the first day of school observing and scrutinizing the other students in the classroom, she barely participated in activities that the kids did throughout the day.

For once she was happy to see her stepdad because she was so ready to go home.

"How was your day?" her stepdad asked. Cindy ignored him, she pretended that she did not hear him.

"Make new friends?" He asked.

"No," she snapped back.

For the rest of the ride home, she remained silent as her two brothers chatted and giggled all the way home.

Later in the evening, her mom came in the room to chat with her, and to inquire about her first day at school.

"How was it?" Karen asked.

"I don't like it," Cindy replied

"What do you not like? It was just the first day, you cannot decide so early, you must give yourself a chance, also give the kids a chance to know you.

"Okay mom, I will try" Cindy quietly replied.

It was difficult to adjust to being at school, but as the time went by, and with the help of Kellie, her stepsister, it became easier.

The years went by quickly and in less than no time, it was time to graduate out of elementary school.

The summer months were uncomfortably hot, with some of the days topping the one hundred degrees mark, but despite the heat, Cindy and her siblings did manage to have enjoy a few of the family organized events.

Cindy was excited about attending middle school, and she counted the days daily, anticipating the opening day of school.

She heard so much about middle school, she could hardly wait to experience what it was like being at one.

Chapter *FOUR*

THE ANTICIPATED DAY WAS here, and Cindy was overjoyed; she was ready to start a new chapter in her tender life.

She woke up about two hours before the bus was scheduled to arrive.

Her mom said, "Cindy did not sleep that much, she was too excited."

She sat next to the window and kept her eyes fixed on the bus stop to see when the first kid would come to the stop.

Seeing the first kid, she jumped up like a grasshopper and skipped across the kitchen then picked up her school bag from the couch, and grabbed her lunch box from the kitchen, kissed her mom, then dashed towards the door.

"What is the rush? It is quite early," her mom exclaimed.

It was like Cindy to not hear her mom. She looked at both sides and when she was sure that it was safe to go across, she rushed across to the bus stop.

She tried to hide her excitement to avoid the other kids from making fun at her.

"Hi Michelle, ready for school?" she asked. "I am nervous."

"Hi Cindy, I am okay, but you can sit next to me."

"Thanks, nice of you to ask."

The school was about two miles from her home, but with the stops and pickups, it seemed like it was much further.

She disembarked from the bus and headed to the school auditorium where her class was scheduled to assemble.

They were informed and instructed where to go and were told of the various procedures and rules that had to be followed.

To her delight and comfort, she realized Michelle was in the same class with her, at least she had someone to talk and hang out with, that was her thinking, but Michelle was not on the same thought level.

She was very shy and reserved, she did not say much, but when she did, it was always to the point in her conversations.

Cindy thought she would be sitting next to Michelle in the classroom, but to her dismay, Michelle sat next to one of her friends from elementary school.

Cindy felt hurt, and disappointed, she could not wait for the school day to be over, could not wait to get to her house.

On the bus trip home, she remained quiet and kept looking out the window to try to get her mind off what happened to her on her first day at school.

The bus finally reached her stop, and it could not have gotten there any sooner for Cindy.

"Bye Cindy," Michelle said as she headed to her house.

Cindy barely opened her mouth, and said "bye," but in her heart she wished that this girl would not talk to her again.

Karen heard the bus pull up and headed to the door to share her daughter's excitement from the joy she had from her first day at middle school, but to her surprise, she saw the pain on her daughter's face, and she knew right away that something had gone wrong.

"Hi darling, what's up? You left so excited now you look like you just came back from seeing a scary movie at school, tell me, what happened?"

"Mom I hate school, I don't want to go back, I really don't want to go back." And she dropped her school bag and ran to her room.

Karen waited a few minutes before she went in to converse with her.

She sat on the end of the bed and remained quiet while her daughter kept crying her little eyes out.

Then she looked up at her mom and said "mom, these kids are so mean, hardly anyone spoke to me; I tried speaking to them and they just ignored me, including Michelle, who lives down the street. "Which house?" her mom interrupted

"The one next to the mailbox," Cindy replied.

"Okay what happened with Michelle?" her mom asked her.

"This morning she said we could sit together on the bus, so I thought we were going to be good friends at school, and at school I found out that we were in the same class, so mom, I was happy because I thought I had someone to talk to, but mom, she went and sat away from me and she joined the rest of the kids, and she ignored me. They looked at the clothes I was wearing like they were ugly or something, they had these fancy clothes and shoes, and thought I did not belong."

Karen eased closer to where Cindy was sitting and gently embraced her, and said to her, "even though I have been out of school for a long time, I can still relate about these behaviors, because these habits will always remain, kids will always be kids. We all went through the teasing and sometimes bullying."

"It's going to take time to get better, but I promise you, it will get better."

Cindy dried the tears from her eyes and hugged her mom a little tighter and said, "thank you mom".

She then joined her brothers and sister Kellie, as they went about doing their tasks, which included homework and other household chores.

As the days went by, Cindy began enjoying school; she made new friends, and became a few teachers' favorite student, and enjoyed the attention that she got because of that.

Cindy was a gifted child; she was good at athletics and music, she also was very smart, she got good grades and was deeply knowledgeable of her subjects, especially mathematics.

She enjoyed playing tennis, but her favorite sport was basketball.

She was selected on the school team and travelled with the team in and out of the city.

They usually travelled with the boy's team because the tournaments were always held at the same time.

Megan and Brianna were her best friends on the team, they became close, they went to the movies, and sometimes to the mall together.

They spent time on the phone but were monitored and had limits set by their parents. On school days they could not talk past 9pm.

They did multi lines where they did group conversations. The girls made the most of their given time, they spoke and giggled about the activities that took place during the day.

"Cindy, you know Brandon has a crush on you, "said Brianna, and they all giggled.

"Not me," Cindy replied, "it is you that he is interested in, he always wants to be next to you when we are travelling."

"Yes, but he is talking to me about you."

They went back and forth with that topic until it was time to get off the phone.

The next day at school, Cindy was so nervous when she saw Brandon, and she tried to avoid him as much as possible.

But as the school term went on, the two became good friends. They went to the movies, to the malls with the rest of their friends, and hung out together.

Eventually, their relationship began to evolve from friendship to boyfriend girlfriend relationship.

Karen, Cindy's mom, heard of what was going on between Brandon and her daughter and was not pleased.

Friday after school, when Cindy got home, Karen followed her to the room and sat on the bed and said to Cindy that they need to have a talk.

"I heard that you and Brandon are awfully close and spend a lot of time together, especially in the hallways of the school. Is that so? Also, you used your friends to go to the malls and movies so you could see him and spend time with him?"

"Mommy, I saw Brandon at school sometimes, but we don't spend much time together, Brandon is always with his friends."

"Someone is not telling me the truth," replied Karen, "anyway, here is what I am going to say to you, whether it is so or not, I do not want you to hang out with this boy, and I want you to spend less time with your friends.

You are almost fifteen, and you are in the eighth grade, you have a lot of time ahead of you to have a boyfriend and all that other stuff, but for now, you need to pay attention to your schoolwork. You are too young to manage that boyfriend stuff. I will be keeping track of you from now on."

"This is not fair, my grades are good, my behavior at home and at school is good, why are you punishing me?" Cindy fumed.

"Your teacher believed that you would have been much better, or you would be at the top of her class if you were not spending all that time with Brandon."

"Miss James is always in people business, so nosy."

"Who said that it was Miss James who told me so?"

"Who else can it be? She is the one that does not like me."

"What makes you think that she does not like you?"

"She is always picking on me, always calling on me first before she calls on someone else, nobody likes this teacher. Huh."

"She calls on you because she saw how bright you are, and she is trying to get you to be even brighter. She cares for you.

Anyway, like I said before, I will be monitoring you. Love you."

And with that said, Karen walked out and shut the door behind her.

Cindy remained in her room a little bit longer than normal, before coming out to mingle with the rest of the family.

As soon as Karen stepped outside to go to the grocery store, which was across the street, Cindy took this opportunity to go to the phone to call her friends to fill them in on what her mom told her, and with the assumption that Ms. James was the one who told on her.

They were all upset and had some choice words for the teacher.

Next day at school, Cindy tried her best to avoid Brandon, but this was very hard to do, because he diligently pursued her until he found her.

"Cindy, I have been looking for you" he said.

"I was busy, and I had a lot to do. I stayed in the classroom for most of the time." She explained.

"I don't believe you. If I am not mistaken, you are trying to avoid me. Brianna told me you were in the cafeteria, I went there, and you were not there. What's up?"

"Brandon, my teacher told my mom that I hang out with you a lot, and that affected my schoolwork, so my mom told me to stay away from you. So that what it is."

"I disliked this lady, she always messes things up, always getting involved in things that do not concern her." Brandon said, terribly upset.

"Sorry Brandon, but we will have to see each other less. I hate it but I have to listen, and I have to obey my mom." Cindy said, feeling so hurtful.

Cindy's friendship with Brandon dwindled a lot during the next few months of middle school, as she obeyed her mom and concentrated on her schoolwork.

Finally, it was time for graduation, and it was time for her to transform from a middle schooler to a high school student.

She graduated as one of the top ten children of her graduating class, despite her lapses in focus during various times of her middle school era.

Chapter FIVE

CINDY WAS EXCITED AND anxious to move on to high school. She was praying that the summer would speed as quickly as possible so her high school experience could begin.

The summer was unlike any other summer for Cindy, there were good and not so good things that happened.

Two weeks after school vacation started, Karen and the rest of the family planned to go to Florida on a vacation. It would be a 10-hour drive. The teenagers were excited about the trip, especially David, because he had just gotten his driver's license and was very eager to drive, but Karen did not feel comfortable with his driving and did not allow it.

They made a few stops before they made it to Orlando. They checked into the hotel, relaxed for a couple of hours before they went downtown to check out the city.

They visited various amusement places and had fun enjoying the rides and the other attractions.

Four days into their vacation, when they had just come back from the amusement park, Cindy received a call from her friend back in Texas, and the news she gave her was not good.

"Brandon was just killed in an accident on his way from playing basketball. He was walking home with his friends, when an out of control car left the road and plowed into them on the sidewalk.

Brandon died on the scene, and Timothy and Jonas were taken to the hospital with serious injuries that included broken bones and lacerations." Brianna told her.

Cindy shouted "no" and she dropped the phone. Her mom quickly came over to her and asked, "what happened?" but Cindy was so distraught by the news, could barely say anything.

After a few minutes, she composed herself and said, "it is Brandon, he is dead."

Karen and the others remained silent for a while, then Karen reached out and wrap her arms around her and said, "I am so sorry, I am truly sorry."

Donald asked, "what happened?" and Cindy said, "I don't know all the details, all I know is that Brianna said that he is dead from being in an accident."

"Can you give me Brianna's number so I could call her?" Karen asked.

"Why? You did not like him, you hated him" Cindy said in an angry tone.

"No, I did not hate him, I was trying to prevent you from making wrong decisions.

I did not want you to get too serious in a relationship that you could not manage because of your age and because of the way you let your emotions affect your thinking, I know you could not deal with being hurt. I was concerned with your education, and this was one of the main reasons that I told you so, and furthermore, I did not say don't talk to him, I said spend less time with him,"

Karen knew it was going to be difficult for Cindy, and she tried to support and comfort her as much as she could.

They packed their belongings in the van, and headed back home, everyone was so quiet as they drove off, not doing too much talking, but thinking of Cindy.

Her mom mentioned certain conversations, but she was not interested in participating.

Cindy called Brianna to find out the details of the accident, and then she relayed what she had learned to the rest of them.

The family arrived home a little past 7pm. Immediately Cindy called Brianna and her other friends.

And without any delay, they came over to her house.

They were in a depressed, broken mood, because of the loss. They hugged each other and cried on each other's shoulders, and Karen and the others that were present, gave their support.

They made plans to visit his mom to give their support, and to find out plans about his funeral.

The summer holidays went by quickly, besides being marred by the horrible accident, that summer was an enjoyable one.

It was a week away from school being resumed, and the excitement for some was noticeable, while others did not really care whether they opened or not.

But Cindy was ready, she had been to the malls and had purchased all that she needed for school.

She was extremely happy, she had been dreaming of this day for a long time, and it was finally here.

She could hardly wait for the first day of high school, unlike middle school, where she had no elementary friends, at high school she was going to be with her same friends that she had from middle school.

Cindy woke up earlier than usual and prepared for her first day of high school, she was all dressed up and she waited eagerly for the bus.

The trip from her house to the school seemed like forever, which is because she was so anxious to get there.

She was very happy to see her friends, and was excited to be in a new environment, but in spite of all this excitement, there was a lonely feeling in her heart. She went to the restroom and sobbed a lot, because she remembered Brandon, and realized that he was not part of their group anymore and never would be again, because he had died over the summer holidays. Cindy was deeply crushed.

Brianna and Megan came into the bathroom looking for her, and they found her crying, and they immediately knew why she was crying, and they hugged her, and they all cried together.

As the days went by, things normalized, and she set up her school agenda. With the help of her teachers, she decided what after school activities she would enroll in.

Cindy and her friends went to try out for the basketball team. Unlike middle school, making the team was much more difficult, because there were so many more kids trying out, and most of them were good at playing the game.

Although she was good at playing the game, she was worried that she would not make the team.

She also tried out for the volleyball team, with the notion that if she did not make it in one sport, she might get picked in the other.

After a few weeks of tryouts, she was notified that she had made both the basketball and the volleyball teams.

Her friend Brianna also made the basketball team, and that pleased Cindy.

The school days seemed to go by quickly, thought Cindy. Feels like yesterday was enrollment, now it is almost the end of the fall term.

So much happened during that first term, and Cindy believed that she had accomplished a lot. Her grades were good, and the remarks from some of the teachers concerning her attitude were positive.

Cindy's mom and her stepdad Donald, always preached to their children about respecting other people, regardless of their status and positions in the society.

The family attended church regularly and heard this type of teaching constantly, so manners, attitude and good habits were imbedded in them.

Chapter SIX

CINDY GOT HER FIRST break for the school term; it was thanksgiving time.

School was out for a week, and Cindy was glad for the time off.

Her aunt and a few other relatives came from California to spend thanksgiving with them.

It was a pleasant atmosphere, they got to spend quality time with each other, her mom had not seen her aunt in a long time, so every little moment was cherished.

There were a few little incidents that happened during the weekend, but nothing major that was any cause for concern or that derailed the fun that they had amongst them.

Karen was emotional when her sister left, but they made a promise that they would not stay that long again before they saw each other.

Christmas season was upon them, and you could tell that it was here, because the weather pattern had changed, and some people started hanging up their decorations.

It got very cold that year, and Cindy did not mind at all, because she got to wear her boots, that she wanted to wear for a while to school; she took pride in her dressing, and she always thought she was a good dresser, and looked amazing in her outfits; she was in top shape because of her athletic activities.

She received many compliments from her friends and even students that she barely knew, and she loved that.

Cindy had come a long way, from being this mean and shy girl from elementary, to this loving and friendly teenager.

She appreciated and respected other people much more than when she was younger. The anger that she harbored within her heart for her father had abated to almost total forgiveness, to the point where she decided she would like to spend her next summer holiday with him.

She discussed that with her mom, who at first was not in favor, but after they reasoned out a few times, she decided to let her go.

The city was buzzing with excitement, because people were busy shopping and preparing for the Christmas holiday.

And the children were out from school and were frequenting the malls and shopping areas.

Cindy received some money from her dad and asked her mom to match it. She took that money and went shopping for gifts for family and friends.

Her stepbrother Shawn had just gotten his driver's license and was eager to drive and to show off to his friends, offered to take her to the mall, and she quickly accepted, because she did not want her mom or stepdad to take her, because they did not have the patience, and from experience, they were always ready to get back home and would hustle her to be quick, but with Shawn, she could shop at her own pace.

Shawn was in the car waiting, that is how anxious he was to drive, and to show off to his friends.

It took him less than no time to make it to the mall, where they met their friends.

Cindy left the boys and grouped up with her friends, Brianna and Megan whom she met at the food court as they had planned.

They were off to their favorite stores, looking and buying when they found what they needed, and at the price that was reasonable for them. They went to the popular stores where most of their comrades shopped, they bought the latest fashions in clothes and shoes.

Cindy's friends were not as fortunate as Cindy was, they did not get much money from their parents like Cindy did, so they were limited to what and how much they could buy.

Cindy and her two friends went into one of the department stores in the mall to look at the latest fashions and if possible, to purchase what they could.

Cindy and the girls were walking past the jewelry showcase when she noticed Megan pocketing a gold bracelet. She was stunned.

She gazed at Megan with a look and expression, like, what are you doing?

Megan looked at her with a fierce look on her face, and a finger pointing in her direction, asking her to remain quiet, and for her to look away.

Then she came up to her and said, "You did not see. I better not hear from the other girls what I did."

Cindy did not know what to do, she said to Brianna and Megan that she was ready to leave, "let us go and find Shawn and David so we can go home."

"What is the matter, Cindy?" Brianna asked, "we said we would be here until about seven."

But Cindy just kept saying, "I am ready to go home."

Brianna asked Megan, "did anything bad happen or did you say anything that irritated her while you all were over there?"

"Not that I know of," Megan replied.

Cindy said bye to her friends, and she and her brothers went on to their home.

David asked Cindy, "what is wrong?"

"Nothing," replied Cindy, "I am not feeling good at the moment."

Upon arriving home, the boys went to their system to play and enjoy the new games that they had just purchased.

Cindy went into the bathroom and shut and locked the door, and she sat on the toilet for a while, playing back the incident that had just occurred in the store.

Her mom, being concerned that she was in the bathroom for an unusual amount of time, went and knocked on the door.

"Cindy, are you okay in there?" she asked.

Cindy did not reply, and the mom asked again, "is everything okay?" Cindy did not answer, but she could hear her sobbing.

"David," she shouted, "what happened today that Cindy is so upset?"

"Mom, nothing that I am aware of, I noticed that she was quiet on our way home, asked her about it, but she said she was okay."

Cindy was in the bathroom debating whether she should tell her mom what transpired at the mall. She knew her mom, and she knew her mom would be angry.

Anyway, she wiped her eyes, and then opened the door and walked out to face her mom.

"Why were you crying? What is going on? Are you sick?" Karen asked, being very troubled by Cindy's action.

"Mom, just something that happened at the mall today. I am not sure if I should tell you because I know you will get angry."

Her mom was getting frustrated. "Come on, just let me know what happened."

Cindy detected the anger in her mom's voice and realized that it was time to tell her what happened.

"Mom, when we went to the mall, we went to Katy department store, and Megan and I were in the jewelry area, and I saw Megan take a bracelet and pocket it."

"What did you do? Did you say anything to her? Did you let her know that that was wrong and that she should put it back?"

"Mom, I was so stunned; I did not know how to act. She also pointed at me to shut up, and she came up to me and said, 'you did not see. I better not hear from the other girls what I did.' So, mom I did not know what to do."

"You see, that is why I kept warning you about these friends of yours. You know if she had gotten caught you would have been apprehended too, since you were there with her?

Now, what are you going to do about it?"

"Mom, what can I do? I will be someone with a target on my back at school."

"Which one do you prefer? Having a target on you at school or at home?

Tomorrow we are going to meet with Megan, I need to let her know that I did not appreciate the trouble she could have gotten you into, and that she needs to find a way to make it right."

"Mom, no, leave this alone, it will just make matters worse, and I will be everyone's enemy, nobody knows, and nothing happened."

"This is not the point, this is totally wrong, and I raised you differently than that, so many things could have gone wrong."

"That is why I did not want to say anything."

"You better not keep things like this from me, you know I am concerned and am making sure that you grow up right and do the right thing."

"I don't know what Donald will say about this"

"Mom, you don't have to tell him, just let this go away."

"You know I don't like to hide things from him, anyway I will let it go for now, but I would hope you will terminate your friendship with Megan, because she doesn't have your best interest at heart."

Cindy was contemplating on not going to school on Monday, because she wanted to stay away from Megan, but she knew if she did, Brianna and the others would be asking questions, so she decided to go; but at the back of her mind, her mother's words were there as a reminder of what she should do or not do.

On Monday, Cindy rode with her brothers in the car, instead of taking the bus to school; she asked to be dropped in front of the hallway to her classroom, where she silently slipped into her classroom without being detected by the rest of her friends.

She did not go out during the break period, instead, she stayed in the classroom to converse with one of her teachers.

The teacher asked her, "is everything okay? "It is unusual to see you in here and not with your friends during break."

"I had to complete an assignment that I started and stayed in to finished it."

The teacher was not convinced of her explanation but left it at that.

Cindy went to the cafeteria to have lunch and was joined by her friends.

"Cindy, why did you stay in during break time?" Megan asked.

"I stayed to complete an assignment that I started earlier."

Cindy pretended that everything was okay, yet in her heart she knew it was not, but to avoid the questioning of Brianna and the others at the table, she kept a smiling face.

She tried to avoid Megan without making it noticeable, but Megan deliberately asked her questions in order to see if she had told anybody about the mall incident.

Cindy knew what Megan was doing, and therefore gave her hints that she did not say anything.

Cindy was very upset at Megan, she disliked her for what she did. She thought she was a different person but found out that she was deceitful, and a bully.

She was now scared of her, she believed she would hurt her if she went against her and let the others know what transpired at the mall

Two more weeks of school before the Christmas holiday and Cindy was thrilled; she planned to keep a low profile, and to stay away from the group as much as possible, so she could avoid Megan.

But it was easier said than done, because Megan was like a fire ant, she stayed on the attack.

Cindy knew Megan was an outspoken person, and always the one in the forefront in their click, but never knew she could be so mean.

Two days before school paused for the Christmas recess, Cindy and Brianna were out in the parking area talking and kidding around and reminiscencing about Brandon; just then Megan came by, but because it was time to be in class, Cindy and Brianna greeted Megan and went into the classroom.

Megan did not like that. She was very upset, she assumed that Cindy was talking to Brianna about her and what she did, so she made some fist gestures to Cindy and looked at her with a mean demeanor.

At breaktime, Megan hustled up to Cindy before Brianna and the others came along, and she questioned her, and accused her of telling Brianna of the mall incident, because she saw them talking. Cindy vehemently denied that she did, but Megan was not convinced.

"If I hear anything about that, I will hurt you or I will make your life miserable."

Cindy was very upset and shouted angrily, "I said I did not say anything to her," and she pretended to be tough, and said, "You better don't bother me anymore, and I think I will tell my brothers so you can leave me alone.'

Megan did not say much after that encounter, but just walked away, she did not want to have any conflict with Cindy's brothers.

Chapter *SEVEN*

CHRISTMAS WAS USUALLY A fun time at the Marcie household, families and friends would come by and they would have a festive time, with lots of food and a great deal of entertainment.

This year was the same, the tradition continued. They attended church, after which they went to the malls to get late gifts before they gathered around to exchanged gifts.

After the Christmas week, Cindy went to spend a few days with her biological father who lived in Dallas Texas. She was longing to see him.

Her dad was very happy to see her and spent the afternoon and evening with her.

The next day, she and her sister Jennifer went to the mall, hoping to get after Christmas deals. The mall parking lots were completely full, so their dad dropped them off at the mall's entrance.

"Dad, we will call you when we are ready," Cindy said

"Not a problem," replied Jason.

Jenny introduced her sister Cindy to her friends that were waiting for her at the food court.

After consuming a few items from the food court, they went browsing and shopping at a few stores.

The mall was extremely busy, and the stores were buzzing with shoppers.

Cindy bought a nice, dress shirt for her dad. She wanted to buy something for her stepmother but decided against it. She knew that her stepmother did not like her, and she could not understand why, but later Cindy found out she was just jealous of the relationship that she and her dad had.

Her dad always made mention of her, and always praised her, and this did not sit well with Joyce, and she tried to drive a stake to that relationship, but that failed.

Cindy observed the way Joyce treated her dad and she did not like it. She shouted at him and talked down to him like he was a kid, and he did not say or do anything about it, she could not believe that her dad had gotten so soft.

Later in the evening, Joyce asked her, "how long are you staying here?"

"Just for a week," Cindy replied.

"I thought you were here for the weekend," Joyce said, and she went into her room and slammed her door.

A few minutes later, she heard an argument coming from inside her dad and Joyce's bedroom.

First it was a loud conversation, but it quickly escalated to shouting and profanity, and from what she overheard, it was focused on her.

Apparently, Jason did not tell Joyce that Cindy was visiting for a week, and she was upset about that, and said some nasty things, which annoyed Jason, and he got very angry, and said, "I have paid for almost everything in here, and am the one paying the bills, don't you think my daughter is welcome here anytime she wants to come?"

That just added more fuel to the fire, and Joyce got angrier, and lashed out with nastier remarks. "Your daughter is not a saint; she is just like the other young girls out there with boyfriends here and there."

Jason realized that this was getting out of control, so he came out and said, "Cindy let's go take a ride down the street."

Cindy was in tears, she felt that this was her fault, had she not come over, this would not have happened.

As she entered the car, she could still here her stepmother fussing and cursing.

"Cindy, don't worry about her, sometimes she gets like that with Jenny."

"Yes, but Jennifer is her daughter, she could do that to her, but I am not her child for her to talk about me like that, this is awful."

Dad realized that his daughter was upset, and wanted to cheer her up, and said, "now tell me, how is it going at school?"

She realized what he was doing, he was diverting from the situation at hand, and she did not mind, because she did not want to waste her time talking about Joyce.

"School is going fine, besides a few little setbacks." And she told him about the incident that happened with Megan.

Her dad was quite upset, because he realized what trouble she could have ended up in.

He admonished her to abandon these friends and find new friends.

They drove to Bobby's pizza and sat and talked for a while, until they felt calm and relaxed enough to go back home.

On their drive home, he said, "my dear, for the remainder of the time that you are here, ignore her, you are here to spend time with me."

They returned to the house, and it was more tranquil than when they left, other than a little murmuring here and there, it was peaceful.

And for the rest of her stay, it remained quiet and peaceful, and they both stayed out of each other's way.

Cindy left after her time was up and was relieved to be back home with mom and the rest of her siblings.

The rest of the Christmas holiday went by quickly, and it was time to go back to school, which she was ready to do.

Cindy decided to take her father's advice concerning her friends and planned to stay away from their circle. This was not going to be easy, but she was determined to give up some of her friends, even though she knew there would be bullying and hatred coming her way.

She slowly drifted away from them. She used all sorts of excuses and schemes to stay away from them.

As she slowly moved away from the friends that were not having her best interest at heart, her grades, improved and that had her in great standing with her teachers and mother.

She spent less time with her friends and spent more time in the classrooms when she had excess time.

Her friends did not like that and asked her if she felt that she was better than them. They tried to make life difficult for her, but she had made up her mind to move on regardless of what they threw at her.

At the end of the school year, she was no longer close friends with Megan and Brianna, but had developed new friendships with a new group of people.

Janet, Patti, Tiffany, Chris and Michael, were more mature than her previous close friends. They constantly spoke of the goals that they had set for themselves, and that encouraged, and motivated her to set goals and to develop plans that would help her achieve these goals.

Her goals were to finish high school, march on to college to obtain a bachelor's degree, and then to proceed to the medical field, because she loved the profession of a doctor or head nurse.

It was summertime again, and Cindy's friends were taking a trip to Europe; they planned to visit England, France and Italy.

They asked Cindy to come along, but Cindy knew that was a hard sell to her mother; she did not know what it would take to convince her. Money was not the problem, but fear was.

She waited until her siblings were out of the house, and it was just she and her mom. She said, "mom, I have finished my homework, do you want me to help you in the kitchen?"

"What?"

"Can I help you in the kitchen and help prepare dinner?"

"I heard you the first time, but because of shock, I said what. Now let me ask you ahead of time, what do you want?"

Cindy slowly proceeded to the kitchen hoping for a miracle, hoping that she would be able to persuade her mom.

"Can I not be a good girl for once and offer help?"

"You could try this with your school friends and your brothers, but not on me, I know you like the back of my hands."

"Come on, spit it out," Karen said smiling.

"Do you remember my friends that came to the house last month?"

"Yes, I do."

"Well, we were talking about the summer holiday, and what we would do for these couple of months, and how much fun we would like to have, and then someone suggested a trip to Europe, and we got really excited, and realized what an adventure that would be. I know you are probably saying that it is expensive, but we figured it out, if we share two rooms, because it would be just the four of us, that will help cut the cost tremendously, and I know my dad would help in covering my trip."

"Are you saying all these things in order to ask me if you can go?"

"Mom you are so smart," Cindy said jokingly.

"Cindy, my dear, I am sorry to have to disappoint you, but you know that is very difficult for me to do, to let you go to the other side of the world with a few friends you barely know. How dangerous that is to have a few teenagers roaming Europe, a strange place by themselves? Strangers in foreign lands?

This is just asking for trouble, my dear. I am not in a position to lose you; I could not live with myself if I allowed you to go and something bad happened."

"Mom, why are you always thinking of the bad things that can happen, what about us going and having a great time and enjoying a great trip, sightseeing and learning other cultures? You always say God will protect his children, am I not His child?"

"Yes, but God gave us common sense, and never asked us to knowingly run into the fire and then ask Him to pull us out."

"My friends' parents are all okay with this, and I am sure that my dad, my real dad, would be okay with this."

"What do you mean by that young lady?"

"Well, my stepdad will always side with you."

"Young lady, you are out of line! Go to your room, and when you come to your senses, we will finish this conversation.

Cindy hastily walked to her room and shut the door behind her, and dove on the bed, and cried for a while, and eventually fell asleep.

Since it was the weekend, she had ample time to think of something to say to her friends on Monday.

She could hardly wait for the weekend to come to an end so she could get out of the house.

First one she saw on Monday was Janet, and she tried to escape to the classroom before Janet could start a conversation, but that failed.

Janet came up to her and said, "Hi Cindy, wow, last week of school, I am so excited, are you?"

At that same moment, Patty and Tiffany came to join them.

"So, is everyone excited and almost finished packing?" Patty asked, with the widest smile on her face.

Janet and Tiffany almost simultaneously echoed "yes we are." But Cindy remained quiet, and everyone recognized the disappointment on her face, and she said, "I won't be going, my mother did not approve for me to go."

"Why not?" Janet asked.

"She did not feel comfortable of me being away that far across the world and she not being with me."

"Oh Cindy," Patty said, "I don't think I mentioned to you, but my parents are also coming on the 3-week trip. They are taking their vacation at the same time, so they could enjoy their vacation and still be there for us."

Cindy felt optimistic, she now had new ammunition to tackle her mom with, she could hardly wait to get to the house.

She was 90 percent sure she was about to be approved to go on the trip.

She got home and was anxious to talk to her mom, but her mom was fast asleep, because she had to work that night. She was a nurse and worked the night shift.

Cindy waited patiently for her to wake up, which happened 2 hours later.

After about a half hour lapse, Cindy went to talk to her mom.

"Hi mom, I found out that Patty's parents are going on the trip with them, so there will be supervision, can I now go?" Cindy pleaded.

"Babe, I understand, but I am afraid that I still can't let you go, I am still not comfortable with the situation, you are so young, and I am not familiar with your friends and their parents. Sorry my dear, you know I mean well."

Cindy was so disappointed and angry, she went into her room, and as a normal teenager would do, she buried her head in her pillow and cried.

Cindy said to herself, that she was going to find a way not to go on their regular family summer trip.

The next morning Karen came home from work, and told Cindy, when she came from school later in the afternoon, they could have a chat.

Cindy came from school and spent a little time with her siblings then went into her room and locked it.

Karen, her mom, walked up to her room and turned the knob and realized that it was locked, and was surprised that it was, because they hardly did that in the house.

She gently knocked on the door and asked Cindy to let her in, but Cindy did not budge, she knocked a couple more times, but she got the same result.

Karen was angry, and demanded that the door be open at once, and Cindy slowly opened the door.

"What is up with you? Why do we have to go through this? Are you so upset that you neglect your brothers and sister out there, and refuse to communicate with those living in the house?"

"Well young lady, you must get things under control; you have to self-check, and you need to do that quickly."

"Life is so not fair, definitely not fair," Cindy said, "some people are so lucky, while some of us always suffer."

"My dear, everything happens in the right time, and you don't have to live your life on luck, but rather by trusting God that His plans will come through in your life. Sometimes spur of the moment situations work but it is much better to take the time to carefully plan things and specifics in your life."

"We can go to Europe sometime during the last year of your high school days. We will go as a family, and I can assure you that we will all have a great time."

Cindy was still disappointed about the trip, but not as angry as she was before. She scooped closer to her mom on the bed, and her mom gently wrapped her arms around her and said, "it is going to be alright buddy."

"Sometimes we just think we are being left out or we are missing out, but God's plans, if followed carefully and obediently, always yield great results and blessings for those who are willing to be led by Him." Karen lectured.

"Mom, how would you know that it is God talking to you? I have listened and watched so many grown people said and done so many questionable things, and kept on saying it is God's will, but the way they lived was so disgusting."

"When I was in middle school, I knew this girl in my class that was always quiet, and kept to herself, her name was Jessica, she barely spoke to anybody, but she would talk to me if she wanted to get something off her mind."

"One day she told me that her choir leader touched her where he was not supposed to all the time, she hated it but was afraid of him, because he told her not to say anything, or else she would be sorry, but I guessed she could not take it anymore so she told me."

"And you mean you did not say anything to me? That is not good."

"But mom she told me not to say anything to anyone, so I did not."

"There are certain things you don't say, but there are things that require you telling someone that you trust, it could mean that you could save someone's life, or you could save someone from pain and other hurtful situation.

You know you could have told me, and I would have found a way to help this young child. I could have let her parents know without them knowing it came from you."

"But mom, she would know it was me because I was the only one she told."

"Cindy, what else are you hiding from me?" Karen asked.

"Nothing mom, I always come to you with my concerns."

"I hope this young girl got some help or found the courage to tell her parents. Does she go to your high school?"

"Mom I have not seen her at the high school or anywhere else, I really do not know."

"Do you have her number? You should always stay in touch with girls in a situation like this. You might be the only help she had."

"Mom, I don't, and I hope she is okay."

Mom and daughter spent a few more minutes together, chatting and discussing various subjects, then they went back to their regular routines.

Chapter EIGHT

THE NEXT DAY CINDY gathered with her sister and her other brothers, as they planned with their parents for their summer trip.

They wanted to go to New York, but their parents suggested that they should take a road trip to the Grand Canyon.

The boys argued with their parents, but it was all in vain, because the parents did not bulge.

"Why New York?" the parents asked.

Donald said, "I've been to New York when I was young, and unless you are going there for something specific, then the city is too busy and fast, and I would not recommend it for a family vacation, especially with teenagers."

"That is the purpose of a vacation for teenagers, to have fun, and be happy doing teenager stuff, and that is what I heard about New York," Joshua said while smirking.

"I can't wait to get to college, then I can go without any obstruction."

At the end of the discussion, the Canyon trip was still what they were going on.

Joshua said, "I dreamt of New York, not Arizona to see a few old rocks."

Donald assured him, that he would love the trip, all he needs to do right now, is to keep an open mind.

They spent the week planning their road trip to the Canyon, making sure that they were well prepared and equipped.

They set off Monday morning on their many hours road trip; they stopped in a few cities, where they refueled, regrouped and relaxed.

These stops made a big difference, in helping to restore energy, and they got to know a few more cities.

It took them two days to get to the Grand Canyon village, where they checked into their hotel.

They spent the night recovering from the driving and from the hectic issues of the road trip.

They spent the next few days enjoying and exploring the Canyon. They went on the sky walks, the rail trains, and through various trails and caves.

One of their most enjoyable activities, was river rafting; everyone said that was the highlight of their trip.

It was time to head home Sunday night. Bedtime was early so they could have a good night's rest and be able to have a safe trip back.

They took less time on the return trip because they had less stops heading home.

They got home about 4 pm on Monday.

They spent the rest of the evening unpacking and relaxing.

Despite not wanting to go on that trip, the boys said they had a blast, and enjoyed every moment of the trip, and admitted they were wrong.

The boys said, "in spite of enjoying this trip, we are still heading to New York next year."

Cindy enjoyed the trip, but it was a far cry from where she wanted to be, she wanted to be in Europe with her pals.

The summer holiday was quickly coming to an end, and Cindy was making plans for her junior year of school.

She had decided to devote a lot of time and effort to her studies for that year, because she wanted her senior year to be as easy and stress free as possible.

On the first day back at school, she met up with her friends and they shared their experiences and details of their summer vacations.

The trip to Europe, as expected, was great; the young ladies claimed to have so much fun, and they were still excited about their trip.

Meanwhile, Cindy was passive and was not as enthusiastic as they were but did exclaim to them that she had a good vacation.

She took every opportunity that she got to try to change the subject of vacation, and to try to place the focus on something else, because she did not want to hear anything else about their European trip.

Cindy selected her classes for the term, and true to her words, she had a loaded schedule.

Cindy's mom was not in favor of that schedule because she thought that it was too much of a heavy load, and despite her pleading, she could not get her daughter to change her mind.

Cindy spent less time with her friends during that school term. She was focused on getting good grades in all her classes, especially in history, since she was not as strong in this subject as she was in the others.

She spent a considerable amount of time in the library researching and acquiring materials that would assist her in her assignments and studies.

Her mother encouraged her to seek help from Uncle Johnson who was very knowledgeable in history. She wanted her to succeed in all her subjects.

Cindy took her mom's suggestion and asked her uncle for help. It paid off, her grade went up significantly, and she acquired a good knowledge of history.

The school term went by quickly, and Cindy was ready for a break; she was exhausted because of all what she had to do, but she was determined to make it to the end.

Cindy did extremely well at the end of her term exams, she even did well in history. She was happy that the sacrifices paid off and was encouraged to continue that path to finish the school year.

At Christmas, Cindy decided to rest a lot, and to skip some of the regular activities she usually did at that time of the year.

She went to the mall on a couple of occasions to obtain gifts for her family and friends, but besides that, she remained home the majority of the time.

January came quickly and it was back to school again.

She knew that she was headed for a tough semester, but she was ready and determined to finish as strong or even stronger than the previous semester.

Despite the heavy school load she had, there was one thing outside of her schoolwork that she was eager to pursue, and she was excited about it.

She enrolled at a driving school, and received a driving permit, and was very committed to get her driver's license.

She attended three days a week after school, and any time she could get her brothers David or Shawn to give her practice lessons, because she wanted her driver's license so badly.

The day finally came when she passed her driving test and obtained a driver's license. She was beyond excited and happy, she told her friends her good news, and promised to take them for a ride.

Her mom was excited and happy for her, yet she was worried, because now her daughter would be going on these crazy streets.

"Mom, can we talk?" Cindy said to her mom.

"I know where you are going with that, but anyway, yes, we can talk."

"Wheels mom, I need wheels," said Cindy jokingly, but hoping her mom would take it seriously.

"Sorry Cindy eventually, but for now it is not possible, but hopefully soon, or better yet, why don't you ask your father? I am sure he will buckle under your charm."

Cindy said she would ask him, and she was confident he would help her.

She was happy that there were only two more weeks of school before the semester end, yet she knew that these were important weeks, and she had to stay committed because those were exam weeks and she wanted to finish strong in her grades.

Cindy did not disappoint, her grades were excellent, and she surprised herself by getting an A in history.

Her mom and stepdad were very proud of her and realized what a determined child this young lady was.

The summer was less stressful than the previous one, she had made the sacrifices, and now she could relax a little bit more, and she knew her upcoming school year was going to be one of her easiest. She was looking forward to her senior year, because she heard so much about the benefits that came along with it.

Cindy's summer was filled with activities, such as camping with the youths of her church, and was deeply involved in VBS, where she mentored the younger girls who attended.

She and her friends went to the movies quite often, they frequented the malls and other shopping areas, she tried to spend a lot of time with them since she barely had time for them during the school year.

"Mom, concerning the promise you made to me in reference to going to Europe this summer for a couple weeks, let us reschedule it for next year summer after I graduate from high school and before I start college."

Cindy began receiving acceptance letters from various universities to which she had submitted requests. She was in no rush to decide which one she would attend, though she had an idea which one she was leaning toward.

Summer sped along, and this was the first summer in a long time that she got to relax.

The first day of the final year of her high school was here, and how excited Cindy was to begin this process that would cumulate all her school years.

She was also anxious, because she was driving herself to school for the first time.

Her dad bought her a good secondhand car, and she was very appreciative to him for doing that.

She made sure she arrived at school after the school bus, she wanted her friends to see her driving and for them to see her car.

She drove past Janet, and she honked her horn to make sure that she noticed her.

Cindy had a few classes that she had to take in her last year of high school, the heavy load last year paid off. She had more free time to do other things that she did not get to do previously, because she was so occupied.

Now that she had her own means of transportation and did not have to rely on others to go where she wanted to go, she was able to accomplish things she had set aside for the time.

She was also more dedicated to playing basketball and volleyball.

She played on the school volleyball team and travelled all over the state with the team. She was very good at both basketball and volleyball and expected to be offered scholarships for both sports.

She expected to receive scholarships for her academic achievements, but she wanted to be awarded all that she deserved, and then choose the college that was the best fit for her.

It was a nice easy fall semester, nothing unusual happened, except for the freedom she had as a senior. She enjoyed all these little perks and benefits that came with being a senior.

Cindy's mom was not satisfied by the way she was approaching her last year of high school but felt that she not making enough effort to get into a good college. Cindy felt the opposite and thought she had it all under control. She sent in the applications to the schools that she was interested in and was just waiting to make her decision.

"Yes, I understand that you sent the applications, but you have to follow up and see what is going on with these applications." Karen admonished.

"Mom, stop sweating, everything will go well, stop stressing."

"Okay, don't say I did not warn you." Karen said, and then left for work.

Chapter *NINE*

THANKSGIVING HOLIDAY WAS A couple of weeks away, and the family was planning for a big gathering this year.

Karen's sister Christine and her husband and their two children were coming over to spend the holiday with them. She had not seen her sister for over fifteen years and was very anxious to see her again.

Michael, she knew from when he was about two years old, but Debbie, who is eleven, she had never met.

It was a long drive from Minnesota to Karen's house, when they got there, they were very tired.

Karen opened the door, and she hugged her sister tightly for a long time, then she greeted Larry, Christine's husband, then greeted the children.

It was quite a reunion for them, and after they shed a few tears of joy, and got their emotions under control, they settled down.

They were so tired from that long trip, all they wanted to do was to go to bed. After eating the meal that Karen had prepared for them, they did just that, and it did not take them long to fall asleep.

The next day bright and early, everyone was up and refreshed and ready to mingle.

Christine and her family got to meet Karen's children. It was a happy gathering.

Christine joined her sister in the kitchen so they could catch up with each other's lives. So much had happened since they had last seen each other, and there was so much to talk about. Meanwhile the children split up, a few of them went to the mall, while the two younger ones stayed home to play their electronic games.

Cindy, Kellie and Debbie stayed in Cindy's room and chatted about boys, movies and other things that interested them.

Thanksgiving was just a couple of days away, so they were busy preparing for the occasion.

Karen bought a huge turkey, and a small hen; she anticipated a bigger than usual gathering, because not only her family and Christine's family would be there, but she had invited a few of the single women from her church.

Tuesday afternoon, Karen began her cooking project, starting with the turkey. She had it defrosting since Monday night, and took it out from the regular fridge, washed and cleaned it thoroughly with lime and vinegar, then seasoned it carefully and left it to marinate.

Wednesday morning, Christine and Cindy joined Karen in the kitchen to assist her in preparing the thanksgiving dinner.

She assigned them a few roles, but the main lifting, she took upon herself.

She continued her turkey project and dealt with the hen. When evening came, most of the cooking was completed except for a few small details, and the completion of baking the turkey, which she always liked to finish on Thanksgiving Day.

Karen was so tired after all the cooking and preparation, and she sat on the couch to relax for a minute and fell asleep right there.

Cindy woke her up and advised her to go to her bed. She took a shower and within no time she was fast asleep in her bed.

Thanksgiving Day, no one woke up before 11am.

Karen woke up early and put the turkey in the oven on a low temperature and went back to bed.

They gathered at 1:30pm for the thanksgiving meal. After Donald prayed, they took turns and said what or who they were thankful for, before they started eating.

The compliments were flowing about how tasty the food and turkey was, and Karen said "Christine and Cindy did a great job" refusing to take all the credit.

It was a pleasant day, with lots of food, and great company and no drama like a lot of families have on Thanksgiving Day.

Around 6:30pm, all the guests had left; just family, including Christine and her family were in the house.

The boys were in their rooms playing video games, and Cindy and the other girls chilled out in her room.

Christine and the other adult members, sat in the living room and chatted. Christine and Karen reminiscence of old-time days when they were growing up, of the good and bad things that they experienced.

The next day, Christine and her family prepared to go back to Minnesota, but before she left, she and Karen shared an emotional moment, and vowed not to stay apart that long again.

Cindy and Kellie hopped into the car and went to the mall to hang out with their friends, and to see if they could find the things they wanted at a reasonable price, seeing that it was black Friday.

They went in and out of the stores, gazing at items and buying a few they found on sale. They then went to the food court and hung out with their school buddies.

About 3pm, Cindy, her sister and their friends were leaving a shoe store, when they saw people running frantically in every direction. She and her group went straight to the parking lot and headed to their vehicles. She inquired from a shopper who came out from the mall frightened, what was going on?

The lady told her that "there were shots fired in the food court area between gang members."

Cindy and Kellie went home from the mall, not stopping at the restaurant from which they had planned to pick up some finger foods.

They reached home still talking about the incident, which led Karen to ask, "what's up? You all are shaking and are back early."

"Mom, there was a shootout in the mall between gang members," Cindy echoed.

"How did you know that it was gang members? Did anybody get killed? How close were you to all that chaos?"

"Mom, we don't know; when we saw everyone running, we ran to our car, and a shopper told us what happened."

Cindy called her friends to make sure that they had made it to their homes safely.

Knowing that they were all safe at home, the teenagers spent a long time on the phone discussing what had happened and how they were feeling.

The incident was broadcast on the 7pm evening news.

According to the news cast, there was an attempted robbery at one of the jewelry vendors in one of the aisles of the mall; the suspects brandished their weapons and the people that were around panicked and started running, which brought about panic and chaos. The suspects were apprehended after a tussle with a security guard. No one was injured from this incident.

"That is why you have to be careful in not repeating and spreading news that you hear from non-official sources. The story is completely different from what you said." Karen and Donald then went to their room.

On Monday, Cindy and her friends still discussed their weekend experience at the mall and laughed at how wrong they were with their information.

Chapter TEN

THERE WERE A FEW weeks left of the Christmas holiday and Cindy could hardly wait. She did her research on the universities that she was interested in attending. She looked at various factors and was leaning towards those that had great athletic programs. She was also depending on her great SAT scores, and her basketball skills to boost her chances of going to the best schools.

She also used her free time, with permission, to drive off the school campus, and she and her friends picked up food from restaurants and did other chores.

And that was basically her routine for the next couple of weeks until school closed for the holidays.

For the first time in a long time, Cindy's family decided to decorate inside and outside rather than just the Christmas tree.

Shopping this year was easier than previous years, because she did not have to struggle to think of what to buy for her brothers, they were grown up now, and gift cards were good gifts for them. For her mom and stepdad, it was easy just give them cash in an envelope.

On Wednesday night, Christmas eve, they completed the gift wrapping, and placed them underneath the tree, and sat around and waited for midnight when it would be officially Christmas.

At midnight, Kellie wanted to open her gifts, but Karen was having none of this.

"We will continue with tradition and open our gifts on Christmas day."

In the morning, everyone gathered around the breakfast table to enjoy their breakfast, Karen always made a special Christmas breakfast, which included a drink called Chau Deux, a French type of drink.

Around 3pm, right before lunchtime, everyone assembled in the living room next to the Christmas tree to exchange their gifts.

At the end of this exchange, some were excited about the gifts they received while a few were disappointed and promised to take them back to be exchanged or refunded.

The few weeks of the Christmas holiday went by very quickly, and it was time to go back to school.

Cindy was excited and emotional at the thought that this was her final semester of her high school life, but she was ready to get it over with.

Monday morning, she woke up and prepared breakfast, which was not usual. After she had devoured it, she sat down for an extended period, because she did not have a first period of class and decided to go in late. She wished all her school days were like that.

Cindy was heading to the cafeteria to meet with her friends. A few boys were hanging out in the hallway that she was passing through, and when they saw her, shouted remarks at her; they whistled, and said some disrespectful things. One of the boys shouted, "hi pretty thing, what is your name?"

She pretended that she did not hear him, but he shouted louder, "I know you heard me, but you are playing bourgie, think that you are all that."

Cindy walked faster in order to get away, but he would not stop harassing her, and three of the four other guys that were with him enjoyed it, while the other guy named Patrick, rebuked him and the other guys for doing that.

They were upset with him and argued with him because he stood up for Cindy, and it had gotten so bad, that they were about to fight, but at the same moment, a teacher was coming through the hallway and that prevented what could have been an ugly situation.

Cindy approached the young man and asked him his name, and then thanked him and then walked away.

She told her friends what had just happened, and they explained to her that these guys are like that, so many people have made complaints against them, but nothing has been done about it.

Cindy and Patrick became friends and as the semester went on, they became close where they were able to go to the movies and the mall with the rest of her friends.

She tried hiding that relationship from her mom, because she knew if her mom found out, she would get upset and would be on her case constantly, so she always included her friends and her sister Kellie, when she went out with him.

Cindy finally decided to mention Patrick to her mom.

"Mom, Patrick has asked me to be his date at our prom, and I told him I have to speak with you first before I give him an answer."

"Who is Patrick?" her mom asked surprisingly, "all these years you've been going to school, I never heard you mention a Patrick, but at this moment, what is going on?" she asked curiously.

"Mom, he is a friend that I made this semester, he is a nice person," and she explained to her how they met, and what he did for her.

"You mean all these things have been happening and you did not mention anything to me? You kept saying everything was alright, there was no problem, and yet you were being bullied and did not say anything to us? I thought we had a better relationship than that."

Cindy realized that her mom was very upset and disappointed, so she knew that she had to choose her words carefully in order to avoid making it worse than it was.

"Mom, it is not like that, you know our relationship is great, I did not say anything because I believed that everything was solved, because the guys never bothered me again. Telling you would have resulted differently; you would have wanted to come down to the school and make a big fuss about it, and that would not have gone down well with my friends."

"Anyway, who is Patrick? Who are his parents?

"I would be crazy if I just let my baby go ahead to a prom with a boy that I don't even know, someone I never heard of. That is not going to happen."

"Mom, this is not fair, it is my prom, I should be able to choose who I want to take to my prom, it is not like anything is going to happen, it is just a companion for the celebration."

"That is what you perceive, but you don't know what is going on in the head of this young boy, you don't even know him long enough to know who he is."

"What about Brian, the young man from church, the one you usually hang out with?"

"Mom, Brian is my church friend, we usually do church activities together, we get along great, but he is not my choice for prom."

"You see, a decent young man, a respectable young man, someone the family knows well, but no, you preferred a no-good intention boy to go to the prom."

"Mom you don't know Patrick, so you should not judge him."

"Neither do you," the mom angrily replied.

Cindy realized that she was not going to win with her mother, so she decided to use a different approach.

"Okay," she said, "I will go with my friends, I know a couple of them that are going together, I will join them."

"I am not going to argue with you anymore, you do whatever you want. You must be back in the house at the time, I set for you.

"By the way, how are you going to purchase your dress? You know these dresses are very expensive."

"Mom, I thought you were going to help me. The money I saved is for when I go to college."

"Well, I am sorry, I don't have the money, I am doing all I can to help with your college expenses plus we have a lot going on now that demands a lot of our finances,"

"I know if I had agreed to go with Brian, you would be different about it, any way I will ask my real father."

"Go ahead and be rude about it, but later you will find out that I was right."

Cindy knew that her mom was just saying these things because she was just upset and disappointed, because things did not go her way, but she knew her mom loved her and would always have her back.

Shawn and Kellie went to Cindy's bedroom to reason with her as they did not want her to mess up their chances of going to prom and they wanted her to be nicer to their parents, so it could go well for them, when their turn came around.

On Monday, Cindy told Patrick what her mom said, and that she would not go to the prom with him.

Patrick was disappointed, but not totally crushed by the news. He felt that this would work out best for him, she could go with her friends, and he would not be responsible for picking her up, but he could still hang out with her, once she got there.

Chapter ELEVEN

THE LAST SATURDAY IN May was prom. Most area schools had their prom slated for that day.

Cindy woke up that day very excited, she was anticipating a glorious evening and night. She did her chores without being reminded to do them, and her mom jokingly said, "prom should be every day, because I would get all my assignments to you completed with no issue and no negative feedback."

Cindy gave a little shrug with her shoulder, and gave one of her signature smiles, and kept walking towards her room.

Around noontime, she went to her closet and took out her dress and laid it on her bed, checking it to make sure it was in tack, she spent a lot of money for this dress. She got the money from her dad.

At 4pm, her friends were at her home, honking, and being loud, they made plans to go to Chang Lee restaurant to have an early dinner before going to the prom, which was scheduled for 7pm but they had to be there by 6pm.

Cindy and her friends Janet, Patti and Tiffany, had a great time at dinner, spent a lot for food and drinks, and got engaged in some juicy conversations before leaving for the prom.

They arrived at the venue around 5.45pm, Patrick was waiting for her, met her at the door, and he walked with her to her seat.

"Cindy, you look amazing, wow, you are beautiful." Patrick complimented.

"Honestly, you surprised me, from the guy I know at school, to how you look now! What a transformation. You are really looking handsome," Cindy remarked.

They then went to their seats and listened to the host of the ceremony giving instructions and directions of how the night activities should proceed.

It was a full night of fun, and the kids were happy, they showed it in the way they socialized.

When the activities were over, they were informed that that the school band was playing at the school auditorium for those who were interested, if not they were free to go home, but some of them left and went to clubs and other plans that they had.

Patrick, excited, came up to Cindy and said, " I have a surprise for you," he gave her a bouquet of flowers and then said, "I have booked a room at Ocean View hotel, your favorite band is there performing for the night, we could go there for a couple of hours and relax and enjoy this great atmosphere, have a late dinner and should have enough time to come back to the auditorium before midnight."

"How come they did not discuss that with me, but did with you?" Cindy questioned.

"Not sure, but that is what it is."

For a while Cindy was excited about the idea, she thought of the band, hotel and all the exciting things offered to her, but after she pondered the thought of what could go wrong, she decided to turn down his invitation.

"Sorry Patrick," she said, all these things that you said and offered sounded good, but I can't go to that hotel, I don't feel right doing that, I don't feel right in my spirit, and most of all, I don't want to disappoint my parents."

"Cindy, they won't know," Patrick exclaimed. We will just be there for a short time, and you will be back in time to catch your ride back home."

"Why can't we just go to the auditorium where most of the students are?" Cindy asked

"Nothing special about being around these uncool kids, I want this night to be special." Patrick said.

"I suspect that you had other plans beside the band and dinner, because I don't see the need for the room. Be honest, what else was on your mind?" Cindy asked.

"The room was for us to spend time together, we have not spent any time together, you don't know much about me, and I don't know too much about you." Patrick explained.

"That is exactly my point, we don't know each other enough to spend 2 to 3 hours in a hotel room, I am afraid bad things might come out of this."

Patrick was visibly upset and made his feeling known to Cindy, after they argued for a couple more minutes, he said, "go ahead, go and hang out with those boring and nerdy kids at the auditorium, I am going to hang out with my friends, and he walked away.

Cindy was completely devastated. She thought he was different from the other boys, but he was just as horrible as the rest of them.

She quietly went to the auditorium with some other kids that were headed there.

Rhonda asked her why she was so sad? She could tell that something was wrong, because it showed on her face.

Cindy chose not to talk about it, but wished that she had driven her car, she would have gone home, but she stayed there being miserable, and waited for her friends to take her home.

Upon arriving at the house, she greeted her parents who were up waiting on her. She then proceeded to her room and shut the door.

Her mom knew something had gone wrong, because her mother's instinct told her so, she was hoping that she did not compromise herself and now was feeling bad and guilty about it.

Donald went to his room, whilst Karen went to talk to Cindy. She gently knocked on the door, and asked Cindy to let her in. Cindy slowly opened the door and allowed her to come in.

"Hi dear, how was it?" Karen asked.

"Terrible, terrible," she answered. The prom event started great, a big gathering, and we had a lot of fun, but after the activities were over, we were instructed to go to the school auditorium where the dance was being held. Some of the students left and went to clubs and hotels, while the rest went to the auditorium.

She was in two minds whether to tell her mom about Patrick and concluded it would be best to tell her, even though she expected her to say I told you so.

Cindy told her mom every little detail of her encounter with Patrick, and said she regretted what she did.

Karen was very upset of how that boy tried to harass her daughter, but she was happy that the date ended that way and not the way he wanted.

She told Cindy how proud she was of her for taking that stand, and for her not backing down. And she hoped that this would be the end of their friendship.

She tried cheering her up and encouraged her to move on from this experience. She lectured her about relationships, and she told her a story about an experience she had when she was about her age. Whether it was true or not, nobody knows, but it was effective in comforting Cindy.

On Monday morning when she went to school, standing next to the entrance of her classroom was Patrick.

"Hi Cindy," he said, "can I talk to you?" he asked.

Cindy just kept on walking; she had purposed in her heart not to have anything to do with Patrick again.

"I don't know what got into me that night, I acted stupidly, I never meant to hurt you, I am sorry "he said as he kept walking next to her.

Cindy said, "bye Patrick" as she entered her classroom. It bugged her that she had to do that to him, because she really did like him, but she had made up her mind and was not going to change it. She said if he could do that on a special night like this, what more would he do if he got another chance? She sure was not going to stick around to find out.

Patrick did not give up, he tried all that he could to win her over again, but Cindy was not interested, she had completely gotten over him.

Chapter TWELVE

THE DAY THAT CINDY longed for from the first day of high school, was finally here, it was graduation day.

She was excited, she had made it, she was graduating, oh what joy she felt, her high school mission was accomplished.

The ceremony was held at the City's football stadium. There were 331 graduating students. The place was packed with faculty, students, family and friends.

Cindy graduated in the top 5 percent of her class. She received many scholarships offers, most of them came from schools she had researched and applied to.

Donald, Karen and her siblings were all in attendance, and they made their presence known, when they called Cindy's name to accept her diploma, they erupted and shouted, and screamed, which got the attention of many around them.

Karen was overcome with emotion, when she heard her daughter's name called. She thanked God for bringing her that far.

After the ceremony, they lingered around for a while, while Cindy and her friends spent time congratulating each other.

They made it home later in the evening and had a small gathering as they celebrated Cindy's achievement.

The next day when everything quieted down, Cindy began looking towards choosing which school would be more suitable for her to continue her education.

She narrowed it down to two schools, one in Florida and the other in California. She wrestled with the decision of which one to choose, but after consulting a few people, and weighing all the advantages and disadvantages, she decided to choose the school in Florida.

She spent most of her summer preparing for her move to Florida. Her life was about to change, she was about to be on her own for the first time in her life. She could not depend on her mom as much as she did before.

Karen also was going to be affected deeply. She had a very special relationship with her daughter and now it was about to be challenged. She said, she did not know what she was going to do without her baby, her only daughter, but she knew that day would come, and she would have to deal with it.

As the days went by, Cindy planned and organized for her move. She gathered things that she needed for her apartment, which was located within a few minutes from the school.

She went shopping for a small refrigerator which she planned to keep in her bedroom.

Cindy knew that she had a roommate, but since she had not met her and did not know what kind of person she was, in term of habits and behavior, and not knowing how it was going to work out, she prepared like she was going to be living in the apartment alone.

Her mom and siblings assisted as much as they could, they wanted her to have an easy transition from high school life to being at college, because they knew it could be hard.

The weekend before her last, before heading to college, she went to spend it with her dad. She knew she had to put up with Joyce, but she was willing to make that sacrifice.

Chapter THIRTEEN

FINALLY, IT WAS TIME to leave home and head to Tallahassee, Florida. School was scheduled to begin on August 17th, so she decided to leave Texas a week early so she could organize and be ready when classes began.

Donald, Karen and Kellie, accompanied her on the trip. Karen rode with Cindy so she could help her drive, while Donald and Kellie rode in the family van.

They left Texas about 1pm that Wednesday afternoon, and headed for Florida, they made frequent stops at the truck pits to re-energize and to gas up their vehicles and to get more snacks.

They arrived at New Orleans shortly after 8 pm and decided to overnight there. They checked into a hotel to relax and freshen up, and to have a decent meal.

They stayed up until about 12.30am, chatting and relaxing.

They checked out early in the morning after having breakfast, and continued their journey, they made a quick stop at a gas station to fill up their tanks, and to check their tires to make sure they had the right amount of pressure, and that they were safe to drive.

After about five and a half hours of driving, they made it to Pensacola, Florida, which was about 170 miles from Tallahassee, their destination.

"We made it," exclaimed Cindy to her mother as they drove into the city of Tallahassee.

They stopped at a restaurant to have a couple burgers and fries before they continued to the college.

"Here we are, finally, I am so tired and worn out," said Karen, "but I am happy that we made it here safely."

The four of them went to the office so Cindy could check in, and to get the keys to the apartment.

The two-bedroom apartment was small but cozy, it came with a stove, refrigerator and a small microwave.

They brought Cindy's belongings to the apartment, which was on the second floor of the building.

Cindy said her roommate was scheduled to arrive on Saturday, and when she arrives, they would decide on the furniture and other necessities for the apartment, but her main concern now, was to get a small bed for her bedroom.

Because they were so tired, they decided to relax for the remainder of the day and planned to take care of what needed to be done the next day.

Friday morning, Cindy and the rest of the family drove into the city to buy a bed and to learn a few places in the city.

They did some grocery shopping, mostly the basic items, she said she and her roommate would decide what else would be needed for the apartment.

She did not mount up her bed, because she was not sure which bedroom she would be in, that was a decision that was to be made between her and the roommate.

"You know we went down to the store and forgot to get a television set?" Karen said

"I did not forget," Cindy said, "but I wanted my roommate to have an input in that, so I waited."

"Not a good idea," Karen said, "you all will have problems deciding which programs both of you want to watch at a particular time, and this could be an issue. I think you should have your own small tv in your room."

Cindy said, "I will wait, at least, I would have discussed it with her, then, if necessary, I will purchase one."

Early Saturday morning, Cindy noticed a minivan pulling up to the parking spot in front of the apartment, after a short glance, she realized that this was her roommate and her family.

A few minutes later, there was a knock on the door, and when she opened, the young lady said, "hi, I am Katy your roommate."

Cindy gave her a small embrace and allowed her to enter.

Finally, she put a face to the name. She had been talking to her on the phone but had not met in person until now.

Katy and her family introduced themselves to Cindy and her family. They spent the next couple of hours getting to know each other.

They discussed their plans for the rest of the day, which included all going to dinner together.

Cindy and Katy decided on the bedroom situation, and the bedroom that Cindy had in mind, she ended up with.

Donald assembled up her bed, while she, Kellie and Karen did the other décor of the bedroom.

Katy, likewise, went with her family to get a bed, and on their return, her dad assembled it for her.

They hung out for a couple hours more, before Katy, and her family left for their hotel.

She wanted to spend the night with them, because they planned to leave early in the morning for their trip back to Louisiana.

Likewise, Karen, Kellie and Donald were scheduled to leave early in the morning, so they all went to bed as early as they could, so they would be well rested for the trip back.

The time came to say goodbye, and this was one of the most difficult times for Karen that she had to deal with in her life.

She started crying from the time they left the apartment.

The relationship that she and her daughter had was unique. Cindy was her only daughter and thus their closeness was unparalleled to any other. She loved all her children, but being the only girl, made it a much more different relationship than the rest of the children.

She loved Kellie, her stepdaughter, but it was not the same as someone that was your own flesh and blood.

Karen embraced Cindy so tightly and kept on crying. Cindy also became very emotional as they said their goodbyes.

They drove for almost 10 minutes, before Karen said a word or responded to Donald, who was trying to cheer her up.

She was happy that her little girl had grown up, and was now enrolled in college, but she was sad that she was going to be out of her sight for the first time and would be exposed to a different world than the one she was accustomed to.

Chapter FOURTEEN

CINDY AND KATY SPENT the rest of the day unpacking and arranging their apartment. They also discussed how they would deal with their privacy.

Karen called about 8:15pm letting Cindy know that they had made it home safely.

The two young ladies sat and shared details of their lives, particularly during their high school days, they also spoke about their families.

Katy revealed that the reason that she chose to attend this college, was because her boyfriend was attending a college in the southern part of the state, which would give them easy access to each other.

Her parents knew that he had left for college but did not know where he had gone. She kept this information from them because she wanted to see him as often as possible, and her parents were not in favor of their relationship.

Cindy told her about the boys she had experience with, the one who died, and the other who tried to play her for a fool on prom night.

"So, you mean you are a virgin? You have not experienced sex yet?" Katy asked surprisingly.

Cindy was uncomfortable speaking about that virgin subject and avoided talking about it.

Cindy was sharp and blunt, "I do not want to talk about that," and said, "I should head to bed now, we will chat tomorrow. See you in the morning. Probably we could take a drive into the city so we could and get acquainted with some of the places."

"Sounds like a good idea; see you in the morning then."

Before she shut her eyes for the night, Cindy called her dad, just to see how he was doing, and to let him know how she was doing.

She could hear her stepmother fussing in the background, complaining about the time of the night that she was calling. She knew she was just being spiteful, because she knew that they went to bed much later than that time, she just wanted to make it an issue.

Cindy was scared to sleep, she had not slept anywhere before without someone she knew in the same house with her; she read a bible verse, prayed, and then she just laid on the bed unable to sleep. She was feeling the loneliness of not having her mom or brothers around.

Finally, she fell asleep, and did not wake up until late in the morning.

She quickly picked up the phone and called her mother to check on her.

Karen was so happy to hear her voice, because she did not get much sleep, because she was worried about Cindy. They spoke for a while before Cindy had to leave.

Cindy and Katy left the apartment and went to the city, only it took a few minutes to get there, because they used the HOV lane.

The two browsed through various stores and other places of interest for a couple of hours. They purchased a few personal items, including small TVs for each of their rooms.

On their way back, they stopped at the grocery store to pick up some food and necessities to last for the next couple of weeks.

Cindy got some sauce, and a frying pan, rice and peas, and a few pieces of chicken parts, and when they got home, she cooked a delicious meal for the two of them.

"Wow, I did not know you were such a great cook?" Katy said.

"My mom taught me how to cook, and to do some other household chores like, laundry, and keeping the house tidy," Cindy said, I know I will miss her, but the way she brought me up, I know I will be able to manage."

"I am not familiar with cooking, and all this stuff; my family is a big one, and when you are the last one of all these brothers and sisters, you tend to get off Scott free; all I did was hang out with my friends, do my homework, and spend time on the phone." Katy said

"That's cool, that meant, you had lots of brothers and sisters to look out for you, and to protect you."

"They did not have to protect me, surprisingly, I was hardly in major trouble, a few little knocks here and there, but nothing too serious that warranted my siblings help, and besides, I wanted to complete high school, I wanted to graduate and make it to college, and now I am in college, and want to earn a degree"

"Great, Cindy said, we will push, and support each other so we can both accomplish that goal."

After a few more hours of talking, and getting to know each other better, they went to their rooms.

Cindy called her dad and spent a few minutes with him, mostly checking up on him to see how he was doing health wise and how he was doing all around.

She also spent some time on the phone with her mom, told her about the adjustments she had made so far, and of her upcoming plans.

Her mom was encouraged that she was handling things satisfactorily. After a few more conversations, they said their good night, and went to sleep.

On Wednesday, Katy and Cindy went to the campus to confirm their classes, and to meet with their counsellors.

Cindy was following her mom's path and focused on becoming a great nurse. Meanwhile, Katy was focusing on her business management degree.

They spent almost the day on campus, organizing, scheduling other school activities, including clubs, and sororities, that Katy was interested in.

After such a hectic day, the two girls stopped at a restaurant to enjoy a meal.

They were halfway thru their meal when this rugged looking guy seated two rows opposite of them, decided to come over to their table, and asked to join them.

"No, we are okay, we are not here for long," Katy said, but he insisted, and got louder each time he spoke.

"Let's go," Cindy told Katy, it's not worth the trouble."

"Oh no, I am not leaving because of this jerk, we are staying here to finish our meal," Katy said.

"Listen man, get out of our space, we are okay, find someone else to bother and harass," Katy said; the man was noticeably angry and upset.

The manager came over to their table and asked the irritating customer to leave. He explained to them that they have a history with this guy, and has continually been thrown out of the establishment.

"Katy, you are tough, now I can see how growing up with those siblings, especially brothers, made you fearless. I now know that I don't have to hire security, because I have you...hahaha," Cindy said jokingly.

"Don't worry, sis, I have your back," Katy said with a big chuckle.

They finally made it home, after a long-exhausting day. They both laid on the couch and dozed off.

When they woke up, they sat down together, and organized their schedule for their first day of classes.

Chapter *FIFTEEN*

CINDY WAS VERY NERVOUS, and excited at the same time, it was her first day as a college student, and this was a new chapter in her life, and she did not know what to expect.

After orientation, she felt a little bit of relief because she met other students that were just as lost as she was.

She gathered all the information that she needed for her classes, then called it a day, picked up Katy, and then went home.

Although the campus was a few minutes walking distance from home, she knew driving was the best and safest option for her.

As soon as she reached home, she called her mom and gave her a detailed account of her day at college.

"Is that what you expected?" her mom asked.

"Definitely not, it is so different from high school, everyone is on his or her own mission, and pays no attention to those around them; it's quite different." Cindy replied.

"From here on, it is all about you and your career, and you are the one to make it happen," her mom encouraged.

"Mom, I hope I can do this, it is going to be so lonely."

"Yes, you can," her mom said sternly. "I did not raise someone who would quit before attaining her goal, you have always been a strong, motivated person who never stops until you have achieved what you wanted, and you are not going to start being otherwise now."

"Sure mom, I will give it my all, and this is definitely my priority."

They spoke for a little while longer, and then hung up.

She then called her dad, before she hastily went to get something to eat from the kitchen because she was very hungry.

After a short chat with him, she picked up the phone and called her brothers David and Joshua and also spoke with her step siblings, Shawn and Kellie.

David and Joshua encouraged her and gave their advice for handling the stress of college life, they were older, so they had experience in this area.

Cindy entered the classroom for her first class of her college life. She was shaking quite noticeably, because she was nervous. She was tempted to sit at the rear of the class, where she could have everything, and everyone in front of her, but she remembered her mom always admonishing her, to avoid the back of classes, because she said it was so easy to get distracted, so she always advised her kids to sit at the front or at least in the middle of their classes.

The professor walked in and introduced herself as Professor Patricia Solomon; she told them she had been teaching at this University for the past 15 years, and that she took pride in what she did, and was always thrilled when she saw her students excel in their studies.

She then went on and asked them to introduce themselves, starting from the front and proceeding to the back.

Cindy froze in her seat because she was the shy type, and did not really know what to say, but she managed, and introduced herself briefly, then sat down quickly.

She realized that this was a different atmosphere from her high school days, and she was now in total control of her education and would have to approach it differently from high school.

This medical ethics class was going to be a challenge for her, or so she thought, because, she had never heard of medical ethics before now.

She also enrolled in three other classes for the semester. Health care techniques, physical assessments, and vital sign measurements.

The semester went by quickly, and the classes were more manageable than she thought they would be.

She made a few new friends during that time and joined a study group.

The medic class that she thought she would have a hard time with, she got an A at the end of the semester, also she got all A's in her other classes.

She was extremely happy about that and planned on using this as a motivation toward her other classes.

"Great job, Dear, I know you had it in you, and you will continue to excel," said her mom.

"Thanks mom, it was better and easier than I expected."

"I am so glad to see my little girl growing up, and you are maturing so quickly. So proud of you, yet I do not want you to get too complaisant, because this is just one semester of the many semesters you must encounter on your way towards your goal, and it will get harder as you go on, but if you continue with good study habits and a right attitude, you will succeed."

"Mom I will miss thanksgiving for the first time with my family, but I will be home in two weeks for the Christmas holiday."

"I can't wait to see you, my dear; your father will also be glad to see you. Jason is always proud of you and would do anything to make sure you are happy.

"Do you want David or Joshua to come and help you drive home?"

"No mom, Katy and I will drive. I will drop her off at her house, and I will spend a couple hours there to rest and refresh, then I will head home."

"Cindy! That is crazy, Karen shouted, "you don't even know these people, nor the area; that is too risky, I am not for that at all."

"Mom, it will be okay. I am not going there to look around the town, just to lay my head down at my roommate's house for a couple hours, what harm can be done?"

"Okay, but be careful, and why don't you have the boys come to meet you in Baton Rouge so they could help you drive home?"

"Mom, I can drive home by myself, I will be alright."

"No, no, not acceptable," her mom replied, being very concerned. "You a young lady, and with what is happening now on these roads, how can you think like that? Suppose you get a flat tire, what would you do? Call your dad to come and meet you there? I know you are stubborn like him, but I know you would not even dare to call him and mention that to him. He would not approve of you driving from Florida to Louisiana, to Texas."

"Okay mom, I will wait on them, and we will drive together."

"Josh will be on the first flight in the morning, so stay home with your friend for the night, don't go anywhere. I feel much better now, knowing that he will be there."

Chapter *SIXTEEN*

THE TWO YOUNG LADIES left Florida early Friday morning and headed to Baton Rouge. They made a few stops along the way and arrived there about 3pm in the afternoon.

Katy slowly drove down the street to her house, which was the last one on the right side of the street, and as she pulled into their driveway, was greeted by her mother and her brother, Dylan.

"Hi mom," she said, "I am home! Any food ready? I am hungry."

"Girl, you must be starving, you did not even properly greet your mom, after being gone for all this time, and you are begging for food?" her mom said jokingly.

"Hello Mrs. Adams, so glad to meet you again," Cindy said respectfully.

"Same here my child, nice to see you again too, I guess you are starving too?"

"I prepared some gumbo for you both, I know my daughter loves it, so I could not have her starving. It is her favorite food, so I hope you will like it."

"I have never eaten it before; Katy spoke about it, but I can't wait to try it."

She really enjoyed it after having a bowl full, and she complimented Mrs. Adams on her cooking.

They sat at the dining table together with her brother, mom, and her cousin that practically lived there, because she spent more time at Katy's house than she spent at her own home.

Cindy asked if she could have some more gumbo because she liked it; that was rather unusual, because she usually was so shy.

"See, I know you were starving too, because I know my cooking is not that good," said Mrs. Adams.

They talked for a while during and after the meal. They talked about college and other things that happened in the area since Katy left for college.

Cindy was very careful about what she said, because she was a shy person, and she was a very private young lady, saying only what she felt you needed to know.

Dylan kept asking Cindy particular questions, like," is your boyfriend at college too?"

"I don't have a boyfriend," Cindy replied.

Katy stared at her brother, and gave him a look, that said, stop embarrassing me, but that did not stop the questions, and he showed a keen interest in Cindy.

"Cindy, after we rest, we could go downtown so I can show you a few places of interest."

"That would be great, especially since I am not leaving to Texas until tomorrow afternoon, I would love that."

She dismissed her mom's command, knowing that she would not know.

They set out and Katy's brother decided that he want to tag along, as expected; Katy was not excited about the idea, but she always looked up to her older brothers, so she agreed to let him tag along.

It was a good outing, they had fun, and they learned some interesting things from the places they visited.

Dylan was a good companion, and Cindy enjoyed his company, as they got to know each other better.

The following morning, Cindy and Katy went to the airport to pick up Joshua, and at his first glance at Katy, he was in awe, he thought she was so pretty, and was mesmerized by her beauty.

"Hi Katy, this is my brother Joshua"

"Nice to meet you," Katy said, "I have heard so much about you and your siblings, I think I already know you."

"Hope they are all good things that my loving sister has told you "And Joshua chuckled.

"Oh no, you were a bad boy, just kidding, they were good things" Katy joked.

It was a fun trip from the airport to the house, with Joshua doing most of the talking, which was unlike him, and that surprised Cindy, but she realized that her brother had an instant crush on her roommate.

Cindy introduced her brother to Mrs. Adams, and to the others that were at the house.

Mrs. Adams said, "you are a handsome young man, and look very respectable too, I bet your parents are proud of you all."

Joshua was so happy to hear Mrs. Adams saying that, because he thought it would score points with Katy, who he was in love with, just by seeing her.

He called Cindy aside privately, and asked her to find out from Katy, if they could spend the night and leave in the morning?

"I can't do that; she already let me spend a night, I can't impose on my friend like that." Cindy replied.

"I am sure she won't mind; she would be glad to have your company."

"It is not my company that you are concerned with, but you seemed interested in her. Anyway, I will ask her even though I am not comfortable about it, and I know mom would not approve, but I will ask."

Katy was thrilled with the idea, and said, "that would not be a problem, I ask tell mom, but I can assure you that it will be okay."

After the confirmation that it was okay for them to stay, Cindy called her mom and informed her that they would come on Sunday instead. They made plans for the rest of the day and evening.

"Cindy, your brother is a very cute guy, and I think he knows that too; he seems like a very nice person to be around."

"Katy, you won't believe, but my brother is head over heels about you, he has the biggest crush on you, and that is why we are hanging around here until Sunday."

"That is cool, and I am glad you all get to spend another day here, now let's see what we can do."

"I love you as a roommate, and a friend, but I do not want to see my brother get his heart broken by you. I know you have a boyfriend that you deeply care about, and this could end up bad for my brother." Cindy explained.

"We are all young, let's see what will happen, it's not like I am getting married next week, or I am set on my boyfriend, only time will tell, let it play out."

"That is what I am worried about, 'play', I know you are a wonderful person, and I would love for you to be with my brother, but I just don't want to see him get hurt."

"Besides, we will be gone tomorrow, and you will be back with your boyfriend, and Joshua would just be a figment of your imagination."

"Don't bet on it, young people are unpredictable, and they have ways of making things happen," Katy said smiling.

Chapter *SEVENTEEN*

Sunday afternoon, about 3:30 pm, Joshua and Cindy left for Texas. Throughout the trip, Joshua would not stop talking about Katy, and would not stop saying how beautiful she was.

"Josh, please don't get too deep into her," Cindy warned. "Katy has a boyfriend, and she is really into him, I don't want to see you have your heart all torn into pieces, so be careful what you do."

"I definitely can win her over, especially with your help, I know it is possible."

"Okay Macho man, turn on the charm," and she laughed.

"By the way, how was your first semester of college?"

"It was more than I expected, so many adjustments to life, and I had to set priorities, and in order to succeed, I had to be disciplined and committed." Cindy explained.

"Wow, my little sister has grown up, and matured quite a bit; four months of college has already made a big difference in your life. Proud of you, sis."

They made it home about 8.30pm and, as expected, her mom was waiting, and was very happy to see her.

After all the hugs and excitement, she freshened up then came back to the table for dinner.

Cindy gave details about her first semester of college, and the difference it made in her life.

Shortly after dinner, Cindy called her dad to let him know that she had made it home safely and would see him during the Christmas holiday.

"Oh, it feels so good to be home in my own bed," and before not too long, she was fast asleep.

Cindy spent the week with her mom, going shopping, and helping with the preparation for Christmas day; they also went to the beauty parlor to get their nails and their hair done.

Friday night, she and a couple of her friends went to the same restaurant, they went to on the day of their prom.

They were happy to reconnect and they had a great night out. They shared their experiences of their first semester of college.

As soon as Cindy entered the door to her home, her phone rang, and it was Dylan.

"Hi Cindy, it's me Dylan, just calling to check up on you to see how you were doing,"

Cindy was somewhat surprised, because she did not expect him to call.

"I am doing okay at the moment, just trying to make the best of my time away from school."

"Your sister told me that you always ask about me; that nice of you, and I am also glad you called."

"Well, I hesitated to call you before, because I didn't want to be a bother to you, but I think about you all the time; you a such a nice and wonderful person, that I want to remain friends with you."

"How sweet of you to say that, but you haven't really known me long enough to come to that conclusion; you haven't seen my bad side," Cindy told him jokingly.

"I know you don't have a bad side; I can tell by the way you act; besides I harassed my sister to get information about you."

"You don't have to harass your sister, you can ask me directly, I will tell you what you need to know, if I feel like it."

"Okay I will," he said, and he sounded very excited, then he said his goodbye, and wished her a good night sleep.

Cindy thought about that phone call for a while and was curious about the interest of that young man. She knew that she liked him but was not knocked out of her shoes about him.

She spent a few minutes with her mom and stepdad before she went to bed.

The next day, she helped her mom with the laundry and other house chores, and later ordered food from Springside restaurant, because on Saturdays, they normally didn't cook, as mom usually took a break from the kitchen.

Later that evening, her brothers took her and Kellie to the movies. They spent almost 2 hrs. at the theatre, they saw some of their high school mates that they had not seen for a long time; also David had a plan and that is why he suggested the movies.

"Lisa, meet my brothers, Joshua and Shawn, and my sisters Cindy and Kellie."

"Hello, nice meeting you all"

David continued, "this is my girlfriend, we started dating a few weeks ago, we are still getting to know each other, but I felt it was fitting for her to meet you all now, while everyone is home for the season."

"I will bring her to meet mom and dad shortly, no words out of your mouths to them, and Cindy, that also goes for you telling my father, I know you are going to visit him."

"You don't have to worry, I won't say anything, you got my word."

They stayed around for a few more minutes with their friends, before they left for home.

"Great taste big bro," Cindy said to David, "she seems like a nice person."

"Agree." Said Kellie, "I like her, you all look like a nice couple together."

The two other brothers began to mess with David.

"Nephew, niece, soon?" Joshua joked.

"Crazy, mom would have a fit, she is the traditional type, which goes by marriage, then children, not the other way around, besides we both have to finish college, before we take that step.

"Man, anything can happen, you never know, this is the crazy generation." Shawn gave his input, and they continued talking about this until they reached the driveway to their house.

Sunday morning, Karen knocked on her children's doors, and said, "wake up, it is time to get ready for church," she echoed.

"I don't feel like it today," Joshua said.

"Young man, don't get on my nerves; please get up and get ready for church. I know you are grown and in college, but as long as you are in this house, the regular rules stand, and that is that."

Joshua mumbled that next time he had a break, he would go somewhere else, where he wouldn't have to be subjected to all these rules.

"Church should be a choice, not a command."

"Whatever, but the rule of this house stands," said Karen.

After this exchange, Cindy and the others left for church, expecting Joshua to meet them there.

Cindy was glad to see her church friends and was happy to be at church. She went looking for Pastor Jim, before the service started, so she could say hi to him; they had a great relationship with each other.

She saw him right before he went into the chapel.

"Hi Cindy, so glad to see you, it is nice to have you home for the holidays, how was school?"

"It was great, learned a few new things, met and made new friends, and had to make a few adjustments, but all in all, it was okay. Thanks for the counseling, prayers and advice that you gave throughout the years, I know they helped throughout the semester."

"My pleasure, glad that I was of help to you. Hope to see you in one of these Christmas services."

The service was a blessing, it was lively, and the attendance was huge, which was usually the case around the Christmas season.

After service, the family went to Johnson's BBQ to have lunch.

"Good food, lots of food, worth the price," David said.

"Yes David, what else? It's what we expect you to say. You love that stomach of yours dearly," Joshua joked.

After a fun filled lunch, they went home and relaxed, the young men watching sports, while the young ladies spent the afternoon watching a few movies.

The next day, Cindy left to spend a few days with her father, she knew it was going to be troublesome because of her stepmother, but she did not really care; she wanted to see her dad.

She got to the house about 11:30 am, and rang the doorbell, no one answered, she knocked and waited. Over 3 minutes passed and no one came to the door, she knew her dad was at work, and was not sure if anyone else was at home, but she said they knew that she was coming, they should have made provision for that, and just as she was about to turn around and leave, the door opened, and Joyce grumbled, "morning."

"Good morning, and how are you doing?" Cindy asked.

"Fine," and Joyce walked away.

Cindy walked into the room that she usually occupied when she visited, and to her surprise, the room was in disarray, the bed was not made, and items were all over the place. She knew her stepmother dislike her, but she did not expect that type of treatment.

A few hours later, Jennifer, her half-sister came home, and she was surprised to see her, because no one told her that Cindy was coming.

"Hi Cindy, surprised to see you, how are you doing?" she asked.

"I am doing great," Cindy replied, I guess no one told you that I was coming, anyway, I am here for a couple of days, I will be leaving on Wednesday."

"So how has life been treating you since I last saw you? How are you doing at school?"

"Life has been good, and my second year at high school has been good so far, I love high school, so different from middle school, I feel grown, now I can get respect from those below me" and she laughed.

Cindy also chuckled, she remembered when she was in the same position.

"Do you want pizza?" Jenny asked. I bought one last night, but only had two slices, so you can help me eat the rest of it."

"Fine, Cindy said, "I could do with a few pieces."

They sat on the bed, and talked and munched on the pizza, and enjoyed a few cans of soda, while Cindy waited for her dad to come home.

Joyce remained in her room, spent most of the time on the phone, she cared not about what was happening elsewhere.

Finally, Jason came home, and he was so thrilled to see his daughter Cindy.

"Hi Cindy, I am so glad to see you, and I am so happy that you made it here safely," and he gave her a big strong hug.

"My two beautiful daughters," he said, and he hugged Jenny. "You all look so much alike, that means, I have to be a handsome man," he laughed.

"Don't flatter yourself," Cindy said, while Jenny laughed.

Joyce shouted from the bedroom, "that's all you do, take credit for things you don't deserve, but when things are not to your liking, you throw the blame on others."

Joyce kept on grumbling as Jason made his way to the bedroom, then her grumbling became a quarrel, focused mainly on Cindy's visit.

Jason said little, while Joyce kept on speaking in a loud tone of voice.

Cindy refused to let the situation bother her, because she expected a hostile reception from Joyce, and her main purpose for her visit was to see her dad.

After Jason took a bath, he put on some dress clothes, and said, "Cindy, we are going out," and he went back to the bedroom.

Cindy did not know who was going out, but at that same moment, she heard Joyce saying, "you just want to spend time with that daughter of yours, what about Jenny and me?"

"You clearly stated that you don't like being around Cindy, so why would you want to follow us?" Jenny chose not to come because she is studying for an exam tomorrow, so relax. Joyce you are so unreasonable, then he came out to the living room, and said, are you ready?"

Off they went to the restaurant which was a few minutes from the house.

They sat down and waited for the waitress so they could place their orders.

Cindy decided on the lobster and shrimp, while Jason ordered the steak. They both had lemonade.

"How was your first semester? Were your classes hard?" Jason asked.

"Dad, college was fun, it was more than I expected, it was way different from high school, but I learned a lot in those few months, not just schoolwork, but about life in general, especially being responsible for my own actions."

"I am so proud of you Cindy; you are truly growing up to be a wonderful young lady. I can't wait to see what you will become a few years from now."

During the two hours at the restaurant, they shared memories, and discussed the future, and their plans as father and daughter.

They also discussed the way Joyce was treating her, and how bitter she was, but they decided to pay little attention to her.

They came back home to more cursing, and fussing, but Jason ignored it, as he promised he would, and spent a few minutes watching television, before he retired to bed.

The next day, after school, Cindy spent some time with her sister Jenny, they visited the mall, and on their way back home they stopped at the ice cream store to have a few scoops of ice cream, before going back home.

The next day, bright and early, Cindy left for home, she was glad to leave.

She was happy to be back home around her mom and other members of the family.

Chapter EIGHTEEN

CHRISTMAS WAS A FEW days away, so Cindy and Kellie went to the mall to complete their shopping, and to hang out a little bit.

While at Michie store, a guy came up to them, and said, "Hi baby," and hugged and kissed Kellie on her lips.

Cindy was surprised, and before she could say anything, Kellie said, "Cindy, meet my boyfriend, James."

"Hi, nice to meet you," then she slowly walked away from the store, while James and Kellie followed closely behind.

On their way home, Cindy said to Kellie, "I never knew, nor does anyone at home know that you have a boyfriend."

"Well, I did not want all the lectures, nor for dad and mom to tell me that I could not have a boyfriend because I was too young, and then compare me to you."

"So why did you invited him to the mall, knowing that I would see him, if you did not anyone to find out?"

"Because I know that you won't snitch on me, and I know that you are cool, and that you would understand. I hope this won't get to them at home."

"Kellie, I am not about to give you a lecture, but I will say that I am not going to encourage you to have a steady relationship at your age. The way I saw you all getting on, I know this is serious."

"Yes, we are serious, we love each other, and there is nothing wrong with us being together."

"If nothing is not wrong with that, why are you scared of telling your dad?"

"Because he won't understand. I know my dad,"

"I don't know why you are putting me in this position," Cindy said, part of me want you to keep your trust in me, but the other part is saying to me, you should not keep this from your mom. I will see what happens."

Cindy, and the rest of the household woke up early to attend the early morning service, because they knew that the later service would be crowded.

The service was great, they had a great program put together, and even though it was early, it was still well attended.

After service, they stayed around for a little while, greeting and chatting with a few friends, then they went home.

The family gathered on Christmas day, and celebrated the holiday where they exchanged gifts, and with traditional foods and drinks. Later they hung around and played games and watched a few television shows, then Cindy got on her phone and called a few of her friends.

The next day, Monday afternoon, Cindy and Kellie went to the mall, just to get away for a while, and to see what bargains they could get.

They went browsing around the stores, bought a few items, then went to the food court to have a snack to eat.

As they were sitting at the table munching on their snacks, Cindy received a phone call from Katy, and from the look on Cindy's face, Kellie knew it was not good news, and she was hoping that it was not news from home.

Cindy said," oh no, what happened? And she began to cry, and said I will call you back, then she said to Kellie, let's go home."

Kellie asked, "what happened?"

"My friend in Louisiana got killed." And that was all she said until she reached home.

Immediately, her mother knew something was wrong, because she could tell that Cindy had been crying, because her eyes were red and swollen.

"What's wrong Cindy? Why are you crying?" she asked.

"Katy's brother Dylan, my friend, has just been killed. I don't know all the details, but I am about to call Katy to find out."

She picked up the phone and called Katy, hoping that she had mistakenly heard what she told her earlier about Dylan, but as she heard Katy's voice, she knew it was real.

"Katy, I am so sorry for what happened, how are you holding up? And how is your mom doing?"

"Not good, not good at all," katy responded, and then she started crying loudly, and Cindy felt her pain, because she knew how close she and her brother were.

"Mom is falling apart, but my other brothers and sisters, and other family members are here, so that helps a lot."

Then Cindy asked, "What happened?"

"Dylan was on his way to the pharmacy to pick up mom's medicine, when he was struck in the head by a stray bullet that came from a gun fight between two guys who were engaged in a road rage incident. He lost control and struck a light pole. He was rushed to the hospital, but he succumbed to his injuries."

Cindy was so heart broken, she could not believe what had just happened, especially when she had just spoken to Dylan earlier in the morning, and he sounded so happy, and so upbeat, she never in her wildest dreams, thought she would be talking about Dylan in the past tense, and she did not know what to say to Katy, because she had no idea how she felt, but she promised to be there for her.

She decided that she would leave a couple days earlier than planned, so she could spend some time with Katy, and she would be able to attend the funeral.

Cindy explained to her mom and the others what happened, and about her plans to leave earlier than she had originally planned.

She spent the remainder of her vacation in a solemn mood; she and Dylan were becoming closer in their relationship, and now this happened. He was the kind of person she could confide in, he was a good listener, and gave good advice, he was winning her heart more and more each day, and now he was gone.

Chapter NINETEEN

CINDY GOT HER BELONGINGS together and prepared for her trip back to college. She planned to leave early in the morning, so she could be there before evening.

Her mom asked to let her brothers drive with her to Louisiana, because of her state of mind, it would be safe for them to accompany her.

But Cindy declined the offer, she said she would be alright, and she could handle it.

Cindy went to bed, but found it very difficult to fall asleep, she thought of her friend who was dead, and the concern on her mom's face because she was driving alone to Louisiana.

She thought about it and decided to allow her brother to accompany her to Louisiana.

Her mom was very pleased with her decision to change her mind, but Joshua was the one who was the happiest, because he was anxious to see Katy, and was eager to give her his support.

It took them about 5 plus hours, to get to Katy's house, it could have been sooner, but the weather was treacherous, so they had to drive slower than normal.

They pulled up at Katy's driveway and saw Katy and a few members of her family on the porch sitting there talking, but from the look on their faces, you could sense the sadness that they were feeling.

Cindy backed up and parked alongside the street in order to avoid blocking the driveway, for those coming and leaving the house.

She came up the steps that led to the porch, and before she could say anything, she and Katy were embraced and crying on each other's shoulders.

Cindy felt the pain that was being transmitted from Katy's body, she was shaking furiously, and she held her so tightly, she knew that was what she needed to feel better.

Finally, she released her grip, and said, "I am so glad that you are here."

Although it had only been a semester, nobody could tell because of the way they carried on with each other, seemed like they knew each other for many years.

"Hi Katy, Joshua said, "I am so sorry about your brother,' and he hugged her, and she said, "thanks, Joshua, I really appreciate it," and hugged him tighter, then released him, and told him, that she was happy that he came. "I wished we had met under different circumstances, but with life, we never know.

Cindy went in, to greet Mrs. Adams, who was sitting on her bed; she looked dejected and confused.

"Good afternoon, Mrs. Adams, please accept my sympathy," Cindy said.

"Thank you, my child, glad you came, I know it means a lot to Katy and the family."

Katy introduced Cindy and Joshua to the rest of her family members that were there.

"Hi Katy, I noticed that you have a full house, and space could be a problem, Joshua and I will go to a hotel for a couple of days until everything settles down."

"Oh no, Cindy, it is not going to happen; most of family members will be going to their homes, just me and my sister, and one of my brothers, will be here. I need you here," and jokingly said, "you can go, but Joshua has to stay," and they laughed, while Joshua blushed with excitement.

After most people left, Cindy, Katy, Joshua, and Katy's sister sat in the room, and listened to music, and listened to Dylan's friends, share stories about Dylan.

Cindy confirmed what she already knew that Dylan was a good and loving person.

The following day, they prepared to attend the wake which was to be held later that evening.

The most difficult part was to get the mother to attend to attend the wake. They pleaded and begged her until she agreed to go.

As they approached the chapel, Mrs. Adams broke down and cried, and called out for her son, and blamed herself for his death.

Katy kept telling her it was not her fault, but the guys who were fighting were responsible for his death.

She believed, if she had not sent him to pick up her medicine, he would still be here, but Katy reminded her, that he did that every month and nothing like that happened, but nothing she said could convince her otherwise.

They went into the building, and after viewing the body, the crying began, and there was not one dry eye in the midst, and as others came in, they joined in, and shed their tears too.

Cindy went up to the casket, and she looked at Dylan lying there, and still could not believe this would be the last time she would see him. She cried but not as loudly as the others, but her pain was just as great as anyone else.

Katy was crying uncontrollably, it was the first time that she was seeing him since the incident happened, and it dawned on her, that this was reality. She spoke to him like he was hearing her, and asked him, "how could you do that to me?" But he laid there motionless, and as peaceful as ever.

Cindy and Joshua, along with a few others, held her up, and comforted her.

The ride back to the house was very painful, everyone in the car was so quiet, and seemed so distant, because they were thinking of Dylan. The mother was still sobbing, and talking to herself, as they approached the house; she was a broken lady.

Cindy wished that there was something else that she could do to comfort her friend, but she knew she did all that she could.

The next two days went by quietly, everyone was preparing for the funeral that was to be held on Saturday.

Throughout the week, the weather was bright and sunny, but this Saturday, it was very gloomy and cloudy, which represented the way the family and community felt, as they prepared to say goodbye to their loving son.

The family took their places at the front pews in the church, as other members of the community continued to fill in the church.

Service started at 11:am and concluded a little past the noon hour.

During the service, two of his friends spoke about him, and gave encouragement to the family.

When the eulogy was given, there was not one dry eye inside of the church.

The preacher spoke to the family, and then went on to preach a few words about life after death and promised them that they would see this young man again, but on the other side this life, in the beautiful place called heaven.

The procession to the cemetery was not too long, because it was located just a few miles from the church.

After the pastor performed his duties at the burial site, he turned over the remainder of the burial ceremony to the ground keepers.

Mrs. Adams and her children, along with other family members, said their last goodbye to Dylan.

And the crying and the comforting continued, this went on for a while, as people filed out from the burying ground.

Katy and her siblings assisted their mom to the vehicle and took her home so she could rest.

Later in the afternoon, some people came to the house to comfort and encourage the family, and to part-take in some of the food and refreshment that the family prepared.

After all quieted down, Katy and Joshua spent most of the afternoon together; they talked, laughed, and enjoyed each other's company.

Cindy was very concerned, she loved Katy, but she was fearful that her brother might get his heart broken, but she knew she could only advise, but the decision was up to Joshua and Katy.

Early in the morning, Cindy and Katy took Joshua to the airport, for his trip back to Texas.

Katy was sad to see him go but promised to stay in touch as often as possible.

"You fancy my brother a lot hah?" Cindy teasingly asked Katy.

"I really do, he is so cool, smart, caring and loving. The future looks promising for us."

"What about your boyfriend?"

"I think I am phasing out of that relationship; he is not making an effort to progress further in the relationship, he is taking me for granted, sometimes I wonder if there is someone else, he is seeing."

Joshua called about 11am and said he had made it safely to Texas.

Cindy wished that the extra week that she was spending at Katy's home, would have been for a different reason, and it would have involved a live and vibrant Dylan, and they would have a great time before she headed back to school, but it was not to be, and she realized how fragile life can be.

She promised not to take anyone, or anything, for granted, because that same opportunity you have now, might not be available for you at another time.

It was time for them to leave to get back to Florida, and the hardest thing for Katy, was to leave her mom and the rest of the family, who were struggling with the loss of Dylan, and head back to college.

She wanted to stay some more, but her mom ushered her to go.

Thankfully for her, she had Cindy who was like a sister to her, and genuinely cared for her, and gave her all the support she needed to go through that tragedy.

The night before they left, they stayed up late into the night, comforting and encouraging Mrs. Adams, ensuring her that she would be okay.

Wednesday morning, they said goodbye to mom and the others, as they prepared for their long trip.

It was a very difficult situation, but they had to manage, and they had to leave.

It was a difficult ride back to Florida, these two young ladies were ladened with heavy hearts, and painful memories, and were overwhelmed by the trauma that they had been through, but they conquered the road, mile after mile, as they inched towards Florida.

Eventually, they made it.

Now they were concerned about their apartment, they were hoping that no one had tampered with it, while they were gone.

And to their relief, it was as they had left it; the only small concern that they had, was a little hike in their light bill, because they left a few night lights, and a television on to deter people from coming in there.

They spent the rest of the evening relaxing. They were very tired, and emotionally drained. Bed was an easy option for them.

For the next few days, they relaxed, shopped, and attended church, and prepared for the resumption of their classes.

After one semester of school, Cindy thought that she was an expert around campus, she knew where to go, and where to find things that she needed, she enrolled in her classes without any hiccup.

Her focus was to stay on track, and to end the semester with excellent grades.

She joined a couple of clubs, and made it on the basketball team, her intention was to stay busy, and to occupy herself as much as she could.

Chapter TWENTY

A FEW WEEKS INTO the semester, Cindy started hanging out with Robin, who she met in one of the clubs. Robin was the total opposite to her. She was far from shy, very outspoken, was very active with her young men, and loved to be entertained.

Their friendship grew stronger as the semester went on, and they frequented each other's place.

Robin lived at the dormitory on campus and had to adhere to the strict rules that governed that portion of the school, but she usually pushed the rules, until she was warned, then would try to follow them.

Katy was not thrilled with Robin frequenting their apartment, she did not like her ways, she said Robin had no respect for herself, furthermore for others. She wanted to confront her on a few occasions, but she did not want to be on bad terms with Cindy because of Robin.

But it got to the point where she could not stomach it anymore, so she approached Cindy and told her what had been bugging her for a while.

"I have noticed since you started being around Robin, and developed a friendship with her, that your attitude toward me, and toward your schoolwork has also changed. I know it is not my place to lecture you, but as a friend and roommate, and I also consider you to be a sister to me, I would like to see you stay the course and finish what you have started with all these great grades."

"Kate, I know you mean well, and you are looking out for me, but as your roomie, and sister by our friendship and my brother (chuckled) I am telling you that everything is okay. I won't be led astray by Robin."

"What do you mean sister by your brother?" Katy asked.

"I have noticed that you have ditched your boyfriend, and are constantly on the phone with Josh, and all Josh talks to me about, is you."

"Okay, I am busted, your brother and I are in a relationship, we did not want to announce it, unless we were positive that this was what we wanted, and sis, we know for sure this is what we want, I love your brother dearly."

"I am so happy for you guys; I could not have asked for a better person to be part of our family."

It was time for spring break, and most of the students were excited to get away for a week, and since it was Cindy's first college spring break, she was looking forward to it.

She had barely finished talking to Katy about Robin, when her phone rang.

"Hi Cindy, guess what?"

"What?"

"We are going to Miami Beach on Monday for spring break, and you are coming with us."

"What do you mean by we? And I am joining? I can't remember discussing that with you?"

"No, but I know you would be excited, so I went ahead and reserved the hotel room for the two of us. The other girls are paired up, and I told them I would pair up with you. So, are you down with it?"

"Robin, let me think about it, and let me talk to a few folks about it, and I will get back to you, as quickly as possible."

"Okay, but I hope you say yes, because I know you would have a great time."

Cindy, straight away related what Robin had said to her to Katy and asked her for her advice.

Katy wasted no time in discouraging her, and told her this was a horrible idea, and told her not to go.

"Don't let Robin push you around, I know you are strong and self-willed, now stand up to this bully."

"I told her I would get back in touch with her, but I am thinking about it, that would be something different to experience," Cindy explained.

"Are you going to let your mom know?" Katy asked

"I don't think so," Cindy replied, "she would worry about me the whole time I am there."

"Can you blame her? Her only daughter in a place like Miami beach, with someone she barely knows, having a wild time?"

"Wow, you sound like my mother; those would be her exact words."

"So, this is a sign that you should not go. We can go a for a couple of days to the beach at Destin, which is a short trip from here," Katy said hoping to convince Cindy.

After thinking about it for some time, Cindy called her mom, and ran the idea of going to Miami Beach with her friends, by her, and as expected, her mom went crazy over the phone.

"Are you thinking clearly? Are you in your right mind? My child, what has gotten into you?" and she went on, and on, not letting up.

"Mom, I have not gone yet, or have made up my mind on doing that yet, it is an invitation, and I said that I would think about whether to go or not."

Cindy pondered the decision in her mind for about a day, then concluded that it was not worth the trouble, and she did not want to stress out her mom.

She told Katy her decision, which brought joy and relief to Katy, and she was happy that Cindy was about to stand up to Robin.

Cindy called her mom and told her that she had decided not to go to Miami.

Karen was so relieved and comforted from Cindy's decision, because she had been troubled since Cindy told her of plans.

Afterwards, she called Robin, and said to her, "I will pass on the trip to Miami Beach."

"Why? You are going to miss out on a great trip, and a wonderful week of fun." Robin said.

"There will always be another time, but for now, I will let that one pass by." And nothing Robin said would change her mind.

The rest of the weekend went by quickly, and Cindy and Katy went shopping, where they purchased a few items for their trip to Destin.

On Monday, Cindy stayed in bed later than usual, and just pondered on a few decisions she had made lately, and the outcome of these decisions.

Before she retired for her night rest, she and Katy spent some time planning their trip to Destin.

They had planned to leave early in the morning to avoid the morning rush traffic, and to reach Destin early enough, where they could have a great day at the beach, and to make it back in the evening, but Katy said to Cindy, "why don't we just book a room at a hotel close to the beach, and spend the night there, and come back home on Thursday evening? This way we don't have to hustle to avoid the traffic, and the 3-hour drive would be less stressful."

"Sounds good to me, that is a great idea" Cindy agreed.

They spent the next couple of hours trying to book a room for that night, but it was difficult, because spring break usually brought a lot of students, and other people to Destin. It took them a while to find a room that was available at a reasonable price.

The location that they desired was not available, so they had to settle for something a little bit further from the beach.

Chapter TWENTY-ONE

BRIGHT AND EARLY WEDNESDAY morning, the two young ladies, with bags packed, and car filled up with gas, left for Destin.

They did one stop at a restaurant to get breakfast, and then continued their journey.

They arrived in Destin around 11am, and went to the hotel and checked in.

The beach was 10 minutes from where they were, so they went there about 1.30pm.

The beach was crowded with people, mostly young people, basically, college and school students.

They secured a good spot, and placed their cooler, and other items there, then they entered the water.

"Wow, what clear warm water, what a contrast from my home beach," Cindy exclaimed.

"Yes, I know," said Katy, "I have seen pictures, but never actually been to one of these beaches until now, and I love it."

They were in the water for a while, then Kate took a break to munch on snacks. She barely left the water, before a young man came over to Cindy.

"Hi" he said, what is your name? I just wanted to come over to say hi."

"And why didn't you come?" Cindy snapped back.

"I did not want to get double rejected, so I took the chance with the one I really wanted to talk to."

"Why would I just tell my name to you, a random stranger?"

"That is why you should tell me, so we can become friends and not remain strangers. '

"So that is what you do? Just go around collecting young ladies' names and numbers?"

"Oh no, not at all, don't judge me like that, I am not that type."

"I have heard these lines before, pick up lines."

"I am curious, do you and your friend live around here?"

"Why would I tell you that? I don't know you; how would I know that you are not trying to harm us?"

"Why would I do that? You see these young men and young ladies over there? These are my buddies, I saw you two over here, so I came over to see if I could make some new friends, anyway, I am sorry for approaching you, please have a nice day." And he started to walk away.

"You don't have to walk away," Cindy said, I am just being cautious, by the way, my name is Cindy."

"And I am Mario, it is my pleasure meeting you."

At that moment, Katy came strolling back.

"Cindy," I saw that you have made a new friend."

"Yes, this is Mario, he came over to say hello, and to make our acquaintance."

"Hi, I am Katy, it was nice of you to come over."

"You all can join us over there, we are getting ready to play a game of volleyball, and we would love for you all to participate."

Cindy and Katy accepted the invitation and walked over with Mario to meet his friends.

"Hello, everyone, meet my friends Cindy and Katy, my new-found friends, they are willing to mingle with us for the next few hours," then he went on and introduced each one to the young ladies.

They chatted, and socialized, before they played a few games of volleyball.

Cindy was thrilled about playing, because basketball and volleyball were her favorite sports, and she was good at both.

When they were through playing, some of Mario's friends commented on how good she was, and how great she played.

Cindy's mother Karen was a good volleyball player, and her dad was great at basketball; she was happy to have gotten the gifts from both.

Katy and Cindy hung out, and mingled for a few more minutes, before they gathered their belongings and went back to the hotel.

They stopped at Sharkie's restaurant to pick up dinner, because they did not want to spend too much money at the hotel for dinner.

Not too long after dinner, Mario called, and Cindy was not thrilled, and did not handle the call well. She later felt bad and blamed her behavior on being too tired.

She promised that she would call him next day and make amends for what she had done.

"New boyfriend?" Katy teased.

"Oh no," Cindy said, "at this time, I am not interested in being in a relationship, and since the death of your brother, I am not eager to be in a relationship right now."

"You really liked my brother, eh?"

"I really did, I can't deny that he was a very nice person, and I will always miss him."

Katy started to sob as they spoke about her brother.

"Sorry, I brought it up," she said, and Cindy talked about something else.

Thursday morning about 11:am, they checked out from the hotel, and drove around Destin to look at the city.

They visited a few historical places, went to the park for about an hour, went to a restaurant to get some food, then went to the beach for another hour and a half, before they started their drive back to Tallahassee.

The drive back seemed a bit longer than when they were going; they were driving at a slower pace. It took them an hour longer to get home, but they did not mind.

Nothing felt better, than to pull up in front of their apartment. They managed to make it upstairs, then went straight to the shower, after which, they sat on the couch, and not too long after that, they both dozed off.

They woke up a few hours later, then went to their beds, and did not wake up until Friday morning.

After breakfast, Cindy picked up her phone and called Mario.

"Hello, who is this?" Mario asked.

"You already forgot me?" Cindy asked.

"No, no, I saw the Texas number, and did not connect the dots."

"That means that you did not save my information in your phone, anyway, I called to apologized for the way I responded to your call on Wednesday night. I was tired from all the day's activities, so I snapped at you. I'm not saying that this was a good reason for doing that, but this was what happened, I am not normally like this."

"It is okay," Mario said, let's put this behind us, and let's start over. We could go out sometime on the weekend, since my school is not too far from where you are, we could have a great conversation while at dinner."

"I am not sure about that, but give me some time to think about it, also thanks for introducing my friend and I to your friends, I appreciate that."

"We all enjoyed you and your friend's company, and we were impressed by your volleyball skills, I guess one day, you will get to teach me some of those techniques."

"Maybe. Mario, I have to say bye for now, I have something else planned for this time, please stay in touch, we have to remain friends."

"Okay, have a great day Cindy, we will talk later."

Mario was dejected. He wished for more sparks between Cindy and himself but promised not to give up.

The weekend was quiet, the young ladies attended a few planned activities, and took in a movie together at the movie theatre.

The next day, they resumed their classes, and it was a little bit colder than usual, and Cindy bundled up, she was heavily dressed, she was buttoned up from head to toe.

"Are you going to Alaska?" Katy asked, while laughing hysterically, this is not Wisconsin, or Chicago, this is Florida, this little chill is as cold as it's going to get in Florida in March."

"Well, I am not used to that, and this is cold to me," Cindy remarked.

"I hope you are not planning to go to class like that. People will look at you like you are crazy."

"Well, too bad, I am going like this, I don't care what people think, I am going to stay warm, come on let's go."

As Katy predicted, some people stared at Cindy, and looked at her, like they had seen a strange creature, but Cindy did not care at all.

When they got back to the apartment, Katy told Cindy, "I admire you, I never thought you would go there like that, but you are tougher than I thought, or more stubborn than anybody I met, but it turned out to be okay."

Cindy said, "my dad always tells me, be the person you want to be, and not the person people desire for you to be."

"Speaking about your dad, I saw his picture on your nightstand, and he is a handsome man, not that I am hitting on him, hahaha, but he is a hunk, and your mom is also beautiful, no wonder you are so pretty."

"Yes, you are hitting on my dad," Cindy said jokingly.

"But your mom gene is stronger than your dad, because you look more like her than him, but your brother, my baby, is the exact picture of this handsome man. Am I lucky or what?"

"Oh, by the way, not that you don't already know, my brother, Josh, is coming here next weekend, to spend a couple days with us, but more you than me. hahaha.

He said, this is one of the few weekends he had off from his basketball schedule, so he chose to spend it with us. He is the star of the team and deserves a little perk."

After driving over 9 hours from North Carolina, Joshua finally made it to Florida.

He showed up at his sister's, and girlfriend apartment, grinning from ear to ear, with excitement.

He embraced his sister, and then hugged his girlfriend tightly, and gave her a juicy big kiss. "I am so happy to see you all," he said, "wished I could have done this more often."

"I can't believe this is my brother, the shy, reserved guy that stayed in the background always, is now smacking a girl on the lips? How things have changed, my brother is now grown." And the girls teased and laughed at him.

Being so tired, from that long drive, Joshua suggested that they order a few pizzas and stay in, instead of going out to the restaurant.

They sat in the living room and chatted for a while, then Cindy excused herself, and went into her room, leaving the two lovers to build their relationship.

They eventually went to Katy's bedroom, where they discussed their future, after which Josh got up from the bed and was heading to the couch to sleep.

But Katy was not in favor of that, she was not intrigued by the idea that he would be out there, and she would be in her room alone.

"I thought you were going to sleep on the bed with me," she told him.

"I would like to, and would enjoy that very much, but out of respect for you and my sister, I prefer to sleep on the couch.

I grew up that way, and I try to avoid temptations as much as possible, and knowing how gorgeous you are, I don't think I would pass that test, and resist you."

Katy was disappointed, but understood him quite clearly, and said to herself, "this is a good man, and I am so happy to have him, and besides, he was so right, because I don't think I would have been able to hold back my horny self, thank to him, I will be stronger the next time, that is how you grow and mature.

After they hugged and had a few kisses, they said good night to each other.

In the morning when Cindy woke up, she was surprised to see Josh on the couch sleeping, but she was happy that he or they made that decision.

Throughout the night, one of her thoughts was, if mom found out that she allowed Josh to come to her apartment, and spend the night in a woman's bed, and she did not say or did anything about it, she would have been furious.

She didn't know how they managed to come to that conclusion, because she knew that was a hard decision that had to be made and was glad they came to that respectable decision.

It was a great weekend, they enjoyed the time that the three of them spent together, especially Josh. He enjoyed spending time with his sister whom he loved dearly, and more so, with his girl-friend, who he intended to spend the rest of his life with.

Early Monday morning, the young ladies said bye to Josh, as he prepared for his long drive back to North Carolina.

"You are beaming this morning," Cindy jokingly said to Katy, "it looks like you had a great weekend."

"Oh, could not have asked for anything better than that, Katy replied, I can't wait until we will be together forever, Josh is awesome, I am so glad you came into my life, because you brought me a treasure."

Chapter TWENTY-TWO

CINDY SET UP A goal, she wanted her grades to be in the top 2% in all her classes for the semester, she wanted to finish her nursing degree at the end of the program, at the top of her graduating class.

The next two months, Cindy stayed true to her commitment, she spent a lot of time studying, researching and completing assignments without hesitation.

In between, she engaged in activities that she was committed to. She also made time for her friends, and went to the movies, when possible, with Katy.

Mario called often, but she did not prolong the calls, because she realized he wanted much more than just friendship, but she was not interested in being anything else but a friend.

She was focus heavily on school at the present time and was not interested in having a romantic relationship.

Cindy had a great semester, with good grades, and she finished her first year of college at the top of her class as she had aspired.

She made the Dean's list and had a high GPA. She was happy to achieve that and promised to do the same in her next school year.

"Hey, can we go and celebrate the end of our first year of college, and your great achievement? Let's go to Florida's Delight and enjoy that great seafood variety that they have."

"Sounds good," Cindy agreed, I am all in, but can we do that on the weekend?"

"Sure, Saturday it is, this way we could have more time, and fun, and not have to worry about the next day's activities. I wish Josh would be here to enjoy with us."

"He was here just a couple of months ago, you already ran out of all the love he poured into you?"

"Yes, like you said, a couple of months, that is a long time ago, I should see my baby much more often than that. You will understand some day, or probably sooner, how it is to be in love, and how absence makes the heart grows fonder. I can't wait for your turn."

"I am not in a hurry to find out," echoed Cindy.

It was summer, and both young ladies, decided not to enroll in summer classes, they both wanted to go home for the summer, but they did not know what to do with their apartment, since they would both be gone for over 2 months. They thought about leaving it closed while they were gone but worried what could happen when others noticed that they were not there, so they had a problem.

But they remembered that Liz, one of their best, and most trusted friends, was staying for summer classes, so they asked her if she would stay there while they were gone.

She welcomed the idea, she was happy to get away from the Dorm for a while, and gladly accepted their offer.

Joshua had a couple weeks of vacation and could be away from basketball for a short period of time, he flew down to meet them, so he could help with driving, and to see Katy.

Cindy spoke to her mom, informing her that Katy would be coming to spend a week with her.

Karen was not surprised, though no one told her of Joshua and Katy's relationship, she had put the pieces together, and her mother's instinct, had her thinking in that direction.

The young ladies, along with Joshua, left Florida and started their trip to Texas. They stopped in Louisiana at Katy's family for a day.

Joshua and Katy told Mrs. Adams about their relationship, and she said, she sensed that would happen, and she gave them her blessings.

The next day, they continued their journey to Texas. It took them over 4 hours, before they arrived.

As expected, mom was thrilled to see Cindy, and Joshua and, although it was less than six months since she had seen Cindy, she appreciates whatever time she could get to spend with her.

David had also made the trip home, and for a few weeks, they all would be home.

Saturday evening, while they were having dinner, Joshua said, "Mom, and everyone, Katy and I are in a romantic relationship, and we are very seriously in love."

"So, she came to spend time with you, not really Cindy?" Karen said sarcastically.

"Funny," Joshua replied. Soon she will officially be your daughter- in-law."

"She must be special," David said, "I have never seen you so passionate about anybody or anything."

"Yes, she is," Joshua responded, "I am so glad that Cindy chose to attend that school, she will have brought home more than a degree." And he laughed.

"You owe me big time, and trust me, when I give you my bill, it's going to be a huge one."

It was a great dinner, the atmosphere was light, so much was shared, and they appreciated each other presence.

Cindy spent the remainder of the evening on the phone with Katy, Liz, Mario, and her dad. He asked her about school, and, by surprise, he asked her if she had a boyfriend, and she quickly said no. She explained that she was not going that route for now.

He was very pleased with her answer and jokingly said, "any young man that want to be with my baby, will have to go through my interview first."

Cindy knew that he said that it was a joke, but knowing her father, she knew he meant it, because, when it came to her, he did not joke around.

Cindy debated within herself, whether to tell her dad or her mom about an incident that occurred with her stepdad.

She knew her dad, and she knew what his reaction could be, and she was not sure if her mom's relationship with Donald would continue, but the last week of high school kept on playing in her head constantly.

Chapter TWENTY-THREE

FRIDAY EVENING BEFORE DINNER, she stepped into the shower, and she was in there for about ten minutes, singing, and enjoying the warm water as it fell on her back, as she normally did. Then she came out to dry and to lotion up her skin, when the door to the bathroom suddenly opened, and there standing in the doorway was her stepdad, Donald.

She was so startled, and embarrassed, she did not know what to do, she wanted to scream, but for whatever reason, she just could not get it out.

She stood there naked, shaking, and frightened, she took her hands and covered her breasts, then tried to reach for her towel so she could cover her nakedness, sobbing vigorously as she did so, as Donald stood there saying "I am sorry, sorry, I did not know you were in there, I just wanted to get a roll of toilet paper, because we ran out in our bathroom."

This infuriated Cindy even more, because she knew he was lying. She knew he heard the shower, he heard her signing, and why did he wait until he did not hear the shower to come in? She knew where the stack of toilet paper was stored.

Cindy was so enraged after that episode, and said, I am going to tell my mom when she comes home.

Donald pleaded with Cindy, and said "please don't tell her, I did not mean to walk in on you like that, I am really sorry."

Cindy insisted that he knew exactly what he did, and planned it all along, and demanded that he get out, and told him, how much she hated him, and never wanted to have anything to do with him again.

Cindy came very close to telling her dad when they were talking, but somehow, held it back, because of the fear of what could happen to the family.

She pondered this in her heart for the past year and more, but this kept eating her up inside, and every time she saw Donald the incident resurfaced in her mind.

She knew she could not let her brothers find out about that, because it would not have ended up good, so she decided not to tell them.

At that moment, her mom came into her room to chat before they went to bed. Again, this issue was pressing against her heart, but she decided this was not the right time to bring this up, and again she said to herself, when would be the right time?

Since the young men were not home, Karen thought this was the best time to find out about Katy.

She recognized that her son was madly in love with Katy, and was seriously thinking of marrying her, so she wanted to know what her future daughter- in- law was like.

"So, Katy will be here next week?"

"Yes, mom, Joshua and I will be going to the airport Saturday night to pick her up, her flight comes in at 7pm."

"I know you have been around her more than anyone of us, what kind of person is she? You have heard how mothers are when it comes to their sons choosing their partners."

"Mom, no need to worry, she is not a hundred percent perfect, but she is way up there in percentage, I am so glad she and I came in each other's lives, she is awesome, you will love her."

"Good to know that she has won your approval, that means a lot to me, because daughters are the hardest critics of other women coming into an existing family.

Saturday evening, Joshua and Cindy left to pick up Katy from the airport, they were fortunate not to have ended up in a traffic accident. A radical driver, going in and out of traffic, at a high rate of speed, just narrowly missed hitting them, and had it not been for God's mercy and guidance, which enabled Joshua to see this driver, and ease back so he could pass, there would have been a serious accident.

This incident had them shaking, they did not say a word until they got to the airport.

At the airport they waited a few minutes for the flight to arrive as they were a little early.

It was not too long before they saw Katy coming in the pathway that came from the baggage area.

"Hi Kate, welcome to Texas," Cindy said, and gave her a big hug.

Joshua was thrilled to see her and quickly embraced her and gave her a peck on her lips.

"How was your flight?" he asked.

"It was okay," she said, "it was the first time that I have flown on a plane, and it was scary, but adventuresome, anyway, I am here, and I am so happy to see you all."

"Before we drive off, can I call my mom to let her know that I had made it here safely? She was worried about me taking this trip by myself."

"Sure,' Joshua replied, "that is important, go ahead, call her."

"Here we are," Cindy told Katy, as they pulled up into the driveway.

"Wow, nice big house," Katy said, as she gazed in wonderment at the house and the others in the neighborhood.

She grew up in a smaller community with nice houses, but nothing like what she was seeing before her eyes.

She thought, Cindy and her family must be rich, and she was even more convinced when she entered the house and saw the layout and what was in there.

"Hi Mom, we are back," echoed Cindy, as her mom made it out from the bedroom.

Then Josh said, "Katy, meet my mom."

"She is my mom too," Cindy said jokingly, and in case you don't know, Katy met mom before."

Karen was happy to see Katy again, and expressed her condolences in person to her, for the loss of her brother.

"Welcome to our home, make yourself comfortable, we are thrilled to have you here."

"Thanks Mrs. Karen, it is nice to meet you again, and thanks for welcoming me to your home."

They sat around for a while, as the family entertained Katy. After a few hours, Donald and Karen excused themselves, and they went to their bedroom.

The young folks, David, Joshua, Cindy, katy, and Kellie, stayed around and talked about college, basketball, and many other things, until the early hours of the morning, before retiring to bed.

Joshua woke up early, before the rest of the family, to prepare breakfast for Katy, just then, his mom came out from her bedroom to prepare for work and was shocked to see him in the kitchen preparing breakfast.

"I need to invite Katy over here more often, I can't remember when I 've ever seen you in the kitchen, doing anything but eating, this girl is a wonder pill, the thing love can do" and she laughed for a while.

"Do you need help?" she asked

"Not really, besides, I will ask Cindy. We will prepare breakfast for everyone, you need to go to work."

"Good idea, but you will have to wait at least one more hour, she would not like for you to wake her up that early, and besides, I heard you all having fun up to the early hours of the morning, and Katy is not going to get up now."

The mother was so happy to see how loving, and committed her son was, she was excited and pleased to see him on the right track, and hopefully, he would be a good husband.

Katy woke up to the scent of fried bacon, fried eggs, and toasted bread, she quickly went to the bathroom, freshened up, then followed her nose to the area where the scent was coming from. She thought that David or Joshua had gone to the restaurant to purchase breakfast, but when she walked a few steps to the kitchen, she saw Joshua and Cindy preparing breakfast.

"You could have woken me up to help with this feast," she said smiling.

"Why would we do that?" you are our guest, and by the way, Josh wanted to impress you, by providing you with breakfast in bed, but mom and I spoiled his plan.

"Must say it smells good, and looks good, and I am pretty sure it tastes good too. I could get use to this, right Josh?"

"No comment, I am not going to incriminate myself with this oath," and he hugged and kissed her on the forehead.

The rest of the week's activities went smoothly.

Josh and Cindy and sometimes David took Katy to several places in Texas, some historical, some entertainment and amusement places.

Josh spent some quality time with Katy whenever the opportunities were available.

On Thursday, which was Karen's off day from work, she requested from Joshua and Cindy, if she could spend a few hours with Katy.

After the family had lunch, Karen and Katy left for the mall.

Joshua was happy that his mom and Katy got to spend time together, but he was hoping that his mom would say all the right things while they were out there.

The two ladies had a good time, they went to various stores, and did a little bit of shopping, mostly Karen, who bought a few items for Katy.

They got along as though they had known each other for a long time.

On their way back to the house, Karen asked Katy a few questions about her family, just to have a better picture of who she was, but besides that, their conversations were more around school and work.

When they came back to the house, Josh and the others were eager to know how the outing went.

Karen just smiled and gave an indication that everything went well.

They were both supposed to leave on Sunday afternoon on a flight to Carolina, with a stop at Louisiana, but Cindy asked Katy to stay another week, and after she got the approval from her mom, Katy decided to stay.

Joshua reluctantly left for the airport, as he made his way back to school. He was going back to North Carolina, but his heart was still in Texas.

Katy had a great time in Texas, and she was extremely impressed with Cindy and her family dynamics, and was very curtain, that she had made the right choice, by choosing Joshua, and by integrating into his family.

Cindy was sad to see her friend leave, but she knew Katy had to spend quality time with her mom, especially, knowing that her mom was still hurting from the loss of her son.

Chapter TWENTY-FOUR

THE REST OF THE summer flew by quicky, but the time spent with her family, including her dad, was precious.

She was able to convince her mom to let her drive back to Louisiana by herself, although her mom was troubled by it, but she was tired of arguing with her daughter, so she gave in.

After stopping in Louisiana to pick up Katy, they made it to Tallahassee safely.

They went up to their apartment and was impressed on how clean it was.

"What did you do, Liz? Are you trying to make us feel bad?' Katy said jokingly.

"I had the time, so I made good use of it, but if you bring it back to the old state that it was in, you will have to answer to me."

They spoke about their summer experiences, and what went right, and what did not, and the great time they had with other family members.

Starting a new school year was exciting for Cindy, she had the experience from year one, and now she knew what to expect. She promised to keep up her grades, and to maintain her status on the Dean's list.

The nurse's curriculum demanded lots of study and focus, and plenty of hard work, but Cindy was committed to do all these things.

It was Thanksgiving, and Cindy decided not to go to Texas, but to spend the time in Louisiana with Katy and her family.

Karen did not like that idea at all, because it was a tradition for the family to be home together for thanksgiving, unless if there was an emergency that would prevent someone from attending.

"Mom, I don't want to do all this driving for just a few days, and besides, Joshua won't be home anyway, he has a commitment at his school."

"Why didn't Joshua tell me that? I spoke to him yesterday."

"Mom, I am sure he will, he was going to tell you in his own time, but I guessed I have screwed that up. Anyway, there should be an exception this year, for Joshua, and me.

We won't be there in person, but we will be chatting with you throughout the season, especially on Thanksgiving Day."

"I am not happy about it, but I guess we will manage."

For Cindy, it was awkward being at Katy's house, because all she could think of was Dylan, who was killed not too long ago.

It was a great thanksgiving weekend, great Louisiana food, and Katy's family showed up in big numbers, which made the weekend even more enjoyable, and appreciated. It was a great way to get your mind off school for a while.

They had a couple mishaps on their way back to Florida, but thank God, they made it back safely.

Cindy was surprised how quickly the school year was moving along, and how much more focused she had to be to stay on course to accomplish her goals.

The semester came to an end, and Cindy was again very pleased with her grades.

Cindy left her car with Katy and went home to Texas for Christmas. Katy stayed in the apartment and invited Liz to stay with her for a few weeks, which she agreed to.

Chapter TWENTY-FIVE

CINDY'S FLIGHT TO TEXAS was rather interesting. On that flight, was Anthony. Cindy disliked him a lot during high school, because he always made fun of her, and tried to embarrass her as often as he could, just to please his friends. She tried to avoid him as much as possible.

She was totally surprised to see him on that flight, and on his way to his seat, which was a couple rows from her, he stopped and said hi to her.

She could not believe it, and she could not believe that she answered him.

Halfway through the flight, he came up to her and asked, if he could sit next to her, since there was no one sitting there.

"No problem," she said, and he retrieved his bag from his seat and came to sit next to her.

"First of all, I want to ask for your forgiveness for the way I treated you through our high school years. I did it out of ignorance, not considering how hurt you were from my insensitive assaults. I am very sorry."

"Man, I hated you with a passion then, you had me fearing you, I would pass another way just to avoid you. There was a time I considered telling my brothers, so they could confront you, but at the last minute I decided against it, because my brothers would do anything to protect me, and I was concerned where it could have led to."

"Right now, I am torn between forgiving you, or ignoring you."

"But since, I have gotten over you, I will forgive you, although, just seeing you today, brought back these bad memories, and ill feelings towards you."

"I do understand if you chose not to forgive me, because I deserve it, but I am different now."

"It is hard Anthony, but with God's grace, I am able to forgive you. I have matured over the years, since I have seen you, and negative things from my past, I try to leave them there, in my past, where they belong. I accept your apology, and do forgive you, and we can move forward with a better relationship."

"Thank you, Cindy, and can I ask where you are coming from?"

"From Florida, that is where I am going to school, what about you?"

"I am coming from Georgia; it has been my home for the last 2 years."

"Do you like it there?" Cindy questioned.

"Yes, I do, I have been going to school, but between school classes, and football, I barely have time to explore the state."

"So, you continued to play football? I am not surprised; you were good at it."

"I obtained a football scholarship and decided to pursue the sport with vigor and enthusiasm, and fortunately, it is working for me so far. I am recognized nationally, and if all works out, and I stay on this path, you are looking at a high draft prospect in the upcoming year."

"Oh, good for you, I wish the best for you, and wish you great success."

As they were coming to the end of the flight, Anthony gave Cindy his phone number, and asked that she call him.

The trip from the airport was short, since Hobby airport was not too far from her home, but on the ride home, Cindy could not get Anthony off her mind. She was amazed how things had turned around from high school to this present moment, where now they could be friends; amazing.

Being home for the holidays, was a relief for Cindy; she was happy to be around family, and friends.

Her mom was happy to see her. She had lots of plans for them to do for the holiday.

But Cindy chose to spend the first three days with her dad, although she hated going to his house because of his miserable wife, yet she loved her dad too much, to come to the state and not go and pay him a visit, also she wanted to see her sister.

She made it back to her hometown and planned to rest and relax for the next couple days, not doing anything major, but small things like decorating, and shopping.

Before she went to bed, she called Anthony, just to stay in touch, and she was surprised to hear how happy he was to receive her call.

After a few minutes of talking, they agreed to go to a movie Saturday night.

Cindy and her mom went shopping and picked up items they needed for the weekend, because of her schedule, she did not have the time to do it during the week.

Around 5:pm, Cindy told her mom that she was going out to the movie with Anthony, a friend from high school.

Her brothers were startled, "Anthony? That same guy, who made your life so miserable at school?" David asked her

"No way, that is not going to happen" Joshua said.

But Cindy said, she had made up her mind, and was going, that is it.

"Who is that Anthony guy anyway?" her mom anxiously asked. "He must have had a bad reputation at school, because none of your brothers approved of you going out with him."

"Mom, he was a mischievous person at high school, and I avoided him at all costs, but he is a different person now, he has grown up, he has changed."

"Do I know him, or his family?" her mom asked.

"Not sure mom, probably you have seen him around, it is a small-town mom."

"Does he go to church, or is he a Christian? You know how I feel about hanging out with people with much different beliefs than you."

"Mom, it is not always about church, there is life outside of that environment."

"You know the Bible is not in favor of dating someone that is not a believer."

"Mom, who said anything about dating? All I said was that I am going to see a movie with this guy, I did not say I was going to a hotel, or somewhere else."

"Watch your mouth, young lady, be careful of what, and how you talking to me, I am still your mother."

"I am sorry mom. I did not mean it that way, I am just not pleased with the way you all made it to be.

I know some of the guys from church who have committed atrocious things against other young ladies, so it is not about church, but the individual.

You have taught me well, and I know what I should expect of a young man, and I will not put myself in a vulnerable position with Anthony, and even though my brothers are not pleased with me for going, they will quickly come if I call or find myself in trouble."

"Not if you don't listen to us," David said,

"I love you all, best brothers in the whole world."

She left them and went to her room to get ready for her date.

About 6:30 pm, Anthony drove up to their house, and parked alongside the roadside, then walked up to the door, and rang the doorbell.

Karen opened the door and greeted him.

"Please come in," she said, "Cindy will be out here shortly, please, have a seat."

David passed by, "what's up man? You take care of my sister and treat her right." He said, then left.

His mother used this opportunity to say her piece.

"I really don't know you, but I know my daughter, and if she chose to go out with you, it is because she trusts you, please respect her."

"Sure madam, I will," and just then Cindy appeared, and Anthony felt relieved.

"Mom, see you in a while, and don't wait up," and she laughed as she said so.

"Not funny," her mom said, "you be very careful."

In the car, Anthony said, "your family doesn't play around when it comes to protecting you, and they let me know that."

"You're lucky my younger brother was not home; he can be brutal when it comes to protecting me."

"I really don't blame them, see how lovely, and beautiful you look. Confession. At school, you looked amazing, and my friends spoke of beauty, and I wanted to reach out to you to show my friends how macho I was, but you did not accept me, so I diverted to all these useless rants, again I am sorry."

After deciding what movie, they wanted to see, they went to sit to the back seats in the theatre, and relaxed, and enjoyed the movie.

When the movie was over, they went to dine at Bruno's steakhouse, which was right around the corner from the theatre.

As they sat at the table, they became more acquainted, and spoke of their past, and their accomplishments, and, what plans they had mapped out for individual life.

Anthony was trying to bring up conversations that were outside Cindy's scope, and she quickly shut them down, then he realized she was not going to let him have his way with her, so he changed the tune of his conversations.

They concluded that they would remain friends, and if anything had to be in the future, they would welcome it if that what it was supposed to be.

After a quiet ride back to the house, they hugged, and promised to stay in touch. Anthony accompanied Cindy to her front door, said goodbye, then drove away.

Karen was up, pretending that she was up looking for some important papers that she had misplaced, but she was too worried to sleep, knowing her daughter was out there with someone she had little trust, and confidence in.

"Mom, what are you doing up? It is way past your bedtime, I thought I told you not to wait up?" she said jokingly.

"You know me, I was not going to sleep unless I knew that you were safely home. By the way, how did your date go?"

"Mom, everything went fine, we enjoyed a movie, went to have a bite, then came home."

"Great, I am glad that all went well. As a mother, I will always be concerned with anything pertaining to my children."

Cindy hugged her mom, and went to her bed, and quickly went to sleep.

Chapter *Chapter* TWENTY-SIX

MONDAY NIGHT, WHICH WAS Christmas eve, the family went to the service, and Cindy was happy to see her friends, and her favorite Pastor, Jim.

Service lasted for about an hour and half, which was longer than normal, due to the programming to commemorate the Christmas season.

When they came back to the house, the family kept the Christmas tradition, they gathered around the fireplace, and wished each other well for the season, and beyond, and then opened and thanked each other for their gifts.

The next day, Christmas day, Cindy spent most of her time on her phone. She called her dad and had a great visit with him on the phone, then she called Katy, and the rest of her friends to wish them a Merry Christmas.

Later that evening, Cindy tagged along with David and his girl-friend Lisa to the movies, after which, they went to the ice cream shop to enjoy some ice cream, before returning home.

Cindy spent a few hours the next day at the mall with Kellie; they did a little bit of shopping, and a lot of time hanging out.

Saturday, she and her mom took a trip to the beauty salon, then went to a restaurant to have lunch.

At night, they stayed up spending precious moments together, as Cindy was leaving the next day to college.

It was a smooth flight back to Florida, hardly any turbulence once they had levelled out in the air.

Katy and Liz were at the airport waiting for her, which Cindy did not expect, because she told them she would take a taxi, but she was happy they came.

"Hi, it is nice to see you all; I knew you missed me I can see it on your faces," and she laughed.

"Here you go, full of yourself, we did not miss you at all, we had so much fun without you," Katy said, but of course she was joking.

Back at the apartment, Cindy almost fainted, when she realized Katy had cooked.

"You did what?" Cindy, filled with astonishment, asked.

"Surprise, surprise, I have learned to cook a few things; I have spent a lot of time with my mom on the phone, and now have the gumbo dish mastered. It was much easier than I thought, but I had been depending on her all my life; I never took the time to cook it. Now the time is coming, when I must cook for a wonderful man, and I want Josh to be proud of me."

"Tastes good, I am impressed, now you have to show me how to cook that."

"Liz also taught me to cook a few Spanish dishes, and for that I am thankful."

As classes resumed, Cindy realized that the lessons appeared to be more difficult, but she was committed to getting good grades, and planned to change her study habits, in order to master her classes.

There were so many new terms that she had to learn and understand as she entered the core of her nursing program, but because she desired to be a great nurse, she made an extra effort to learn them.

Some of her friends reached out to her for help with their studies; they knew that she was smart, and was doing good in the classes, so they relied on her a lot.

Robin particularly, depended on Cindy constantly to assist her in her assignments. She took advantage of Cindy's kindness, which led to resentment from many of Cindy's other friends. She was also a bossy type of person, who always thought about herself and no one else, and that infuriated the others.

"Hi, Cindy, spring break is next week, are you coming to Miami Beach with us this time? Last year you said you join us this year. Are you going to keep your promise?' Robin asked.

"I will let you know by week's end," Cindy replied.

At the apartment, Cindy ran the idea by Katy, but as expected, it was met with resistance.

"I don't think you should go. Robin is not the best person to go on a trip with. She is not a responsible person, and it is all about Robin, and no one else, she will leave you stranded, she is not reliable.

"I understand that, but I just can't go from home to school, and back to home routinely, I need to have some fun every now and then and going on that trip will provide that."

"Anyway, since your mind is made up, and there is nothing I can do to stop you, I am cautioning you to be careful."

Cindy called Mario, her friend, and told him about her plans for the break, and he insisted on taking the trip with her, but she rejected his companionship because she had plans to invite Anthony.

"Hi, Robin, I have decided to come on the trip, please give me a call back, so we can make arrangements.

Later that afternoon, Robin called back, and she and Cindy finalized all details for the trip.

Anthony was very excited and happy for the invite from Cindy and accepted it immediately. He was in favor of all the details, except for Cindy sharing a room with Robin. He tried to persuade her to get a separate room, and he would pay for it, but she refused. She wanted to have fun, but she still wanted to maintain her dignity.

She told Joshua about her plans for spring break, for which he was not in favor with, but he realized that she was grown, and he could not prevent her from doing what she wanted to do, and he could only advise.

Although, if she had told him about Anthony, he would be saying something else, and would have gotten their mother involved.

She told her mom, told her mom that, she was taking a trip with her friend to Miami, but did not give her many details.

Chapter *Chapter* TWENTY-SEVEN

MONDAY MORNING, THE FUN began. Robin came by, along with 3 other friends, to pick up Cindy, then off they went to Miami. Robin was the driver for the first leg of the trip. They were singing loudly to the songs on the radio and asserted that the fun had begun.

About an hour into the trip, they were pulled over by the state police for speeding; although they pleaded and begged the police for a chance, he joked, and laughed with them, but still penalized Robin, and gave her a ticket. She was very upset, and underneath her breath, said a few choice words directed to the officer.

The next five and a half hours of driving was shared among the three other young ladies, they did not let Cindy drive, because they were not familiar, nor confident in her driving ability.

Music blasting, ladies laughing loudly, the young ladies entered Miami Beach. This was a routine trip for three of these ladies, and they knew exactly what they were doing.

They soon pulled up to the hotel, and checked in.

The hotel was buzzing with college students, who were eager to participate in spring break activities.

After securing their belongings in their room, the three other ladies came into Robin and Cindy's room to join them, and to plan their next move.

Cindy knew from their conversations, that she was in for a rude awakening.

"There is action at South Pointe Beach later this evening, big party, who's in?"

Robin asked.

"Count me in," said Tameka, "me too," said Kizzy, "not sure," said Grace, "give me some time to think about it."

"I am out, I am not coming with you all, I need some time to relax."

"Relax? You came here to have fun, and to forget about your worries for at least a week, come on." Said Robin, and two of the other ladies sided with her.

Cindy spent the rest of the night on the phone with her mom, Katy, and Anthony.

The next day, Anthony arrived, checked into his hotel room, then went to the hotel where Cindy was.

Cindy went to meet him in the lobby, then they went up to her room.

Robin was sound asleep, after a night of partying, and reveling on the town, so they decided to take a drive up to North Beach where they had lunch, before taking a walk on the beach.

The relationship between the two of them was getting more serious daily. Cindy loved the way Anthony carried himself, and she loved how mature he was.

About 6pm, they went back to the hotel room. Upon entering, they met all the young ladies sitting in there.

"Hi, this is Anthony," Cindy said.

"Anthony, these are my friends from college. This is Robin, Kizzy, Tameka, and Grace."

"Nice to meet you," they said.

"You look familiar, I feel like I've seen you before, do you play football?"

"Yes, I do," Anthony replied smiling.

"Quarterback?"

"Yes," Anthony replied.

"You are on television all the time, your school lost in the last National championship game."

"I have brothers who play and are hoping to be like you, in a good school, and eventually professionally."

After an hour with the young ladies, Anthony said he was going back to his hotel, and he invited Cindy to come with him.

She thought about it for a while, and wondered to herself, if that was a safe thing to do, but for whatever reason, she trusted Anthony, and believed he would do the right thing, so she said yes, she would tag along.

"Are you going to bring me back here tonight?"

"I thought you would spend the night, and come back here in the morning?'

"That's not going to happen. Are you bringing me back here or not?" she demanded.

"For sure, I will, if that is what you want."

The hotel was less than ten minutes from where she was staying, so they got there quickly.

Cindy was very uncomfortable with her decision and realized that she was taking a risk, but she promised to be careful, and she was happy to get away from the ladies; this way she would not have to deny their invitations to go clubbing.

The two sat on the bed and became more familiar with each other, they asked and answered various questions, and they revealed their likes, and dislikes, then Cindy asked Anthony, "how come you never told me about you being a big star football player at your school, and at a national level?"

"We went to the movies, dinner, and other places, and you never told me; what are you hiding from me?"

"The reason I did not tell you is because I wanted you to choose me for just me, and not because I was a star football player."

"You have just insulted me; "you think you being a star would cause me to fall for you? You really do not know me, and I don't know you, and yet I am here with you."

"Don't get mad," I did not mean it that way, I just wanted us to be together and not be linked to football. Anyway, I am very sorry, I did not mean for what I said to come out like this."

"Let me make it up to you, and before he had finished saying that he put his hands around her, and before she could react, he had his lips on hers.

She was so shocked and uncomfortable; she did not know what to do.

She felt like pushing him off, but she felt a chill going down her spine, she was stunned, at least for 20 seconds, then freed herself.

"What happened? Did I surprise you? Not enjoyable?" he asked while smiling.

But she was not smiling, she was upset. She said, "this is not the way I anticipated my first kiss would be like with you? I wanted it to be more romantic than that, not you forcing yourself to it."

"I have never been in a serious relationship before, and that is why I wanted to take my time and do the right things, I want to enjoy every detail of the journey, but I guess I am too slow for you."

"Again, let me say I am sorry. I just keep messing up but let me say that I am honored to be the first one that you allowed to kiss you."

"I did not give it to you, you took it without my permission," she snapped back.

The two were quiet for a couple of minutes, then Anthony got up, and paced the floor a couple of times, before sitting back on the bed.

"What do we do now?" he asked.

"Take it slow, let us get to know each other, what I have is precious to me, and if you are the one to have it, that won't be withheld from you, but I have my standards, and requirements, and I don't want to go from one man to the other. I want a lasting relationship, something with meaning, and I believe I have found that with you, am I wrong to believe that?"

"Of course not, I do respect you, and will continue to do that, you are special, and I definitely want to be with someone that is that special."

Anthony came down to Miami Beach, with a different mindset; he thought he was coming to party, have fun and sex for a week, then head back to school, feeling macho, but it did not go according to his plan.

He hugged her, and told her he was in it for the long haul.

She was feeling so emotional and vulnerable, and thought to herself, if he did not take that approach, she didn't know what would have happened, how she would have responded, because she was feeling an excitement that she had never felt before, and her hormones were acting up differently than ever before, but she was glad that she did not have to make that decision.

Cindy knew if her mom knew where she was at this present time, she would have had a heart attack, but again she thought to herself, that she was an adult, and was entitled to make her own decisions.

"Hungry?" Anthony asked.

"Yes, I'm starving," she said.

"You should feel comfortable around me and be free to say whatever you want to."

Anthony knew he had found a special, precious young lady, and he knew her from high school, and knew that she always was proper, so he did not want to lose her, yet he had decisions he had to make, which would be difficult for him when he got back to school.

"Hotel food, or you want something from outside?'

"I think we can go out," Cindy replied.

The way she was feeling, she wanted to get away from the vulnerable position that she was in.

"Picking it up, or eating out there?' he asked

"Let me see. I think we should eat out there, then take a walk on the beach front."

"Cool," he replied. "Sound like a plan."

After a wonderful outing, they went back to the hotel. They talked for a while before they kissed, and this time, Cindy enjoyed it, because it was done with passion and affection, and they cuddled up and kissed some more, before Cindy, panting with passion, said, "can we go now? please take me back to my hotel."

"Something I did?" he asked.

"No, it is me, and I think the best way for me, is to go to my hotel." The situation is too intense for me, and I can't handle it."

When Anthony heard that, he pressed some more to see if he could get her to stay a little bit longer, because she was on the verge of giving in, but she insisted that he take her back, and he complied.

Upon her return to the hotel, she met her friends getting ready to go clubbing. Samantha, planned on staying.

"Coming?" Kizzy asked, "you know you have not been out with us yet?"

"I know, but I will pass again tonight, I am tired."

"Ah ha, fireworks happened in your neighborhood?" and they all laughed.

Cindy never told them that she had never been to a club, and that she grew up in the church.

After they left, Sammy asked, "how was your time with Anthony?"

"It was good, and that is all I am going to say." And she laughed.

Samantha tried her best to get details from her but was not successful. Cindy would not give that type of information to someone she hardly knew.

Her phone rang, and it was her mother.

"Mom, what are you doing calling at this time of the night, aren't you supposed to be sleeping?"

"I could not sleep, my mind was on you, so I was worried, and decided to call you. Where are you? Are you okay?"

"Mom, I am in my room with Samantha, and I am doing okay, no need to worry. I am fine, and will be fine, so you can stop worrying and go and get some sleep."

"Okay I will, take care of yourself."

"Love you mom, talk to you in you in the morning."

She spent at least half an hour on the phone with Mario and a few minutes with Katy before calling Anthony.

They spent at least two hours on the phone before she retired to her bed.

The last day of their trip, the young ladies went to a beach party, while Cindy and Anthony went on their own.

Mid-morning, they went to the beach, to swim, and sunbathe, and played a little bit of volleyball. Anthony discovered how competitive, and how good Cindy was in the game.

Later that day, they drove to Miami to do a little shopping and sightseeing; it was the first time Cindy had been to Miami, and she loved it.

After having dinner in one of Miami's popular restaurants, they went back to Miami Beach.

Since it was their last night before they headed out the next day, Anthony wanted to spend some quality time with her. She thought that was a good idea.

She chose her hotel instead of his, even though her friends were not there, she knew that would be security for her, because of the anticipation of them coming home anytime.

Anthony was all about passion that night, and sometimes he got too excited, and tried to push the envelope, but Cindy shut him down.

They expected the others to come in anytime from their outing, so Anthony hugged, kissed her and said his goodbye.

After he left, she felt so lonely, she did not think she would miss him that much.

She thought of the times in high school when she cried because of his cruelty, and now she was crying because he had to be apart from her, who would have thought that.

She went to sleep before the others came in, which was a good thing, because she did not want to be drilled and questioned by them.

Chapter *Chapter* TWENTY-EIGHT

IN THE MORNING, THE young ladies decided that they would head back to Tallahassee about noon.

They volunteered Cindy to be the first driver, since she did not go out with them, they said she was not tired. She tried to get out of it, but to no avail.

She asked that someone stay up with her, if only for the first 20 minutes, because she was not familiar with the area, and would not know where to go.

Samantha, the most considerate one, volunteered.

But they did not go to sleep as they said they would, but instead they were all over Cindy with their accusations, and said she was not a good friend to go out with, and that she used them in order to come and spend time with her boyfriend. Samantha had to asked them to stop with their pettiness, and to leave Cindy alone. She told them, if it did not go the way they wanted, not to invite her again, but for now just let it go.

Robin did not like Samantha defending Cindy, and got on her case instead, and they had a big argument, until Cindy said she was going to pull over and stop driving if that continued; that is when they cooled off.

At last, they made it back to the school, and the ladies dropped off Cindy at her apartment, and the continued to their dorms.

"Back at Cindy's apartment, Katy and Liz were waiting, and were happy to see her make it back unharmed.

"How was it?" Katy asked. "And please give us details of the trip."

"Yes, everything, leave nothing out" Liz said, as she bubbled with anticipation.

"First of all, the young ladies are mad at me because I did not spend much time with them."

"Why not? I thought you all went together as a group?" Katy said.

"Yes, we did, but my friend came from Georgia, and this changed everything."

"I did not know you had a close friend in Georgia, is she from your hometown?" Katy asked.

"Who said that it was a she?"

"Oh, it is getting better and juicer," remarked Katy.

"My friend Anthony, who is from my hometown, was my partner in crime for the week."

"Anthony and I went to the same high school, but we were not friends, actually, I hated him, because he made my life miserable, but on my way to Texas this past Christmas, we met on the same flight and things changed after that."

"How comes you never said anything about him?" Katy asked.

"I just wanted to keep this quiet, and I did not want you filling Joshua with information."

"That is what you think of me? Shame on you Cindy but come on, details; I am waiting."

"We spent most of the week together, going to lunches and dinners, spent time on the beach, and lots of time at the hotels."

"Hotels? You mean that you all were at separate hotels?" Katy asked, being inquisitive.

"I found out that he is the quarterback for his school football team, and the school played in the last championship, and he was all over the television giving interviews because of their success. I was mad at him because he did not tell me that, but I found out when I introduced him to the group that I went with, and they knew who he was."

"I was mad at him for not telling me, but we made up."

"We made love, and I almost allowed him to pass the boundaries that I set for the relationship."

"Boundaries? You mean the sex boundaries?" Liz asked.

"Definitely, Cindy replied, "but we came close." It was so hard for me, my mind was saying one thing, but my body was saying another, but after getting hold of myself, the mind, and heart prevailed."

"Basically, those are the details of my trip."

"You mean you did not go out to the activities?" Liz asked.

"No," Cindy replied, "I had my own agenda."

"I see why the ladies were mad at you." Katy said.

Joshua called later in the night and told Cindy, he heard of her adventure, and hoped she knew what she was doing, especially when it came to Anthony, and he hoped mom didn't find out.

"She won't find out because you will not tell her, you don't want to spike up her blood pressure, and be responsible if something goes wrong."

"Cindy, I hate when you do that, but I hope you did not compromise yourself and put yourself at risk for pregnancy, and turn away from your studies?"

"No worries, big brother, your sister did not have sex, if is that you are concerned about, I have my standards and dignity to protect."

"So, you are really into this guy? All I have to say is be really careful, go into that slowly, and let it develop, don't rush it."

"Thanks brother, much appreciated, that is why I always love you."

"Yeah right, also leave Katy out of it, she only tells me because she cares about you. Talk to you later."

"Cindy, I hope that you are not mad at me for telling Josh, because I felt that I had to," Katy explained.

"I am not going to say that I approved what you did, but mad? No, but I know if I don't want Josh to know something, I better not tell you."

The next day Cindy set up her guidelines and plans of how she would approach and finish the rest of the semester.

She remembered it wasn't too long before she started college, and now she was already approaching the end of her sophomore year.

The next few weeks she remained focused; she wanted to finish the semester with good grades.

It was hectic, the workload was heavy, but she managed, and finished the semester with excellent grades.

Katy thanked Cindy for being in her life and helping her with her studies, which enabled her to get A's in her classes.

Cindy reminded her, that she was the one who put in the work and determination, so she needed to pat herself on the back for her accomplishment.

Chapter TWENTY-NINE

CINDY DID NOT GO home for the summer, but got a part time job at OBC clinic, which was a few miles from her apartment, and she was so excited to get her first job and could hardly wait to start.

Cindy called her mom, and as usual said, "hi mom, how are you doing? How is it down there in Texas?"

"Hi dear, how are you? And what do you need? Because when you call me in this manner, it is usually that you need something, or there is something that you want to talk about, what is it?"

"It is nothing, it is just a daughter calling to check on her mother. By the way,

Her mom, interrupted, "I knew it, there was something, I know you, my daughter."

"Mom, all I am saying is that I have found a job and will not be coming home for the summer."

"My dear, I am not surprised, you have always been a stubborn child, and when you told me last summer that you would not come home again for summer, I believed you."

"Mom, it is not like that, I want to take a few classes this summer, and I want to earn some money; I am tired of asking you for money."

After the two of them went back and forth, each one claiming to be right, the mom conceded, and congratulated her on her new job, and wished her well, and asked her to be careful.

She enjoyed the summer job and was content to have earned her own money, and not have to ask her mom for money; she felt that she was growing up to be a responsible adult.

Also, during the summer months, Cindy spent a considerably amount of time with her boyfriend Anthony, who visited her often.

As Cindy started her junior year, she decided to get back into sports. She tried out for the basketball team, and after a few tryouts, she was selected to be the point guard of the team.

She knew that she was not working on making it professionally, but she just wanted to be on the team and be part of the school's history.

She stayed focused on her grades, while she incorporated basketball into her schedule.

Cindy, Katy, and Liz made plans to surprise Anthony during the fall at one of his games.

Cindy was so anxious; she could hardly wait.

But for now, she was just concentrating on classes.

As she started her first day of class, she said, I can't believe it is already my junior year, I am so much closer to the end of my program, but I must remain focused.

It was going to be the most challenging of all her years, because she was scheduled to do most of her clinical classes and would have to visit different facilities.

Chapter THIRTY

THE THREE LADIES, SET aside the second weekend of September to attend Anthony's football game.

They booked a hotel room for the weekend.

They left Florida at 10:30 Friday morning and headed North on I-75 towards Georgia. The trip took about five and a half hours, with Katy doing most of the driving. They checked in the hotel about 6pm and spent the night watching movies and having fun.

Cindy spent an hour on the phone with Anthony but did not give him a clue that she was in Georgia.

They woke up Saturday morning, ready, and excited to go to the game. Cindy could not wait to see Anthony play for the first time.

The game was scheduled for 11 am in the school stadium, and it was sold out, and would be televised nationally.

Their seats were close to the playing field, in so much, they could identify the players, and Cindy was worried Anthony might spot her, so she tried to be as elusive as possible.

When Anthony and his offence came on the field, Liz and Katy shouted as loud as possible, and shouted Anthony's name.

Although they had never met him, he had won them over by what Cindy had told them. All that time Cindy tried to hide from his view.

The game was closely contested, and at halftime, Anthony's team was up by a field goal.

After a short interview with a reporter, Anthony ran to the locker room to be with his teammates.

Cindy and her friends, planned to go down close to the sideline when there was about a minute left in the game, so they could have easy access to Anthony.

What a game it was; with a couple of minutes left in the game, Anthony and his offense took the ball from their own 10-yard line, drove down the field, and scored a touchdown with 7 seconds left in the game.

As time expired, the fans stormed the field because they were so happy they had just beaten their chief rival.

Cindy, Katy, and Liz used this opportunity to get on the field and close to the vicinity where Anthony was.

He was surrounded by reporters, camera men, and teammates, as they celebrated beating that team, and holding on to their number 1 position.

Cindy was excited. She was looking forward to seeing Anthony's reaction.

Cindy carefully inched, and maneuvered her way forward, closer to where Anthony was; she made it to the front, and hid behind one of his teammates, just waiting for the interview to be over with so she could pounce on him, but when she looked to his right, she noticed about three young ladies waiting for him, and immediately, she had a bad feeling , but she convinced herself they just wanted to see him like everyone else; as soon as the interview was over, she saw him head to where they were, but that did not deter her, she continued with her plan.

As her friends watched, Cindy ran towards Anthony, as though it was an ambush, and she embraced him, and shouted "surprise."

Anthony stood there like a deer caught in the beam of a headlight. He remained frozen for about a minute, not sure whether it was the shock of seeing Cindy, or the fact that he had gotten caught in an awkward situation.

Meanwhile, Katy, and Liz joined Cindy at the front, to be part of the surprise.

But being the quarterback that he was, Anthony came up with a split-second decision, and said, "Cindy, what a surprise, nice to see you, but ladies, I must run to the locker room quickly, I have a reporter from the network waiting urgently on me; I will be back soon."

One of the young ladies turned to Cindy, and said, "hi, my name is Laura, I am Anthony's fiancée, and these are my friends, are you his fans, or his friends?"

"We are his friends," Cindy quietly said, we are here to support him, anyway nice meeting you all, tell him Cindy said she had to leave."

Cindy was so hurt, she could barely put one foot ahead of the other, because she felt so weak, and had little energy left in her.

"Why didn't you tell Laura everything that had been happening so she could deal with that dirty scum bag?" Katy said, as they drove away from the venue.

But Cindy just kept on gazing at the ceiling of the car, and said nothing, sat there like she was in another world, as they made it back to the hotel.

About a mile from the hotel, her phone rang, and it was Anthony, but Cindy chose not to answer it.

As soon as they got to their room, she spread out on the bed, face down, and cried bitterly.

The others tried to comfort her, but she was not consoled.

Eventually, she felt asleep, and did not wake up until the next day.

"Hi, how are you doing this morning?" Katy asked, concerned about her friend and roommate.

"Doing better than yesterday," Cindy replied, "It still hurts, but it is good that I found out now than later about all this mess, when I would be fully committed in a relationship with him."

Her phone rang, and it was Anthony again, this time she answered, and said to him, "you have the nerve to call me after the way you embarrassed, and humiliated me?"

"Let me explain," Anthony pleaded.

"There is nothing to explain, there is nothing that you can say that would make me like you again. How dare you, Anthony?"

"If you had told me you were in a relationship, and you would have to make a choice, or was going to break up with that person even though it might have been a lie, I would have felt better, because I would not have been blindsided like I was yesterday."

"Sorry Cindy, but this is not how I wanted you to know that I was in a relationship that I was planning on getting out of because of some hurtful experiences. I really love you."

"Man, I was so stupid, I hate myself for falling for you the way I did."

"I never meant to hurt you Cindy, I am so sorry, I really don't want to lose you."

"Anthony, after this phone call, I don't want to ever speak to you again. I never thought the first person I gave my heart to would have torn it up so quickly, and into so many pieces; imagine, I almost gave you, my virginity? Had I not fought hard against my emotions, I would just be another one in your list, another feather in your cap, so you could have boasted to your friends."

"Boy, you don't know how much I dislike you for hurting me that badly."

"Can we still communicate?" Anthony asked, hoping to patch things as time went by.

"Right now, you are the last person I want to keep communicating with."

"Cindy, I won't give up on us, I am going to keep fighting until we become one again."

"There was us, but this don't exist anymore, not after the weekend. And the sad thing about it, I was madly in love with you, that is why I felt it to my core."

"Bye, Anthony, you are now a memory." And she hung up the phone.

She immediately started crying, when she realized how much she had loved this guy, and what could have been.

Katy tried to comfort her, but could not ease her pain, so she let her cry, and thought that might help her; she left her and went to the bathroom.

While she was in the restroom, Josh called, but she left her phone on the couch, so he called Cindy's phone.

"How sis, how are you doing? Is Katy anywhere close by?"

"I'm okay. Katy just went into the restroom, and her phone is out here."

"What is wrong?"

"Nothing, I am okay"

"Are you and Kate fighting?" Josh asked, because he could tell from her voice that all was not well, and Katy went to the restroom without her phone that was not a normal thing.

"Cindy, it is me that you're speaking to, and I know something is wrong, come on spit it out."

She recognized in his voice, that he was getting angry, so she told him what just happened to her on the trip.

"This piece of low life, this guy is never going to change, I wish I could get my hands on him."

"Josh it's okay, I will get over him as time goes by, although it hurts right now, but this too shall pass. I know you're about to say 'I told you so,' but we are all entitled to make mistakes, even stubborn girls like me."

"All I'm going to say, is, I hope you learn from your mistake."

They made it back to Florida later that afternoon and said that they were happy that they made the trip, or else, they would never have found out what was going on with Anthony.

The next day she went back to class, but she was not totally focused, the breakup with Anthony was still fresh on her mind and interfered with her studies.

Over the next few weeks, her grades dropped but not dramatically, but she had to get a hold of her emotions, and refocus on her studies, that was the reason she was there, and with the help of her friends, she was able to get back on track.

Chapter THIRTY-ONE

For Thanksgiving, she bought a ticket and went home to Texas; her mom was surprised, because Cindy had not said she would be coming home, and since she missed the last one, her mom assumed that she would just stay at school.

But Cindy needed the family time in order to help her heal from her miserable ordeal.

This year, everyone planned to be there for the holidays.

And to Cindy's surprise, Katy came strolling in with Josh.

"What are you doing here? She asked surprisingly, "You did not tell me that you were coming to Texas?"

"I did not know until yesterday after you left. Josh called, and said, 'guess what? I have purchased a ticket for you, and we are going to Texas. I was surprised, but happy."

"Cool, I'm glad that you're here, makes the holidays even more enjoyable."

"Josh, why don't we surprise dad? Let's go and spend a day with him, and you can introduce him to Katy."

"Not this time Cindy, one day is not enough time. When I come back for the summer, at least I will have a couple of weeks, I will visit him."

Cindy left on Tuesday morning, and surprised her dad, sister, and Joyce his wife, and as usual, the reception from Joyce was cold.

She, dad, and Jenny, her sister, went to a restaurant to have dinner. They had a lot of fun, and they tried to stay out as late as possible, because they knew, that awaiting them at home, was the miserable lady.

The next morning Jason knocked on Cindy's door, hugged her, said goodbye, and left for work.

Cindy left not too long after that, back to her home. Even though it was a short visit, she enjoyed every bit of it, she always loved being around her dad.

Thanksgiving was special as usual, with family traditions. Everyone had an enjoyable time, and they were all happy to see each other.

It worked out where Josh and Katy had the same flight as Cindy back to Florida, which made the flight more relaxing.

Cindy knew that once thanksgiving was over, Christmas was less than a month away, so it was back to hard work with her classes, so she could finish the semester strong.

After her disaster with Anthony, Cindy promised to be more careful if she ever got into a relationship again. She didn't want to be that vulnerable again.

Cindy had a great Christmas holiday season; she did not go home but stayed with Katy and Liz.

They went to a few Christmas activities and visited the theme park.

She also had a few visits from Mario, who tried very hard to be in a romantic relationship with her, but she told him, as much as she cherished the friendship they had, she wasn't willing to put that at jeopardy, for something that would not work, because she knew she did not love him in a romantic way.

Cindy played basketball during the spring semester, also she did not follow the young ladies on their spring break trip, but rather stayed home and relaxed, and did a few activities with Katy and Liz, and she practiced for their big basketball tournament, in which they had to play Miami, which was their chief rival.

Excitingly, they beat Miami by seven points, which was a great win, because this was a conference game.

She had a great game, with good numbers, and her floor management helped them win.

Because of that game, her popularity increased among the other students, especially the guys, but she was being careful not to let her guard down.

Cindy's team finished the season with only two losses, and won the collegiate championship. She was known nationally because of her stelar play.

Cindy and a few of her teammates, along with Katy and Liz, went to an NBA game in Atlanta, and the trip was worthwhile, because there she and her teammates were introduced to the crowd at halftime. She also got to meet some of the NBA players.

A few of the players knew who she was, and spoke to her for a while, and exchanged numbers with her, and promised to stay in touch.

Cindy was tempted to forgo her senior year at college, and to accept an offer to play professionally; she gave it a great amount of consideration, but after discussing it with her mom and brothers, she concluded that she wanted to graduate, and playing professionally was not what she wanted to do at that time.

Chapter *THIRTY-TWO*

CINDY KEPT IN TOUCH with Kirk, whom she had met during her visit to Atlanta, and chatted on the phone with him regularly.

She had promised that she would not get into a romantic relationship any time soon, but as they got to know each other more, they developed a friendship which progressed into a romantic relationship, but she told herself to take it slowly.

Katy and Liz tried to discourage her from having a romantic relationship with Kirk, but Cindy loved to do things her way, and was always a stubborn person.

Joshua was very upset with her when he heard what she was doing, but as he told her, she was grown and entitled to make her own decisions, whether he approved or not, but he still wanted to give his input. He loved his little sister dearly and would love to see her do the right things, and he would love for her to be happy.

"Cindy," he said, "are you going down this road again?"

"No Josh, I am going down a different road, they are two different people, and I am not going to rush into it, I will be careful, and will take it slow."

"You know that I am around these basketball guys, and from the stories I have heard from them, they are horrible, I would not like any family members, or any of my friends to be with any of these guys."

"I am going to run this by mom."

"Oh no, you won't, that would be my decision, you stay out of my business."

"What has become of my little sister, this is not you, what happened to the sweet little church girl that I knew growing up? Please don't lower your values.

"Well, I have grown up, and am looking at life differently; with reality, and not fantasy."

"I am hoping that you know what you're doing," Joshua remarked.

"I will be fine," Cindy snapped back.

As soon as she got off the phone, she approached Katy and told her she was not pleased with her telling Joshua about everything that happened in her life.

Katy did not accept the accusation from Cindy lightly, and the two of them argued, and said some hurtful things to each other, which caused a rift in their relationship.

Cindy called her mom after these two confrontations, hoping to feel better after talking to her.

"Hi mom," she said, "how are you doing? I am checking up on you."

"Hi dear," her mom replied, "you just crossed my mind, how are you doing? Are you okay?"

"Sure mom, all is alright, how is Texas? Hopefully I should be there for thanksgiving."

"So, you are not coming home for the summer, at least for a couple weeks?" her mom asked.

"No mom, I am planning to work, as I need money, during my senior year at school. There are a number of activities that I have to attend.

"Well, your brothers are coming in the last two weeks of August; I hope you will change your mind and make the trip."

"I will think about it, but no promises, mom.

"Also, mom, just want to say, that there is a young man that I started dating; his name is Kirk, and I met him last year in Atlanta; we have been friends since, but now we took it to the next level, and are now in a relationship."

"Is he a student?" Karen asked curiously.

"No mom, he is a professional basketball player."

"Is he a Christian? Does he go to church?"

"Mom, I am not sure if he goes to church; he lives in Atlanta. Also, I know that he is a very nice person, and he cherishes me"

"I don't like the sound of that; I don't trust these athletes; they use people, then dump them"

"Mom, Joshua is a basketball player and is getting ready to play professionally; is he going to be like that?"

"Don't group Josh in the same category as these guys Josh is a respectable, God-fearing young man,"

"That is what I'm trying to say to you mom, there are exceptions to that type, and I believe that Kirk is an exception."

"Anyway, I hope you know what you are doing."

"Mom, stop worrying, I will be okay."

She hung up so that she could spend some time on the phone with Kirk. They spoke for a while before she retired to her bed.

Cindy had been working minimum hours throughout the semester; now she approached her manager and asked if she could work full time for the summer months as she wanted to accumulate more financially, and without any hesitation, he approved her request, and included a small raise because he loved her work habits and her attitude toward the patients.

Cindy loved the health field and could hardly wait to graduate and become a licensed nurse.

She hardly spent time with Katy and Liz like before; she devoted most of her time to Kirk, and every opportunity she had, she would be around him and his friends. She was keeping her eyes and ears open to monitor him; she did not want to be caught in the same situation as Anthony. And after doing her research, she found out that he had no other girlfriends, and no illegal activities.

Although it had been only a few months of dating, they acted like they had been in a relationship for years, and many were of the same opinion after watching them.

July 4th weekend, Cindy left Katy and Liz and went to Atlanta to spend the long weekend with Kirk.

She did not regret it; it was one of the best 4th of Julys she had ever experienced in her life.

He treated her like a queen; he made sure his friends noticed her and he flaunted her beauty amongst them. They participated in so many activities that she was worn out.

Cindy dreaded going back to Florida on Sunday she had such a wonderful time with Kirk and did not want to leave.

She made it back to Florida about 8pm, and had to take a taxi, because she could not reach Katy or Liz on their phones, and this was by design, because Cindy did not communicate with them while she was in Atlanta with her friends.

Cindy arrived at the apartment, and immediately quarreled with Katy for not picking her up.

"What happened to the great relationship we had? We were like sisters, but now you have brought it down to being roommates." Katy said.

"Nothing is wrong. Things happened that needed adjustments, and that is all I did. I met a great guy, and I have included him into my life, which has given less time with you and others, but we are still cool." Cindy said.

"I did not expect that our relationship would end up like that, but like you said, life changes as you grow older, so I have accepted it, and wish the best for you, going forward."

"I can't stay long chatting tonight, I'm very tired, and am going to bed; I'll see you in the morning," and with that said, Cindy went to her bedroom.

Chapter THIRTY-THREE

JULY 7TH, ABOUT 7.35 in the morning, Cindy's phone rang, and it was her mother calling.

"Hi mom," she answered, being sleepy and grouchy, why are you calling so early in the morning?" she asked.

"Brace yourself; I have sad news," her mom said.

Instantly, Cindy's body shivered, and immediately she started crying, not even knowing what the sad news was, because she knew when her mom called that early, it had to be something major.

"What is it mom?" she asked.

"It's your father. He was in a vehicular accident, and I am sorry, he did not survive."

Cindy only heard your father, and she dropped the phone, and screamed.

Katy rushed into Cindy's room to see what was going on.

Cindy was on the floor, and said "no, no, this can't be true."

"Cindy, what's wrong, what's going on? "Katy demanded, but Cindy just kept on saying "no, not my dad."

"What's wrong with your dad?" Katy asked, and then her phone rang, and it was Joshua, and then she knew for sure, that something bad had happened.

And then Joshua told her of his father's accident, and of his passing from his injuries.

Katy reached out to Cindy, and hugged her tightly, as Cindy cried on her shoulder.

"I am so sorry that this happened, I'm sorry for your pain." And Katy stayed quiet, and allowed her to cry, because she knew that would help ease the pain.

Katy called Karen to find out more about what happened.

"Mrs. Marcie, this is Katy, I am so sorry about Jason's death, please accept my sympathy."

"Thanks Katy, and how is Cindy holding up?"

"She is not taking it well, but we will get through it together; I will be here for her and Joshua."

"Thanks, Katy, thanks for being there for my son and daughter."

"Mrs. Marcie, what really happened?" Katy inquired.

"He was on his way to work, when a drunk driver, ran a red light, and slammed into Jason's truck, he was injured very badly and died on the way to the hospital."

"Who is drunk that early in the morning?"

"It was a long weekend because of the holiday, and people were still celebrating into the wee hours of the morning, when they drive drunk, unfortunately, they put peoples' lives at risk, and have no concern who they kill. And the law is so lenient to them." Karen said.

"I agree, harsher punishments need to be given to people who take someone else's life because they were driving drunk."

"Thanks, Mrs. Marcie, be strong, and I will talk to you later."

"Take care my child, and keep an eye on Cindy, she is going to need a friend to lean on; she was very close to her dad."

"I will be there for her," Katy confirmed.

Cindy woke up a couple of hours later, and asked Katy, "was I dreaming? I heard some news about my dad, is that true?"

"Oh dear, I wish I could tell you otherwise, but unfortunately, the news you heard was true."

"I spoke to your mom while you were sleeping, and she explained to me what happened."

And Cindy related to her, all that her mom said.

"I will call her in a minute, did Josh call?"

"Yes, he did, he is devastated, he wanted to talk to you, but I don't think it was a good idea to wake you up."

"I will call him after I speak to my mom."

"Katy, I should have gone home for at least the beginning of summer, I would have spent a couple days with him, now this."

"Cindy, don't do that to yourself; you did not know this was going to happen, and you were planning to go home later in the year."

Cindy called her mom, and was still shaking because of grief, and her mom was relieved to hear her voice.

"Oh, Cindy baby, I am so happy to hear your voice, I was very worried about you, how are you holding up?"

"Mom, I can't believe that is happening to me, why dad? Why did he have to die? Why couldn't he survive?"

Then she stayed quiet for a while, because she was trying to process everything in her head.

"Are you there?" her mom asked.

"Mom, I can't believe he is really dead; it hurts so much because I did not even get to say goodbye. If I had come home like you suggested, probably he would still be alive. He usually takes the day off when there is a long weekend, and I am with him."

"No, no, Cindy, don't do that, this had nothing to do with you. One idiot ran a red light and took his life, some things in life are beyond our control, and this was one of those things."

"I wish I could get my hands on that murderer right now; he killed my dad and robbed me of my happiness. What was he doing drinking that early in the morning anyway? Monday morning? What a low life of a person."

"Cindy, don't do that, this is not how I taught you to deal with adversity."

"But mom, this is different; we never had to deal with adversity this great, he took my dad away from me, and I am never going to hug, kiss, or talk to my dad again," and the tears kept flowing down her cheeks.

Her mom was overtaken with grief, and sobbed, as she tried to comfort her daughter.

"Mom, I am about to call Josh, and then I will see how soon I can get a flight to Houston; talk to you soon."

"Okay, David will be in tonight, I am not sure when Joshua will be here."

She was not in the best of terms with her Josh, because of Kirk, but she knew at that moment, her best friend and brother was who she needed, so she reached out to him.

She called him, and he was anxious to talk to her; he knew what she was going through because he was going through the same thing, and he knew how close she and their dad were.

Joshua encouraged her to be strong, and offered his support to her, and told her they would get through it together, and he strengthened her.

They planned their flights to coordinate where they would be on the same flight from Florida to Texas together.

Cindy checked her phone and saw that Kirk had called many times, so she called him, and he expressed how worried he was when he could not find her.

"It has been a couple of rough hours for me."

"What you mean? What 's going on?" he asked, very concerned.

"I received sad news; my dad passed away from an accident. So, I was and am still devastated."

"Oh baby, I am so sorry, why didn't you call me earlier? I would have been down there already."

"After I got the news, I cried myself to sleep, I got up a few minutes ago, and I called my family, and now I am calling you. You don't need to come over, because my brothers and I are making our plans to go to Texas."

"Okay, I will come with you to Texas."

"Oh no," Cindy replied; "that would not be wise, not in a situation like this; I would have to present you to my mom and the rest of the family, I think this is a bad idea." Cindy said, "I hope you will understand."

"I understand," Kirk replied, "I just wanted to be there for you."

"It's okay, I know I have your support, and I appreciate that. I will keep you informed."

Joshua called and said he had booked a flight for mid-afternoon on Tuesday to Texas, and that he would be coming to Florida, and that they would take the flight from there. He said he would be in Tallahassee by about 9pm.

Chapter THIRTY-FOUR

After a 5-hour drive, Joshua was at Cindy's apartment.

What a relief when Cindy saw her brother; she quickly hugged him and cried on his shoulder, while Joshua tried to hold back his tears.

Katy and Liz accompanied them to the airport, they were to come to Texas later for the funeral.

David picked them up at the airport, and was happy to see them, but he was very sad because of the situation that brought them home.

"How are you both holding on, especially you Cindy?" he asked.

"I am doing a little bit better now, but it still hurts," she replied.

"It's tough, but we will get through this," David assured them.

As soon as they entered the house, Cindy was enveloped in the arms of her mom, and there she sobbed exceedingly.

"Mom, why did God have to take him so early in his life?"

"My child, God has never made a mistake. He is all knowing, and there is always a reason why He does things, and whatever He does, is for our best, even when we don't understand it, and it makes no sense to us, we still have to trust Him, He knows what He is doing."

"Mom, I am hearing you, but it's still not making sense to me, so many wicked and evil people live long lives, and nothing bad happens to them, yet people who are living good lives, are usually taken away from their families, and loved ones. I don't get it."

"Cindy, even when we don't understand, we still have to keep on trusting Him. I don't have all the answers, but I believe he takes some of his dear children earlier than expected, because he is saving them from something that could draw them away from Him later in their lives."

"Let me ask," Karen said, "did anyone of you call his wife to offer condolences, and to find out what plans are being made for his funeral?"

"Mom, she might be glad that daddy is gone. I don't care to call her," Cindy exclaimed.

"None of this nonsense." Karen said furiously. "That is not the way I raised you, not with that attitude, I don't care how hurt you are right now, this is not the right attitude and approach to take."

"Mom, I spent time with them often, and she treated my dad horribly, and for this reason I don't like her, and never will." Cindy remarked.

Josh and David sided with their mom, and reiterated, that this was not the time for that attitude, but that did not change Cindy's mind and feelings towards Joyce.

Joshua called Joyce and offered sympathy on behalf of his family and he spoke to his sister Jenny, and encouraged her to hang in there.

"Oh, thanks Joshua, I really do appreciate that, it is so sad what happened, I am still in shock, never expected that."

"Joyce, I know now is a difficult time, but please keep us informed of the plans and details of the funeral and other things that you have in mind."

Joshua conveyed her sentiments, but Cindy said she was insincere and she was the cause of his death.

Karen said, "I know this is a hurting period, but lashing out at others is not the right way to handle your pain, it will only make it more painful."

"I am tired, and worn out," said Joshua, "I will see you guys in the morning." And he went to bed.

Meanwhile, Cindy got on the phone to talk to Kirk, and he annoyed her, because he thought she should have allowed him to come to Texas, so she limited her time on the phone, and went to bed.

Falling asleep was difficult for her; she saw images of her dad in her mind and could not believe that she would never see him again. It took her a long time before she finally fell asleep.

In the morning, they gathered for breakfast, then they started on the plans for the burial of Jason. They contacted Joyce to find out what she had already done, and what she was doing now, and how they would team up with her to make sure everything ran smoothly.

After their conversation, they assigned responsibilities to individuals of the things that needed to be done in order to make sure things went according to plans.

July 18th was set for the viewing and memorial service, while the funeral was set for July 19th, at 11: am.

Joyce offered for Cindy and her brothers to stay at the house when they came for the funeral, but Cindy refused the invitation. She said she would prefer that they go to a hotel, where they could be close to her mom, Donald, and Kelly.

The brothers knew that was not the reason she wanted to be at the hotel, but to avoid any more confrontations, they agreed with her and declined the invitation.

"And besides," Cindy said, "Katy, and Liz are coming for the funeral, and Joshua, you would not want your girlfriend staying at Joyce's house; that would not be cool."

Chapter *THIRTY-FIVE*

JOSHUA AND CINDY FLEW to Dallas on Wednesday; they wanted to help get things organized for Friday, and Saturday, and to spend some time with their sister, knowing what she was going through.

Some folks came in as early as Thursday morning, and by nighttime, the hotel was buzzing with family and friends.

Cindy was so happy to see her grandmother, whom she had not seen since she was about 4 years old; she could barely remember her features, but she spoke to her regularly, so she was thrilled to meet up with her.

The relationship between Karen and her mother-in-law was not at its best; Karen resented Marian because she said she hated her for Jason and she meddled in their relationship constantly, and thus, she did not want anything to do with her, but she assured her children that she harbored no hate for her, just disliked her interference.

Cindy said to herself, I know my mom said this to maintain her Christian image, but deep down, I know my mom hates my grandmother, I know she has confessed to God on many occasions about this lady.

Friday evening a lot of people showed up to pay their respects to Jason at the viewing and memorial service.

Cindy met uncles, aunts, and other family members that she had never met before, some she did not even know existed.

Cindy decided not to view her dad's body, because she wanted to keep and cherish the image of a happy joyful father. Some people tried to convince her, but she stuck to her decision.

The evening was a solemn one for the children of Jason, they came to realize that this was reality, and could not be changed, and their dad was gone forever.

Cindy had Katy and Liz to lean on that night, and she needed their shoulders, because she broke down a few times.

The trip to the hotel from the chapel was a quiet one, hardly anything was said, there was too much sadness to be in any other mood.

Back at the hotel, Cindy went into her room, and asked to be left alone, but her friends did not think that was a good idea, and insisted that Liz stay with her, and after arguing, she finally gave in and agreed to the company.

She sat on the bed for a while just gazing at the ceiling before she started communicating with Liz.

She turned off her phone and she knelt, and Liz knelt with her, and they prayed to God for strength, for her and the family.

She then turned her phone back on, then retired to bed.

Chapter *THIRTY-SIX*

SATURDAY MORNING, THE DAY of the funeral, Cindy woke up very depressed and sad, as she prepared to attend the most painful event of her life.

She was asked to join her family at the breakfast table, but she declined, she had no desire for food.

She rode to church with her best friend and brother Joshua, who she heavily depended on.

They arrived at the church early, ahead of the others, and had the opportunity to view the body before the crowd came in, but like before, Cindy refused to view the body, and stayed in her seat.

Cindy was surprised to see the large turnout for her father's funeral, she knew him to be friendly, and loving, and kind, but she had no idea, that he was so well known in the city where he lived.

It was a lovely service, painful, but not too sad, because the death was sudden; a lot of the people were still in shock, but most of them said he was in a better place.

During the eulogy, Cindy broke down again, which was expected, but she was surrounded by family and friends, which gave her much support.

At the burial site, it was more intense, because this was where they said their final goodbye to Jason, and this is when Cindy felt it the most, she was beside herself, but her mom was like a rock for her and her brothers.

Jenny came over, and hugged Cindy, and they cried together, and comforted each other, until it was time to leave the graveyard.

From the graveyard, most people went to the recreation center, where they gathered for a few hours to celebrate Jason's home coming. They socialized and enjoyed the food and drinks that were catered.

Cindy did not go to the center, but went to her hotel, she just wanted to be alone; but Liz stayed there with her.

After Josh took them to the hotel, he went back to the center to meet up with his mom, girlfriend and the other people that were there.

He tried to cover up his hurt by pretending to be okay, but deep inside, he was hurting, because he remembered Cindy asking him to visit their dad a few months ago, and he declined, so that was eating at him.

A few hours later, Karen came back to the hotel, she checked on Cindy to see how she was doing, then went to her room to relax, she was very exhausted, both physically, and mentally.

The next day before they left Dallas, Cindy went to visit her grandmother who was staying at a different hotel.

The grandmother told her stories of her dad that she was not aware of, and she told her about some things in his past, that none his children knew about.

Cindy knew of his basketball career but did not know how passionate he was about it; she did not know that he suffered a major injury, which derailed his dreams of making it professionally.

Now she knew where his children got this passion for the game from, and where the talent came from.

The ride back from Dallas seemed to be so long for Cindy, who was eager to get home.

Finally, they made it Houston, turned in the rental, then went home to relax, after a weekend of hurtful emotions.

Cindy stayed another week with her mom before returning to Florida, while her brothers, along with their girlfriends, left on Tuesday morning.

Chapter THIRTY-SEVEN

DURING THAT WEEK, CINDY and Joyce were on the phone, discussing Jason's items.

Jason had a will, which would be available for sorting out his main items, but there were certain items, like clothes and other smaller items that needed to be sorted.

Jason had assigned Joyce, and Cindy to be joint Executors on his will, so they had to work together to execute the will.

Cindy hated that, but she knew her dad did that on purpose, so they could mend their relationship, in case something had happened to him.

Cindy did not care about his high school items, she just wanted his college items, such as his basketball trophies, and other sports memorabilia, and she was hoping that he had listed that in his will, so she wouldn't be fighting over it.

Leaving her mom this time, was so much more emotional, though she tried to hide her emotions concerning her Ex-husband Jason's death.

But Cindy knew, on the inside, she was hurting, just like every-one else, because even though they were divorced, they remained friends.

Kirk had obtained Katy's number from Cindy before Jason's death, so he called her, and they planned to meet Cindy at the airport.

She saw Katy, but Kirk was lurking at the back, and then caught up with them, and said, "hi Cindy,"

She turned around, and saw him, she was surprised, and turned to Katy, and said, "you were on this too ah?"

"It was all Kirk's idea, I just helped him along."

"I missed you so much baby, how are you doing, and coping?" he asked.

"I am doing much better; it has been a rough couple of weeks."

"We will go through it together; I will be in your corner."

"Thanks, honey, your support means a lot to me."

They reached the apartment, then Kirk said, "I think we should go out and have something to eat."

"You two love birds go ahead; I will stay home."

"Yeah, I don't feel like it either, I have no appetite," Cindy said.

But after much pleading, and pleading, she submitted.

At dinner, Kirk spoke about many subjects, but stayed clear of anything that would mention or refer to her dad.

She seemed to have a great time at the dinner, and for the time being, did not think of her dad's situation, but enjoyed the time with Kirk very much.

It took only a few minutes to get back to the apartment, which was a couple miles away.

Katy and Liz were waiting for them to come back; Liz wanted to make sure that she was okay before she left for her apartment, but Kirk asked her to stay a while, he wanted to get to know, Cindy's best friends.

They spent about an hour together, before Kirk and Cindy excused themselves and went to the bedroom.

He cheered her up, and encouraged her to be strong, but also, he tried to be intimate with her, but he tried to go too far, and Cindy was having none of that, and she let him know how she felt, which he understood, and apologized for his behavior.

He spent a few more minutes, before leaving for his hotel.

Kirk left early in the morning back to Atlanta. He later called her to report that he had made it safely and reminded her how much he loved her.

Back at work, Cindy's boss and coworkers, embraced and comforted her, and tried to make her feel as relaxed as they possibly could. They knew how much her dad meant to her because she spoke about him all the time.

Chapter THIRTY-EIGHT

THE NEXT COUPLE OF weeks that followed, Cindy went into a deep depression, and she spent most of her time alone; she spoke very little on the phone to her family and friends, which raised concern among them, especially her mom.

She assured her mom that she was okay but just needed time to recuperate, and to sort out things.

Karen asked Katy to monitor Cindy's behavior, and to keep her informed if anything out of the ordinary developed.

The relationship between Katy and Cindy had improved since the death of Jason. Katy remembered how much Cindy helped her when she lost her brother, and she wanted to return the favor to her, and to provide a shoulder to her that she could lean on.

She approached her and asked if they could go to Seabreeze to have dinner, along with Liz?

"That's fine, we could do that. What about 7: pm?"

"Sounds good to me, I will notify Liz."

It was a busy Saturday night, as expected, so the ladies knew that it would be a little while before they would have their dinner;

they requested to seat outside on the balcony which overlooked the highway and a portion of the lake.

They chatted while they waited for their food. They spoke about school, work, and anything that came to mind.

The topic finally drifted to Cindy and Kirk's relationship, and to Katy and Liz's surprise, Cindy, for the first time, was willing to speak about it.

She told them what she loved about him and also told them about his eagerness to take her to bed.

"Not that I don't want to go to bed with him, but I have my standards and values, and I want to stick to them; also, I'm afraid that as soon as I give in to him, our relationship might change, and he will fizzle out of the relationship. I am basing that on my observation of his behavior, the pressure he is putting on me to give it up, that is a red flag to me."

"Cindy, follow your instinct, don't be pressured into doing what you don't want to do, don't do it for him, you have to think of what is in it for you too." Katy admonished.

"Pleasure, that is what that is in it for me, this hunk of a guy, hahaha, just kidding, never been there, don't know, but I can't wait to go there, but I still want to do it the right way."

"You are so right, Cindy," Liz said, "I did not say anything to you all, but now that Cindy said that, I will say, I went through that.

"I was really in love, and I thought Jessie loved me, and like you said, after I gave him my virginity, after 4 months, we were no longer together. He slowly showed less interest in the relationship and eventually moved on. I regretted that to this day."

"Oh, I am sorry that I brought this up, and brought these bad memories back to you, I am so sorry." Cindy apologized.

"No need to apologize, I have moved on from that, although sometimes it flashes through my mind, and honestly, I am glad I told you all, thanks Cindy, I feel like a load has been lifted from my chest."

"Good for you Liz, and I am proud of you Cindy." Katy expressed.

Just then, the waiter came with their food and inquired if they needed any more drinks.

"No thanks," Cindy replied, "we are good."

There was silence at the table, as the ladies devoured their food, they acted as though they were starved and had not eaten for days.

"Kate, I'm glad you thought about this outing, I needed this, I needed the fellowship, always a pleasure being around you all, although sometimes I shut you out, but it is done in love."

"Always my pleasure, my friend, by now, I have learned how to approach, and appreciate our relationship."

"What are you doing?" Katy asked, as she reached for the bill. "No, no, this one is on me."

"Thanks," they both said, "we appreciate that and are grateful," Liz said.

They left the restaurant in a great mood. Cindy stopped at the campus to drop Liz and then she, and Katy continued to their apartment.

They sat on the couch and watched a few programs on TV.

"Kate, I miss my dad badly, especially at nights, I always called him before I went to bed, and he always had pleasant things to say to me. I wished he had survived, even though he would have been crippled, I would have felt better, because I know he would be there and I would take care of him."

"I know how you are feeling because I went through it with my brother; even though it didn't happen the same way, I know the pain is the same. I was hoping Dylan and I would have grown up together, hear his children call me aunty, and my kids talk about their uncle, but God had other plans, although, I don't think that it was God's plan for him to die like that, but I preferred that he is gone to meet God, than to suffer, and not be able to do anything for himself."

"I was hoping that my dad would be the one walking me down the aisle, while staring my husband to be straight in his eyes, sending a message to him, like "if you don't take care of my daughter, you will answer to me," and I wanted him to be there for my graduation, saying how proud he was of me, but all these things won't happen." And the two young ladies shed some tears before they went to bed.

"Kate, do you want to go to church today?" Cindy asked.

"Sure, we could do that, we need that about now in our lives, I don't know if Liz wants to join us; although I doubt it, she loves going to her church. But I will still ask her."

"Liz, we are going to church in a couple hours care to join us?" Katy asked.

"Sorry, Kate, but I will pass today, because I have plans to go to my church; maybe another time."

"Hahaha," I told you she would say that" and she could not stop laughing.

The church was a few miles from the campus, it only took them a few minutes to get there.

"Katy, I can't believe we are this close to the church, and this is the first time I am attending service here, shame on me."

"Sometimes it takes a painful occasion to get us back on track, and this was what happened to you.

"God speaks to us in so many ways, and somehow, He will get our attention, whether we like it or not."

"It happened to me with my brother, and now with you and your father. It is up to us to learn from these experiences."

Chapter THIRTY-NINE

THE SERVICE LASTED ABOUT an hour, and they both talked about how meaningful the service was, and how much they needed to renew their faith in God.

When they got back to their apartment, Cindy called her mom to check up on her, as usual, and when she told her mom that she just came from church, her mom almost fainted, because she did not expect that.

"I have been praying for you continuously, hoping that you would find your way back to being close to God. Since you went to college, you have been going the opposite way from God."

"Mom, I did not realize how quickly I had drifted from God, and the values that I learned from you and others, I just let them slip away, but dad's death brought back the reality of life to me."

The next couple of weeks, Cindy buried herself with work, she got permission from her supervisor to work overtime, so she did that to occupy her mind, and to think less of her dad's death.

She spent lots of time with the young ladies; if she was not at work, she was with them, when they were available.

Cindy's relationship to Kirk had reached a standstill; there were two factors, Cindy believed were responsible for that; she believed the long-distance romance played a big part in that, and she believed that her refusal to have sex with Kirk had a lot to do with it. She refused to worry about it and planned to concentrate on graduating college. She loved Kirk but was not going to make the same mistake as in the past.

At the end of the month, tired from the heavy workload, and being depressed from all that she had been through, Cindy said, "Kate, why don't we take a week's vacation and get away from Florida for a short while?"

"I can check with my boss tomorrow and see if he will allow me to leave on short notice, if he does, then we are on our way." Replied Katy.

"Sounds good," said Cindy, "I will check with Liz to find out if she would be able to accompany us."

The next day Katy got the answer from her boss and was anxious to meet Cindy.

"Hi Cindy, guess what?'

"You got it, you cannot hide your emotions, whether sad, or happy, they just come out."

"I spoke to Liz, and she is in favor of joining us."

"I was thinking," Cindy said, "why don't we be adventurous and go across to the Bahamas for the week? That would be great."

"That sound like a great idea, but there is a problem, the money." Katy replied

"I would be happy to chip in most of the cost. For instance, I will take care of the hotel room if you all could take care of your flights."

"I think we could do that, let me call Liz to find out what she thinks."

"Bahamas, here we come, "said Katy, "we are about to leave our mark on the Bahamas. When we leave, people are going to say,' the three sisters were here.' Hahaha," Katy laughed.

"You are so crazy girl, don't know what I would do without you, my brother is so fortunate to have found you."

"Again, it is all because of you," Katy replied

Chapter FORTY

"THE FLIGHT TO THE Bahamas was almost 4 hours long. It was a smooth and calm flight, and once they landed, collected their baggage, and boarded the taxi, Cindy said, "let the fun begin, we are going to forget about all our troubles for at least a week, and we are going to have a great time."

They made it to the hotel very quickly because the hotel was not too far from the airport.

They unpacked and were ready to have fun.

Cindy shifted the curtain and looked outside the window, and shouted, "wow, look at the water, it is so blue, can't wait to get in it."

The two other ladies came over to see what she was talking about and totally agreed with her.

Monday morning, they woke up early, and went to the hotel courtyard where they had an enjoyable breakfast.

After returning to their room, they planned their activities for the remainder of the day.

They first decided to go to the beach, and when they looked out of the window, it was already crowded this early in the morning.

They quickly changed into their bathing suits crossed the street, and they were right there.

They spent a few hours in the water, and Katy, and Cindy laid on the sand and got tanned from the sunlight, while Liz relaxed in the hammock.

When it was time to leave, Liz was reluctant to go, but they reminded her that they had other plans, could enjoy the beach, every day of their vacation, so she left with them.

They completed the activities that they had scheduled for the day. When they returned to their room, they were so tired, and took a nap before they went out for dinner.

They capped the night by going downstairs to the lounge and enjoyed the entertainment that the hotel had scheduled.

The band was awesome and played music that the young ladies were familiar with, and they danced wildly, and enjoyed a couple glasses of wine, and champagne before they called it a night and went back upstairs.

The days that followed, found them exploring Nassau, and other areas in the Bahamas; they visited places of historical interest, as well as entertainment venues.

During their stay, they were fortunate to see the island annual festival, where the people reveled crazily. Cindy, Katy, and Liz enjoyed, and participated in a few of the activities of the festival.

The crowd was made up of the locals, and lots of tourists, and they all partied like there were no cares in the world.

While in the Bahamas, they made a few new friends, especially male friends.

There was one guy named Mathew, who was madly in love with Liz, and took care of her local needs like coconuts, mangos, and some other items.

He asked her to marry him so he could come to America with her.

She thought he was joking, but after conversing with him for a while, she realized that he was serious.

She sadly had to turn him down, because she was there to have fun, not to get involved in a relationship, especially being so far from Florida.

Katie was blunt with those that were interested in her; she let them know quickly that she was not available, and they would be wasting their time.

Alex, a front desk clerk at the hotel, was interested in Cindy from the first day, they came in, and throughout the entire week, he begged her to have lunch or dinner with him; the more she turned him down, the more persistent he became, until she finally gave in, but said it had to be in the hotel's restaurant.

That was a win for him, and he quickly accepted her conditions.

At the table, he told her that she was one of the most beautiful young ladies he ever saw come through the hotel doors; he even went so far as to say, "your parents must be angels, to bring forth such a pretty person."

And he was right, because Cindy was a very beautiful young lady; she had a good blend of her father and mother.

With all his efforts to warm his way into her heart, Cindy, unfortunately, had to break his heart, and dash his chances, when she told him that she was already taken, and in a serious relationship, but would like to remain friends with him.

He agreed to be friends but felt very dejected from her rejection.

When she came back to the room, her friends were eager to find out how her date was, and she gave them the details, and the sadness she felt when she broke his heart.

Chapter FORTY-ONE

THE NEXT DAY THEY woke up and prepared to go back to Florida.

Cindy said to the others, "so sad, every good thing must come to an end, I wish we had three weeks here," and she said that with sadness in her voice, because she knew that she was going back to reality.

"Although, I missed my beau," Katy said, "I am in total agreement with you, it should have been three weeks."

"I am in agreement with you all, I will miss Mathew, such a nice guy"

"I see someone is in love; you might have to come back and get him, and bring him to Florida," Cindy said jokingly.

"Not so easy, and not so fast," Liz replied, "any relationship I enter into again, has to be like Katy's, or close to it."

"Thanks Liz, but thanks to God, who brought Cindy into my life, who brought Josh into my arms. I am grateful to both."

When they arrived back in Florida, Joshua was at the airport waiting for them.

"Josh, what are you doing here? What a surprise," Katy said.

"You mean you didn't know he was coming to pick us up? I thought you were part of the plan to surprise Liz and me,' Cindy said.

"No dear, it was all his idea, but I am glad he did.

"I missed you so much, and I just wanted to see you as soon as I could."

"Or you were scared of the Bahamian boys that were trying to hit on her," Cindy said laughingly.

"No way, I am established and totally secure, and she can't find a more handsome one like me."

"Don't fool yourself, these guys were hot, and aggressive, but there is none in the world like my Josh."

"Are you all hungry?' Josh asked.

"Yes, I am," Cindy replied, "don't know about the others, but I am starving."

"Same here," Katy said, "me too," Liz said.

Josh took the ladies to Blue Ocean seafood restaurant, one of the best restaurants in the city.

The young ladies shared their experiences of their trip with Joshua, and he was happy that they enjoyed their trip.

After the waitress came and took their orders, Joshua excused himself, and had the waitress place an engagement ring on Katy's plate, alongside her appetizer, properly covered to prevent detection, and he instructed the waitress to serve Kate last.

As Katy uncovered her plate, she noticed the small black box next to her croissant.

"What's this?" She asked, as she stared at it with astonishment,

Then Joshua went down on one knee opened the box, and said, "Kate, my dear, will you marry me?"

Katy flew from her chair, and hugged him, as he stood up, and said, "yes I will, definitely will."

Everyone at the table was surprised and happy for the two them, and offered their congratulations, and their blessings to them.

"Kate, you are definitely part of the family now, just one more step to seal the deal, and you will be a Gregaben. Sis, I love you."

"And Josh, my brother, congrats, you are always a great guy, and an amazing brother, I know you will make a great husband, and eventually, a great dad."

Joshua thanked everyone for their encouragement and their support, and then they proceeded to end their dinner.

The ride home from the restaurant was nothing but quiet, because everyone was so happy, especially Kate.

Cindy called Kirk, to let him know that she had made it home safely, but his reception was cold, and he sounded like he was annoyed about something; she did not want to get into an argument so she got off the phone as quickly as she could.

"What's wrong Cindy?" Katy asked, after she saw the expression on Cindy's face.

"Kirk is acting like a jerk," Cindy replied, "I have no idea what's gotten into him, anyway, I am about to go to bed, it has been a long and interesting day. Good night to you both."

The following day, Cindy called in sick; she wanted to rest and catch up on her sleep.

On Tuesday, she was welcomed back to the clinic with embraces by her co-workers; they inquired about her trip, and she gave them details.

The next few weeks, she went back to her regular routine; work, home, and meeting with Kirk off and on.

Chapter FORTY-TWO

THE RELATIONSHIP WITH KIRK was not as great as she wanted; she often got mad at him for things that he did that were inconsiderate, and then, he would win her back with something amazing. One time he was a bad guy, and the next time she was saying how amazing a guy he was.

The summer holiday was finally over, and it was time to get back to classes.

But right before signing up for her classes, Cindy decided to take a break from school, and to skip this semester. Cindy claimed that she had too much on her mind, with the death of her father, and her rocky relationship with Kirk, she needed the semester off.

That did not sit well with her mother, who chastised her for that decision, but realized, she was not in control anymore. She tried to make her see the importance of continuing, and getting it over with, and shared with her the pitfalls from when people take breaks from their studies, but nothing she said, swayed, or changed her mind.

Cindy continued her full-time schedule at work and did as much overtime as she was allowed to do.

Meanwhile, her brother Joshua was drafted to play basketball professionally, and would be moving to Orlando.

Cindy was excited about that, and she knew her dad would have been so proud of him

Cindy was saving as much money as she could, and only bought things that she needed; she considered herself a miser.

Cindy planned on going home for Christmas, she had a special gift for her mom.

Karen had always wanted to go on a cruise, but could not go for various reasons; one of them was finance and though she made a reasonable amount at her job, but there were so many needs that required most of her money,

Cindy thought, this coming spring would be the best time to go.

She saved the money for that purpose, and said she would inform her mom when she got home for Christmas.

She wanted her mom to have enough time to fit it in her schedule.

She could not wait to spend some quality time with her mom alone, far away from everyone, and everything.

Cindy realized that since she mentioned to Kirk about her friendship with Mario, that his attitude toward her changed.

He tried to be nicer than before, and his calls were more frequent than before, and he stopped taking her for granted.

Kirk was jealous; he hated that Mario was in the picture, although Cindy promised him that she would not do anything to hamper their relationship, yet he kept saying that he did not want to lose her.

Kirk purposed in his heart to be more active in Cindy's life and was going to be more visible in the relationship and try to spend more weekends with her, whenever possible.

Cindy appreciated the attention, but she was concerned with his new possessive attitude.

Chapter *FORTY-THREE*

ON FRIDAY SEPTEMBER 10TH, Cindy's 21st birthday, Kirk decided to surprise her. He corroborated with Katy and Liz to organize a birthday party for her.

All the plans were completed and the guests were notified.

Kirk wanted it to be a complete surprise, and he did everything possible to make sure it was.

He told Cindy that he would be in Florida on Wednesday and Thursday because he had a meeting with a prospective business partner but promised to fill her in with the details later.

Kirk checked into the hotel on Thursday, as the party was scheduled for the Friday, and he booked the ballroom at the hotel for that occasion.

On Thursday night he called Cindy, to let her know he could not spend time with her, because he was tired from the two days of activities, but planned to spend the rest of the weekend with her.

Cindy argued with him for a while, but realized she was not going to win, so she conceded, and waited for tomorrow.

She knew that he knew that Friday was her birthday, because she reminded him all throughout the week, and she had an idea, and feeling, that this was the reason he was in Florida, but she had no idea that he had this massive celebration planned.

Early Friday morning, Kirk called Cindy to wish her happy birthday, and then asked her where he would fit in her birthday plans.

She was given the day off to celebrate her birthday, so she laid in bed for a couple more hours.

She woke up about 10:30 in the morning, said her devotions, then went into the kitchen to prepare breakfast, but to her surprise, and delight breakfast was already prepared.

"Happy birthday, my sister and best friend; I do hope you will have a great day. Welcome to the adult world, hahaha, you thought I was going to let you fix yourself breakfast today? Not a chance." Katy said.

"Thanks sis, that is why I appreciate you so much, and for your information, you are just 3 months more adult than I am, and by experience, I am more adult than you. Hahaha."

A few minutes later, Kirk came to pick her up, he had a few activities planned for her birthday.

After they left her apartment, they drove almost 3 hours to Jacksonville, where they went shopping, to the beach, and then went kayaking on the river.

Cindy was very impressed with the food they had at the five-star restaurant he took her to.

The trip back to Tallahassee took longer because they made a few stops along the way.

They got back about 6:30pm. He dropped her at her apartment and told her to be ready by about 8:45 pm, for their dinner appointment.

Cindy gave Katy a lovely pair of earrings she bought for her from her shopping spree in Jacksonville.

"Thanks Cindy, they are beautiful, but today is your birthday, I am the one that should be giving you, but again that is the type of person you are, loving and always looking out for others."

"Liz and I are going to the movies tonight, I wished you could have come with us, but we know you will have a great dinner with Kirk."

"I am about to take about an hour nap before Kirk comes by. You all enjoy the movies; I will hopefully join you next time."

Katy was happy to hear that she was going to nap, because she knew she would be able to dress for the birthday party undetected by Cindy.

Chapter FORTY-FOUR

KIRK WAS AT THE apartment, at 8:45, and Cindy was all dressed up and waiting.

"Wow, my dear, you look amazing, and you are even more beautiful tonight," Kirk complimented Cindy, as he opened the car door.

"Thanks, Boo, I am trying to keep up with you," she said jokingly.

They drove down Seaside Blvd. where the hotel, and several fancy and expensive restaurants were located.

She was tempted to ask him if they were going to one of these restaurants, but decided against it, and to just wait and see.

"Oh, Cindy, can we just stop at the hotel for a minute? I forgot something important that I need."

"Not a problem Kirk,' she replied.

He pulled up at the hotel and told her it would only take a few minutes.

The valet attendant came up to him and was given the keys.

Cindy said, "you don't need to valet park, I will wait here in the car for you."

"Oh no, I would not do that, it is too dangerous, how could I leave a lady in a car alone in the night in a busy place?"

"Sorry, I was not thinking about that, I thought it was for a short period of time, and could have waited, but you are right," and with that said, they went to his room.

They spent two minutes in the room and headed back down-stairs, when he told her that he did not find what he was looking for, and most likely left it in the gym on the second floor; let's hope that it is there."

"What is it that you are looking for?" she asked.

"Something I bought for you, I can't tell you what it is, so it is pointless to ask."

They took the elevator down to the second floor; his plan was to open the door to the lounge like it was leading to the gym, but it would be the lounge.

He held her hand, as they made their way toward the gym. He called them from upstairs to let them know that he was on the way.

He reached the lounge door, and said, 'let's pass this way, it would be faster," and he opened the door to the deafening sound of surprise! Surprise!

Cindy stood there shocked, and surprised. She had no idea that was what they had planned for her.

Everyone sang happy birthday, they sang in all different chords, and tones, but who cared? They were just happy to be there for the celebration.

Cindy, after the shock had worn off, said, "I should have known, because Katy, and Liz going to the movies on a Friday night without me? Unheard of. That should have tipped me. Anyway, great job guys, I did not have the slightest clue this was happening."

She hugged Kirk, and said, "You are the best, that is one of the reasons I love you so much."

After a few speeches, the party went to full swing.

Kirk had many of his teammates and friends there. Katy had invited some of their college friends.

Kirk went about the room, proudly introducing his girlfriend to everyone he came across, and the compliments Cindy received were tremendous.

The party started as a formal setting, but quickly became loud, and boisterous.

Cindy joined her friends, as Kirk did the same.

About 12:30 am, the door opened, and in came in Joshua; Cindy and Katy were beyond shocked, because neither knew that he was coming.

They ran towards the door and screamed and hugged him, and that got the attention of those who were there.

And Cindy gladly introduced her brother to everyone and took him to Kirk, and formally introduced him.

Kirk chatted with them for a few minutes, then went back to his buddies.

"I did not know that you were coming, you and Kate, pulled a fast one on me." Katy said, "I am just as surprised as you, I had no idea."

"You think I was going to miss my little sister's twenty first birthday celebration? Not going to happen.

"You are so slick, all these questions you were asking me, was because you had your plan. Katy said.

You are full of detective skills; I must watch out for you."

At that moment, Robin, Kizzy, and Samantha came up to them, and Robin asked, "who is this handsome guy? He is so fine."

Robin, this is my brother Joshua, and before she could finish introducing him, Katy interrupted and said, "this is my fiancée, and he is not looking for anyone, so take your eyes off him."

Robin made a remark, and she and her friends walked away.

The party was swinging, lots of food, and plenty of drinking.

About 1:30am, Kirk and Cindy left the party venue and went to Kirk's room.

The two decided to take some time away from the crowd for a few minutes, to spend some quiet time together.

"Thanks, Kirk, it has been an amazing day, and wonderful night, you have really made my 21st birthday very special."

"It is not done yet, we are still celebrating, check this bottle on the table, very expensive, and of the best quality, and that is because you are very special to me."

He took the glasses and the bottle of wine and put them on a tray and laid it on the bed.

"Kirk, you know I don't drink alcohol."

"I am not asking you to get drunk, just a small amount to celebrate you."

"Okay, just a little bit. Okay, enough."

"Wow, this is strong Kirk."

"Not really, it is because you are not accustomed to drinking, so it seems strong to you."

"Kirk, that is enough, that is your second glass, you will be drunk before you realize it."

"I am good, this is mild, not a big deal."

After chatting for a while, the two drew closer to each other, and Cindy rested her head on Kirk's chest, as he was stroking her hair, and told her how lucky he was to be with her.

"The feelings are mutual," she said, "you are a real gentleman, that is one of the reasons I trust you, that is why I am here with you right now."

"Oh, this is Katy calling, let me answer her quickly; I'm sure she is just concerned about me."

"Hi Kate, oh no, I am not away from the hotel, I am here with Kirk in his room, I am fine, will be down before everyone leaves."

"Great friends, and family you have."

"No Kirk, no more, the bottle is almost empty."

"Kiss me, not a peck on my lips, a real kiss, you know what, let me show you how to do it."

"Okay Kirk, relax, you are getting too aggressive. Take your hands out from there. What happened to the gentleman that was here a few minutes ago?"

"Cindy, I love you, I want to make this night special for you."

"It has already been special, I enjoyed it, and am still enjoying it, if only you could keep your cool, and control yourself."

"Cindy, I cannot help myself, because you are so beautiful, and enticing, I just want you to feel good."

"Okay kirk, stop acting like that, you are scaring me."

Kirk was not listening to what Cindy was saying, his attitude had changed, he no longer wanted to be just there with her, but now he wanted to know her.

"Stop it Kirk, get your hands off my breast, you are hurting me, stop it, leave my bra alone, what are you doing?"

Cindy stood up and was heading towards the door, and Kirk came and blocked her.

Cindy began sobbing, as Kirk became more aggressive.

"I want you so badly, Cindy, I really do."

"Kirk, the right time will come, I will be all yours, but now Kirk, not now."

"I can't control myself; I have to have you, I love you."

"Kirk no, as she struggled to keep her underwear on, no, stop, you are hurting me, stop, stop." She cried.

But he would not, he had determined to have sex with her.

"Kirk, please, I don't want to lose my virginity like this, please Kirk, no." and she fought as hard as she could, but he overpowered her, and held his hand across her mouth, and took his other hand, and pulled on her underwear, leaving a small hole in it, and tossed it on the bed.

She gave it her last effort, she tried hard, but to no avail, she tried to scream but could not. She kicked, and kicked, until she could not kick anymore, then the dreadful thing happened, he penetrated her.

"Ouch, ouch," she cried, as she felt the pain of him being inside of her, she was crying hysterically, as he continued.

Finally, she just laid there quietly, as he did his thing, she just sucked up the pain and hurt, and wished that it would that it would be over.

After Kirk reached his climax, he stopped, and laid next to her.

"Sorry, Cindy, sorry, what did I just do? I don't know what got into me, I am so sorry."

Cindy laid there quietly, in pain, weeping bitterly. She never had been hurt so badly in her life, she wished she could die at this moment, she did not know what to do.

Yet, she felt so guilty for allowing that to happen.

Only if I did not trust this guy, if I had not come up to his room to be alone with him, that would not have happened, who can I tell, who will believe me, because I was not forced into his room.

All these things she pondered in her heart.

Her mind was all messed up at the time, and her heart was broken in a million pieces.

Kirk took a fast shower, dressed, and left her there, and went down to the lounge, where there were still a few people left.

Joshua, Katy, and Liz approached him, and asked him "where is Cindy?" because they saw him come back alone.

"Oh, she is taking a small nap. I will wake her up in a while, she will be down before it is over."

Joshua was uneasy about that, he was worried, and said if she was not down in 10 minutes, he was going up there, a matter of fact, let me call her.

She sounded sleepy, but said she was okay and would be down soon.

Kirk was with the few of his friends that remained there, and they were laughing, giggling, and having a good time, meanwhile Cindy was upstairs miserable.

She got up to make her way downstairs, but when she saw the blood on the sheet, she became really upset, and cried, and came to the realization, that what she feared, had really happened.

She sat at the edge of the bed, wondering what to do next, and she knew that Katy and the others would come up, if she did not go down soon.

She took off the sheet, and shamefully put it underneath the bed, then she went to the shower, where she stayed for a long while, as she washed herself from the blood, and other bodily fluids. She cried bitterly as different thoughts crossed her mind.

She got out of the shower, and was drying, when she heard the knocks on the door. She knew it was not Kirk, because he had a key; she wrapped the towel around her, and went and peeped in the keyhole, and saw it was Katy.

"One minute Kate," she said faintly.

Right away, Katy knew that something was wrong, she could tell by the sound of her voice.

Cindy dried her eyes, put her ripped underwear on, and with the towel around her waist, she opened the door.

"Are you okay?" Katy asked, "we saw Kirk came downstairs without you, and the way he acted, prompted me to come and check on you.

"Honestly, is everything alright? I am your sister; you can talk to me."

"You look like you have been through some trauma."

"I am fine, Kirk and I went through some misunderstanding, which caused me to be angry."

"Did he hit you? What did he do to you? Don't hide it from me.'

"It is okay. Right now, I don't want to talk about it, I will sort it out later."

"I knew something went wrong. I can see a few bruises on your neck, and other parts on your body, that meant you all were fighting, and who knows what else happened?"

"I am furious. And he came downstairs, like everything was okay. She is taking a nap," he said. "That good for nothing jerk."

"I hope when you go downstairs, Josh, doesn't see these marks, because it would get ugly down there."

"Come on, take me home, we don't have to go back to the party, we will call Josh and let him know that I was not feeling well, and I asked you to take me home."

"I am going back to tell Josh and Liz that I have to take you home. I will come up with something believable to tell them, you wait for me in the bathroom downstairs."

"Cindy apparently had a couple of drinks too much; she is in the restroom. I am going to take her home. Liz, ride with Josh, so he won't ride by himself at this time of the night."

"Okay," said Joshua, "we will let the others know, that she had to leave, as a matter of fact, I will tell Kirk, and he will tell the others."

"Hi Kirk; Cindy left. She was feeling terrible so she went home." Joshua told him,

"Why didn't she call me, and tell me that?"

"Are you crazy? You left her upstairs in a room sick and all alone, and you are down here enjoying yourself, and she should call you, and tell you crap? Man get a life."

Kirk began swearing and acting the fool. "Who are you to tell me what I should do?"

Liz stepped in and convinced Joshua that they should leave before the confrontation turned ugly.

On the way home from the hotel, Katy tried her best to get more information from Cindy, but Cindy would not offer any. She did not say much, and you could tell that she was hurting, and just wanted to get to her apartment.

Katy vowed that she would find out what happened in that room; she said she would not stop until she got to the bottom of it.

She was convinced in her heart that Kirk raped or attempted to rape Cindy; she saw to much evidence that led to her suspicions.

Cindy went directly to her bed when they made it home; she took off her shoes and spread herself across the bed and fell asleep quickly.

Katie took her phone and took pictures of the bruises on Cindy's neck, and the marks on Cindy's body, especially the deep bruises that were on her thighs, which convinced her even more that there was a struggle between the two of them, and she wanted this for evidence, if it came to that.

She was hurting for Cindy. She thought, how can someone so wonderful and loving go through all that pain? She doesn't deserve to be treated like that.

Not too long after that, Joshua, and Liz came, and inquired about Cindy, but Katy made an excuse for her, and told them, she was not feeling good.

Chapter *Chapter* FORTY-FIVE

CINDY WOKE UP ABOUT 11: am the next day and was still in a daze.

Joshua and katy had gone to the store to get a few groceries, so the apartment was very quiet.

She went to the bathroom to take a shower, but before she did, she sat at the edge of the bathtub, for a minute; while sitting there she noticed the awful gap on her thigh, then it finally hit her, that she was not dreaming, that what she went through was real.

She went to look at the mirror, and saw the scratches on her neck, and thought, wow, these are horrible.

She went and sat on the toilet, and just stared at the ceiling, as thoughts raced through her mind.

"Should I tell someone? Or should I not?" she said to herself. "If I do, will anyone believe me? Or would they blame me for what happened?"

Right now, I am feeling worthless, devastated, never thought this would happen to me.

She finally went into the shower, and stayed there for a long time, as the water poured down on her head, and unto her body.

"If Only the water could wash away the shame that I am feeling right now, if only it could take away the pain, and the broken pieces of my heart, only if I had wings, I would fly far away, never to return." And Cindy broke down again and cried, until she had no more tears to cry.

She finished the shower, dried, and lotioned herself and waited for the others to come home.

"How am I going to explain the scratches, and bruises on my neck to Josh? I will let him know that I had a fight with Kirk, but I won't go into deep details.

"Hi guys, did not see you when I woke up, I thought you eloped."

"Funny. You were fast asleep, we did not want to wake you up, so we went shopping without you." Katy explained, "Josh was very worried about you, especially after last night."

"Yeah, what happened last night?" Josh asked.

"Well, it was a great night, which turned into a nightmare."

"I 've never known you to drink. And it was so bad you ended up being sick, I knew it was a special day to you, your 21st birthday, but out of control? I would never think that for a moment." Josh said.

"Josh, I am not a drunkard, it so happened, that I let my guard down, and was enticed by Kirk to have one drink which I did, but honestly, I was not drunk, I was just hurt by the fight I had with Kirk."

"You mean that guy hit you, and you hid this from me? And made me believe that you were drunk and not feeling good? Girl, now I am mad, not at Kirk, but at you for deceiving me, and letting this guy get off scott free."

"Josh, I know you, things would have gotten out of control, and I would not want you to get hurt, because of my negligence. Kirk and his boys can be vicious."

"Tell me that this is it with you and that jerk, but it is not over between him and me, our paths will cross again."

"It's definitely over; this guy has become my number one enemy."

While they were speaking the phone rang. It was Karen, their mom.

"How are you, Josh, and Katy doing? How was the surprise birthday party? They got you good," Karen said.

"Mom we are doing okay, Josh, and Kate are right here next to me. It was a surprise to me, it was a huge party, only person that was missing, was my dad, I know he would have enjoyed it. I can't believe he is gone."

She said this to change the subject as she did not want to go into details about the party.

"Hold on, talk to Josh," and she handed the phone to him, and she made a sign to him, that he say nothing to her about her fight.

She spent a few more minutes with her mom, before assisting in preparing lunch.

While at the table, Joshua noticed the scratches, and bruises.

"What the heck? This must have been a big fight, for you to be that injured, and I am getting even madder now than before."

"Josh, can we drop the subject? i cannot undo the stupid mistakes that I made; I want to forget this episode in my life and move on."

"Enough about me, did you guys set a date yet? I mean for the wedding."

"We have a few dates in mind," replied Katy, "but we haven't decided which one is best suited for both of us, but don't worry, you will have a big part to play in planning it."

"Fine, don't wait until I am old and gray to have it. Hahaha.

"By the way, anyone care for the movies tonight? I want to clear and relax my mind."

Josh looked at Katy, and she nodded her head, and he said, they were okay with the suggestion, also they would call Liz.

At least, for a couple of hours, Cindy had her mind on something else, instead of the horrible things that happened to her.

She was happy to be around family and friends; she knew that this was part of the healing process, but also realized, that there was a long, and hard road ahead, and life would never be the same.

Chapter FORTY-SIX

THE FOLLOWING DAY, SHE decided to visit Liz's church, just to be in a different atmosphere. She enjoyed, and was blessed by the service, and promised Liz, to visit again another time.

After a weekend of twist and turns, it was time to head back to work on Monday.

Cindy's co-workers were eager to get details about the party, because a few of her co-workers, who were in attendance, spread the word of who her boyfriend was. He was well known, because of his fame in the basketball world, so they were excited they had met him, and were anxious to find out more about him from Cindy. If they only knew, what he had done to Cindy, they would think of him differently.

Approximately two hours later, a courier came into the center to deliver a lovely bouquet of flowers and asked for Cindy. He approached her and handed her the flowers.

She took the flowers, and pretended to be happy to receive the flowers, but she took them and laid them on the table in the break room. She took the card, and went to the bathroom, and read the words that were penned.

"Sorry Cindy, I am so sorry, and ashamed for what I did to you, I don't know what got into me, I hope you will forgive me for doing that to you. PS, I still love you."

The note just enraged Cindy more, she was trying hard not to cry, she did not want to send out any signals, that there was trouble between her and Kirk, she did not want her co-workers getting into her private affairs, she did not want them to know that Kirk and her were over, especially, not after a celebration like she just had, and a few of them were witnesses to it.

She placed the card in her pocket, and asked, "does anyone want these flowers?"

"Why?" asked Dr. King, better known as Junie, they're beautiful, and should mean a lot to you; why not take them home?"

"I am not a flower person, and it would be a waste; why can't someone from here enjoy them?"

"Okay, I will let one of the ladies take them home, just don't know which one I will let have them."

Before leaving for home, Cindy stayed in the parking lot, and texted Kirk in response to the card that he sent.

She typed, "you got the audacity, and the nerve, to write to me, and to send flowers to me? After what you did to me, you think I care about some lousy flowers? You think I care to see, or hear from you again? I don't believe you, and to think, I was so much in love with you? Unbelievable."

Kirk replied and said almost the same things that he jotted on the card.

Cindy put her phone in her bag, and said "bye you jerk."

She said she would delete him from her phone, but thought about it, and said, these texts and other information might come in handy, so she decided to leave them in there.

Cindy tried daily to put the memory of that incident out of her mind, but it was more difficult than she thought it would be.

She leaned on her best friends, Katy, and Liz for support on a regular basis. She gave them lots of her evening time, tutoring them with their classes. Any small space of free time that she had, she plugged something in there so her time would be occupied.

Cindy had no clue, but was informed by Katelin, one of her co-workers that Dr. King, had a crush on her, and that he was very disappointed she was seeing Kirk.

She observed him a couple of times, staring at her and pretending he was paying attention to something else.

They had a great working relationship between them, and had become close friends, but she had no idea he felt this way towards her. She wished she knew before she had gotten involved with Kirk.

She always like Junie, but never thought of having a romantic relationship with him, but she believed, if he had showed her that he was interested in her, things could have been different.

Chapter FORTY-SEVEN

As THE SECOND MONTH approached, and she still did not have a period, she began to worry, and was deeply concerned.

Nothing happened, and she knew that she was in trouble. She had an idea that she might be pregnant, but she was hoping that this was not the case.

She made an appointment to see another doctor, instead of her regular doctor, in order to keep this quiet.

The doctor ran a few tests just to confirm what he told her before, that she was pregnant.

Cindy was heartbroken, and upset, not that she did not want a child, but this was not how she envisioned seeing herself bringing a child into this world.

Cindy sat in her car and wept bitterly, "what am I going to do?' she asked, "What am I going to say to my mom, and others in my circle?"

It took her a long time to reach the apartment, she stopped at the public park, which was about 3 miles from her apartment, and sat in her car shedding tears, and wondered what she was going to do about her situation.

Katy was at class, so she was alone in the apartment, and she cried some more, until she was weak, then she laid on her bed and fell asleep.

The following day, she called in sick from her job as she was not in the best frame of mind, to perform her duty effectively.

Katy was back from her only class for that day and was surprised to see Cindy home because Cindy hardly took time off from her job, unless it was urgent.

"Are you okay?" Katy asked, "it's unusual to see you home at this time of the day."

"I am fine, but I just needed some rest, and to clear my mind a little bit.'

The two sat on the couch, and chatted, and spoke of Kate's upcoming wedding, and the excitement they both anticipated concerning the wedding; just then Cindy's phone rang, and she glanced at the number, and recognized that it was the doctor, so she sprang up from the couch, and went into her room to take the call.

That raised suspicion to Katy, then she went to her door, and shouted, "is everything all right?"

Cindy did not respond. Katy waited for a minute, and asked the same question, still no response, but as she listened attentively, she could hear her crying.

"Can I come in?" she asked, if it is not too much trouble.

Cindy slowly walked to the door, and swung it open, "please come in," she said in a low, and sad voice.

Katy embraced her, not knowing what it was, but knew that something was wrong, and allowed her to cry on her shoulders for a while.

When she ceased crying, Katy asked, "What is going on? What is wrong? You know you can confide in me, I am always here for you, don't be afraid to talk to me."

Cindy thought about it, and figured, she must tell someone, because this drama was eating her up ferociously, and outside of her mom, Katy was one of the only people she could trust, and confide in, so she decided to tell her what was going on.

"I am trusting you," she said, while she was sobbing as she was talking, "you, and you alone are going to hear what I have to say, and I am trusting that it will remain between us two.

"Oh definitely, you can trust me on that, I have your back.'

"I was raped. Kirk raped me, and the tears just kept on coming. I told you that we fought, well yes, I fought as hard as I could to keep my virginity, and my pride, and dignity, but my strength was not strong enough to prevent it from happening."

"We were okay for the first few minutes that we were in the room, and suddenly, out of nowhere, he changed, and acted like a wild animal. I begged him to stop, I pleaded with all that was in me, but to no avail.

He was so much stronger than I was, so he overpowered me, and he penetrated me, and had sex with me against my will."

"Kate," she said, I don't know which hurt the most, the penetration, or my dignity. Katy, I hate myself for allowing it to happen, I should have never trusted him, and accompanied him to that room, what was I thinking? How could I have been so stupid and not see through him? How could I let my guard down and be so careless?"

"It's not your fault Cindy, you were in love, and the way he presented himself to you, and the way he treated you, it was almost impossible to think something like that would happen."

"He won your confidence and trust, then he exploited you, he used your goodness as your weakness, and took advantage of you. He is a low life, and he will get what he deserves."

"Katy. I am pregnant."

"Oh no," and she hugged her, and they both cried loudly.

"What am I going to do?' Cindy said, I always wanted children, but not like this, it is killing me to know that I have this rapist child inside of me. Oh Lord, what did I do? And what am I going to do?"

"I can't tell Josh, and mom, and not Liz, this is to remain between the two of us. I can't tell the police, they won't believe me, because he did not force me into the room, and see how long I waited to tell someone., and where is the evidence?" they would ask.

"What did I do in my life that has me being punished like this?"

"I tried to be a nice, and loving person, I tried not to harm others, and here I am, with a truck load of problems."

"You are a kind and loving person, there is no one else I would rather have as a friend, and sister than you. Bad things sometimes happen to good people, and you are a perfect example, but we will get through this together."

"How far along are you?"

About six weeks, the doctor said.

"Katy, I don't think, I am going to keep the child, as much as I love children, I just cannot fathom me having a child that came about because of the criminal activity. It's a crime, he raped me."

"I understand all that, but please don't rush to a decision right now, you are not in the best frame of mind to make such a major decision like this. Please wait a few days, and we can sit and talk about it."

"Okay, but not a word to Josh, or anybody else, I am counting on you." It's very hard for me to keep such disturbing information from Josh, if he finds out that I hid this from him, I don't know what would become of our relationship, but as a true friend, I am giving you my word, that I will honor my promise."

Friday evening while they were relaxing, Katy asked, "is this a right time to continue the discussion we started a few days ago?"

"There is not too much left to be said about the issue, I have made up my mind, I am not going to keep the baby."

"So sad, I am, and will support you, and be there for you, as much as I can, but this time, you don't have my support, because I am totally against abortion. I don't condone what happened to you, a matter of fact, I am so angry, that it caused me to be sick, but I think there are other alternatives, please reconsider, and don't do something that you would regret later."

"Thanks for the talk, you are a great person."

Chapter FORTY-EIGHT

TWO DAYS AFTER SPEAKING with Katy, Cindy set up an appointment to have the abortion done.

She did not tell Katy about it, because she did not want to be deterred from doing it.

Shortly after Katie left for class, Cindy took a cab to the clinic where she was scheduled to have the procedure done. On her way there, she thought so many times, to ask the driver to take her back home, but when she remembered Kirk, she continued to the clinic.

The procedure took a while, and was extremely painful, and the weight on her mind, knowing what she was doing, affected her even more.

She grew up being totally against abortion, she was taught that it was wrong, but now that she was caught in this situation, she ignored what she had learned, and had believed, and did what she thought was right for her now.

She stayed at the center for a few hours, until she had recovered enough to go home.

She called Katy and asked her to come and pick her up.

"Where are you? Is everything okay? You sound like someone in a lot of pain.'

"I am at the Tronto clinic."

"Where? Did you? No, I don't believe you went along, and did it?"

"Katie, I am in too much pain to argue with you, are you coming or not? I left the car, so you could pick me up."

"Sure, I will be there shortly."

Katie arrived at the clinic in less than 10 minutes, and felt sorry for Cindy, after she saw how she looked.

She quickly went to the passenger's side, and opened the door, and assisted her into the seat.

After they left the clinic, making their way back to the apartment, Cindy began to cry, when she realized what she had done.

"Katie, I am so sorry that I went did this, I thought that was the best option for me, but now that it's done, I am feeling so guilty, I believed, I have taken a life from someone. I don't know how I am going to live with myself for doing that."

"I wished you had not done it, but since you did, you can't bring it back, this is not reversible, from here on you just have to live with the decision that you have made, it is not going to be easy, but you have to try to put this behind you and try to move forward."

As soon as they got to the apartment, Cindy went straight into bed, for she was having serious pain.

Katy was heartbroken, and she was disappointed, but she knew that there was nothing that she could do now, because the operation was done, and what she needed to do was to support and be there for her best friend, who was in a bad place.

This was a day and a weekend Cindy would never forget, but she knew also, that she had to move on with the rest of her life and to make better choices in the future.

She went back to work on Monday and acted normally because no one knew what she did over the weekend.

The next day Junie, the doctor, asked her out to lunch and she accepted.

He came in about 1 pm, and asked her if she was ready

"Are we going out somewhere?" she asked, "because you have your keys, and you are not wearing your doctor's coat.

"Yes, we are going to the restaurant down on 6th street, I have some extra time today, which allows me the opportunity to get out of the building and away from cafeteria food today."

Cindy was glad to be invited and relieved to get out of the building for a while.

The food and atmosphere were great, but most of all, she enjoyed the company of Junie.

They enjoyed great conversations about other things besides work.

Cindy did not tell him of her ordeal that she just went through because she did not want it leaking out in the office, not that she thought he would, but she was not willing to take that chance.

Back at the office, some of her co-workers were lambasting her. They accused her of being with Kirk and with Dr. King.

"Who does she think she is?" said Juanita to Benda.

And Brenda replied, "she thinks she is better than us, because everyone thinks she is cute, but she ain't cuter than me and I sure ain't gonna bow down to her."

"Why all these negativities? You all pretend to be friends with her when she is around and behind her back, you all talk bad about her. That is not good."

"Katelin, whose side are you on? She just became part of our staff and you are so into her."

"Juanita, I am not like you all, I am either a friend or not; I am not a pretender and I am her friend, a true friend."

Later in the day, when the opportunity presented itself, Katelin told Cindy what happened earlier, and admonished her to be careful around these ladies.

"Wow, it never crossed my mind that these ladies were so evil.'

"Just watch your back and be careful, people can be jealous of someone else, and use other things to disguise it, just be smart around them."

"Thanks Kate, I do appreciate it."

Later in the evening, Cindy told Katy what happened during the day, and Katy quickly encouraged her to hold on to the doctor. "This might be the healing you need to get your life back on track." Katy said.

"I understand that, but I am not in a hurry to go down this road again," she said.

Her focus was to finish her degree by the end of the next year, seeing that she had taken a semester off, she was determined to finish by December.

In the meantime, she planned to work as much as possible, and to save as much as she could.

Chapter FORTY-NINE

As SOON AS THANKSGIVING came, Cindy left for Texas; she missed it last year, and her mom was not pleased with her, so this time she was the first one there.

All the members of the family came for the occasion, this was their first big gathering since Jason's funeral.

Karen was happy to have everyone home for thanksgiving, and she and Cindy prepared a variety of dishes for the occasion.

As usual, they had a great family gathering. They had great food, wonderful fellowship, and they were thankful for the family they had.

The next day, Karen and Cindy went shopping. They were so happy to spend time away from the others. They discussed a variety of subjects, and on a few occasions, Cindy was tempted to tell her mom of her recent ordeals, but at the end, withheld the information.

This time thanksgiving holidays were different, for the first time Cindy did not have her father around and did not have to go and visit him. His death still brought pain to her.

After a great weekend, the siblings made ways to get back to their colleges.

David and his girlfriend left around midday on Sunday, while Joshua and Cindy left later in the afternoon.

Their journey back included a stop in Louisiana, where Katy joined them, after spending the holidays with her family.

Cindy, and Katy made it safely back to Tallahassee, and Joshua continued to his destination.

Cindy tried hard to get her life back to normal and she spent a lot of her time working; she used that time to occupy her mind in order to avoid thinking of all the negative things that had happened to her recently.

Cindy scheduled her vacation around the Christmas holidays because she planned to assist David and his girlfriend Lisa, with their wedding.

Being home for Christmas was like therapy for her; she needed to be around family; she needed to draw strength from them.

She wished Joshua could be there, but he was busy with his hectic basketball schedule.

David and Lisa were making plans for a big wedding, they planned for 200 guests, which did not include their families.

Karen was putting a lot of her energy in the plans for David's upcoming wedding, and she was drained. Karen loved all her children and tried not to show favoritism to one more than the other.

Cindy saw the way she looked and informed her of the plan that she had for both during spring break.

The Christmas vacation served its purpose, for Cindy was rejuvenated and anxious to start back to school in the spring.

When Cindy came back to Florida, Katy noticed a difference in her attitude. She was more vibrant and spoke more positively and was in a good mood most of the time.

I am thrilled to see what a great effect Texas had on you; girl you are like a brand-new person."

"Kate, home is always home, it doesn't get any better than being around family who cares and loves you."

"Since you love Texas so much, and you have two more visits planned for next year, we have decided to keep you at home as much as possible; we have decided to get married in June in Texas.'

"Congrats, my sister, I am so happy and excited for you, and I can't wait to celebrate you."

"It will be quite a summer; my graduation in May, Joshua might be in the playoffs, and then, this huge milestone, our wedding; it's going to be very hectic, but I am ready."

"I know both of you, and I know you will handle it fine."

Cindy went back to part time work, while she concentrated on her studies. She took up a full schedule for the spring semester as she was determined to graduate in December.

She scheduled the few days that she had to work a week to mirror Dr. King's schedule so she could be close to him; she did not want to lose their friendship, and she was hoping it would develop into more than friendship.

He was happy to hear that she was going back to school to continue her studies and he promised to assist her in way he possibly could.

She was ready to tackle her classes in the same manner that she did before, when she was on the Dean's list. Her goal was to graduate with distinction.

Luckily for her, she could complete her clinicals at the clinic she was working at. She was happy about that; she would see Junie more often than she thought after she registered for school.

The hectic schedule, plus David's wedding was weighing on her physically, and she was happy to get the break to go to the wedding.

Chapter *FIFTY*

CINDY HAD NO CLASSES on Friday, so she left Florida on Thursday evening and arrived in Texas about 9 : pm.

Katy and Liz wanted to stay at a hotel, but Cindy would have none of that. She let them know that there was enough space at their house to accommodate them for the weekend, so they agreed to stay there.

Traffic at the house was busy for the days of the occasion, family and friends from near and far were invited to celebrate.

It was Valentine's weekend, and love was in the air, so besides David's wedding, there were many other activities that happened for that weekend

Cindy was part of the bridal party and was excited; she had not been in a wedding for a long time, the last one was her dad's, and she hated it, but did it for him, but this time was different; she enjoyed being a part of it.

The ceremony was beautiful, her brother looked more handsome than ever, and her sister-in-law, was such a beautiful bride, and the way they exchanged their vows was a pleasure to witness.

The reception was fun, with lots of food and drinks, and lots of celebrating.

Cindy met up with Mark, an old church friend, who had a crush on her when they were in high school, but even though she had liked him, she thought that he was too quiet, and acted like he feared people.

They hung out for most of the reception and agreed to stay in touch. They both had plans to move back home after graduation, to help build up their community.

Meanwhile, Liz was introduced to Michael by Cindy (he was her cousin.) They instantly connected and planned to stay connected.

After the wedding and weekend activities ended, they went back to their various homes and cities.

David and his new bride went on their honeymoon to another country, they planned to relocate to Houston when they returned.

For Cindy, it was back to school and her studies; her next planned trip to Texas would be for spring break.

Cindy stayed in touch with Mark; they conversed about so many things: they talked about the past, they shared some of their future plans with each other, and their relationship was getting closer the more they chatted with each other, but Cindy was not in a rush to go into another deep relationship, she just wanted to be close friends for the time being, though she was liking him more as the days went along, but the love that she had was for Dr. King, but she was hesitant to tell him that.

After a month of hard work, it was spring break, and she went to Texas to meet her mom, so they could go on the cruise that she had surprised her with.

Chapter FIFTY-ONE

The ship left Galveston on Sunday and headed to Mexico on a four-day cruise.

When her mom boarded the ship, she was so amazed by the layout and the inside of the ship.

"Wow, Cindy, this is like a hotel," she said in amazement. "I heard people talk about what was aboard these ships, but never in my wildest dreams did I ever think, I would be seeing it with my own eyes. So far I am loving it."

"I am glad, mom, that you are a having a great time, that was my expectation when I bought the package; this is the least I could do for a mother as loving as you."

The two of them exited the ship along with some of the other passengers to take a small tour. They visited a few of the country's historical sites, and did a little bit of shopping, before returning to the ship.

The next two days, they enjoyed many activities on the ship, and they enjoyed the time they got to spend with each other, without having to worry about husband, children or work.

As the ship turned towards home, Karen said to her daughter, "I had so much fun, I wish it was longer, I never thought I would have loved it like I did; I'm sure we'll do it again, and next time it will be my treat, and it will be for a longer time."

They disembarked and retrieved their parked vehicle, and slowly made their way home.

"I can't wait to tell Donald about the trip and see if I can convince him to go on a cruise in the near future, he is not one who likes being on the water."

Cindy spent the rest of the break with her family and left on Saturday back to Florida.

"Kate, you have to, you definitely have to take a cruise one of these days, I am telling you, that would be one of the most exciting, and enjoyable things you would ever do in your life. I had the most fun, and so did my mom; she can't stop talking about it."

"I will definitely consider it; I would have to convince Josh, but with your help, I'm sure he will."

"Lately, we have been so busy with his basketball, my graduation, and the wedding; it has been driving us crazy, but a good crazy, it is a kind of busyness that I like."

Cindy finished the semester, as expected, at the top of her class, and was very proud of herself.

She attended Katy, and Liz's graduation and felt in a way, that she was not part of their graduating class, but knew she needed that semester off, so she was okay with that, and said that would push herself more to make it to the end.

Mark kept on trying to push their relationship to more than what it was, but because of her feelings for Junie, she did not want to commit to him.

Chapter FIFTY-TWO

CINDY WAS EXCITED BECAUSE Junie invited her to have dinner with him; she was hoping that he was going to tell her about his feelings for her.

He came to pick her up at her apartment; Katie, and Liz was gazing through the window trying to get a glimpse of him and his vehicle, but they did not have to do that, because Cindy invited him to come upstairs to meet her friends.

They rode off, and went to Meggy's Steakhouse, which was about twelve minutes from the apartment.

It was a lovely restaurant, the atmosphere was inviting, the ambiance superb, and most importantly, the food was tasteful.

They ate until they were full; Junie had a couple glasses of wine while Cindy had a glass of virgin pina colada.

They conversed while they ate but did most of their talking after they had finished eating.

They spoke about a lot of things and tried to stay away from subjects that dealt with work.

Then Junie said, "Cindy, from the moment you came to the clinic, and I saw you, I was mesmerized by your beauty, and then after I got to know you, I realized what a gem you were, not just beautiful outside, but your spirit was also beautiful. You are such a loving and spiritual person, and you drew me to you, and I was excited to realize I might had found the love of my life. I tried different little ways to let you know that I was interested in you, but you unintentionally kept shutting me out."

"The day you came back to work after your birthday bash, and I found out that you were seeing Kirk, that news hurt me so badly; I was miserable inside, but tried not to show it; at work I put on a happy face, and even though I was happy for you, when I was alone at home, I was torn to the core, but realized that there was nothing I could do at the time, but to accept it, and that is what I did."

"You might be wondering why I'm saying all this to you, or where I'm going with this. I don't know how you feel about me, or if I'm even making sense to you, but don't think of me negatively, because of how I felt for you, but I honestly want to wish you and Kirk the best life together and I wish you will be happy.

I am hoping that we will keep our friendship; I have accepted what it is, and have moved on, I am now seeing a young lady I met recently and am planning to get engaged soon."

"What? "Cindy exclaimed, and remained quiet for a while, with a stare of disbelief and disappointment on her face.

Slowly recovering from the shock, she asked, "how long have you been seeing each other?"

"About a month ago, but it seems like longer than that, because of the way we are connecting."

"I honestly wished that it would have been you, but you don't always get what you desire in this life."

"Yes, you can, you could still be with me, I am not taken, I have been living a lie for a while now. I left Kirk on the weekend of my birthday. He treated me so badly, he hurt me so badly, that I now hate every fiber of his being," and she began crying, "I kept a poker face so that the people around me, especially in the clinic, wouldn't talk bad about me, but all this time, I've been hurting."

"I always had feelings for you, but I hesitated to tell you so, I did not want to put myself out there, and then get rejected, so I kept my feelings to myself, hoping one day we would be able to connect romantically. I told my roommate and friend how I felt about you, yet I found it hard to tell you."

Cindy bowed her head, as the tears ran down her beautiful face.

"I am so sorry Cindy, I am sorry that this is the way that we had to say what was in our hearts, I wish we had done this earlier, but as much as it pains me to walk away from a relationship with you, because I deeply care for you, I have given my commitment to Jessica and I can't walk back on it now."

"Oh, how I wished that you had not shut me out before or had told me the things that you just said to me, we would have been married a long time ago. Why did you protect this jerk of a guy?"

Cindy did not reply, she was too stunned from what had just transpired.

She was saying to herself, when will I ever get a break? What did I do in life that I am now being punished for?

Then she said, "Junie, I am not blaming you, or mad at you for what you told me; I was not expecting this tonight. When you invited me to dinner, I thought this was the night we would announce the beginning of a romantic relationship, never in my wildest dream did I expect what just happened."

"Again, I am sorry Cindy, I do care about you, and I am hoping that you will not hold this against me and that we can remain great friends."

"Junie, can we leave now? I just want to go home right now."

"Not a problem Cindy, let me take care of the bill, and we will be on our way."

On their way back to the apartment, Junie tried in vain to cheer up Cindy, but she was very hurt and would not entertain his sweet talk.

He thanked her for coming and promised to be close with her, if she would allow it.

She told him thanks for the invitation and the dinner, and said she was willing to remain friends with him, if he desired it.

Katy and Liz were anxious to hear about the date; they could hardly wait to hear the details of the evening.

As soon as she entered the apartment, they were at her for the details.

"Well, I am sorry to say that it was a bag of mixed feelings."

"It started fine, I mean great, lots of fun, and great conversations, but it ended up not good for me."

And she went into detail about what happened, and all that was said between them, and of her disappointment.

"Why didn't he just tell you all these things on the phone? Why did he have to bring you out there, build up your hope, and then just crush your spirit?" Katy asked

"I don't think that was right," Liz agreed.

"Anyway, if it was meant to be, it would have happened, I am pretty sure that the right one will come along, or is already there, but you chose to neglect it," Katy said.

"You're so right Katy, and I have been through worse and have survived, so this too will pass."

Later that night, Cindy called Mark and spent a long time with him on the phone. They spoke of so many things, including their days at high school at church, and of Mark and his crush on her, and of Mark's desire to make the crush a reality.

The next few weeks were very hectic because of her devotion to Kate's wedding plans, and as the maid of honor, she wanted to make sure that everything went according to plans.

Joshua was distraught, that his team lost in the third round of the playoffs, but he was glad that he would have a bit more time to assist with preparations for the wedding.

With work and wedding preparations, Cindy didn't have much time for anything else, and the little time she had was spent all on Mark.

She was anxious for the wedding day to come because she was happy for her brother and friend, but also, she was anxious to see Mark, because he was one of the invited guest and he promised to be there.

The day of Joshua and katy's wedding was finally here, the anticipation was over, the guests kept pouring in and the atmosphere was full of excitement.

The wedding ceremony was flawless and everything went as planned.

The bride was as beautiful as ever and her groom held his own and not forgetting the bridal party, they were amazing.

The reception was fun-filled, although it was a huge crowd.

Cindy and Mark had the time of their lives, they made the best use of the time they had together, Cindy did not know Mark could be so loving and affectionate, he really did surprise her, he was not that boy that she thought was nerdy when they were growing up.

What a great weekend it was, it was a wedding, family reunion, and the reconnection of friends and loved ones. Some people were sad to see the weekend come to an end.

Cindy and Liz left for Florida without their best friend Katy; she and her husband, left for their honeymoon, and afterwards, she would move to Orlando with her husband.

Chapter FIFTY-THREE

Before graduation Liz had given up her dorm and had moved in with Cindy and Katy for the last few weeks, but her plan was to move back to her hometown in South Florida until she decided what she wanted to do; she and Michael had broken up, and she was now seeing Shawn, Cindy's stepbrother.

Meanwhile, Cindy was supposed to graduate in December and to remain in the apartment. She was okay with it but was still a little bit scared of living there by herself, and the traumatization of Kirk, still loomed in her head, and often brought back anxiety.

Liz offered to stay with her until she graduated. Cindy was quick to accept her offer and thanked her for being such a good friend.

"You don't have to contribute anything, just you being here is a great comfort to me,"

"No, I won't do that, I will contribute my share in keeping the apartment."

The two existed very well together, more cohesively than anticipated, and became close friends, like sisters.

On the weekends that Cindy was not completely overwhelmed with schoolwork, they would go to the movies, and other activities.

In September, they went to Ohio, to spend time with Cindy's boyfriend Mark.

They had a great time and were treated like queens by Mark and his friends.

Mark graduated in May, and was now working at a huge corporation, and had a great job that he loved.

Cindy was counting the days when she would graduate, where she would be in the workforce, making lots of money, and being free from college life.

When November came, they went to visit Shawn in New York, and to say they had a good time, would be an understatement.

This was a first trip to New York for both, and they were amazed by the people and the life of the city. They were surprised by how busy the city was, and the night life; they realized why it was said that "the city never sleeps".

They wished that they could be there more often, which Liz's desire might just come true, because Shawn was very much interested in being with her forever.

They made it back to Florida on Sunday evening and were worn out from all the activities in New York.

"What a big contrast between the two places" Cindy said to Liz, "it is like night and day, New York is so busy, hectic, and full of life, while here it is so quiet, laid back, and sometimes boring, but I still love it.

"New York is a place I would like to visit probably once a year, for about a week, then go right back to Texas."

"I'm the opposite, I would love to live in New York, and the way things are going, I might just do that."

The next day, Cindy came back from class very excited.

"Hi Liz, the end is in sight, I found out today that my graduation date is December the 12th, so now I have a conclusion to my studies."

"Oh girl, I am so excited for you, wishing you nothing but good things going forward."

Cindy called her mom and informed her of the date, so she could put it on her schedule; she also informed her that, she would not be coming home for Thanksgiving.

She decided to stay with Liz for Thanksgiving, seeing she put her plans on hold so she could be with her in the apartment, she saw it fitting to spend the holiday with her,

They purchased a small smoked turkey, and prepared some of their favorite dishes, and made lemonade and fruit punch, and bought some sodas, and they relaxed, and enjoyed their Thanksgiving dinner.

Then they enjoyed watching a few movies together.

As the date for graduation drew closer, Cindy became nervous because she was so excited; she could hardly contain herself. She was so grateful to God for giving her the strength and faith to make it, because she went through so many things which could have derailed her from ever finishing school, and now one of her goals in life was just a few weeks away from being met.

The day before her graduation, with her mom, brothers, and best friends present, Cindy sat on the couch and began weeping, and they that were present, knew instantly why she was crying, she was heartbroken because her dad was not there, not alive, to see her graduate and to celebrate with her.

On the morning of the 12th, she woke up and said, "to God be the glory, had it not been for you Lord, I would have never made it, I would not have been graduating today, and the pain and struggles that I have been through, only your grace could have seen me through. Thank you, Lord."

After all was said and done, and everything was in place, they left for the ceremony.

Chapter FIFTY-FOUR

CINDY LOOKED AMAZING; SHE had her hair done differently and had an amazing dress that she bought with the money that her dad had saved for her. She received so many compliments on how well she looked.

It was a great ceremony, the speeches were short and to the point, and some were entertaining. The guest speaker was considerate with his speech, he chose to be reasonable with the length of his speech, which was educational, informative, and encouraging.

Cindy graduated with honors, and in the top percent of her graduating class, like she desired to, because she always said, she wanted to graduate with distinction.

On her way to receive her diploma, as she marched down the walkway, her family and friends made their voices heard, they were loud and shouted at the top of their voices, where she could hear, and where others would take notice of how proud they were.

"Wow, she said, "it is real, I have made it, I have graduated," and she was a little bit emotional at that moment, but quickly got hold of her emotions, for she knew she had pictures to take and did not want to mess up her mascara.

Cindy said her congratulations, thanked her teachers and friends, then left for home.

But the celebration was not over, because Joshua, David and Mark, along with some others, planned a small gathering with family and friends, to help Cindy celebrate her accomplishments.

Karen was so proud of her daughter for her perseverance and patience, that she was overwhelmed with emotions, and she hugged her, and told her how proud she was of her.

Katy and Cindy embraced, and they cried on each other's shoulders, because only the two of them knew what Cindy went through, and how much courage it took to overcome the mental, and physical trauma, that she suffered under the hands of Kirk.

They celebrated until about 11: pm, before they rested from all the day's activities.

The following day, Cindy, Joshua, Katy and Liz, took Karen, David, Donald, and others, to visit certain places in Tallahassee, and surrounding cities.

Later that evening, Cindy invited Mark to come over to have dinner with the family.

The restaurant was very busy, because it was a Saturday night, and because of all the visitors that were in town for the different graduations that took place.

The family asked to be seated outside, because there were many members in the group.

While they waited for their food, they spent time talking about things that happened in the past, tricks that Cindy's brothers played on her, when she was much younger, and they laughed, and joked around.

Mark finally joined them; he got lost, when he left the hotel and had to ask questions in order to find the restaurant.

He was escorted to their table by the waitress and was seated next to Cindy.

"Hi everyone, this is Mark my friend, he is from my hometown, and some of you might know him, but to those that don't, you can introduce yourselves.

The food was delicious, and the way they interacted with each other was great to witness.

Before they left for their hotels, they asked the waitress to take a group photo of them.

They then left to their hotels. Cindy stopped her mom, and called Mark over, and formerly introduced him to her as her boyfriend.

They spoke for a short while, before Mark left for his hotel.

Donald, Karen, Liz, along with Cindy went back to the apartment.

Later that night when Cindy was in her bedroom, her mom knocked on her door, and asked if she could come in.

"Please do mom, I know you have questions."

"What made you say so?" Karen asked, as she entered the room.

"Mom, I know you, and I saw that expression on your face earlier in the evening, so I was expecting your visit."

"Mark, I can't believe how much he has grown up, I remembered when he was so quiet and withdrawn, and stayed away from many activities because of his shyness; he has come a long way."

"Sure mom, he has, but is that what you came in here to say? Is there something on your mind that you want to talk about? Mom, I know you well."

"Okay, how long have you two been dating? And how serious are you with the relationship?"

"Mark and I reconnected at David's wedding, we stayed in touch, but we were not an item yet, but as we get to know each other more, we slowly developed feelings for each other, and here we are."

"At the moment, we are moving slowly; we are hoping to be in this relationship for a long time, hopefully for life."

"My dear, Mark seems like a pretty good guy; he is a handsome young man and has done well so far; I know his family, and they are good people, so all I can do right now, is offer my blessings on your relationship."

"Thanks, mom, coming from you, it means a lot; I cannot be any more pleased than that; you have always been a good judge of character, so getting approval from you is truly appreciated."

"Cindy, everything will be okay, and I will pray for you and your new beau."

"Beau? Mom you are into things," hahaha.

"I will be coming home two weeks from today; I hope I will be able to get this furniture sold before I leave for home."

"Are you going to drive by yourself? Or you want Donald and I to come and accompany you."

"Thanks, mom, but I will be alright, Mark is going to accompany me on the trip."

"Why wait until after Christmas to come home? You could leave on Wednesday and be home in time for Christmas."

"Mom that is when Mark will be available, so I made arrangements to accommodate his schedule."

After family and friends left, Cindy began her preparations, for her departure from Tallahassee.

She sold the things that she was not taking back to Texas and made arrangement to turn in her apartment on the day she was leaving Tallahassee.

Their last night in the apartment, Liz, Cindy and Mark stayed up late talking, celebrating, and Liz and Cindy reflected on their stay at the school.

They planned on keeping their friendship as tight as possible and promised each other that they would not let 3 days pass, before they heard from each other.

Liz was the saddest, because she had never had anybody so close to her in her life, not even her family; she would miss Cindy.

Chapter FIFTY-FIVE

SATURDAY MORNING, CINDY AND Liz hugged and cried as they said their goodbyes, as Mark and Jessie, Liz's brother, watched them; they admired the love and friendship these two ladies showed to each other.

Difficult as it was, they had to part. Liz and Jessie left for Parkland Florida, while Cindy and Mark were on their way to Texas.

Cindy asked to be the first driver, but Mark said no, he was not in favor of her driving at all, he wanted to drive all the way.

But Cindy, stubborn as she was, argued about it and insisted that she help with the driving. Finally Mark obliged and said she could drive the first 3 hours.

After stopping to get fuel and a few other items, they were on their way to Texas.

Mark was true to his word and as soon as she had driven 3 hours, he had her pull to the side, away from traffic, and he got behind the wheel.

It was a relief when they crossed the Texas State line; they knew they were not too far from reaching home.

In a few more hours, they were home.

Karen was so relieved when she saw them pulling up in the driveway.

"Thank you, Lord," she said, "they made it home safely."

Cindy unpacked, before settling down for dinner.

Mark stayed with them for almost an hour, after which, Cindy said she would drive him to his parent's house.

"Cindy, don't go alone, let Donald come with you; it's not safe to go out at this time of the night by yourself."

"Mom, I will be alright; I can manage, and it's not that far from here; I will be back before you know it."

"It's not the distance; it is still too dangerous.'

"Okay Kellie can go with me."

"You're just as stubborn as your dad was, always have to have your way."

Cindy still had bad feelings toward Donald; she didn't know if she had it in her to forgive him, and she could never trust him again. The drive took about 8 minutes to Mark's house, and she was about to head back home, when Mark beseeched her to come in to meet his parents.

"Dad, mom, meet Cindy. She is the young lady I spoke about, and this is her sister Kellie."

Cindy was surprised; she did not know that he had mentioned her to his parents.

"Hi, I'm Jacob, and this is my wife Laurie; I've heard about you from Mark, and he won't stop raving about you, but now I can see one of the reasons why. You are very beautiful."

"Thank you, sir, I am happy to meet you and your wife."

"You don't have to call me sir, we are now family, so feel free to call me Jacob, and I know the same goes for my wife, we prefer the casual way."

"We know your family and they are nice people, so I'm glad that Mark chose you."

"How is your dad? I know he lives in another city, but I'm hoping that you are staying in touch."

"Dad."

"It's okay, Mark, I am okay with that, I am getting over it."

"Sir, my dad passed away recently, he died in an auto accident."

"Oh, dear, I am so sorry to hear that; my condolences to you. I am sorry that I brought it up."

"It's okay, you didn't know, and it's something I'm learning to accept."

"Anyway, it was nice meeting you, but I think I better head back home before my mother loses her mind."

"The pleasure was all ours, be careful going back, and say hello to your family on our behalf."

Mark walked Cindy and Kellie to the car and gave Cindy a peck on her forehead before she drove away.

"I love him, he is so cute and handsome; you both will make pretty children," Kellie said.

"Oh dear, you are way ahead of us, it is going to take a while before you see little ones tagging along, but I'm glad for your approval; I will let him know how much you are taken back by his handsomeness."

Meanwhile, Jacob, and Laurie were complimenting Mark on his choice; they were very satisfied that he chose Cindy.

They were also happy that she had moved home; they were hoping that would encourage him to move back home too.

When Karen saw the car coming down her street, she breathed a sigh of relief; she knew how reckless the younger folks in the neighborhoods drove and how dangerous it was on the streets.

Cindy was extremely tired from her trip from Florida; she took a bath and went into her room, and not too long after, she was asleep.

The next day Mark came to pick her up; they went to breakfast and had some delicious pancakes, waffles, and eggs.

They spent about an hour at the restaurant before going to the mall.

Even though Christmas was a few days ago, Mark still wanted to get some gifts for the people that he didn't have a chance to give them.

From the mall they went to Dolphin's restaurant.

As they sat at the table, waiting on their meal, Mark said to Cindy, "you know every time I look at you, I see you getting prettier; I did not think it was possible, because you are already so pretty, but miracles do happen."

"Oh, thanks, Mark, you are so flattering; what do you want?" she said jokingly, as she blushed.

"I wish I didn't have to leave you here and go back to Ohio; my mind will not be at peace, not that I don't trust you, or not that I don't have confidence in my charm, but love, you are an eye catcher."

"You know you can change that? You can always move back home; that would be awesome and eventually one of us must move if we are to stay together."

"Eventually, I will, especially, since I want to make you my wife, not too far in the near future."

"I didn't know that you were thinking that far ahead, but I am so thrilled that you are, that just made me feel better."

I had a few dates, and a few ladies that I was looking at, but the chemistry was not there, and I did not feel for them, the way that I'm feeling for you; it's different, I don't even know, I can't explain it, but you are special."

"Well, I am so glad that our paths crossed again, and we were given the opportunity, by the Lord, to reconnect, and Mark, I care for you and love you dearly."

"I must say that you have made my lunch much more enjoyable, you have added so much more spice to it, and I truly love you too."

From the restaurant, they went downtown to the under-ground stores and restaurants, where they did more shopping before going home.

"Thanks for a great day, Mark, I had a wonderful time.'

"You are welcome, babe, I will see you a little bit later this evening."

Karen was delighted with the way the relationship between Mark and Cindy was developing; she was very fond of Mark.

As Cindy entered the door, she said, "last night Mr. Jacob asked me to say hello on their behalf."

"Oh, thanks, we might see them in church soon."

"I love the way you and Mark are getting along; you are developing into a fine young couple."

"Mom don't include me for dinner, Mark and I are going to have dinner soon."

Early the next morning, Cindy drove Mark to the airport, for his flight to Ohio.

Chapter *FIFTY-SIX*

CINDY WAS HAPPY TO be back home; she had accomplished her goal that she had set, and now she was making plans to enter the workforce fulltime.

She still had a big challenge ahead of her; she had to pass the state exam so she could obtain her nurse's license.

She devoted the next month to studying, and she prepared diligently for the exam.

On her first attempt, she passed the exam with no difficulty.

Cindy received many work offers from major hospitals and other medical companies

She analyzed and did research on most of the companies she received offers from, and after consulting with a few people, she accepted an offer from one of the hospitals in the medical center, where she always wanted to work, but she was faced with a small set back; it was about 25 minutes from where she lived.

But she took the job because there were many advantages to taking that job, and she was willing to accept the little set back until further plans.

After she was hired, Cindy first purchase was a vehicle. She traded in her old car and bought a fully loaded SUV.

Cindy loved working at her place of employment; she was welcomed by her co-workers; they were friendly and patient with her.

It was a better atmosphere from her previous job, where she had worked with a few back stabbers, and some nonprofessionals, with exceptions like Dr. King and a few of his aides.

Cindy kept in touch with Dr. King; his last communication, he informed her that he was set to get married in June, and she would receive an invitation from him soon.

She was not sure if she would attend, because there were so many emotions attached to Dr. King.

Driving to her job from her home was becoming a struggle to Cindy; she hated the traffic, a drive that was supposed to be about 25 minutes, sometimes took her about an hour.

Cindy approached her mom and told her of her intention to move to an apartment.

Her mom was perturbed by the idea of her daughter living alone in an apartment.

"Why do you want to do that? she asked, Are you not comfortable over here?"

"Mom, it is not about being at home, it's about other issues."

"I hate the traffic, it frustrates me. I want to live closer to my job, so I can get to and from there faster, and thus, will have more time to rest."

"Cindy, this is dangerous. Imagine how vulnerable you are going to be. You will be an easy target for those vultures out there. I am concerned, I am deeply concerned."

"Mom, there is no need to worry, I am planning to get an apartment close to the medical center; there are lots of nurses that lives in that area."

"I'm not planning to move right away; I hope to move at the end of September, which is about six months from now."

"What did Mark say? How does he feel about that?"

"I haven't yet spoken to him about that; actually, I'm about to call him to discuss it."

But knowing the type of person she was, she wasn't going to change her mind, whether Mark agreed with her or not.

In the quietness of the night, when her mom and stepdad went to bed, Cindy called Mark.

They spoke for a while, before she brought up the idea of moving out of her mother's house, into an apartment.

Mark was stunned by Cindy's suggestion, and questioned her about her decision, and told her how concerned he was.

"You know how dangerous that can be?" he asked her, "there are too many variables that can lead to negative results."

"Mark, I'm aware of what you are saying, and I'm pleased that you are concerned about my welfare, but look at my side of it. I am so frustrated with the traffic, I am always tired because of it, I can't work overtime because of the traffic and distance; it is not feasible for me, and besides, most of the nurses are living close to the center."

"I understand all that, but my main concern is your security; that's what bothers me."

"Mark, I have six months to ponder this idea, so for the next few months, I will be enjoying my time with mom."

"Okay, I am hoping that you will make the right decision."

Not too long after her conversation with Mark, Mario called; he told her of his new relationship, saying he found a soulmate, and said how happy he was.

She congratulated him, and wished him well, and although she was not involved with him romantically, she still felt awkward, after he told her.

She always thought he would be there as a backup, in case she had to turn to him. She felt rotten for feeling this way and chastised herself for thinking that.

Cindy was getting better at what she did on the job, and she desired to move it into the management level.

She had great teammates who helped her to be a more effective nurse; she also had good relationships with her patients.

Karen and Cindy tried to schedule their off days to mirror each other so they could spend quality time together.

They went shopping often and visited the salon on occasions.

Karen encouraged Cindy to be involved in more church activities, but she knew once Cindy moved to her apartment, she would not be going to church as often as she did now.

She was also concerned with her safety, and dreaded to see her leave, and she was hoping that their relationship would remain strong.

At the end of august, beginning of September, Cindy started her search for an apartment to move into by October 1st.

She looked in the medical center area, which would be a quick drive to her job.

She narrowed her search to 4 good complexes, but ultimately, it came down to the one that was closer to the job, although it was the most expensive amongst the four, but it fitted her needs more than the others.

"Mom, she said, "I have found an apartment, and I will be moving at the end of the month; in the meantime, I will be living with you for the next two weeks. It's a stone's throw from my workplace."

"My issue is that you will be living alone, and that bothers me; a young beautiful lady, going in and out of an apartment by herself all the time that is troublesome, and that is going to keep me up at nights."

Chapter FIFTY-SEVEN

CINDY MOVED INTO HER apartment on October 1st, as planned.

The following week on their day off, she and her mom went furniture hunting, for a bed, and a dining table, and planned to buy a few more pieces of furniture the following week.

Her mom made sure that she was there when the furniture was delivered; she wanted the people who delivered the furniture to believe that she was an occupant at the apartment.

It took about a month to set up her apartment as she wanted it to be, and had it almost fully furnished, except for a few items, which were not needed at the time.

Cindy felt good, like she had grown; she was now her own person, and could come and go whenever she felt like, she was completely independent now, and was free to roam about in her own space, without worrying who she might offend.

For the first two weeks, Cindy basically slept underneath the bed, because any noise she heard during the night panicked her and she barely slept.

She questioned her decision to go on her own, but she vowed to stay the course.

She spent lots of time on the phone with Mark; he helped ease her fears at night, and kept her company until she fell asleep.

Cindy became good friends with Sarah, her co-worker, who often came by to keep her company.

Cindy invited Liz to come spend the thanksgiving holiday with her, and with no hesitation, Liz accepted the invitation. She also asked her mom to join her for the dinner, although she dreaded being around Donald, but she knew for her mom's sake, she had to tolerate him.

Joshua called Karen, his mom, and told her that he was coming home for thanksgiving, but Karen informed him that she was going to Cindy's place for thanksgiving dinner.

"Even better yet," he told her. "Katy and I will give her a big surprise. Please help her cook so we can have some good food," he said jokingly.

"I wished David could have made it, but he said he promised his mother-in-law that he would have thanksgiving with them, and he didn't want to go back on his promise, nor disappoint his wife."

Mark also planned to surprise Cindy on Thanksgiving Day. He gathered all the information that he needed from her to locate the apartment without arousing her suspicion.

Cindy and Sarah stayed busy all-day Wednesday, shopping and preparing for the dinner.

They prepared and seasoned their turkey and left it out on the kitchen counter to marinate.

They then worked on their entrées and other items, like appetizers and desserts.

Cindy was unaware that her mom was also doing some cooking to bring to the feast.

Had she known that Karen was cooking, she would have discouraged it, because she wanted her mom to relax, but Karen was making provisions for the others that Cindy knew nothing about and she was making sure that there would be enough, as well as a variety of food.

Cindy stopped cooking long enough to go pick up Liz at the airport.

Liz was thrilled to see her, and they embraced and greeted each other.

Liz was impressed with the progress that Cindy had made; she complimented her on her vehicle and her cozy apartment.

Liz was introduced to Sarah, who joined them in the kitchen where they continued with the remainder of the cooking.

They had so much fun; they laughed, joked, and Liz and Cindy shared some stories from their college days.

Cindy was happy, she was in a good frame of mind and things were finally clicking for her.

She was preparing dinner for the seven of them, not knowing that there would be three more attending.

Early Thursday morning, Karen, Donald and Kellie showed up at Cindy's apartment. "Mom, why? You were not supposed to be cooking? This was supposed to be your time to relax, this was one of the main reasons I asked you to come over.

"You know it is hard for me not to cook a little something, I had to chip in somehow."

"Mom, this is not a little something, this is a lot of food that you prepared, we won't be able to consume all that food."

"You will have to save the leftovers for a later use."

About 11:am, Karen asked Donald to go home to make sure the back door was locked, "I think I might have left it unlocked."

But Donald knew that this was his cue to pick up Joshua and Katy at the airport; they were scheduled to arrive about 11:30 am.

Sarah and her boyfriend Dave came in. Cindy introduced Liz to Dave, Kellie, and Karen.

A short while later, there was a knock on the door, and Sarah went to see who it was, but she did not know any of the people at the door, because she had not yet met Donald, and she did not know Joshua.

Karen introduced Sarah, to Donald, Joshua and Katy.

As Karen let them in, Cindy was coming out of the bedroom, and she screamed with excitement, because she was so happy to see Josh and katy. She was surprised to see them; she had no clue at all that they were coming. "Am I seeing right? Is that Josh and Katie? Or am I imagining things?'

"Sis, you thought you could have this big celebration without us. Well, it wasn't going to happen."

She hugged them and got emotional because she was filled with joy, she always loved to be around Katy.

"So, mom, you knew about this plan? That is why you did all that cooking, now it's making sense, and Donald did not have to go home, he was part of the plan. You all got me, but I love it."

Cindy did not care for big celebrations anymore, since her disaster with Kirk, but she was hoping this one would turn out positive.

She barely finished introducing Josh and Katy to Sarah and her boyfriend, when she heard a knock at the door, she wasn't expecting anyone else, so she was hoping that it was not the complex security, who came to address their loud noise, but when she opened the door, she almost fainted, in shock to see Mark at the door.

She had no idea he was coming and neither did anyone else.

"You thought I would let you have your first thanksgiving bash at your new place without me? Think again."

Cindy stood there for about a minute, speechless, not knowing how to react, then she grabbed him, hugged him, and kissed him.

"Any more surprises? Is anyone else coming?" she asked.

Then she introduced Mark to Sarah and Dave and said to the others, "a few of you already know him, and some of you might have seen him at the wedding, but now I am officially introducing him to everyone as my loving boyfriend."

"However, I am beyond thrilled to have all my friends and loved ones here for Thanksgiving; I could not have asked for a better Thanksgiving; I love all of you guys."

And in unison, they replied, "we love you too."

"Guys, give us about 30 minutes, and we will be ready to commence eating." Cindy said.

Karen joined Cindy and Liz in placing the food on the table; she ignored Cindy's instruction to sit like the others, but these words fell on deaf ears. Karen insisted she had to help.

The table was set, and everything was in place. They gathered around and held hands, as Karen said grace, and gave thanks for the fellowship.

They were enjoying their food, and busy talking, when Katy took her fork, and tapped her glass to get everyone's attention, and said, "guys, I have some good news. There is soon to be a little Joshua, or Katy to come into this world to help with all this food."

"You are pregnant? Yes, yes. Congratulations to both of you, I am so happy for you, I can't wait to spoil this child." Cindy exclaimed.

"Thanks, Cindy," Katy replied.

"What a blessing," Karen said, "I am so happy to hear the news of my first grandchild; again, I give God thanks."

Everyone in the room gave their blessings and congratulations to Joshua and Katy.

"How far?" Cindy joyfully asked.

"Roughly about six weeks. We found out from the doctor three days ago, but Josh and I decided to wait until we came for thanksgiving to share our news."

"It has been an exciting and surprising day for me so far, and I am not sure what else is in store, but I will stay alert."

At the end of the celebration, everyone was happy for a joyous day, and they were very grateful.

Later that evening, Mark, Cindy and Liz went to his parent's house to spend a few hours with them.

His mom offered them dinner, but because of all the food they had eaten during the day, they said, they would have to pass on the offer.

Laurie was not happy about that and kept insisting that they should have some of her food.

Cindy compromised and said, she would have a small portion.

"Cindy, you don't have to do that to please us, if you are full, you are full; we are just glad you came by to spend some time with us," Jacob said.

But Laurie would not give up. "It is on the table; do you want me to fix a couple plates for you?"

"Mom, we will take care of this, thanks for preparing it."

Cindy could sense the anger in Mark's tone, yet she knew that he was trying to please them both.

Chapter FIFY-EIGHT

FRIDAY, CINDY AND LIZ went to Karen's house to spend some time with Joshua and katy, the newlyweds, and soon to be parents.

They spent the day with them, but later decided to stay the night.

"Where is Mark?" Karen asked.

"He wanted to spend a couple days with his parents, which worked out great for both of us."

"So Preggy, how is the baby coming along and how are you doing" Cindy asked.

"I'm doing okay, and the baby is doing fine, I hope."

"How is the mood?" what food nauseates you? Or is it too early for that?"

"She is very moody and eats everything."

"Josh, this question was for Katy, you would not know anything about what I asked."

"Thanks sis, you always have my back, and I am learning to deal with the difficulties of the first trimester."

Later that night, when they were in a private setting, Josh said to Cindy, "what really happened that night with Kirk? I know something went wrong, and it was more than you told me. I ran into Kirk a few times since that night, and he tried to avoid me on both occasions; he acted like I was supposed to confront him about something."

"Joshua, we have dealt with the happenings of that night already, and I don't want to deal with that again, I don't want to relive those moments again. All is well, I assure you."

Katy was cringing in her chair, but she remembered her promise to Cindy, so she held her peace, but she felt very guilty holding back from her husband.

"Cindy, any wedding bells yet?" She asked in order to change the subject and to avoid any further discussions on that painful night.

"We are not there yet, but we are heading in that direction, I don't know what he's thinking or planning, but I hope we are not too far from the 'I do.'"

"What are you wishing for? Boy or girl?"

"Just a healthy baby, that is all."

"Josh you?"

"Same here," he quickly replied.

"I don't believe either one of you, because I know you all have a preference."

"I would love a boy to carry my name, and to do man stuff with, but if it's a girl, I would be as equally happy."

"Honestly, the truth is I just want a healthy baby, I just can't wait."

Karen and the others returned from shopping. Liz was happy she got to spend time with Kellie and Donald, her future in-laws.

It was a weekend well spent, they got to hang with Josh and Katy, and they were all there to love upon Karen, and nothing negative happened; they were all very pleased.

Mark and Cindy spent Sunday morning talking and planning. Mark was not comfortable with Cindy living alone in an apartment, in a huge and busy city as Houston.

"I will be living in Ohio for a few more months, then I will be moving back to Texas."

Cindy was happy to hear him say that, although she was not sure if she wanted him to give up the great job he had, but she knew one of them had to give up their job for their relationship to stand a chance. They could not live in different states and have a successful relationship.

But Mark had made up his mind and he was not going to let anything deter him from moving back home.

As he promised, he spent a few more months in Ohio, then moved back to Houston.

It did not take him long before he found a great job, making even more money than the one he had left in Ohio.

He lived with his parents for two months, before he notified them that he was moving to his own apartment. His parents were not in favor of that decision because they had the space, and they were alone, but he wanted his space.

Cindy tried to get him to move in with her, against her mom's wishes, but he did not want to, he wanted to respect her, and said they would move in together when they were married.

"Then what is the purpose of moving to Houston? I thought you wanted to make sure that I was safe?"

"At least I am here in town, that counts for a lot."

"Yeah right, if an intruder enters my apartment, I will tell them that Mark is in town, and that will take care of that."

Mark tried to please his parents; he did not want to disappoint them by living with a woman without being married.

And it was a tug of war. He did not know what to do, his parents on one end preaching to him about not living a life of fornication, while Cindy was pressuring him, because she was scared.

Eventually, it was up to Mark to make a decision, and after six months of living in his apartment alone, he asked Cindy to move in with him.

He said she was at his apartment anytime she was not at work, and he was not sure why she was paying for a place that she did not stay at, plus he cared for her safety; he knew she was vulnerable living by herself, which was an invitation for something bad happening.

Cindy felt guilty for having him go against his parent's teachings, she wanted to stay on their good side, but she also wanted Mark to be happy, and she wanted to feel safe and to sleep in peace.

Mark said it was a tough decision, but at the end of it all, he just wanted to know that she was safe.

Cindy only had three weeks left on her lease, but it did not matter to her, she moved in with Mark right away.

Within two weeks, she sold most of her furniture, to friends, her co-workers.

Not only did Mark's parents fuss about his living situation, but Karen, Cindy's mother, was displeased, and very disappointed in her.

She scolded her, and told her that, her decision went against the values she was taught.

Cindy reminded her mom that she was the one that was constantly reminding her of her safety and now she was against someone that she cared about, coming to her rescue to protect her.

"Mom, it is not like Mark and I are strangers; we are planning to get married soon, so this should not be a problem."

For the next year, the two lived together against the wishes of their parents.

At first it bothered them, but as they became more comfortable with each other, they worried less about what others were thinking about them.

They had a happy, enjoyable life together; Mark treated Cindy with lots of respect, treated her like a queen and Cindy appreciated him very much and tried to please him as much as possible.

They went on vacations to Latin America, and to the Caribbean on three occasions, and planned to go again.

The way they acted among other people commanded the admiration of many of their peers.

Karen was overjoyed to see how lovingly Mark was to her daughter and how much he cherished her. She knew he loved her, but she did not expect that level of commitment from him, she was very satisfied.

Although Mark's parents were against them moving in together, they were pleased with the way Mark and Cindy honored each other and could hardly wait for when they would be married.

Cindy did not expect Liz to get married before her, but such was the case.

Chapter *FIFTY-NINE*

SHE AND MARK FLEW to New York, and on the plane, Mark noticed that Cindy was so distant, lost in thought, and he assumed and believed that she was thinking about when her turn would come. She always believed among Katy, Liz and herself, that she would be the first to get married.

Mark had his plan, but he was waiting on the right moment to put it into place.

In the taxicab on their way to the hotel, in Brooklyn, Mark said to Cindy, "I saw you deep in thought on the plane, what were you so concerned about?"

"Nothing really, I was just reminiscing about the good times that Katie, Liz and I had throughout our time living together and was thinking that they were both going to be married people."

And Mark interrupted, "but you are not?"

"Not really, kind of, I really don't know," Cindy mumbled, "and things happen when they're supposed to," and then she changed the subject, and said, "New York is always busy, would you like to live here?"

"Not really, I love the laid-back life, Texas suits me fine."

They checked into the hotel and after settling down, they called Liz to let her know that they had arrived safely.

The next day, they met up with Shawn and Liz.

"Girl, your face is glowing, you must be very happy and excited that this day has come; you have been dreaming about it for a long time."

"Happy Oh, that's not the word, because I am beyond that; I am overjoyed."

"Liz, I am so glad to be a part of your wedding, and I am so thankful to have a friend like you, who thinks so highly of me."

"Are you ready prepared for your big day?"

"Could not be any readier than this, and I am definitely pre-pared."

The wedding ceremony and reception went great; it was not a huge wedding, but it was well-organized, and the groom and bride were remarkable.

Mark and Cindy spent a couple days in New York, before they left for Texas.

They were exhausted from their trip and went to bed soon after they got home.

Cindy had scheduled the next day to be off, so she did not have to hustle to get up in the morning, unlike Mark, who had to wake up early for work.

Chapter SIXTY

FEBRUARY IS BEAUTIFUL IN Houston; the cold weather is usually on its way out and makes way for a beautiful springtime.

Mark and Cindy spent lots of time outdoors; they visited the blue bonnet fields to see their beauty.

On one of their walks in the park, Cindy asked Mark if they could get a dog; she loved animals, especially dogs.

At first, he disliked the idea, but with her persistence, he gave in to her request, and said they would.

For his 24th birthday, Mark planned a small celebration. He invited some of his friends and some of Cindy's friends, along with family members.

On March 1st, a day before his birthday, Mark and Cindy went to the county animal shelter to adopt a puppy.

Cindy was excited when she saw the young puppies, and they looked so cute. She did not know which one to pick but finally settled on a beautiful black Labrador puppy.

She was so happy; she talked all the way back to the apartment.

"What are you going to call him?" she asked Mark.

"It's your dog, you should name him," he told her.

"No, I want you to name it," she exclaimed.

"Okay, here is what we are going to do, we will both come up with names and on Sunday we will reveal the names, and then we will choose the best one."

But Mark actually had other plans; he had something up his sleeve.

Cindy woke up early that morning, because it was Mark's birthday, she went to the kitchen and prepared an enticing breakfast and laid it out on the table which was decorated after he went to sleep the night before.

"Hi Markie, wake up my boy, breakfast is ready, it is March 2nd, your birthday, and I have prepared a delicious breakfast."

"Oh dear, I am so honored, no one has ever done this for me, I will be right there."

They joked and laughed as they enjoyed the breakfast.

"I need to have birthdays more often, like twice a year," Marked joked.

"I would have taken you to lunch this afternoon, but I did not see the need, as we are having a celebration later today; I think we should starve until then, this way, we can eat to our contentment. Agreed?" she laughed.

"Agreed, besides, I'm going to be busy preparing for the party."

The guests started arriving around 6pm, and by 7:30, almost all the invited guests and family were there.

The celebration started quietly, but soon was full of laughter and chattering, and the music was swinging, although they tried to keep it as low as they possibly could, because of their neighbors.

The celebration was in full swing, everyone was occupied doing something, when Mark got everyone's attention, and said, "I got Cindy a puppy yesterday, and she is thrilled about it, but we could not come up with a name for him, so we came to the conclusion that we would both come up with names by tomorrow, and we would choose between our choices the best one suited, but I have decided to reveal my name tonight, while everyone is here, this way I can have your advice."

"Cindy, please bring the puppy from the crate, I have put a ribbon around its neck, and attached, is a small box with the names that I have chosen."

Cindy carefully opened the box, and stood there speechless; she could not believe what she saw in there. She opened her eyes wide, as she stood there shocked and surprised, she saw the huge diamond ring inside of it.

"What is it?" her mom asked.

Then Cindy showed them what was inside the box; Mark knelt in front of her, and said, "Cindy, will you marry me?"

"Yes, yes," she said excitedly, "I will, I surely will," and she hugged and kissed him.

And all that were present gave their blessings and wished them well.

"By the way, there was a name in the box, but I saw the ring first."

And the room was filled with laughter.

"The name he chose was Happy, and I love it, I think it describes the dog, and also me, so we will stick with this name."

Karen was so happy of what had just transpired, because it bothered her that they were living together without being married; that was not what she envisioned for her daughter.

Likewise, Mark's parents shared the same sentiments.

The party continued until the wee hours of the morning, before everyone left.

"What a birthday celebration that was; I got my wife to be, a new dog, and the blessings of family and friends, what more can a chap ask for?"

"Oh, you wait and see, the celebration is not over yet, it is scheduled to end with fireworks," and with that said, she led him to the bedroom. They enjoyed love making, but they did not get into any sexual act.

Cindy wanted to attend church in the morning, but did not because she was so tired from all the activities of the night, and said, she would stay and rest.

Mark and Cindy used this time to discuss their future, including a wedding date, and how many guests they planned to invite.

Chapter SIXTY-ONE

Two MONTHS HAD PASSED since the day of their engagement, and they decided to get married in June of the upcoming year, but they withheld telling others, until a future time.

Both were having enjoyable careers and they loved what they did.

Mark was just promoted to manager of his department, while Cindy kept getting good reviews and increases in her salary.

They were living and enjoying a great life. They travelled frequently, and did lots of fun things together, and most people thought they were the perfect couple.

But it was not always as rosy for them as some people thought, because they came very close to breaking up last thanksgiving.

It so happened, that thanksgiving night, after they came from Mark's parents' house, and dropping Liz at Karen's, they got into a heated argument on their way back to the apartment. It all started because of what happened at Mark's home.

Mark tried to be fair and did not give his mother total blame for what had happened; he thought Cindy made too much out of it, and that infuriated Cindy, who felt that his mom was inconsiderate, and just had to have her way.

But that was not the main issue that almost split them up, that was just the beginning of the argument.

As the saying goes, "the best part of breaking up is making up," so after their argument, they admitted that this petty situation should not bring such hostility in their relationship and decided not to go to bed with them being mad at each other.

But here is where it almost went off the rail.

The two began being intimate with each other, and their passion grew stronger for each other with every minute of them getting deeper emotionally, but when it came to having sex, Cindy pulled away, and withdrew herself immediately.

Mark was furious.

"You need to stop. You keep doing that all the time, anytime we get to this time, you shut it down, and leave me in a bad position, what is going on?" What are you hiding from me?'

And Cindy began to sob, as the memories became alive to her once more, and she knew this was the time, she had to tell Mark, if she wanted to save her relationship. She had to lay it out, she had to come clean, and tell him everything, and allow him to make his decision.

"I know you are going to be disappointed with me after you hear what I am about to say to you. You might even give up on our relationship," and she continued to sob.

"Mark, I am not a virgin."

He sat up quickly, and was in total bewilderment, shocked, and in disbelief.

"You sure had me fooled, why didn't you tell me that before? Why wait until now, after all we have been through, and all the plans we have made? I would never have thought that, because of the way you acted and the things you said to me, and because of your church upbringing. You got me, and I am not sure if I can trust you anymore, you have deceived me, and I am not sure of our relationship, because it is based on a lie."

Cindy buried her head into the palm of her hands and wept bitterly.

"Who was this guy? College guy huh?"

"Mark, this was not supposed to happen, it was beyond my control."

"What do you mean it happened beyond your control?"

Before he could ask the question, "were you raped?" Cindy took control of the conversation.

"I was with this guy named Kirk, and we were in love, well so I thought, I completely trusted him, and I did everything to make him happy, so on my 21st birthday, he held a huge, surprise party for me, and invited my friends, and his elite friends. He was a professional basketball player.

The party was extravagant, and vibrant with lots of people. My best friends and my brother were there, and we were all having a good time, but Kirk persuaded me to go to his hotel room, he said that there was something he wanted to discuss with me, and promised we would be coming right back to the party, but this was the biggest mistake I ever made in my life.

I normally do not drink alcohol, but for some stupid reason, I allowed myself to be persuaded by his pleading, and I ended up drinking, but I was not drunk, but from there onwards, everything went downhill, and oh that pain, though I fought with all my might, I cannot even talk about it, but let me just say, I fell asleep, and when I woke up, I knew I had lost my virginity to someone I did not consent to, it happened against my wish.

I hated this guy, and I hated myself for allowing me to be victimized like this." And she kept crying.

Mark felt her pain, and cradled her in his arms, and said, "honey, I am so sorry, sorry you had to go through that, that had to be very painful."

"I am very sorry for the way I behaved, although, I believed you should have told this to me earlier, I would have supported you.

But don't worry, I am here for you now, and we will go through this together, and you will overcome that, and you will have a great life, going forward."

"I wanted to tell you earlier, but I feared losing you, and I hated thinking about it, because I am traumatized each time I think about it, seemed like yesterday to me. That is the main reason that I don't celebrate my birthday anymore."

At the end of it all, they woke up next morning, cuddled in each other's arms.

And they promised to move forward from all that had transpired, and to build a great future together.

They had a great Christmas season, spent most of it with family and friends. Cindy had mended her relationship with Laurie and hoped that they would continue to grow their friendship.

Chapter *Chapter* SIXTY-TWO

THIS THANKSGIVING, THEY PLANNED on spending it with Joshua and Katie in Florida.

Cindy was scheduled to work on thanksgiving weekend, but managed to switch with one of her co-workers, who owed her a favor.

Joshua, and Katy lived a few miles from the airport, and this was by design, because Joshua travelled often, because of his profession.

Cindy hugged her brother and Katy, but quickly made her way to her nephew Kevin.

"Oh, he is so cute, what a handsome baby, he mirrors both of you, not one more than the other, good for him," and she hugged and kissed him, and just could not get over his cuteness.

"Sorry to bring this up, but I wished dad was here to love up on this bundle of joy."

"Kate, you look good, you still have that glow after the birthing of your baby."

"What about me?" josh asked jokingly, "don't I look good too?'

"Hahaha, someone is jealous. You look good too my brother."

"Hopefully, mom and Katy's mom will get to see him soon, we planned on visiting them during the Christmas season." Josh said.

"Oh, we might miss you because we are planning to spend Christmas with Shawn and Liz in New York.

"Also, we have set a wedding month, the exact date we have not set, but the month is June."

"We haven't told anybody yet, so keep it quiet, because our plans are not concrete yet."

"Oh sure, and congratulations to both of you, I know sis, that you will make a good wife, and I have confidence, Mark will be a great husband, and Mark, now your eyes are closed, even though they are wide open, you can't see other ladies, so, welcome to the club." Joshua said laughingly.

"Josh, stop scaring the guy, it is not like that, you get what you put into it."

"You all are so funny, and besides, Mark and I are practically married, we are just going to make it official."

"I know we are going to be together for ever, I believe in God's keeping power." Mark said, with a grin on his face.

"Okay, it is time to start the thanksgiving dinner process, who is going to join me in the kitchen?"

"I am," said Cindy.

"I was speaking to the men, I want to check out their cooking skills, I know their moms taught them well."

"She taught us boys, to eat all of our thanksgiving meal, and not to let any go to waste, I have been doing that faithfully." Josh joked.

"So true Josh, you have been eating, that is so funny, but I love it." Mark could not stop laughing.

On Thursday, everything was in order, the food and drinks were prepared, and everything was ready.

The gathering was small, just the four of them, but the atmosphere was great, you could feel the love that enveloped the gathering.

After dinner, they watched a couple of movies, and relaxed, and spent time on the phone talking to loved ones and friends.

The following day, they drove to Tampa, which was about an hour, and 45 minutes away, spent a short time there, then went to Clearwater.

The water was nice and clear, but not as warm as the summer months, but they still enjoyed being there.

They spent about an hour going through the busy stores and restaurants that were located on the strand.

Driving back to the Orlando area seemed like it took forever. They were tired and eager to get home.

They had planned to go downtown later in the evening to listen to a few local bands, and to have a night out on the town, but changed their minds, because of their weariness.

Mark and Cindy left Florida Sunday afternoon and arrived in Houston in the evening. They went to bed earlier than usual so they would be well rested for work the next day.

The week flew by, and before not too long, it was the weekend again.

Mark and Cindy went to Karen's house with a purpose in mind, they went to inform them of their wedding date.

Karen was just coming from her Saturday evening shopping, which she normally did on the weekends that she was off.

"Hi folks, what brought you to this part of the country?' she asked jokingly.

"I came to receive all the goodies that you bought for me while you were out there shopping; I am still your daughter you know?'

"Okay, still my daughter? Well carry the groceries into the house."

"Funny, but you got me."

"You all are so hilarious, but I love it," Mark said, as he carried the groceries into the house.

As they sat at the table to have dinner, Cindy said, "Mom, Mark and I have decided on a date for our wedding."

"Good, that is great news, I have been waiting for that news since the day of your engagement."

"We have decided to get married in June of next year, the exact date, we will let you know in a couple of weeks."

"You are so good together; I could not hope for a better person to be with my daughter. You have made her a happy person, and I am sure the same could be said on her behalf too."

"Coming to church tomorrow?" she asked.

"Not tomorrow, but we will soon." Cindy answered.

They stayed with her a few more minutes, before they said, bye, and promised to see her soon.

"Mark, I thought we were going to your parent's house tonight?"

"Cindy, it's too late, they go to bed early on Saturday nights so they can be at church early on Sunday morning."

"So, when are we going to tell them?"

"I will call them tomorrow and share the news with them."

"I would have really liked to tell them in person, I would love to see their facial expressions, but you know your parents best, so I trust you."

As he said, Mark waited when he knew that his parents were home from church, and he picked up the phone and called them. His father answered and jokingly pretended to be his mom answering.

"Dad, I know it's you; stop trying to imitate mom, you know we're close, and where is that beautiful lady anyway?'

"Laurie, come to the phone, it's your ugly son," he said jokingly, as he handed the phone to her.

"Hi, son, it is nice to hear your voice, we just came back from church. We missed you at church."

"Mom, we did our praying at home."

"Mom, I'm calling to let you know that we have set a date for our wedding; we have decided to get married in June of this coming year, but as to the exact day, we will let you know soon."

"Hey Jacob, Mark said that they have set a wedding date."

"Mom, you can discuss that later. I will give you details when we confirm the exact day."

"Oh, my son, I am happy to hear that, because I hate to see you living like this. My God does not like this, and I did not bring you up like this."

"Mom, this is not the time for a lecture, and I will talk to you soon"

"How did your parents react?" Cindy asked.

"They were happy, they can't wait for the wedding."

"They are happy for us, but they want to see us living as a married couple, instead of this living arrangement." Cindy replied.

"I could tell by the way you were answering, I got to know you really well my boy." And she laughed.

The next couple of weeks, they prepared for their trip to New York.

They had an issue with where to leave their dog.

Cindy knew that her mom did not have the time to take care of a dog, although her mom said they could leave it with her; she would be able to handle it for two weeks, but they decided that was not a good idea.

Mark's parents said it would be great company for them, yet Mark did not feel comfortable with that, and said, he would take it to a doggy day care, but Cindy was not in favor of that either, so they settled on Mark's parents.

"New York, here we come, are you ready for us?" Cindy said.

"I am sure it can handle us, the famous celebrities," Mark said sarcastically.

Chapter SIXTY-THREE

IT WAS A BUSY Saturday morning, and to avoid having Shawn come through the traffic, Cindy suggested that they take a taxi to the house.

"There is not a time we come here, that it's not busy night and day is the same with lots of movement, and you said, you would love to live here?'

"Mark, New York is perfect for me, I could move around, and no one would pay notice of me; I love that."

"You know how much I hate the cold weather, so that is already a setback for me, and I love the slower pace of life, so New York is a no, no, for me." Mark said.

This is going to be our first Christmas in New York, and whether it is cold or not, we are going to enjoy it to the fullest; we are going to make the best of it, agree?" Cindy asked.

"Agreed," Mark responded, even though, he was saying that just to please her.

"Welcome to our home, I think the last time you visited, we were still living in the apartment, is that so, Liz?"

"Sure right, Shawn, we moved a couple of months after they left, do you remember I was about to call Cindy and tell her that we were moving to a house, but you said don't tell her because you wanted to surprise them when they came back?"

"Well, we are surprised, and we love it; it's very spacious, I hope one of these rooms belongs to me, or rather, us." Cindy said.

"Mi casa, es su casa," Shawn said, "you are forever welcome here."

They had a couple days left to do their shopping and Cindy was hoping to spend most of the time doing just that.

"Mark, you can tail along tomorrow if you can keep up with me."

"Funny, you think I will let you go in the streets of New York by yourself? That's not going to happen."

"Way to go, Mark, being protective and taking care of the one you love." Shawn said.

"I sure don't want anything negative to happen on our trip and as long as I can prevent it, I will." Mark replied.

"Honey, don't take this that seriously, you know that I was kidding about that. Liz will be with me and I know you would come too."

Monday evening, the four of them were extremely tired from all the walking they did, going from store to store, and from the hustling that they did.

"You know we still have to go out tonight for a little while; my friend from work invited me to a gathering tonight and I promised him that we would be there, so I think we should go even if it just for a short time."

It was much better than they anticipated; they thought it was going to be a rowdy gathering, but to the contrary, it was a small family gathering.

On their way home, they witnessed a minor accident.

Going through one of the downtown streets in Manhattan, they saw a vehicle swerving in and out of the lane, and eventually ran into a mailbox, and stopped at a newspaper stand.

Before Mark, and Shawn could get to the vehicle to see if the driver was okay, he backed up, and drove away, still wavering in and out of the lane.

"Was he hurt, is he okay?" Cindy asked. She was a little bit shaken from what she had witnessed.

"Welcome to New York," Liz said, "what you don't see here, means it does not exist."

They made it home, and Cindy said, "thank you Lord for bringing us home safely."

Christmas day came and went by quickly. It was a cold snowy day, so they stayed inside most of the day.

The next day they went to see what bargains they could find in the stores so they could finish buying their gifts to take back for their friends in Texas.

Cindy dreamt of experiencing New Year's Eve in New York. She, Mark and Liz bundled up, and prepared themselves for a long day and night, as they gathered in Time Square with the huge crowd who were there to welcome the new year.

They enjoyed being in that environment, the atmosphere was vibrant, lots of music, and entertainment, beyond their expectations, it was a surreal experience.

Then it was time to drop the ball to welcome the new year, and the counting started, and the massive crowd joined in the countdown, the people roared, and they got louder and louder, the closer the count got to one. And finally, the ball hit the ground, and there was a loud shout, and they were hugging and crying, and all types of things going on at that time.

Mark embraced Cindy and kissed her, and they wished each other prosperity for the new year.

"What an experience," Cindy said, "I wouldn't trade this experience for any other entertainment activity anywhere else in the world."

She asked Mark if they could make this an annual trip going forward but Mark did not commit to that proposal.

Mark and Cindy thanked Shawn and Liz for the great time that they had in New York, and thanked them for their hospitality, and for being such great friends.

Later in the afternoon, they departed for Texas, with Cindy vowing to return. Mark was glad for the trip, but not as excited as his Fiancée was.

Chapter SIXTY-FOUR

ONE WEEK AFTER THEIR trip from New York, Cindy felt sick; she wasn't sure whether it was something she contracted in New York or whether it was food poisoning, because most of the illness had to do with her stomach.

She visited her doctor who was in the medical center where she worked.

After explaining to her doctor how she felt, he ran a few tests and procedures, and came back with a diagnosis.

"Hi Cindy, I have good news," Doctor James said smiling.

Cindy felt relieved, because she worried that she had been compromised with a virus from her trip to New York.

"Great Doc, what's the good news?" she asked.

"My friend, you are pregnant."

Cindy remained frozen for a while, unable to say anything, because she was not expecting to hear that, she thought they had taken all the precautionary measures to avoid getting pregnant, and now this.

"Are you not happy of that great news?" the doctor asked.

"Yes, I am," Cindy replied, "just surprised, and confused," then she went into detail as to why she felt that way.

After recollecting her thoughts, she was happy to know that she was carrying Mark's child, and she hastened to get home to deliver the great news to him.

As expected, he was taken aback from the news, and was shocked for a moment, then he became very excited and hugged his mate, and congratulated her on the conception of their first child.

"How far along are you?' he asked.

"About six to seven weeks,' she replied.

Cindy was excited, yet traumatized, because thoughts of her previous pregnancy came racing back into her mind, although, the circumstances were different, yet it was still hard to overcome the bad feelings.

She was so happy she cried, because this time her pregnancy did not come about because of a rape, but instead, it was not forced, and even though, she still wanted to be married, before having a child, she was not angry because it did not happen like that, but she was overjoyed that she was having a child with someone who cared for her, and would love her child, just as much as she would.

They sat there in amazement, as Mark rubbed Cindy's stomach, and smiled; he could not believe that he was going to be a father and was anxious to tell the world.

"If it's a boy, he should be named Mark Jr. but if it's a girl, she should be called Lacey."

"Mark, don't you think that you are way ahead of yourself? We have a long way to go."

"First, we have to make sure that the baby and I are okay and healthy, then we can proceed with other details."

After a week had passed, Cindy worked up enough courage to tell her mom, and broke the news to her that she was pregnant.

Karen was very excited for her and Mark, and was happy to have another grandchild, but still took the opportunity to let her know that this was not what she envisioned for her, pregnancy before marriage, a child out of wedlock.

Though Cindy explained to her, that they were still getting married in June, and that the child would not be born out of wedlock, Karen argued with her, and said, that it was conceived before marriage and that was what it was.

Cindy related her mother's sentiment to Mark, and told him, how upset she was, and how angry she was with her mother for being so glued to her religious beliefs, yet not having the compassion of Christ in a situation like this.

"Come here. We are not going to make these things our problem anymore, going forward, it's our lives, and we are going to live according to what pleases Mark and Cindy. We will be open for advice, but the last say will be with us. I love you and now even more, so avoid being stressed, and let us enjoy our lives together."

"I am about to call my parents; I know what they are going to say, pretty much the same thing as your mom, but like I said, it is our lives.

As predicted, his parents were happy for the news of their first grandchild but were disappointed about the way it came about.

"Mark, I think we should hold back on our wedding, we should wait until after the baby is born."

"But I thought you wanted to be married before you had this baby?'

"Not really, I know it's the right thing to do because we love God and were brought up being taught that having a baby outside of marriage was wrong, but we have already made the mistake, having a wedding to justify or to hide our fault is not going to make it right."

"My Lord, whom I serve, understands what I did, and He is not holding it against me, so neither will I. I am going to trust Him and move forward and trust His forgiveness."

"Well said, my dear, and I am with you all the way." Mark said.

The next few months, Cindy felt miserable, she was struggling with her 1st semester of her pregnancy, she was often sick, and was very moody, and Mark had to learn how to deal with that situation. He exhibited his patience, and his maturity, besides, he loved his fiancée and did whatever he could, to make her happy.

Chapter SIXTY-FIVE

MARK AND CINDY FOUND out that they were having a boy, and they were happy to know that. Mark was extremely happy, he always desired having a boy that would carry on his name.

The months leading up to her due date, Mark took special care of Cindy, he made sure she stuck to the right diet that the doctor prescribed, he also encouraged her to keep up her beauty habits, so he made certain that her hair was well groomed, and that she went to work looking as beautiful as usual.

Her due date, August 23rd, was about a week away, and Mark and Cindy had her bag packed and ready to go, in case of an abrupt emergency.

Saturday night, Cindy and her friends were home having a social event, when she felt an abdominal pain; she winced and continued with her activities, but the pain became more intense, and more frequent, and then there was a real sharp pain, which got the attention of those around her, and they realized that she was in labor.

She quickly called Mark, who had just left to go to the store around the corner to pick up a quart of ice-cream. He spun around and came right back to the apartment.

The trip to the hospital was rather short, because they lived a couple blocks from the hospital.

Mark went up to the Nurse's desk, and took care of the admission details, while Cindy was wheeled to the labor and delivery area.

The nurses took her vital signs and prepared her for delivery.

They frequently checked on her to see how much she was dilated, and they kept the doctor informed.

Mark was nervous, that was a first experience for him, and he acted like it, he would not stop talking, until Cindy going through her pain, could not take it anymore, called him out, and asked him to be quiet.

The nurses informed him that if he could not handle the pressure of the moment, they would ask him to wait in the waiting room, until he was needed.

At 2:15am, that Sunday morning, Marcus Jason Jackrose, came forth into this world, he weighed 8lbs, 10 ounces, and was 23 inches long.

Those that were in the waiting room, were happy and joyful, especially Mark and Cindy's parents.

Mark was the happiest man on earth at that moment, he was reunited with Cindy, because they had him to wait in the waiting room, because he could not handle the process of the birthing.

He sat on the bed next to Cindy and stroked his hand through her hair, as she looked at him lovingly.

Mark was beaming with pride; he had become a father.

Cindy quickly forgot the labor pains, after the nurse laid her little boy upon her chest.

And she and Mark said a thankful prayer, and then celebrated.

Cindy did not have to stay in the hospital beyond two days, she had no major complications, and she was feeling well, and the Doctor said, it was okay for her to leave.

Cindy was blessed to have so many people support her after she left the hospital.

The grandparents were there to advise and help her navigate from pregnancy to being a mom of a newly born.

Marcus was a pleasure to be around, he was happy most of the time, except when he was in need. He was surrounded by many who loved him.

Mark, believed this was the best thing that happened to him, while Cindy was forever thankful; she had not been sure if she would be able to have any children after what she did with the first; she never forgave herself for what she did, and regretted it constantly; she also worried that she would have problems in labor, but fortunately, for her, Marcus came with no difficulty.

Marcus stole the attention from Mark. Cindy shifted most of her time to care to him, but Mark understood and did his best to make sure the family was happy.

For Marcus first Christmas, they took him to Florida to spend the weekend with Joshua and his family.

Josh and Katy were thrilled to meet their nephew, and to introduce their son to his cousin.

They had a great weekend before returning to Texas.

Marcus was fortunate, Karen had retired, and volunteered to keep him when his dad and mom were both working.

He sometimes spent time at his other grandparents, they were very fond of him, and bought him lots of toys and other items.

Mark and Cindy had no problem when they wanted a night out by themselves to enjoy each other's company, although sometimes Cindy's mind was not with their date, but on her little boy.

Cindy would call every hour to see how he was doing and this annoyed his grandparents, especially Laurie.

She called Mark and told him how infuriated she was. "I raised you all your life, and look at you, an excellent young man; I did not abuse you, what makes your mate think that I am not able to take care of my grandson for one night, that she has to keep calling every minute to check on him?"

"Mom, first, she is not just my mate, but my fiancée, I understand how you are feeling, but I also see her point, not that she does not trust you, she is just missing her son.

Please, mom, don't let this be a problem, enjoy your time with your grandson, and I will talk to Cindy."

"What's up? What did your mother say?" Cindy asked.

"She was not too happy about you calling so often to check on Marcus."

She said, "she did fine with me, why it would be any different with her grandson?"

"Mark, I understand what you are saying, and how your mom is feeling, but I am sure, when you were Marcus's age, your mom felt the same way that I am feeling now. It is a mother's thing, I wished I could explain it better, but it is a feeling, also I promise to be better, less aggressive."

But with all that said, Cindy still could not sleep, she was concerned about her boy, and could not wait for the morning to come, so she could pick up her son.

In the morning, she woke up and was ready to go, when Mark told her to wait for a while; he asked that they go and have breakfast, after which they would go and pick him up.

Cindy did not like the idea, but Mark pleaded with her, and she agreed.

"Cindy, you know we were supposed to discuss our wedding last night?"

"I know, my body was present, but my mind was not there at all. Sorry about that."

"But I thought we had decided on putting it off for a later time?'

"Yes, we did, but we did not conclude. We need to set a new time and date."

"Sure, can we discuss that later tonight?'

"Yes, we will. I just want you to know that I am eager to get married to you."

"Oh Babe, I know, and I know the feeling is mutual."

"Okay lady, let's go and get our prince, I can't wait to see him."

They made it to the house in less than no time.

Marcus was in the bedroom with his grandfather and was laughing loudly; they heard him as soon as they entered the house.

"Hi Mom, we are here," Mark said.

"Dad, how are you doing? What are you telling my boy? I heard him laughing from the parking lot," Mark said jokingly.

"We are doing okay," his dad replied, "and Marcus is still in one piece."

"Mr. Jacob and Ms. Laurie, I am sorry for the way I came across to you but this was not my intention, I was just trying to cope of not being around my son, but I trust you."

"My child, I know what I said, but I was just angry, but I know how you felt. When Mark had to go to the day care, I almost had a breakdown, so I have been there, but you don't need to worry when he is with us, because we love him just as much.'

On their way home, Cindy said, "your mom gave us an option: We could leave him at their home a couple days in a week in order to give my mom a break, but they live further away from us; we will have to think about it."

"As soon as we get married, we are going to buy a house closer to our parents so we won't be faced with that dilemma."

Later that night, as they laid on the bed, they talked about their wedding and settled on a valentine's day wedding, since it fell on a Saturday.

Chapter SIXTY-SIX

FOR THE LAST FEW months, Mark has been complaining of head-aches that he has been experiencing, and Cindy asked him to go visit the doctor, but he kept putting it off, saying he would, but kept procrastinating.

Finally, he could not bear the pain anymore, so he made an appointment with the doctor.

His private doctor did all he could but referred him to a neurol-ogist, who had him to do an MRI scan, so he could have a better diagnosis on what was causing the frequent and painful headaches.

After going through the scan, the doctor noticed a mass on the brain, and decided to run further tests to determine whether the mass was benign.

Mark and Cindy were very worried and were hoping for a neg-ative result.

The doctor called after three days, and asked Mark to come in to see him.

That bothered Cindy, because of the fact that he asked him to come in; it did not seem like the news was good, but she was hoping that she was wrong, and all would be well.

Mark and Cindy approached the door, and gingerly, stepped into the office and informed his receptionist that they were here to see Doctor Joseph.

After a few minutes, Dr. Joseph came to the window, and said, "come in you and your wife," not knowing that they were not married, but assumed that they were. "Have a seat."

"Son, the news is not good. I wished it was different. The mass we saw on your brain is cancerous, and it is very aggressive, but with treatment, and lots of prayer, anything is possible.'

Mark remained frozen for a while, his mind locked in disbelief, while Cindy was sobbing furiously, she could not believe what she was hearing.

Mark held on to Cindy, and said, "we are going to beat this, we will."

Doctor Joseph assured them that he would do everything in his power to ensure that he would get the necessary treatment he needed to help him fight against the cancer.

"We have to start treatment right away, because this is an urgent situation. I have contacted Doctor Ahmed, he is one of the top oncologists in the country, and fortunately, he resides in our city."

"Here is the number of his office, you should contact him as soon as possible to set up an appointment, I have told him all the details of your situation, so he is waiting on your call."

"Thanks, Doctor, we really do appreciate that, we will contact the Doctor, as soon as possible, and get the treatment that Mark needs to get him healthy. Thanks again." Cindy expressed.

The two of them left the office feeling so dejected, but holding on to hope, and praying that the treatment would work, and Mark would be back to great health.

On their way home, they remained quiet because they were so sad because of the news that they had received.

Finally, Cindy said, "honey, we have to believe, we have to tap into our faith, God is always on our side."

She said this, but in her mind, she was wavering, because she knew that it was extremely serious. She also doubted her prayers, because she knew that she was not in the best standing with God.

But she kept encouraging him. "We will fight this; you have to be here for our son Marcus." She told him.

As soon as they got home, Cindy called the Doctor, because Mark was too depressed to call, and she set up an appointment for him.

Then the scary thing, calling their parents to relate the news to them.

Mark called his dad, he thought it would be less painful if his dad relayed the news to his mom, instead of him.

"Dad, how are you doing?"

"Fine, what's up? What's going on? You specifically asked to speak to me, that is not normal."

He said, "dad, I have some bad news, "

"Is Marcus, okay?" his dad asked.

"Dad, you went straight away to Marcus, you didn't ask if Cindy or I were okay, but automatically thought that it was the Marcus"

"Most of the time when a young father or mother calls their parents, it is usually about their children, anyway, I'm sorry, what is it son?"

"Dad, I just came from an appointment with the doctor to check on frequent headaches I have been having, and I found out that I have brain cancer.'

Mark did not hear anything coming from the other end of the phone, siolence for a minute or two.

"Dad are you there?" he asked.

Quietly he said, "I am still here."

"How bad is it?" he asked tearfully.

"Jacob, what's going on?" Laurie asked.

"It's Mark," he said.

"I know it's Mark, I was the one who gave you the phone, what's up with Mark?'

"He had bad news, he just came from the doctor, and found out that he has brain cancer."

"What?" and she took the phone from Jacob.

"What is going on son? What am I hearing? Is that true?" she asked faintly.

"Mom, I found out that I have brain cancer, but mom, don't worry, we will all beat this together."

"Son, I am so sad to hear that," and she cried as she listened to him.

"Mom, I have to go to take care of a few things, take care of dad, and don't worry, everything will be okay.'

"I know that was hard for you to do, but I am glad you got it over with, now I am faced with the task of telling my mom.'

"Do you want me to call and break the news to her?"

"No, thanks, but I think I should do it. Here, hold on to Marcus for a while."

She went into the kitchen, got a glass of water, then sat on the couch, and dialed her mom's number.

"Mom, hi, how are you doing? How was your day?"

"I am doing fine, how are things over on your side? Are Mark and Marcus doing, okay?"

"Not doing too good."

"Okay, what's going on? I can tell from your voice, that something isn't right."

"Mom it's mark."

"What, are you having problems?"

"Mom, it is more than that."

"Come on, you are scaring me, I can't take another one, after your dad."

"We went to the doctor today, and we got some bad news, we found out that Mark has brain cancer."

"Oh, no, no," she said, she was so loud, that Donald came quickly to see what was wrong.

"How bad is it?"

"Doctor said it is very aggressive, and we have to address it with urgency."

Then Karen put on her mother's hat and encouraged her daughter.

"God is good, He will see us through this." She calmly said.

"Can I speak to Mark?"

"Mark, everything will be alright, don't give up, we have to fight against this, we will keep on praying."

"Mom, thanks for the support, with God's help, I will be okay."

The following day, Cindy requested a day off from her job, and she accompanied Mark to the oncologist office.

Dr. Ahmed welcomed them and explained to them the plan that he had laid out for them to follow in treating Mark's condition.

After listening to Dr. Ahmed, Mark was optimistic, about the operation, and the beginning of his treatment.

The next few months were tough for Mark and Cindy, they made a few adjustments to accommodate the time they had to spend at the doctor's office and taking the treatments.

The operation was a success, and the treatment was working effectively, but Mark knew he still had a long way to go, but he was committed to the challenge, so he had a positive mind set, and vowed to get better, so he could be there for his son.

Mark was improving satisfactorily; his doctor was pleased with the progress that he had made.

Cindy accompanied Mark to his last session of chemo treatment, and when it was over, they went over to the bell that the hospital had set up, which patients ring to signify the end of chemo.

They joined hands, and together they rang the bell as hard as they could.

They were happy that Mark had come to the end of that harsh treatment. These were nine rough months, but they glorified God that He gave them the strength to go through it successfully.

They called their parents, and gave them the good news, and thanked them for the prayers that they offered on their behalf.

"Young man, daddy will be with you more often now, I am sorry for all the time I neglected you, but it was necessary, now I am all yours."

Marcus looked at him straight in the eyes and acted like he understood what his dad said to him, and Mark choked up, as he kissed him on his forehead, and thanked God that he was given time to be there for him.

"Let it out, Mark, don't stifle the tears, men are allowed to shed tears too," and she reached out to him, and hugged him.

"I missed celebrating, my son's, and my wife to be birthdays, but I will make it up to you all in the near future." Mark said to his loved ones.

"Oh no, you did celebrate our birthdays, you are here, and your health has improved drastically, I could not wish for a better birthday gift."

"But your birthday is next week, and we are going to celebrate." Cindy said.

"We have so much to be thankful for, we can't take it for granted. I will organize a family gathering, and we are going to celebrate you."

She picked up the phone and called her mom. "Karen," she said, and she started laughing, because she always addressed her mother by calling her mom, so this was funny to her.

"Who are you calling Karen, young lady?" and she chuckled.

"Mom, tell me that you don't have anything planned for next Saturday?"

"No, I don't, I will be home."

"Great, I am having a small get together for Mark's birthday, and to give God thanks for His goodness. It will be just family and a few friends."

"Oh, David and Lisa are coming home for the weekend, so this is a good idea, it worked out well."

At first, when everyone saw Mark, they were sad, knowing what he went through, but after he spoke to them, the mood changed to celebrating.

And the celebration was more joyful than they expected. There was lots of laughter and joking around, and they all had a swell time, and were happy that this celebration took place.

Mark thanked Cindy for organizing the gathering, and for lifting his spirit.

Sunday morning they attended church; their parents and other church members were surprised to see them, they had not attended this church in a while.

The pastor acknowledged their presence, but also said some things in his message, that Cindy knew was directed to her and Mark.

At first, she was upset, but then she chose to ignore it, and took in the rest of the preaching.

They mingled for a short while after the service was over, then left for one of her favorite BBQ restaurants with their parents, and David and his wife Lisa.

While at lunch, Mark felt this was the best opportunity to inform everyone of their decision that they made concerning their wedding.

"Since we are all here, let me say that we have set a time and date for our wedding. It will be in February on Valentine's Day, but we will give you all more details later down the line."

"Congratulations, Mark, and also Cindy, but why not sooner?"

"Mom, let's not make this an issue, we carefully planned this, and we are going to stick to our plan.'

"I am so happy for you; this is the best way to go." Karen said. "Is it going to be a big wedding?"

"We are still in the planning stages mom, but we will fill you in on the details later, but most likely, it is going to be average"

Mark and Cindy, decided to have family members and a few guests at the wedding; they did not want a big wedding, but they wanted something elegant.

They hired a wedding planner, and told her what they desired, and from there on, they were basically hands off.

Mark, "can you believe it?"

"Believe what?" Mark asked.

"Marcus will be two years next week, oh my, how time has flown by."

"For sure, we are going to do something special for him this year, last year was a tough one."

Mark was almost at full capacity at work, which was an indication that his health was getting so much better.

As promised, Marcus had a great 2nd birthday celebration, and he got a good gift from his parents.

Also, Mark reminded Cindy that her birthday was coming up soon, and he was going to celebrate it with flare.

Cindy did not care to have one, but Mark insisted; he did not want to take anything for granted.

"You can't live in the past, you have to move on, that is the only way you will overcome what happened to you."

"It is easy for you to say, it did not happen to you, so it is easy for you to plan and move forward." She said angrily.

"Cindy, I am sorry that I said anything, I did not think you would look at it this way, forget that I ever said anything. You always say that I never listen to you, but here you are, ignoring my advice.'

"Hold it there, pal, you did not listen to my advice, I nagged you, yes I said it, nagged, I told you on numerous occasions, to go to the doctor, when the headaches had just started, but you ignored my advice, and see what happened."

Mark was furious, "so you had all these things on your chest, all the time that you were encouraging me, and you never said anything, until now? I just found out how you really feel."

Mark said, "I am going to take a walk, I'm going to the mailbox."

Cindy waited patiently for his return, and as soon as she heard his footsteps coming up the stairs, she went and open the door for him.

As soon as he entered the apartment, she hugged him, and told him how sorry she was, and that she was not holding anything against him, and that her support for him was genuine, it is just that the trauma of that birthday still got to her.

"I am sorry, and I should not use that as an excuse to take it out on you," and again, she apologized.

After they patched up things between them, they took Marcus to the ice-cream shop, to get a few ice-cream bars, then they went to the neighborhood park to relax, and enjoy the fresh air.

Marcus had a great time, he had them chasing him, as he ran all around the park.

As soon as they put him in his baby seat, before they even strapped him, he was already asleep, he had spent all his energy running around.

The wedding plans were coming along perfectly, and on schedule, although it was still a long way off.

They were hoping that it would happen, because they had put it off twice, for legitimate reasons.

Cindy chuckled, and laughed, as she related to Mark about a marriage proposal, she received from one of her patients at work.

He asked her to forget about Mark, and to marry him, he said, he would give all that she needed. He said he was rich, and that his ex-wife did not love him, but loved his money.

"Mark, I thought that he was joking, but he was serious; another nurse on the floor told me what he said, and she said, this guy was obsessed with me. It is flattering, but this is scary, I am going to try to avoid him as much as possible."

"My girl is hot, hot, can't be resisted," Mark teased, "this is good stuff."

"Are you off from work, this weekend?"

"Yes, I am," Cindy replied.

"Why don't we go to Galveston, and spend the weekend there?"

"Sound like a good idea to me," Cindy replied.

Chapter *SIXTY-SEVEN*

FRIDAY AFTER WORK, THEY packed their bags, along with Marcus necessities, and headed to Galveston.

Traffic was tight going down to the Island, but they were not in a rush, they said, whenever they got there would be okay with them.

Summertime in Texas is very humid, and many find solace at the beach.

At that time of the year, it is always been busy on the Island, and finding First class hotels is hard to come by, and if you do find any, they are very expensive, but Mark, did not mind, for a good relaxing weekend, he said it's worth it.

Getting back to the mainland on Sunday afternoon, was almost as hectic as when they were going to the Island, that happened because there was a couple of minor accidents, which caused a major backup.

When they got to the house, they were so tired from the traffic, that they went to bed early, right after Marcus fell asleep.

Cindy's birthday was a few weeks away, and Mark suggested that they should go to Mexico for the weekend of her birthday, and this time she did not hesitate, but accepted the invitation.

The Friday before her birthday, they drove to the airport, and left on a non-stop flight to Mexico.

The flight was about 3 hours long, they got there early in the mid-morning, and went to the hotel, and checked in.

Mark tried to convince Cindy to let Marcus stay with one of his grandmothers, but he failed. She said if Marcus stays, then she stays, she was only going to Mexico if Marcus came along.

He did not want any big argument, so agreed to let Marcus accompany them.

He knew that there would be less activities that they could do with a child, but all that mattered to him was the happiness of his family.

After they had rested for a couple of hours, they went down to the hotel terrace to have something to eat.

Marcus stole the show. Everyone was so into him, they said that he was so cute, and irresistible, they just had to pinch his cheeks.

The food was delicious, they ate until they were satisfied, then made it back to their room.

After an hour had passed, they dressed in their bathing attire, and went down to the beach.

They took turns going in and out of the clear water, then they both went with Marcus alongside the edge of the shoreline.

Marcus was amazed with the water, and the small waves.

After a long period on the beach, they returned to their room.

The following day, they planned a visit to an old fort which was in the historical district of the city, this fort had been built in 1617.

Knowing that they had a long day ahead of them, away from the hotel, they decided to have breakfast at the hotel before they left for the day's activities.

While at breakfast, Mark left the table to visit the bathroom, and at the same moment, Brenda, and her family came in to have breakfast, and she noticed Cindy at the table.

"Hi Cindy," she called, "what a surprise."

"Hello Brenda, it is so nice to see you too."

"Meet my husband, and my two boys. This is your son? He is so adorable."

They spoke for a while about what had been going on in the clinic, since left.

Brenda gave Cindy details about her ex-co-workers, including Dr. King.

But as the adults spoke, the kids ventured off without them noticing.

Eventually Mark came back from the restroom, and Cindy introduced him to Brenda, and her husband, but when she turned around to introduce him to her sons, she noticed that they and Marcus were not there.

Cindy panicked, but Mark spotted them going to the beach; he quickly ran towards them, and held on to Marcus, and brought the boys back to their parents.

"I let go of his hands for one second, and within a minute he was gone, I am so sorry, it happened so quickly," she said, as she apologized to Mark.

"Had I stayed another 5 minutes in the bathroom, we could have had a tragedy on our hands," Mark said.

As they went back to the room, they argued about what had just happened.

Mark brought up the fact that he suggested that Marcus stay home with his grandparents, and that would not have happened, but Cindy snapped back at him.

It took about an hour, before the two of them brought their communication back to a civilized level.

They put away their differences, and made up, and then agreed to continue with their day's activities.

Apart from the morning's incident, the rest of the weekend was flawless, they enjoyed the sights, and the adventures.

Later in the evening, they sat on the balcony of their hotel room, which overlooked the beach, pool, and terrace.

They sat there and were entertained from the live band that was playing on the terrace.

Marcus fell asleep, and after tucking him in bed, they shared a private session between them, after which, they prepared their belongings, before they went to sleep, for their trip back to Houston.

In the early morning, they left for the airport, to take their flight to Houston.

They arrived in Houston, and before they went home, they went to their favorite restaurant to have lunch.

On their way home, Cindy was very quiet, and seemed distant, and Mark assumed that she was thinking of what almost happened to Marcus in Mexico.

But he chose not to ask her, because he did not want any confrontation, if that was the case.

Mark tried to avoid stressful situations, both at home and at work, he was very mindful of what he went through with his health.

They got home and sat on the couch after they laid their baggage aside, but because they were so tired, they napped there for a short period of time.

Cindy, when she woke up, prepared a light meal for them before they retired for the night.

Before Mark left for work, Cindy thanked him for a wonderful weekend, and for the great birthday gift.

Cindy's mind was on Dr. King; after she spoke to Brenda in Mexico, she called him on the job, to avoid any issue with his wife.

The nurse hesitated, and told her Dr. King was busy, and she would not be able to transfer her call to him, but Cindy insisted that she had to talk to him, and that it was very important.

After being so persistent, the nurse finally put the call through to Dr. King.

"This is Dr. King; how can I help you?' he asked

"If you desire to," Cindy replied.

"Is there a problem Mrs. Jackrose? Are you in distress? I can't remember meeting you, but how can I help you?"

"Junie, this is Cindy," and she laughed.

"Did you get married? Because I can't recall your last name being Jackrose. Did you forget to send my invitation?"

"Not yet, this is my fiancée's last name." hopefully in February, it will be my last name, for keeps, and consider that your invitation"

"Don't play around, I need a formal invitation, and by the way, what prompted you to call me today? And seeing you did not call my personal phone, but called me here, is everything okay Health-wise?"

Cindy told him about Mark, and what he went through, and told him how he had recovered satisfactorily.

"How are you and your wife doing? What is the total in kids, six, seven?" and she laughed jokingly.

"I know you expect me to be fruitful, but I am not that fruitful, my quiver can only hold so much, but seriously, I have one beautiful little girl, and you know if she is beautiful, she looks like her mother."

"Looking for compliments for your wife, or sympathy for you? No chance."

"Enough about me, what about you? How many kids do you have? And where are you working? And how are you being treated at work, and at home?"

"I have a three-year-old son, he is as handsome as his dad."

"I don't know his dad, but if he looks anything like his mom, he is one handsome dude."

"Well thanks, I see you still have that crush on me, see how you are flattering.?" And she laughed jokingly.

"You are right, I never stopped thinking about you, I am always hoping that everything was okay with you.

"My wife and I are doing okay, although sometimes the things that she does, makes me question her motives for being with me, but that is another story, for another time."

"I have to say goodbye for now. I have taken up so much of your valuable time, and by the way, I am doing fine, and am being treated good at work, and excellent at home."

"I always have time for you, so feel free to connect with me anytime you feel the need to."

"Okay, I will, and you will get your invitation. Take care my friend, and until then, be good."

Cindy felt good after speaking with Junie, she was happy that she had a friend that she could depend on and could tell of her issues.

Chapter *SIXTY-EIGHT*

LATER THAT EVENING WHEN Mark came home, she could tell that he was upset.

"What's up buddy?" she asked him, you came home not your usual self, what's going on?

"This guy at work is trying to push me to the limit, he is constantly not following instructions, and pretends that he doesn't understand what I am saying to him, which I know is false, because I hear things around in the office, how he planned to make my life miserable, because he said, he was the one that was supposed to be promoted, but instead they promoted me."

"Honey, don't stress out about this, it is not worth your time, just be careful with this guy, and keep eye on him, but otherwise, just continue to do your job, and run this by your manager."

"I wish it was that easy, but I will talk to my manager concerning this matter."

"Thanks for your support, I can always count on you."

"Cool, but take my advice, and stop stressing, it is not going to do you any good."

The next day, Mark did as Cindy told him, he spoke to his manager, but Chris, saw him in the office, and just knew that he was reporting him, and made note of it.

The next few weeks, he was quiet, and did not get in Mark's way.

Mark noticed the change in his attitude, and was very pleased with that change of attitude, and hoped it would last.

Cindy informed Mark, that she was scheduled to work on Thanksgiving weekend, so he would have to go to his or her parents for dinner, or they could order some food, and have dinner when she got home.

"I will be okay, Marcus and I will go to my parents, then swing by Karen's."

"Sounds like a plan. We will be ordering food at work, so I will be fine."

"I called mom, and she will be cooking, and will be expecting to see you and Marcus."

David and Lisa were also coming home for Thanksgiving, and Karen was very happy, especially when she found out that Lisa was expecting.

When everything ended, Mark and Marcus made their way home, where Cindy was patiently waiting.

"How was it?" she asked.

"Great," Mark replied, "also we found out that Lisa is expecting."

"Let me call David, how come he did not tell me," she said.

"Because it was a surprise, he wanted to reveal it at Thanksgiving dinner."

"Hopefully, I will see them at Christmas, if not, at our wedding."

"Oh, speaking about wedding, the planner called, and said, she had secured the Jeffers's banquet hall, on Meadows Lane for the reception."

"That is a good location, and a good place to have it," Mark said.

"Cindy do you realize how close we are to that wedding date? Once Christmas is over, it is all quick pace to that date."

"Mark, I can't wait, I have been dreaming of this day for a long time, I can't wait for this to happen."

The rest of the weekend, they spent at the mall, at the park, and at church.

The following few weeks were very busy at work, for Cindy, the Christmas season, always had the most emergencies, and most of it had to do with alcohol, and the busiest time of the year.

Because of all the actions that took place at the hospital, Cindy was extremely tired, and could hardly wait for her time off, so she could get away from these hectic schedules, and the madness of the season.

Mark and Cindy packed a few items in a travelling bag, and took Marcus, along with Happy their dog, and went to David and Lisa's house, to spend a few days, where they could relax and enjoy some family time; also, Cindy was longing to see Lisa and was eager to help her with her pregnancy.

Since Christmas day was in the middle of the week, Cindy and her family planned to stay at David's until Sunday.

David was thankful that his baby sister came to spend Christmas with them; he always loved being around her, and she had developed a good relationship with Lisa, his wife.

On their way back home, Cindy told Mark, "That was a great relaxing weekend, oh, how much I needed that, I hope I can get another one of these weekends, before the wedding.

Mark was in total agreement, and said, "they should make it happen."

Chapter SIXTY-NINE

On New Year's Eve, Cindy and Mark sat on the couch and followed the activities that were taking place in New York, and as they watched the gathering in Time Square on the television, Cindy said to Mark, "I wished that I was there right now."

"Not me, once is enough for me, and I am very comfortable on my couch watching it," Mark said smiling.

While they were watching, and listening to what was going on the television, they heard various sirens echoing in the background; at first, they thought it was on the television, but soon realized that it was in their vicinity.

And almost instantly, the breaking news notification came up on the screen, and the reporter announced that there was a massive explosion that just occurred a few minutes ago.

It was reported that a trailer that was used for storing and selling fireworks had exploded in the Brooks neighborhood.

"From all those sirens that I heard, it must be very bad, I hope that you won't be called to go in to assist."

"If I have to, I will gladly go, I am always thinking of helping others first before I think of anything else."

They were listening to the news on the radio, while they kept watching the concert and performances that continued around the globe.

The report came in that five people had lost their lives, and seven were injured, two seriously.

This news put a damper on their spirit, but there was nothing they could do to change the circumstances of what had happened.

They continued enjoying the celebrations, and continued to watch attentively, as the host, and hostess, continued the countdown in Time Square, toward the new year.

As they came closer to the finale, the people shouted and screamed at the top of their lungs.

Marcus, woke up, and came looking for his mom; he could not sleep because of all the noise from the fireworks that were going on in the neighborhood.

The ball landed on the ground, and the celebrations went into high gear.

"This is going to be a good year for us," Mark said, "I can feel it."

"I believe so too," replied Cindy, "we will accomplish much, and we will put all the negatives behind us."

Then she leaned over and gave him a big kiss.

"Ewe, mommy, what are you doing to daddy?" he barely could talk, but he wanted an explanation.

"My dear, mommy loves daddy, and is just letting him know that."

"Poor boy, like he knows what love is, and this image is going to be on his little mind for a while, but hopefully we will get the opportunity to explain it to him.

"What are we going to eat today?" Mark asked.

"Not sure," Cindy replied, "I think I will make a good soup like my mother usually does on New Year's Day."

"Actually, I was thinking of going to the restaurant on Smith street to have some black eyes peas; there is a saying that eating them on New Year's day brings you luck." Mark said.

"Listen to you, I thought you said, that you don't believe in luck? I can see your mom going off, if she hears you saying that. You know she doesn't believe in luck, but blessings."

Off they went to have some black eyes peas.

Cindy was not complaining about that, in contrast, she was happy, she did not have to toil and do any cooking that day, not that it was a bother, but it was a relief.

"Good food, eh?" Cindy expressed.

Mark could not disagree with her, "yes it was, I really enjoyed it."

"I have been passing by here quite often, but never thought of going in, but now I know why they are busy most of the time, the food is good. I will definitely add this to one of my favorites."

Cindy's cousin, Johanna, was moving in with them so she could babysit for them, she planned on being there on January 2nd, and Cindy was looking forward to that, she had a nice relationship with her.

When they got home, Cindy prepared a few sandwiches, along with the leftovers from the restaurant, for Mark to take to work the next day.

Cindy took the day off, so she could welcome Johanna.

She was so happy to see Johanna, she knew that Johanna coming to live with them would be a great help for them, especially going through the stress of the upcoming wedding.

Johanna fitted in right away, and was excited about the wedding, and helped wherever she could.

Mark came home, and Cindy introduced him to Johanna, who had Marcus sitting next to her, he was already getting close to her.

The next few days that followed, they worked on their wedding plans, they had received almost all the rsvp cards from the invited guests.

On the weekend, Cindy went to her seamstress to get the finishing touches on her wedding dress, and after she did a few minor adjustments, the dress fit perfectly, and Cindy loved it.

She said, "for the next three weeks, I am going to watch what I eat, because I am not going to put on one pound more, I have to look good on my day."

Preparations continued for the next two weeks, as the day inched closer, and the nerves started to come into play, for both.

Cindy was anxious for the day to come, while Mark was eager for the day to pass.

They continued to help with the organizing until the day before the big day, then they released everything in the hands of those that were designated for the planning and organizing.

Finally! It was wedding day, everything was in place, and everyone was excited, especially the parents of the couple.

The bridal party was on top of everything, ensuring that all went according to plans.

The guys were punctual, and ready to get the action going.

Mark was nervous, and waited patiently, as he stood at the altar with his support team.

Cindy shed a few tears when she remembered her dad and knew that he was not there to walk her down the aisle, but after she composed herself, she prepared to go and meet her prince.

As she walked down the aisle, the pictures, and flashes, came from every corner of the church, as many wanted a picture of her.

Her beauty was immaculate, she was sparkling, her smile could have lit up any dark room.

"Beautiful bride,' that was all you heard from those that were present, as she walked.

Mark stepped down, and gently clasped her hand from the father giver, and held on tightly.

The pastor, who knew both, from a very young age, performed a lovely ceremony. The signing was great, and the songs that were chosen, were very passionate ones.

It was quiet as they looked each other straight into the eyes, as they said their vows to each other, and looking straight at them, was little Marcus.

When it came to that part of the ceremony, where the pastor said, "you may kiss your bride," Mark probably gave the longest kiss that was ever given in that church, Cindy would never forget that moment.

Then the pastor said to the couple, "I now pronounce you husband and wife, what God has joined together, let no man put asunder, go in the peace of the Lord."

The day that Cindy dreamt about for a long time was now a reality.

There were smiles and cheers and congratulations hurled at them, as they walked down the aisle, as husband and wife, for the first time.

After all the pictures were taken, and many gave their blessings, and their well wishes, they left for the reception.

And then the fun began.

The pastor blessed the food and the gathering, and gave a short encouraging speech, before turning over to the master of ceremony.

Sam was ready. He looked at his agenda and began by serenading the newlyweds.

He then called on a few chosen people to say something to the couple and warned them to be brief.

The couple took to the floor to perform their dance, and who knew that Cindy could dance so? She was not a party girl, but her moves were current and timely, she looked like she had been practicing.

The fun continued until the wee hours of the morning, but without the newlyweds; after handing over Marcus to his Granny, they left for Galveston.

Chapter SEVENTY

MARK'S DESIRE WAS TO go to Paris for their honeymoon, bur Cindy did not want to leave her son for a week with someone else while she was that far away.

She promised Mark that they would take that trip soon; by then Marcus would have spent enough time with his grannies that would have enhanced her confidence in leaving him with them.

They arrived and checked into the hotel about 10:15 pm.

Mark had already spoken, and informed the hotel staff, what he needed to be done on their behalf.

He told them that this was his wedding night and he anticipated great service.

They were given a room, overlooking the ocean, and the strip, and could view some of the activities that were taking place there.

The room was decorated nicely, with some lovely bouquets of flowers, and Mark had them spray in the corners of the room, a few drops of her favorite perfume, and on the table were two bottles of well chilled champagne.

On the drawer next to the bed, was an expensive bottle of the finest wine.

Cindy was impressed by the length that Mark went through to make sure that she would have a great night.

They went into the bathtub, and laid in the warm bubbled water, and they played like two kids, having fun in the water, after which, they went into the shower, and helped each other in bathing.

Cindy then slipped into the elegant, revealing, silky lingerie, that Mark bought her not too long ago.

Mark was in his birthday suit and was ready for the occasion.

He then turned the lights off and had the room in total darkness.

"Whoa," Cindy softly said, "are we going to play hide and seek? "Cindy said jokingly.

"Why not?" Mark laughed.

Then he went to the other side of the room, and turned on the other light switch, and a blue soft light, that he had them put in, came on.

"Oh my, this is romantic, I love it," Cindy said, as she blushed, and looked at Mark passionately.

Mark quietly came up to her, and hugged, and kissed her, then he poured some champagne into the glasses, and he took his glass to her mouth, while she simultaneously, did the same to him.

He then took the lotion that he bought secretly for that special moment, and he poured a small portion into the palm of his hands, and passed it gently on her face, then he took a bigger portion, and lotion her neck, and shoulders, and he slowly, slid off her top, and lotioned her upper body, then worked his way to her lower body.

"I know you are not a drinker, nor am I, but for this, our special night, we could have some wine, which will do us good."

She knew she could trust him and agreed to have some wine.

They continued with their night of passion, they made love to each other, in different ways, they did not hold back anything, they went all the way to the wee hours of the morning, until they fell asleep in each other's arms.

Cindy woke up early, about 8 o'clock, and ordered breakfast. She woke up Mark about 9:30am, and they sat on the bed, and enjoyed their breakfast, while they sat there, Cindy said to Mark, "I am so amazed by your performance last night, I know we had some great times before, but last night, you were above and beyond, that sex was out of this world, best I ever had, kudos, to you."

"My Dear, I have been holding back, I was giving out about 80%, because I wanted to save the 100% for this night, I wanted to shine, but there is plenty more from where this came from, just request it, and it is right there."

Cindy jokingly said, "you are so full of yourself, here you are like Tarzan, beating on your chest, but honestly, you did shine."

"Cindy, we have to get married once a week, so we could feel this way all the time."

They rested, and relaxed for another hour and a half, before they checked out, and made their way back home.

"Honey, that is a night that I will never forget," Cindy said.

"Babe, same here, a matter of fact, the whole weekend was very special."

"I looked at you, coming down the aisle, and I saw the most beautiful lady on earth coming towards me, and I said to myself, boy you are so lucky, well blessed."

"Thanks, and that is how I saw you too, very handsome, and charming, and I considered myself very fortunate."

They reached their apartment around 1:30pm, and Mark said, we could leave Marcus at your mom's until the evening time, and we could spend some more quality time with each other."

"Mark, I know you are still in that mood, because you had a great night, and I suspect that you are trying to give Marcus, a brother or a sister, which is not likely right now, but I am only going to stay with you for the next 2 hours, and then, I am going to get my baby."

They made it to Karen's, and knocked on the door, because she left her key home, and Karen said,

"I thought you weren't coming back tonight. What? You don't trust me with Marcus?" and she laughed.

"Yes, we do, that is why we left him with you, but I missed him."

As they entered the house, little Marcus came charging onto them, and shouted, "mommy, mommy."

"Daddy is here too; you did not miss daddy?" Mark asked him, smiling.

"So, you are legal now huh, and I am very proud of you guys, and it was such a beautiful wedding, my congratulations to you again, and I will continue to pray for you."

"Thanks mom, we will take all the prayers that we can get."

"Oh, your gifts from the reception are at Mark's parents' home, are you going over there when you leave here, or go pick them up another time?"

"I think we'll get them at a later time, right now, we just want to get home and relax, Johanna is coming back from her parents later this evening; she will watch Marcus while we try to get some rest."

They both scheduled the next couple weeks off, so they would have the time to get the gifts and sort them out.

"See you later, mom," Cindy said.

"Bye, Mr. and Mrs. Jackrose. I have been waiting a long time to say that, and it felt good saying so. Bye Marcus, granny will see you soon."

"Hi mom, how are you and daddy doing?"

"We are doing okay, are you all coming over?"

"Not today mom, we are too tired, but definitely tomorrow, if it is God's will."

"I am so happy son, that you and Cindy are now married, I waited for that day for a long time."

"Mom, I know you are happy, not because we love each other, but because we are not going to live together and not be married."

"Either way, I am happy for you."

"Mom, I will see you later, say hi to dad."

"Thanks, Mark, you stood up well for us, I like that." Cindy said to him.

"We are moving forward in our lives, we are not looking back, we are married now, and we don't need to deal with what we did before. Mark continued, "baby, I love you, and I will do all I can to defend you, and our son."

"Really appreciated it Mark."

The rest of the weekend, they just stayed home and rested.

On Wednesday, they went to see Mark's parents, they spent some time with them, and then collected their gifts, and left.

When they got back to the apartment, they placed the gifts into the closet in Johanna's room.

"Hopefully, we won't keep them in there too long. I called the realtor yesterday, and he said, he has a house for us to look at, as soon as we are available.

"Since we are off this week, why don't we just take care of that?" Cindy said to him.

"Let me call him and see if he is available tomorrow, if he is, then we will go, if not whatever time he could go this week, we will go."

After breakfast on Thursday, Mark and Cindy, along with their son Marcus, went to meet Hai at the location he directed them to.

The Jackrose' were impressed with the house and where it was located and asked Hai to continue with the sale process.

The house was in Senhouse, which was an upscale neighborhood, and it was situated between their parents and their jobs, it was very close to Mark's job.

Hai worked very quickly to get the sale of the house completed, he let them know when the closing was, and how soon they would be able to move in.

Cindy was very excited; she dreamt of owning a house, and now it was going to be a reality.

Chapter *Chapter* SEVENTY-ONE

ON MAY 20TH, THEY moved into their house, the first thing they did, was to invite the pastor to come and bless the home.

After they had organized and purchased most of what they needed for their house, they sent invitations to family and friends to come and celebrate with them.

"There is a big difference between leasing an apartment, and owning your own home, I'm so glad for Marcus, now he has so much space to play and to roam around." Cindy said.

In August, Cindy said to Mark, that they should hold a birthday celebration for Marcus, for his 4th birthday.

"I will invite my friends and co-workers to bring their young ones to come and celebrate with Marcus."

"You know your birthday is next month? Well, we are going to celebrate big."

"I am not sure about that, but I will think about it."

Texas is hot in the summer, but this year it was hotter than usual, and many spent time at the beach in Galveston, but Mark and Cindy wanted a change from the normal and decided to go to Destin, Florida, to enjoy a week on the beach.

They had been going nonstop from the time they had been married and they needed to get away to enjoy some leisure time.

When they returned to Texas, they felt so much better; they were well rested and less stressed.

Marcus' birthday celebration was successful, and he and the other kids had a blast.

Three and a half weeks after, Cindy had a great celebration for her 28th birthday; many of her friends gathered to celebrate with her and her family.

The next couple of months, they planned for the Thanksgiving holiday weekend.

Everyone voted to have the celebration at the newest house in their group, the Jackrose house.

Thanksgiving week, Katy and her son arrived on Monday. She had asked Mark and Cindy if she could spend at least a week with them, and that Joshua would join them later.

Late Wednesday morning, Shawn and Liz arrived. Shawn planned to stay at a hotel to avoid overcrowding, but Mark and Cindy were completely against his suggestion and assured him there was enough space to accommodate him and his wife.

Wednesday evening was like a little reunion, the close-knit circle of friends were together again, Cindy, Kate, and Liz, being the core of the circle.

So much had changed since they last lived in that apartment in Florida.

There were weddings and additions to families, young ones who would be the new generation.

They told stories and talked of the future, as they gathered that night, cooking and laughing, and having a great time.

Thanksgiving Day, the rest of the guests arrived, including Mark's parents, and Karen, along with Donald. Some of Mark and Cindy's friends showed up.

They had lots of food and drinks, and lots of laughter and fun.

The ladies congregated together and spoke about things that interested them, while the guys gravitated toward the football games that were on tv.

What a great time they all had, before it climaxed later that evening.

The following day, the three young ladies, left the children with their dads and grannies and went to the mall to shop and hang out.

"Just like old times," Cindy said, "we are together again."

"Feels so good to let the dads babysit while we roam the malls," Katy said.

"Although I don't like to be away from my little Pookie, I must say, being around you ladies, makes it worthwhile. We should make this an annual tradition, going forward," Katy suggested.

"Fine with me," Cindy agreed.

"I am all for it," Liz said, "it feels good to get out of New York every now and then."

"Hahaha, you all caught us today. I wonder what the conversations were like? You all got to talk about us freely."

"Josh, no sweat, it is just a small, reversed role, and let me say, it felt good." And Katy laughed,

And all the ladies that were there, agreed, and laughed loudly.

The remainder of the week went by quickly.

Joshua left early Saturday morning because he was scheduled to play a game on Sunday. Most of the other guests left on Sunday.

The following week, Mark and Cindy started decorating their house for the Christmas season.

They bought lots of decorations, since it was their first Christmas at their new house.

They wanted Marcus to have a great time, a time he would remember.

They did the decorating inside, while they hired a contractor to do the outside of the house and yard.

The few weeks that led up to Christmas day were very busy; it seemed like more people were out shopping this year, than previous years.

Everywhere was crowded, it made it hard for them to get what they needed.

And yes, the traffic was a mess; it took a long time to go from one point to another, and it was frustrating.

Christmas day was beautiful for those that loved the cold weather and snow, which was unusual for Texas.

Donald, Karen, and Kellie, who was home for the holiday, came over to enjoy the day with Cindy and the family.

After eating, they opened their gifts, most of which were for Marcus. He was so excited and started playing with his toys immediately, especially the little truck he sat in and could drive himself around.

Joshua gave him a child basketball hoop, hoping that he would turn out to be a great player.

Mark left the ladies and went into the bedroom to watch basketball, because his team was playing, but unfortunately, his team lost, and he was disappointed.

He came out when Karen and Donald were ready to leave, and said, "it was nice having you over, thanks for coming, we enjoyed your company."

"We had a great time, and you did a great job with the decorations; next year I will have you do my house," Karen said jokingly.

After they left, Cindy said to Mark, "I noticed you went to hide and to be away from my folks."

"Not really, you got it wrong. I wanted to watch my game, and I didn't want to take over the tv in the living room, knowing that you would want to watch it."

"Donald was lost around us, I thought you should have invited him to come and watch the game with you."

"Cindy, I was not sure if you would accept Donald being in your bedroom."

"Anyway, this was just a little misunderstanding, hopefully it will be different the next time."

"Honey, tomorrow I want to go shopping to look for a BBQ pit, hopefully I will get it on sale, seeing it is the day after Christmas."

"Sound goods, I might tag along."

"Not a problem since you are paying, "he said, also, I need to call the homeowners association office to see what their policies on fireworks are, because I want to get a few and celebrate the new year. There is an open field around the corner where I could do that."

"But Mark, that is dangerous, I don't know if that is a good idea."

After debating for a while, Mark scratched the idea.

He got up early Sunday morning and prepared the chicken, and a few strings of sausages and left them there to marinate.

After service, he rushed home, and went straight at it; he was so anxious to try his new grill.

It took him a long time to get everything completed, but at the end, it was worth it.

He got lots of praise from his wife, Karen, and his parents, who came over because they were invited.

"Good, now you can ease up the cooking duties from me."

"Not really, I've heard you are not supposed to eat too much of BBQ meat, because it is not healthy for your lungs."

"Nice try, Mark, hahaha, your lungs, why not your colon or intestine?" she laughed.

Monday at work, one of his friends invited him and his family to a gathering on New Year's night, but   Cindy was not inclined to go, and after they had a strong discussion, he declined the invitation.

It was a good thing they didn't, because something terrible happened that night at the gathering.

One of the kids that was there at the house was outside with some other people watching fireworks, when a stray bullet struck him in the shoulder.

He was quickly rushed to the hospital where they performed surgery on him.

When the news reached the Jackroses, they were so sad to hear the bad news, and were happy that they had decided not to go.

Mark thanked God for keeping them from going and knew He worked everything for their good, and he apologized to his wife for the argument he had with her concerning going to the gathering.

In their neighborhood, there was a great display of fireworks, and it lasted for a good while.

As midnight approached, Cindy said to Mark, "honey, I can't believe it's already a new year, seems like only a few months ago, we were celebrating and here we are again."

"Babe, that is why we can't take any day for granted, we have to make the best of each day God blesses us with."

"Well said, honey, life is too short to waste even one day, we have to appreciate every minute that we are allowed to exist."

They did their traditional devotion, right around midnight. They thanked the Lord for seeing them through the old year and they trusted him for the upcoming year.

When they woke up later in the day, Cindy cooked a simple meal, and after they ate, and relaxed for a while, and went to the neighborhood park to spend some time with Marcus.

When they got home, they were all tired, and Marcus was already asleep, and they were happy about that; they stayed up for a short while, and then went to bed early.

Mark and Cindy had planned to go to Paris for their anniversary, but changed the time to September, around Cindy's birthday. They planned to have a low-key celebration for their anniversary.

Chapter SEVENTY-TWO

FRIDAY MORNING, THE DAY of their anniversary, they left for San Antonio to spend the weekend. They stayed at a hotel overlooking the riverwalk.

Saturday morning, after breakfast, they took Marcus to the amusement park, and that took most of the day; they got to the hotel and after having dinner, they went to the riverwalk, to walk around, and to do a little bit of shopping.

Later they went up to their room and sat on the balcony to watch the boats go back and forth on the river.

It was a very busy night on the riverwalk; because it was Valentine weekend, many came to the riverwalk to celebrate their love.

After a lovely, peaceful, and relaxing weekend, Sunday afternoon, they drove back to Houston.

Since they were both off Monday, they bypassed their house and went to visit their parents.

They stopped at Mark's parents and spent a few minutes with them, and as expected, they were happy to see Marcus, their only grandchild.

Laurie asked Mark when they would be getting another grand-child, and Mark made it clear to her that he was not the one in control, but God was, and He would do it in His own time.

"But are you trying? "She asked.

"Mom, let's leave that alone, it will happen at the right time, don't worry."

"Don't get so upset with me, I was just being curious, no need to be hostile."

"I am sorry, mom, if you took it that way, but that is not what I meant."

"Okay, okay, leave these folks alone, these are grown folks, we don't need to be in their business." Jacob said.

They spent a few more minutes there, before they left for Karen's house.

"What a surprise, "Karen said, "I did not expect to see you all."

"Since we are off tomorrow, we decided to come over and spend some time with you. Are we cool or what? Cindy said laughingly.

"You all are always welcome here, especially Marcus, he is more desirable to see than the three of you all standing here," Karen joked.

They spent almost two hours with Karen and Donald. They got home close to midnight.

But they did not go to sleep until about three in the morning.

Cindy said to Mark, "it looked like you were trying to fulfill your mother's wish last night, you were in that kind of mood, let's hope it did not happen."

"What do you mean by not wanting it to happen? I thought you wanted another child?"

"Yes, but not at this moment, I am thinking, say the next year and a half, when Marcus is a little older."

Mark knew that arguing with Cindy was a waste of time, because once her mind was made up, it would take a miracle to change it.

It was that time again, another celebration, Mark's birthday.

But they decided to have a low-key celebration, amongst them.

The four of them went to dinner at his favorite restaurant.

Later at home, Cindy had ordered a small cake, so they had some of it, along with some wine from a bottle Mark had purchased a while back.

While celebrating, Mark said to Cindy, "honey, I am getting old, twenties flew on by and I don't want my thirties to pass me by without Marcus having a brother or a sister."

"Stop stressing, what will be, will be. You will have your child soon, you are still young, you are now in your prime of your life, and I have evidence of that."

"Thanks, babe, for the flattery, I like it," he said blushing.

Chapter SEVENTY-THREE

Work was getting very hectic for Mark, not because of the work itself, but because of the toxic environment.

Although, he was liked by most of his co-workers, there were a few who disliked him, and made it very difficult for him to perform, like he would love to.

Chris had eased up with his pressure, but recently was back at him with more intensity than he had before.

Mark promised him that if he continued with his nasty attitude, and if his production kept going down, then he would leave him with no choice but to let him go.

Chris did not like what Mark said to him and promised not to take his threat lightly.

Mark came home one evening and told his wife that he did not want to work with his company anymore, and he would look for another job with another company.

"Honey, I am so sorry that you have to go through this dilemma and have to give up something that you worked so hard to achieve, but whatever you choose to do, you have my full support."

"If you want to leave now, you can, I know it won't be easy, but I thank God that he has put us in a good position, that we can sustain until you find something that you would love to do."

"Babe, I won't quit until I find something first, I would not do that to you, not if it's in my control, and besides, I am not going to let someone run me from my job, I would have to leave on my own terms."

"All that is true, but people like that, you don't take their words lightly, I like to be safe, anyway, be on your guard."

"That is one reason, I have not let him go, because I want to keep him close."

A few months after Mark had that conversation with Cindy, Chris left the job, he told his friend that he had found another job.

That was great news for Mark, and when he told that to Cindy, she could not have been happier.

Mark was relieved, although he still had a few who were against him, but not to the extent that it caused fear or discomfort.

Mark was thankful that he did not have to look for another job, he was sure that he could deal with the rest of the disgruntled associates, but the worst of the bunch was gone.

The next few months were peaceful and enjoyable at work, and Mark was less stressed.

He was ready to enjoy his life, and to be more involved with his family.

Chapter SEVENTY-FOUR

I*t* finally came the time to visit Paris, after putting it off on numerous occasions.

They booked their flights and their hotel room and planned to be there a few weeks.

Cindy felt comfortable leaving Marcus with her mom, he was bigger and older, and her mom was home fulltime, and she had Johanna to help her, because she decided to stay with Karen instead of going back home.

They woke up early Sunday morning, and make sure that Marcus was okay, and all his stuff were in order, before taking him to Karen.

Jacob took them to the airport early Sunday afternoon, they had to be there at least an hour and a half before their flight, because they were travelling internationally.

The flight to Paris took almost 11 hours, it was a non-stop flight.

The trip from the airport to the hotel was relatively short because of the proximity of the hotel to the airport.

As soon as they checked in, Cindy called her mom to let her know that they had made it there safely, and to check on Marcus.

"Did he miss us; did he cry?"

"Of course, he did," she replied, "but he is okay now."

"Okay, we will talk to you later, we are tired from the flight and about to take a nap."

She and Mark did not wake up until 8 pm.

She called her mom again, then they went downstairs to have something to eat.

As they sat at the table, Mark said, "finally, after much planning we are in Paris, we are going to make the best of it, you and I are going to have a great time over here."

"There are not too many things that I can recall, that have you more excited than how I am seeing you now, I am happy for that, because I want you to be happy."

They stayed up late into the night, preparing an agenda, and setting up schedules for their time in Paris.

They listed several places that they desired to visit and planned on how they would get around and how everything fit into their budget.

The first thing on their list was the Eiffel Tower.

"If I don't go anywhere else, it would not matter, but I must go there. I heard and saw too many images of that tower for me to miss it."

Before reaching the tower, they were impressed with the area Champ De Mars, the place where the tower was located. They felt that welcoming feeling and the warmth of the environment.

"Oh my, the tower is all that I heard about and saw in pictures, I am sure glad that I got to see it," Mark said to Cindy.

"Yes, it is beautiful and interesting," Cindy replied.

They took lots of pictures of the tower and of them by, and in the tower.

During the few weeks, they visited, Louvre Museum, they went on a sightseeing cruise on the Seine River, they enjoyed the Moulin Rouge cabaret show, and to conclude, they visited Versailles Palace. They also dined at some of the most exquisite restaurants.

Cindy said to Mark, "these few weeks we did so much, we visited so many places, and had the greatest of time, we spent quality time together, I cannot complain, but must say thank you, these were a few of the most wonderful weeks in my life."

"I love you dearly, Mark, and would not want to be with anyone else but you."

"That saying see Paris and die,' now I understand why people say so, but the dying part, I am not ready for. I still have a lot to offer to you, Marcus and my friends. I would love to bring Marcus here when he is older, I am pretty sure he would enjoy it."

They finished packing their bags, and suitcases, and then made sure that they had their transportation for the airport arranged for the morning.

They then went to bed and before falling asleep, they made the best of their last night in Paris.

They had a smooth flight back to Texas, they slept most of the flight.

"I loved Paris, but it is sure nice to be home in America." Mark expressed.

Waiting for them at the airport were Karen, and their little man Marcus.

As soon as he saw them, he quickly detached from granny's hand, and bolted towards them with all the speed that he could muster.

Cindy hugged and kissed him, as she told him how much she missed him.

"Mommy, granny give me ice-cream by the place." Marcus said excitedly.

"You are telling on me young man?" Karen said jokingly.

"You all look pretty relaxed, that means you all had a good time." Karen said.

"Oui, oui, bon time," Cindy replied, as she laughed at her half French, and half English.

On their way from the airport, Cindy said they would just spend the rest of the day at Karen's and would go home in the morning.

They were so tired, that they went to bed at the earliest opportunity, and did not get up until later that evening. They stayed up for another couple of hours, before they went back to bed, and did not wake up until the morning.

When Donald and Karen came back from church, they, along with Marcus, and Johanna, left for home.

Monday morning, when Cindy went back to work, her manager requested that she come to visit her in her office, as soon as she had some free time.

Cindy was concerned, because she knew she had been gone for a week, and she was not sure if something came up while she was gone, because she could not recall having any issues with anyone before she left, so she was nervous.

Around 10:15am, when she completed her assignment, she hesitated for a while, then got the courage, and went into the office.

"Hi, Ms. Joseph, here am I," she said nervously.

"Please have a seat, and can you please give me a minute, while I wrap this up?"

"Sure ma-am," Cindy replied politely.

"Now, you might be wondering why I asked to meet with you, and a thousand things might be going through your mind, but there is nothing to be worried about."

Cindy took a deep breath and felt less nervous than when she stepped into the office but was still concerned.

"Nicole the head nurse is set to retire at the end of the year, and I was wondering if you would be interested in taking up that position? You do not have to give me an answer now, but please consider it."

"I will, I mean, I will consider it, and will get back to you with an answer shortly."

"Thank you for considering me, I really do appreciate that."

"You have done well, and you have a great attitude, and most of the other nurses think highly of you."

Cindy could not wait to get home to share the news with Mark.

"Hi Mark, hi Johanna. Come here my little champion, Marcus, how was your day? Did you behave today? You were not nutty today, I hope."

"Mommy, see, I wrote my name, I count 1. 2 .3 .4 .5, as he moved his fingers as an illustration.

"Good, who taught you that?"

"Mommy, Johna," and he pointed to her.

"Great job, Johana, I really do appreciate that, thank you."

"Mark, I have something very important to discuss with you when we settle down later."

"Should I be worried or concerned?" he asked.

"No, you did not do anything wrong, well not yet." And she smiled and walked away to the bedroom.

He followed her quickly to the bedroom, "are you pregnant?" he asked, hoping that she was, "a little Frenchie?"

"You wish, but no, I am not, and besides, we just came back, one week ago and you expect to have a baby?" and she laughed at him.

"Mark, here is what happened at work today. My manager called me into her office to address an important matter. I was worried and honestly, I was scared, because I did not know if anything had happened that involved me while I was gone."

"I hesitated to go in, but I said sooner or later I must face her, so I worked up the courage and went to see her. To my surprise, she offered me the head nurse position because my current head nurse is set to retire at the end of the year."

"I told her I would get back to her shortly with my answer. So, what do you think I should do?"

"I am excited, but yet there is doubt in my mind, if I am able to handle the job because I am so timid; how will I deal with these grown people?"

"I am looking at you, and all that you are going through with the people you supervise, I don't know if I would like to go through that."

"Come here, my dear." And she sat next to him, as he embraced her and said, "I know you can do this, it is because of the way you worked and carried yourself, you are chosen to lead this team."

"You can do anything, if you put your mind to it, you are not coming from the outside to do this, you are familiar with these nurses, just continue to be you, and they will continue to respect you, and if anything, negative comes along, I know you will deal with it, You did not go looking for that job, it came looking for you, that is confirmation that it was sent to you by God. So congrats, on your new job."

"My turmoil at my job should not discourage you from excelling at your job; our jobs and environment are totally different."

"Thanks babe, for the pep talk, I am feeling much more confident now, I will let her know by Friday."

"After work on Friday, we will go out to have a celebration dinner, and that is on you, because you can afford it," and he enjoyed teasing her.

As planned, Cindy told Ms. Joseph that she would accept the position when it became available at the end of the year, and she thanked her for offering the position to her.

After dinner, they dropped off Johanna and Marcus at the house, and went to the movies.

On their way home from the movies, Mark was in disbelief, "how can you sleep in an action movie like that?" he asked Cindy.

"Simple," Cindy replied, "when your body is so tired, and your mind is occupied with all sorts of things, it doesn't take much to sleep in a movie theatre."

They were surprised that their little man was still up when they got home, he was waiting for them. Johanna said, he has been fighting sleep, and it did not take long for him to soundly fall asleep once they were home.

Before retiring to their bed, Cindy asked Mark about the upcoming thanksgiving, and if he had any suggestions for the weekend.

"Not really," he responded, "but it should be someone else's turn to host, I think David."

"I will check with mom tomorrow to inquire about that. David hates hosting anything, but if it's his turn, he will have to."

The next day, she found out that it was his turn, and her mom assured her that he would host it.

Chapter *SEVENTY-FIVE*

MARK'S SITUATION AT WORK had gotten much better, and thus his stress level was way down from what it was. The employees that were hostile towards him were more appreciative of him now, and he was enjoying his job again. This all happened when Chris left. He was the influencer and instigator of all the hostility, and Mark kept thanking God that he had left.

Cindy's upcoming promotion was not made public, her manager did not want any rift among the crew, she wanted to wait until the said time, before she informed them.

Most of the family and friends came to the Thanksgiving celebration, and surprisingly, David and his wife did well in hosting it, and Cindy commended them for a job well done.

Thanksgiving is never done with this family unless some shopping takes place.

So early Friday morning, they went to the mall, and shopping outlets to see what bargains they could get.

Cindy tried to get most of her Christmas gifts and presents.

Sunday, most people left.

Shawn hated that he had to go back to the bitter cold, but he said he still would not trade New York for anywhere else.

Later that night, Cindy said to Mark, "why don't we go to New York for Christmas?"

"Cindy, you know I am not a fan of the cold, what makes you believe that I want to be there for Christmas?"

"Honey, I would love for Marcus to see and experience snow; he would love playing in it."

"Don't use Marcus as your bargaining chip, he would not have the slightest idea of what snow is."

"Also, Mark, when I get that new position, it will be hard for me to get my vacations, around Christmas time."

"Anyway, if you don't feel the need to go, we won't go, I will be okay with that too."

"So now you are trying psychology on me, trying to make me feel guilty?"

"Mark, if that is the way you feel, we definitely don't have to go."

At the end of all that going back and forth, they agreed to go.

For the next two weeks, they organized their affairs, including accommodations for Happy the dog, which they decided would be at Mark's parents.

Jacob was to come by and turn on the lights and take care of certain things in the house.

They left Texas on Sunday in the evening, by choice, so that Marcus could see New York Skyline at night, because they were certain he would enjoy the lights.

And he did not let them down. He was so excited, and would not stop pointing, and talking, especially as they were descending, and Johanna also enjoyed seeing that beautiful landscape. She had never been that far away from Texas, and had not flown on a plane, much less at night.

She was amazed by all that she saw, and was awestruck, when they drove downtown Manhattan.

They made it to Brooklyn, at Shawn and Liz house, and were greeted and welcomed by both.

"You must be hungry; I prepared some light food for you."

"Thanks, Liz," Cindy said, "we really appreciate that," as they went to put their bags in the bedroom.

"Johana, you can make yourself comfortable in the room at the end of the hallway."

"Thanks, Liz, and I love your place, it is lovely."

"Oh, thanks, Johanna, we tried our best to make it homey."

The following day, they went downtown to do some shopping and sightseeing, and you could imagine how thrilled Johanna was to see the beauty of New York; she was surprised to see all the people on the streets, coming from Texas, this was unusual for her, she had never seen a place that busy.

They made it back to the house and were very tired from all that walking; for the remainder of the day, they relaxed.

Christmas eve, they stayed up late wrapping gifts and doing other things; thus they got up late on Christmas day.

They all chipped in and got the meal on the table as quickly as they could.

It was cold and snowing outside, so they tried to stay as warm as possible.

But Cindy was excited, she hustled with her meal because she was eager to get outside to take Marcus to play in the snow.

Mark went with them for a couple minutes and took a few pictures, then went back into the comfort of the warm house.

Meanwhile, Marcus, Cindy and Johanna, were having a ball, as Shawn and Liz looked on, and laughed, as they saw the fun Cindy and her partners were having.

Then Mark joined them again, this time for a longer period, and took more pictures, and videoed them, then retreated to the house.

Finally, Cindy said, "that is enough, let us go in."

"Mark, I am so glad we came, that was a lot of fun, and I am sure Marcus enjoyed it, and won't forget that experience."

The day after Christmas is always filled with bargains at the stores, and they did not hesitate to take full advantage of that.

It was quite an outing for them, the team from Texas, got to ride on a train for the first time in their lives quite an experience for them.

"Thank you, Mark and Cindy for inviting me to come here with you, I cannot be more thankful than I am right now, I am having a great time, thanks again," Johanna said.

They continued sightseeing and their exploring New York for another hour and half before returning to the house.

They were excited, waiting on the celebrations for New Year's Eve.

Cindy had desired to go to Times Square for the dropping of the ball, but with Marcus, that was difficult; she would have to leave him with Shawn, and she did not want to put him through that, and furthermore, Mark said he would not go, because he said, once you had experienced it one time, that was all you needed.

As the hours passed by, the anticipation of the new year grew more exciting, as folks filled in the square, and took their places as they anxiously waited for the entertainment to begin.

An hour before the ball dropped, they gathered in the living room, and watched the various activities that were taking place throughout the world.

They got their champagne, and other snacks together, as they waited for the New Year.

There were entertained by all the personalities that performed, and listened attentively, for the start of the countdown.

The crowd got louder, as they came closer to the end of the count, then finally, the ball dropped, and there was singing, dancing, and shouting, as well wishes were shared amongst the crowd.

And the fireworks were seen coming from all directions.

They, in the house, toasted each other with their champagne, and extend wishes to each other, as they all hope for a prosperous New year. They celebrated until the early hours of the morning.

The ladies remained in their beds for a while, but the guys got up to watch their football games.

After dinner, they sat in the living room, and shared their wishes, and dreams for the New Year, and for the future.

Because they had to travel next day, they went to bed early.

"How quickly a week and a couple days went by," Cindy said, as they headed towards the airport.

As expected, the airport was very crowded, as people who travelled for the holidays, were coming and going.

Shawn, and Liz, hugged and say goodbye to the Jackrose family, and Johanna, then left for home.

Approximately half an hour into the flight, they fell asleep, when they woke up, they were preparing to land into Houston.

Donald was there at the airport, waiting on them.

On their way home, he filled them with in with information, and the news that happened while they were gone.

Cindy, and the others, spent the night at her mom's house, the next day, they went home.

They spent the rest of the week preparing for their work week.

Chapter SEVENTY-SIX

MONDAY MORNING, WHEN SHE returned to work, Ms. Joseph asked to see her, at least this time she was not that nervous, because she knew what it was about.

"I would like for you to complete a few documents, so we can make it official that you are now the head nurse."

Cindy carefully went through the documents, and after discussing a few concerns, she completed the signing of the documents.

Ms. Joseph, called for a short meeting, and informed the nurses that were present, that as of Monday, Cindy would be the new Head Nurse.

She said, she would inform the rest of the crew, and would send an email to the company's website.

Cindy was very happy, although she feared the unknown, but she remembered her talk with her husband, and told herself she could do it, and she promised to do a great job.

She came home, and said "Mark, it is official I am the Head Nurse of the department."

Again, he congratulated her, and told her how proud he was of her, and assured her that she would do a good job.

"Thanks, dear, I could not have done this without your constant support. We will officially celebrate this achievement Saturday night."

They visited Karen and told her the good news, and she was very happy for her daughter, and congratulated her, and wished her well in the position.

The nurses, on Monday, ordered a cake, and organized a small luncheon to celebrate her new position.

She was moved by their kind act and assured them that she would do her best to make sure they enjoyed their work, and that the department would be run efficiently.

She thanked them for wanting her to be their leader.

The next few weeks, Ms. Joseph guided Cindy in her new role, and Cindy, being a fast learner, grasped the new materials, quickly, and easily. She also was good on retaining information, and was good at following instructions, and directions.

For their anniversary, Mark and Cindy went to Galveston, and spent the weekend at the hotel where they spent the night of their wedding.

This time, it was different, because they brought Marcus and Johanna with them.

Their son enjoyed playing at the beach; he loved the sand and water.

As they laid on the sand and watched him play, Mark said to Cindy, "I can't wait when we will have another little Mark or Cindy running along with Marcus."

"I know," Cindy replied, "but we are almost ready, soon we will be working on that, patience my friend, patience," and she poked at him.

"You realize God has been good to us. He blessed us with a wonderful son, two great jobs and a wonderful family, and great friends."

"Although we were not in the place where we were supposed to be with him, He still blessed us, because he loves us unconditionally, I hope we can emulate that type of love in our relationship, as we mature and grow."

"And speaking about growing older, your birthday is a few weeks away."

"Yes, I know, how quickly that came about, seemed like yesterday, I was a teenager, now I am heading toward middle age." Mark sounded disappointed.

"Be thankful, young man, so many did not make it past thirty, and I know, most of their family members wished that they were still here, so we will be thankful that you are here." said Cindy.

During the weeks that followed, Cindy planned with her mom and Mark's parents to organize a birthday bash for Mark.

The celebration took place at the community center in Karen's subdivision.

Many of Mark and Cindy's friends, and co-workers attended, along with family members.

They had a great time, and Mark appreciated the effort that was put into it, by his wife and the rest of the family.

"Mark, I must say you still look good, you look like you are in your early twenties, except for the little pouch that you are developing, which I hope you keep under control."

"Yes ma-am, always to the point, that I can count on, or else you would not be Cindy."

Cindy and Mark's relationship grew stronger by the day, they learned to tolerate each other and to make each other feel comfortable, but most of all, they respected each other.

The summer this year was extra hot and unbearable, which caused them to be engaged in lots of inside activities, they tried not to be outside unless it was necessary, or when they visited the beach.

Marcus was in his last few months of pre-school and was on his way to kindergarten in the fall.

They planned a birthday party for him, and invited his day care friends, along with their parents. By chance, they chose one of the coolest days of all the hot days to host the Saturday afternoon birthday party.

Surprisingly, almost all the invitees showed up. The kids had a great time, they played a variety of games and ran around the grounds.

The adults also had a great time and were glad for the little outing, and they interacted with each other wonderfully.

"Wow, what a day," Cindy exclaimed, "these kids took all the energy from me, and left me drained."

"Mark, I need a vacation just to recuperate, agree?"

"Definitely, these kids are full of life, and they just keep going on with no intention of stopping, that is until they sit down and fall asleep wherever they rest their heads."

"I am glad we did it though, I know Marcus will remember that day."

"And there will be pictures to jog his memories," Mark said.

"All these birthday celebrations are getting more emotional to me, especially as I get older, it means more to me each passing year, and we are not done yet, we still have you, my dear, to celebrate."

And out of nowhere, he said, "Lord, I am so thankful to have this lady in my life, to call my wife, she is more amazing than I ever expected, and to top it off Lord, you added this bundle of joy called Marcus to strengthen our relationship. Lord, I don't deserve all this goodness from you, but again this is who you are, amazing and awesome." And Mark was overwhelmed with emotion, and was like a different person, like he had an encounter with an invisible being.

Cindy noticed that too, and wondered what brought this on? But she did not say anything, just pondered that in her heart.

Chapter SEVENTY-SEVEN

MARCUS' FIRST DAY OF kindergarten brought great emotional feelings to his parents. Mark was so proud of his little boy, and took lots of pictures and videotaped every little move that he made.

"Cindy, doesn't he look like a little Mark? Sharp, handsome and intelligent."

"Mark, you're full of yourself, but honestly, I am glad that you are a proud papa, many of the other kids, don't have any male figure to see them off to their first day of school."

After lingering around the school premises for a little longer, Mark left and went directly to his job, while Cindy and Johanna went home.

Later in the week, Mark began planning for Cindy's birthday bash. He told Cindy, this might be the last big celebration, because after you reach your thirties, you scale down with these extravaganza celebrations.

"I am in agreement, after a while, it just becomes a ritual and loses its meaning."

Mark did it big; he invited a lot of Cindy's friends to join her family in celebrating her birthday, and he had quite a lot of his friends there too.

Everything went well, and most people left happy and satisfied.

Cindy was very happy the way it turned out, and was very grateful to Mark, and all who helped to make it worth remembering.

Katy, Joshua, Shawn and Liz, with the guile of Mark, all came to surprise her.

But the person who surprised her the most, was Dr. King; she invited him, but he did not reply so she did not think he would attend, but to her delight, he did, and she was extremely happy to see him. She had a strong friendship with him, and was always glad to be around him.

This was a weekend to remember, Mark organized this bash like it was a wedding reception. The food was plentiful and tasteful, and the drinks were in abundance.

The festivities went into the early hours of the morning.

Seeing Josh, Katy, and her nephew, was a pleasure for her, and for Cindy, that made the event worthwhile.

Most of the guest left on Sunday, but Katy and Kevin her son, stayed back, they planned to stay a couple more days with Cindy and the family. They left on Wednesday.

Friday evening, Cindy suggested to Mark, that she wanted to upgrade her vehicle, she wanted to trade in the one she had, for a new one, and he agreed to her suggestion.

In the morning, they left to go to a few dealerships, she was very happy, she did not think Mark would go along with her suggestion, but was she glad, he did.

They found the SUV that she wanted, although the salesman tried to persuade her to get something else, but she had decided on her choice, and nothing that he said could make her change her mind.

She drove out of the dealership, with a fully loaded SUV, like she wanted.

"You have worked so hard, you have gotten a promotion, I believe, that you deserve to have what you desire."

"You can trade in your truck; you have been driving it for a while."

"This is going to be with me for a while longer, I can't see myself getting rid of my truck right now. As a matter of fact, I am going to have this truck long enough to turn it over to Marcus." And he laughed as he said so.

They went to church on Sunday with their new vehicle, so their parents could have a peep at it, and they wanted church to be the first place they went with their vehicle, as a way of saying thanks to God.

The last few months, Mark had been very involved with church activities, he was assigned to mentor the young boys from the youth group, and they loved him and looked up to him.

After service was over, Cindy persuaded her mom to walk with her to her vehicle, and the mom was very surprised to see her new vehicle and congratulated them on their purchase.

They also surprised Mark's parents, by driving up next to them, right before they were ready to leave.

From church, they went to have lunch at the BBQ restaurant, which was a couple miles from the church.

They had a great lunch then went home.

The weather was lovely that day in September, so they decided to sit outside on the patio, and watched Happy run back and forth, as Marcus tried to catch him.

Then Mark popped the question again, "Marcus is past five, and we are not getting any younger, when are we going to try for another child?"

"Boy, you won't give up on that eh?" she replied and laughed loudly.

"You made a promise, and I respected that, now you have to keep your end of the bargain." Mark emphasized.

"Of course, I am going to keep my part of the bargain, we will see what happens."

"Look, see Marcus out there, see how handsome he is, and see how much he desires someone to play with, that is why he is harassing Happy, with a child like this, and a wonderful couple like we are, why wouldn't we not desire another child?"

"We will, my dear, we will."

"We don't have a lot of time, let's not wait until it is too late." Mark replied.

They stayed in the backyard a little while longer, but as it was getting dark, they went back inside, so they could avoid the mosquitos.

Mark, then hooked up his recordings of Marcus at his birthday party, and looked at the recordings again, and was just as excited to watch it, like he did, when he first watched it.

"Is this part of your scheme to send a message to me?" Cindy asked.

"No, it is not, I am just trying to enjoy my boy as much as I can."

"Mark, I am off Labor Day weekend, do you have any plans for that weekend?"

"Not really, I planned on spending quality time with my family."

"Well, my co-worker is having her 40th birthday celebration in Austin, and she has invited us, what do you think about going?"

"If it was a wedding or something of that sort, I would have considered it, but for this, I will pass." He replied.

"I will BBQ on that weekend, and will invite our parents, and a few friends, and we will have a good time."

"Babe, I just wanted to get away, I wanted a different environment, different crowd, but I guess that won't happen."

Mark realized that his wife was disappointed with his answer, and that he would have to be ready for the fallout that was coming his way.

As expected, the next couple of weeks were filled with mood swings from his wife, but he expected that, and he was prepared to deal with the various situations as they came along.

Mark went on with his plans that he had for Labor Day weekend.

On Saturday, he woke up early and prepared to BBQ some chicken parts, and some sausage links.

His parents and Karen brought a few other entrées to add to what he already had.

Cindy did very little, she barely got involved in organizing anything. She was not pleased with his decision that he made a couple weeks back, and she was not going to pretend that it was okay to be dismissed, like she was.

After their parents and friends left, Mark confronted Cindy and expressed his disappointment in the way she behaved.

And the two got into a heated argument and said things that they were not supposed to say to each other.

Later that evening, Mark approached Cindy and asked her, "was all this necessary? You mean you are carrying a grudge for two weeks for something that is so trivial?"

"That is what I am talking about, to you it is simple, and of little value, but just ignoring my input and feelings, is that okay?"

"Anyway," Mark said, "I don't want to fuss about this anymore. Let's put this behind us, and let's move forward, I think we are better than that."

And with that said, he tapped her on her shoulder, and asked, "agreed?"

And she shrugged her shoulders, and said, "whatever."

Within the next couple of weeks, they worked out their differences, and were back to being buddies again.

At work, Cindy was very happy. She excelled in her new position. The push back that she expected from her nurses did not come, but rather, she was surprised how much they gravitated to her new implementations.

Ms. Joseph complimented her on the progress that was made in the department and was pleased with the level of respect she earned from the rest of the nurses.

Cindy believed that this was her calling, and she was very passionate about what she did.

Mark was also enjoying his job and was doing well as a supervisor.

He was more at ease since Chris left the job.

His co-worker and friend Joel told him he met Chris at a store, and said, Chris told him, that he was out of a job, and he also said that Chris blamed him for being out of a job.

Mark assured Joel that all these misfortunes were on Chris, he said, Chris made the decision to quit the job, and to pursue a different avenue in his life, so being out of a job, was his doing.

At the end of the month, Halloween weekend, Mark and his family, along with Johanna, went to Austin, just to get away, and to have some quiet time, and to enjoy some activities.

Saturday morning, Johanna stayed with Marcus, while Mark and Cindy went to the hottest thing in the city that weekend, the college football game.

It was a nail bitter throughout the game, but at the end, the home team won by a field goal.

Later that evening, they all went downtown Austin to have dinner and to browse around.

By night's end, they were tired, and they longed for their beds.

The next day, they checked out early from the hotel, and drove around for about an hour, had lunch, then made their way back to the Houston area.

Chapter SEVENTY-EIGHT

THE NEXT FEW DAYS, Cindy, alongside her husband, and her siblings, planned a surprise birthday celebration for Karen their mom, who was turning 65 years on November 10th.

They secretly planned, and organized the celebration, without Karen knowing what was going on.

The birthday fell on a Wednesday, but they chose to celebrate it on Saturday.

Donald was in on the plan with them, so it made it easier to pull off the surprise without her being suspicious.

David, Joshua, and Shawn, with their families, came in Saturday morning, and hung out at Cindy's house.

Cindy invited Karen's friends, and gave them instructions how to proceed, in order to maintain the secrecy of the event.

Cindy had contacted her mom a few days ago, and invited her to a surprise party, she was holding for Mark, and she said, she would be there.

That day the weather was perfect, God contributed to that occasion. A small cold front came in early in that morning and brought some pleasant temperatures.

Karen and Donald were prompt that night, they were there a minute after 7: pm.

"Hi Cindy, we are here," she said, when she entered the door, "and where is everybody? And where is Mark?"

"I sent him to the store, whenever you hear him pull up, you and Donald will go to the guest room, and stay there until I come to get you, capeesh? I have given the signal to the others, so it should be happening shortly.

Cindy pinned the flag on the door to let everyone know that it was okay to come in.

She opened the door, and motioned to them to keep quiet, then she let them in quietly.

After she was satisfied that most of the guests were present, and had them hide, she went to the guest room, and brought out Karen and Donald.

Karen came out with anticipation of surprising Mark, but to her shock, she was the one who was celebrated.

As she approached the living room, Cindy turned on the lights, and people sprang from all directions, and shouted, happy birthday, and they sang happy birthday to Karen.

She stood there frozen and speechless for a moment. She was in total disbelief when she saw David, and Joshua, along with their families, coming from the direction of Cindy's bedroom, she bowed her head, and was very emotional, then she looked at them all, and said, "thank you."

"David, Joshua, you all were involved in this plan to give your mom a heart attack?" and she laughed jokingly.

Then Joshua said, "Mom, we could not let you pass your 65th birthday without a celebration, you have been here all these years for us, this is the least we could do for you, and by the way, you are now a senior citizen, understand?" and he amused himself with laughter.

"We were, and we are right to this day, very blessed to have you as our mom, you are one special lady, and we thank God for a gem like you." Cindy said emotionally.

Karen was overwhelmed with emotion and expressed her gratefulness to her kids.

After the speeches were over, they went into party mode, and mingled with each other. There was lots of food and drink, and they all had a swell time. It was a night filled with laughter and fun.

At the end of the activities, Karen thanked everyone who attended, and expressed her gratitude to all who made it possible, and to all who helped her celebrate this milestone.

She was pleased to see Mark's parents, and most of her friends from church, and some of her ex-co-workers.

After church on Sunday, those that did not have to travel, and some other friends, joined Karen, Cindy, and some others, to finish the celebration on the beach.

There were lots of food and drinks left from Saturday night and wanted to consume as much as possible of what was left.

When it was all over, and everyone had left, the Jackrose spent their Monday off to relax and to recuperate.

"Babe, I am so proud of you and your siblings, for going above and beyond, to make sure that your mom had a memorable birthday."

"Mark, you played an equal part in making sure it happened, so kudos to you too.'

"I would do anything to ensure that you are happy, you're being happy, makes me happy too." Mark explained.

"Thanksgiving this year, is to be hosted by your parents, I wonder if they remember that," Cindy said to Mark. "Please give them a call, and remind them, so they won't be scrambling at the last moment, or if they are not able, we will host it here."

"I will call them; we are having it at their house."

At the same instance, Mark telephoned his mom.

"Hi mom," he said, "how are you all doing?'

"We are okay, is everything okay?" she asked, concerningly.

"Yes, we are okay, I was just checking to see if you remember that you and dad are the hosts for thanksgiving this year."

"Oh yeah, we remembered, we spoke about it this morning, we have made plans, and we are presently working on a few things for that day."

"If you need our assistance, let us know, I want to make sure everything goes well without any big issues."

Cindy promised to help with the cooking, because she knew that would be a heavy task for Laurie to handle.

A few days later, Cindy called everyone who were supposed to attend, to get confirmation of their attendance.

And everyone she contacted, verified that they were coming, so at least they had an idea how many Laurie and Jacob were cooking for.

Shawn and Liz came in one week earlier because they wanted to spent time with Cindy.

Cindy was happy for that because Liz would help her with the cooking.

Cindy and Liz stayed up late at nights talking about their days in Florida, and reminiscing about old times.

Katie joined them on Wednesday mid-morning, and it felt like a reunion, although it was not too long they were together.

As the guys argued and talked about sports, while watching television, the ladies occupied the kitchen, and tackled the cooking while they joked, laughed, and had fun together.

Karen had asked Katie to stay with her, but Katie had kindly declined, because she wanted to be with Cindy and Liz; she did not want to miss the opportunity to relive some of the past joy that they experienced during their college years.

The turnout at Jacob and Laurie's was huge, it was the biggest group that they had so far, since they started the thanksgiving tradition.

What brought about the great turnout, nobody knows, but there were a few theories that were floating around.

They gathered for prayer, but before Jacob prayed, he said, "Mark, I have a big surprise for you," and then out came out Debra, his sister.

They had not seen each other for several years because she had been living in Switzerland for a while.

He was happy to see her and was glad she made it home for thanksgiving. He hugged her for a long time.

Jacob said the grace, and they lined up, some plates were filled to the brink, while others barely had anything.

They took their food and gathered in little niches here and there, the guys were glued to the games that were on the television. Katie, Cindy and Liz had their own clique, and Mark spent most of his time with his sister Debra, they had so much to talk about.

There was an incident which came about, but as quickly as it was kindled, it was quickly extinguished.

Mostly everyone had a great time. People started filing out by 7pm, and by 9pm, mostly everyone had left, except for the family members and few close friends.

They stayed up late with Debra, asking her about Switzerland, and other European places, with the intention of visiting there soon.

Friday morning, they took the rest of the food and drink, to Cindy's house, and they that remained, gathered there to continue celebrating.

Debra, who tagged along, was very much impressed with Mark, and Cindy's house. She complimented Cindy on the interior decorating of the house, and joked with Mark, and said, he had nothing to do with the decorating.

Later in the afternoon, they dove to one of Houston's most famous malls, and as expected, it was very crowded. Some people came to do shopping, but most of the younger people came just to hang out.

They went to several boutiques and name brand stores, and purchased a few items, mostly for the kids.

They stopped by the food court to get a few items of fast food to munch on.

Before leaving the mall, they stopped at the skating rink, so the kids could enjoy watching people skate.

The children became restless and cranky because they were tired, which was an indication that they had to leave for home.

Even the adults were tired too, and some of them joined the kids and took a nap.

After they were well rested, Cindy asked, "what is on the agenda for tonight?"

"What about movie night?" Mark suggested, "we could rent a few movies and get some popcorn and have a great night."

Most of them agreed, the only problem they had was choosing the movies that they wanted to watch. Everyone had a movie of their choice, but at the end, they had to compromised and they had to vote on the movies that they would rent.

With corn popping, along with other snacks and drinks, the folks enjoyed the movies, and had lots of fun throughout the time that they stayed up.

After a fantastic weekend, Joshua, Katie, Shawn and Liz, and their kids, returned to Florida and New York.

Debra had another week with her family. She stayed a few days with Mark, and Cindy.

Mark took a day off from his job to spend time with her, while Cindy used her day off to go around town with her.

Friday after work, Mark collected his family, together with Johanna, and went to his parent's house to spend the night.

Cindy left early Saturday morning because she had to work, the next two days, but Mark, and the others, stayed at his parents until Sunday afternoon because that is when his sister was scheduled to leave.

Cindy joined her family at Jacob's house to accompany Debra to the airport, as she made her way back home to Switzerland.

"Mom, Dad, it was such a blessing to see you, and to spend time with you again, take care, I love you all," she embraced and kissed them.

"The pleasure was all ours, we enjoyed having you home, and you have a safe flight back home." Jacob said.

Her mom just hugged her and wished her a safe trip back home; she was emotional so she could not say much.

"Sis, words cannot express what these two weeks meant to me. It was such a heartfelt feeling and such a blessing, to re-establish that close sibling relationship again. I am praying that we will maintain that relationship, and that we will see each other more often than we used to. Take care, I will see you soon."

Debra hugged Mark, and reiterated her love for him, and promised to stay closely in touch with him.

And to Cindy, she said, "it was such a pleasure meeting you, I probably had seen you at church before, when we were kids, but I can't recall, but I am so happy that I got to spend time with you and to really know you, and sis, you are special, you are a sweetheart, and I know my brother is in good hands, he has found himself a gem."

"Marcus, my baby, take care, aunty will see you soon. I know you will be okay because you have great parents."

And with all that said, she hugged them again, and went to the gate, then onto the plane.

Mark dropped his parents off at their house and proceeded with his family to their house.

On their way home, Cindy said to Mark, "honey, I barely hear you speak about your sister, the most you said is that she is living in Switzerland, and that was that, but the way you all related these two weeks, I could swear that you were the closest siblings"

"We were not the best of siblings, we were more like acquaintances, not even friends because of favoritism by my parents, and when she left to go to England to study, I was happy, then I heard she had gotten married and moved to Switzerland with her husband; I was relieved because I knew she was not coming back. We never had gotten to patch our relationship, so that is why, I did not say much about her, but when I saw her, my heart was happy, so I knew I had to make things right, so here we are, and I loved it."

"I am glad you did make up, because I can see how much that meant to both of you, especially you, see how emotional you are, just talking about it."

"You are her older and only brother, and that makes you feel proud, to have someone to look up to you, and I know you were there for her at school, ready to defend her if the need had arisen."

"Exactly, that is why I am pushing for a sibling for Marcus."

"I knew you would go there because I left myself wide open for you to jump on the opportunity to make your plea. Anyway, we will start working on it next weekend, when everything is calm, agree?"

"Oh sure, agreed," and his face lit up when he said that.

Early Monday morning, Debra called to say that she had made it home safely, and thanked them again, for a splendid two weeks.

After speaking to Debra, Cindy, since she was up, prepared breakfast for her and Mark before they left for work.

She boiled 3 eggs and toasted a few slices of bread, and added a couple slices of cheese, along with some hot chocolate.

"Two eggs for me?" Mark asked surprised.

"Yes sir, I am preparing you for our upcoming project, I want to make sure that you are capable."

"Hahaha, funny. You have jokes, I will show you. Just wait and you will find out."

After making sure that Johanna and Marcus were occupied, the two of them kissed and left for their jobs.

Chapter *SEVENTY-NINE*

MARK, IN HIS MORNING huddle with his team, suggested that they should have a Christmas luncheon, apart from the company's annual celebration.

"Great idea," one of his colleagues remarked. And the rest of the team agreed, so they set it up for Monday, the 23rd, a day before the company's party.

In the huddle, he encouraged the group to avoid too much stress activities this Christmas season, and to be careful of their surroundings, because this is the season where so many negative things happen, and he said to enjoy family and loved ones.

Later in the day, he and two of his co-workers, who have been friends with him since he started to work at the company, went to lunch at one of their favorite BBQ spots, where they usually hung out for lunch.

While they were there, one of Mark's favorite Rocket's basketball players walked in, he had a few other players with him.

Mark felt compelled to approach him, to let him know how much he admired him and was a diehard fan.

He was very approachable and very humbled, and that impressed Mark. He spoke to him briefly, and he asked one of his buddies to get him a Rocket's cap that he had in the vehicle, and he signed it, and handed it to Mark.

Mark thanked him and went back to his table.

He was so delighted to have met and obtain his hero's autograph.

He went back to work excited, he could not wait for the day's work to end, so he could rush home to tell his wife of his day's adventures.

After they took off their work clothes and showered, they came to the living room and sat on the couch, then Mark asked Cindy, "how was your day?"

And Cindy went into detail concerning a couple of patients she had to interact with when they had disagreements with a couple of nurses.

Then she asked, "and how was your day?"

And Mark wasted no time, he spoke briefly about his plans with his co-workers, but he was so excited to tell her about his encounter with his basketball hero, and showed her the signed cap, as evidence of his meeting with him.

She was happy for him, because she knew how much it meant to him, and she knew he was going to cherish, the signed hat.

He took it and locked it up in the safe where he had his valuables.

After taking a bath, he sat on the couch and watched football.

Cindy, in the meantime, prepared dinner, then talked on the phone with her friends, Katy and Liz.

The next day at work, Mark and his buddies discussed the football game.

Apart from a few meetings and a couple of projects, the day was quiet.

Mark left work a little bit earlier than usual, since there was not much work to do that day; he stopped at the store to purchase a few grocery items.

When he got home, he changed his clothes and began cooking.

Cindy came home and was astonished to see Mark cooking.

"Are you okay?" she asked

"Funny," he replied, "I do cook sometimes."

"Yes, hamburger and chicken on the grill, but here you are in the process of cooking regular food?" scary, she joked.

"So right," he said, "I know you would like to finish."

"Anyway, I am not making fun of you, actually, I am thankful that you started dinner."

Dinner was ready by 8pm. After seeing Marcus to his bed, and having read his bedtime story, the couple, along with Johanna, sat at the table to have dinner.

"Yummy, good job Mark," Cindy complimented.

"Thanks, but you did most of the cooking, I started, but you did the heavy lifting, all I did was the minor stuff."

"Don't know who did the cooking, but I know it is delicious, and I am enjoying it."

"I am glad you are enjoying it, Johanna, and don't be bashful, eat as much as you can."

"Yes," Mark chimed in, "it is buffet style, eat as much as you can."

Once dinner was over, and the dishes were washed, the three of them sat in the living room, and took in an episode of their favorite comedy show.

They said good night to Johanna, as she left for her bedroom, and after a few more minutes in the living room, Mark, and Cindy went to bed.

"We need to do that more often, because it turned out to be a wonderful evening."

"I agree," replied Mark, "once I get the opportunity to leave early from work, like I did today, that would not be a problem."

He reached out and embraced her, and said to her, "I am so blessed and fortunate to have you in my life, you've completed me, I without you, is like the sea without salt."

"Cindy, my boo. I really do love you, and will continue to do so, forever."

Cindy being emotional, with her head resting on Mark's chest, responded, by saying, "I am the fortunate one. There were several instances that happened earlier in my life that indicated a doomed future, but after I embraced your love in my life, my life has been very enjoyable and fulfilled.

So, with no hesitancy, I can truly say, Mark, honey, I honestly love you."

All the love talks and teasing led to them being passionate with each other, before they dozed off.

Cindy was off next day, and hence, was not obligated to wake up early, unlike Mark, who was scheduled to be at work at a certain time.

Unfortunately, he forgot to set his alarm to assist him with waking up, thus, he was already late for work.

Cindy tried to convince him to call in for the day, since it was their slow period at work, but Mark chose to go in.

Johanna allowed Marcus to go and kiss and say goodbye to his parents before she took him to his school.

Mark hugged and kissed Cindy and set off to work.

Cindy quickly went back to her bed because she was so sleepy, because they stayed up late into the night.

Chapter EIGHTY

MARK APOLOGIZED FOR BEING late to his manager and then joined the meeting that was in progress.

After the meeting, he went into more details to his boss, concerning his lateness, but he and his boss had a great relationship, so they just laughed it off, and moved on.

Not many activities happened during the day because of the Christmas season, many of the employees were off on vacation, so the few that remained at work, were there to man the offices and do the necessary work.

Before Mark left for home, he and his friend Sam spent a couple of minutes in the parking lot chatting. They planned to go to the Rocket's game on Thursday night.

Sam planned to drive to Mark's house after work, and they would drive together to the game. They lived near of each other, so they usually carpooled to different activities.

Mark and Sam left the parking lot and headed for home.

Mark stopped at the supermarket to get a few items and went to the gas station to fill up his tank so they wouldn't have to stop tomorrow before they went to the game.

He pulled up to the outside pump got out of his truck, and took off the cover in order to pump the gas.

Just at that moment, Chris pulled up alongside his vehicle. He had been following him from the time he left the parking lot from his job.

He made a few comments to Mark, blaming him for not having a job.

Mark gently answered, "Chris, you are the one who left, I had nothing to do with that."

"Yes, you did that, you made it difficult for me and you reported me."

"Chris, sorry man, but I don't have the time for this argument, I am going to get gas and then head home."

The driver on the other side of the pump heard the commotion between the two men, and realized that they were having a heated argument, so he took his phone and began recording in secret what was going on; he also captured both license plates.

Chris said to Mark, "you are going home to your family, and I can't get to mine. Well man, I can't let that happen."

And with that said, Chris pulled out a handgun aimed it straight at Mark, and shot at him, then sped away at a high rate of speed, which caught everyone's attention.

The bullet struck Mark in his chest, and he slowly crumbled to the ground.

"Call 911, someone call 911," someone kept saying. Within minutes of the shooting, the place was swamped with emergency vehicles and personnel.

The crowd grew larger as onlookers gathered around.

As the police officers tried to take control of the perimeter, the life flight helicopter landed.

Mark was loaded into the chopper, still unconscious, as it left for the medical center.

The policemen inquired if anyone saw what happened, and the one who recorded the whole episode, presented to them the recording.

The officers immediately called in the information to headquarters and asked that an APB be put out for Chris. He gave them the vehicle description and license plates number and told them which direction it went.

Cindy heard all the sirens that were coming from close by and wondered what had happened.

Then she said, "let me call Mark, because he is usually home by now, and if he had stopped at the store, he still would have made it home by now, and if anything, he would call and say that he was running late."

She dialed his number, but it kept ringing, then went to his voice mail; she left a message and asked him to call her right away.

She waited a few minutes, and when he did not call, she called him again, and she got his voice mail again. She began to panic.

Cindy then called Sam and asked him if he knew the whereabout of Mark.

"Mark and I left work about 2 hours ago, and I saw him take the exit that leads to the grocery store. Is everything okay?"

"I haven't heard from him, and when I call him, I don't get a response, and I am worried, Sam. I am hearing all these sirens in the area."

"Yes, I am hearing them too, it seems like something awful happened, but I believe Mark is alright, probably caught up in traffic and not able to get to you."

"I hope so, I really hope so."

As soon as she hung up with Sam, her phone rang, and she was hesitant to answer it, because she had a bad feeling, and she did not recognize the number, and that troubled her more.

She, finally said, "hello, "and then as soon as the caller identified himself as a police officer, she dropped the phone and began crying.

"What's wrong, Cindy? What's wrong?" Johanna asked, and started crying, not knowing what was going on, but just because of Cindy's reaction, she knew it was not good.

She quickly ran to the phone to see if the caller was still there. "Hello, she said, "is anyone there?"

"Yes, I am," the caller answered, "and who are you?" he asked.

"I am Cindy's cousin, and the babysitter."

"I am sorry," he said, "I am sorry to be the bearer of bad news, but there was a shooting this evening, and unfortunately, it involved Mark. He was shot, and was taken to the hospital in critical condition, again, I am sorry."

Johanna let out a screeching scream, it was so piercing that it frightened Marcus.

"No, no," she said, "that can't be, noooo."

Cindy laid on the floor, screaming, and crying, and kept calling Mark's name, and said, "you don't do that to me, Mark."

"Cindy, the police said, he is alive, let's believe he will make it."
Johanna called Karen and told her what happened.

"What? I will be right there," she said, and hung up the phone.
The news spread quickly in the area.

Cindy phone rang and she did not answer, but Johanna picked
it up , and saw that it was Mark's father calling.

"Hello," she answered.

"Tell me, that what I am hearing is not true," he said.

But from hearing her cry, he knew what he feared might be
true.

Johanna had never heard a grown man cry before, and that
broke her down immensely.

She heard a grown man cry like a kid.

Just then, the doorbell rang; it couldn't be Karen, she could not
have made it there that soon.

She did not want to let anyone in, except the immediate family.

She went to the door, and to her surprise, it was Karen, "how
did she got here so quickly?" she asked.

Karen came in screaming, and reached down to the floor, and
picked up her daughter, and embraced her, and they both cried
loudly.

"Johanna, stay with Marcus, and don't let anyone in.

Karen and Cindy drove to the medical center and went straight
to the emergency room to find out what was going on.

They met Mark's parents there, and when Cindy saw them, she
broke down again, crying hysterically.

Mark's mom Laurie was taken to a room, because she was about
to pass out.

The doctor told the family that Mark was still in surgery, and more information, would be given as soon as possible.

Cindy and the rest of the family, were in the waiting room, praying and hoping that everything would turn out okay.

After about 5 hours of surgery, the doctor came out to report.

He said, "the surgery went well, he is stable, but in critical condition. We have placed him in a medically induced coma, and we will see what happens from there.

"Can I see him?" Cindy asked.

"I am not sure that is a good idea, seeing your condition, and he can't see you nor hear you."

"I just want to see him, please doctor."

"Doctor, I am her mother, and I am also a nurse, I will go in with her to make sure she is okay."

"Okay, I will also ask one of the nurses to go with you, if any situation arises, she will take control and secure the place."

Mark laid there, unaware of the presence of Cindy and Karen.

Cindy held his hand, and she spoke to him, she was hoping that, even though he was in a coma, he would still be able to hear her.

"Babe, I am so sorry for what happened to you, please don't quit on us, fight, don't give up, keep fighting for us, I know you will beat this," she was crying, while she was saying this to him.

Karen also joined in and encouraged him to keep fighting.

The nurse said it was time to leave, so Cindy kissed him on his forehead and told him how much she loved him, and she and Karen said goodbye to him.

The dad waited to go in to see his son, but the nurse said, he couldn't at this time.

Cindy pleaded with the nurse until she gave in and allowed him to go in for 5 minutes. She said, she was doing him a favor, and that he should be out of there then.

The mom was not sure she would be able to keep her emotions under control, so she was not allowed to accompany the father.

He stared at his son laying motionless on the bed, not knowing that he was there, and Jacob felt the strength leaving his body, but he had to stay strong for the family.

After a few more minutes, Karen said, it was time to go home, but Cindy hesitated, she did not want to leave, she wanted to stay there until he woke up.

But Karen pleaded with her for a while, and eventually, she agreed to go home with them.

When they got home, Johanna, updated them of the news that was reported.

She told them that Chris was apprehended about 2 hours after the shooting.

She gave Cindy a phone number so she could call the officer who was working on the case.

Cindy did not want to be at the house alone, so her mom said they would move in with her until things quieted down.

Cindy went to the hospital daily, she talked to Mark every day, praying and hoping that he was hearing what she was saying.

The day came when Mark was scheduled to be taken off the medically induced coma, and Cindy and the rest of the family, were all present to hear what the prognosis was.

It did not take too long, before Dr. Armstrong approached them.

"He has been brought out of the coma, but he is still critical, and very weak, but has made a little progress, keep praying, and hoping for the best.

"Doctor, can I go and see him?" Cindy asked.

"I will ask the nurse to accompany you to his room."

Cindy, carefully and fearfully, approached his bed; she realized, that he was in serious condition. He barely could open his eyes, but for the moment, he did also recognized Cindy.

She squeezed his hand, and he responded with a feeble squeeze of her own.

She spoke to him constantly, and told him to fight, and not to give up, and that they were praying for him.

Karen, and his parents soon joined her, and instantly, they realized that he was in bad shape, and it looked worse than they expected, yet they had to keep their hopes high, to encourage him, and to support Cindy.

"I have prayed, and am praying for you to come through this, you just have to be strong and not give up," Karen said.

Five days later, Dr. Armstrong called the family and asked if they could come down to the hospital.

Upon hearing that request, Karen and Mark's parents, along with Debra, who came in the night before, knew that the situation was not good.

Cindy, who was already at the hospital, waited on the others to come, but she knew that what the doctor was about to say was not good, she felt it in her stomach, but she kept hoping for the best.

Dr. Armstrong led them to a private room and told them, that he didn't think Mark was going to live much longer, and he encouraged them to say their goodbyes, and said how sorry he was.

They were in disbelief. They cried and comforted one another.

Cindy was weeping bitterly, she was in agony, and kept calling for Mark.

She cried until she had barely any strength left in her.

"Why God?" she asked, "why did you take him away from me and his son? It's not fair; it is just not fair." And she kept crying.

Cindy requested to be at his side, she wanted to hold his hand.

The Doctor said, she was not in the right frame of mind to handle it, but he allowed her to go in with other members of the family.

His mom, declined to go in, she could not bare watching her son take his last breath.

They camped in his room, as they realized, that the end was near.

Laurie, after she was persuaded by her daughter, came into the room, looked at her son, and cried painfully.

About 11pm, she told Debra she had to get out of the room, and Debra walked her out. She said, "I can't watch my son die."

Her grief was great, her only son was about to exit this world.

Cindy, Karen, and Jacob, remained in the room, they wanted to be there for him, they wanted to be there till his last breath, until the very end.

December 23rd, around 12.35am, Mark began his exit from this world. He stretched his body, and gave a big sigh, then he was ushered into eternity, at 12.42 am.

"Oh, no, no, Mark, you can't do this to me, you can't leave, what am I going to do without you? You can't leave Marcus. Oh Lord, Lord," and she continued to cry in agony.

She laid her hand on his chest and wept bitterly.

She refused to let him go, when they came in to wheel him away.

Karen had to assist, in order to free her from the body.

Since this was a criminal case, the body was now part of the investigation.

Karen had to persuade Cindy to leave the hospital because she was hesitant to do so.

Cindy was going through one of the worst periods of her life, she never thought, after the rape, she would go through something so painful again, and now this.

"Mom, what am I going to do?" she asked, what am I going to tell Marcus when he asks for his dad?"

"You will be okay, Mark's parents, and I will make sure that you will be okay."

Chapter EIGHTY-ONE

CHRIS' CHARGES WERE UPGRADED to murder, and he was denied bond.

Many of Cindy and Mark's friends, and co-workers called to extend their sympathy and support to the family.

The incident had been on the news from the time it happened to the present day that is how many of her friends found out.

Cindy let Johanna, handle the phone calls because she was not ready to speak to all those who were calling.

Dr. King called and asked to speak to Cindy but Johanna denied him, but took a message, and gave it to Cindy.

Cindy quickly called him back.

"Hi, this is Junie," he answered.

"I am sorry that my cousin did not let you talk to me, she was just following orders."

"I am so sorry to hear what happened to you, my deepest sympathy to you, and the rest of the family."

"Thanks, my friend, your call means a lot to me."

And they continued speaking for a long time. He promised to be there for her and to assist in any way possible to make life easier for her.

The next two weeks were the most dreadful two weeks of Cindy's life.

Preparing to bury the one that you loved so dearly, was not going to be easy. But with the help of family and friends, she would manage.

The funeral was set for January 12th.

But until then, Cindy and Mark's family had to live with the memories of Mark and the pain of not having him around.

Cindy tried to explain to Marcus as best as she could, that his dad had gone to a great place in the sky, called heaven, and that he was with Jesus, but he still did not understand.

Friday morning, the day of the funeral, started as a blur to Cindy, she was numb to everything around her.

She dreaded for 3pm to come, because that was the time of the viewing.

Family and friends came from all over to attend the funeral of Mark, and to sympathize with Cindy, and the family.

Most people that were there, went to view the body, but Cindy decided she did not want to see it, but Joshua convinced her to, and she went to take a final look at him, and touched him, and said, "I love you baby, and always will.

Joshua held her up, as she cried, and he said to Mark, "rest in peace, my brother, I will miss you, but I promise, I will be there for the family, I will see you on the other side." and then he led her to her seat.

The casket was closed for the final time as the pastor began the service.

He gave a solemn opening remark, and he encouraged Cindy and the parents, and the rest of the family, to be strong, and asked them to continue to trust God, and to lean on Him in this difficult time.

Sam, Mark's good friend, did the first reading, while Joshua did the second.

Debra, his sister, read the eulogy.

It was very touching, especially, after she said, "when Mark was in his early teenage years, he did not have any close friends, many labelled him a nerd, and he was bullied. I remember him telling me that there were a couple of young ladies in the church he had liked, but feared approaching them, but I guessed when he went to college he changed, because I was shocked when I came home to see the beautiful young lady he had chosen to be his wife.

Mark was one of the most loving young men you would come across, he treated everyone with respect, and cared for all who came in his path."

And she continued reading the eulogy, and there was not one dry eye in the service.

Cindy felt it even more, because she knew what was said about him was true.

After the eulogy Cindy, with the assistance of Joshua, went up to the pulpit to read a poem that she penned for him.

"My dearest Mark, I know you left us, but it was not by choice.

My heart is aching, my soul is desolate, as I continue to hear your voice.

And it is telling me, be strong for me and for Marcus,

But honey, I can't lie, this is tough and painful, because dear, this is a big loss.

Cindy could not continue, because she broke down.

David, her bigger brother, came up to help Joshua support her, and Joshua took the paper from her, and continued reading the poem.

"It was my hope that we would grow old together, enjoying God's blessings,

Never once it did come into my mind, that you would be here, early in your life, in a casket.

Our plans and wishes that we had for our future all shattered totally,

Now I am left here alone, not knowing what to do, not knowing how I am going to function emotionally.

Oh, Lord, help me, I don't know how I am going to live without Mark,

Who is going to be there for us, who is going to have my back.

Dear God, why did you do this to me? Why did you have to take Mark so soon?

And here I am, having a farewell service for him this bright Friday noon.

But God: it does not matter how angry I am, and how miserable I am feeling right now,

I still must acknowledge your love for me, and your will must be done, and I will continue to come to you, and bow.

I love you Mark, I really do, and will continue to love you. Bye Dear."

The brothers supported her and escorted her to her seat.

The pastor said a few more words, and then brought the service to an end.

The procession left the church and headed to the cemetery, which was about 10 miles, from the church.

The burial site was in a new area of the cemetery.

The Pastor and the rest of the participants gathered around the site, and sang a few songs, after which, the pastor gave a farewell speech, then concluded the service. The groundkeepers lowered the casket in the ground.

As the casket started to descend to its final resting place, the family and friends laid flowers and other items on it.

Cindy was out of it, she had to be taken away to avoid any unfortunate happening.

From there, many went to the community center, where there was food and drink prepared for the family and others, who came to say goodbye to Mark.

Cindy, Joshua, Katy, Liz and Johanna chose to go home instead, while David, Lisa, and Karen stayed at the community center.

Katy still had some time left before she had to go back to her job, and after discussing it with Joshua, she decided to spend some time with Cindy.

Karen was pleased with Cindy's decision to move in with her until she felt comfortable to go back to her house.

Chapter EIGHTY-TWO

THE NEXT FEW WEEKS were difficult for Cindy, she had to adjust not having Mark around, and to embrace the role of being a single parent.

Marcus did not understand what was going on, so he kept asking, "where is my dad? And when is he coming home? And what was he doing in that box?"

Karen tried to explain death to him, and told him his dad would be gone for a long time.

She was hopeful that as he grew older, he would understand, and would be able to cope better.

Cindy wanted to put her house up for sale, but her mom discouraged her from doing that.

"It is too early to make such a decision, let time heal you for a little bit, then you will be in a better position, and you will have a clearer head to make decisions.

Cindy could hardly wait for the case of her husband's killer to commence; it was scheduled to begin on July 16th.

Debra was reluctant to leave her parents, as she prepared to go back to her home in Switzerland, because she knew how tough it was going to be for them, but she had no choice, she had to get back to her family.

"Cindy, the invitation still stands for you to come and spend time with us, I think this would be the right time to come which would help you with the healing process."

"I will, as soon as the right time comes along."

And they embraced, and said goodbye, and wished each other well.

Cindy accepted the offer from her brother and Katy and went and spend a couple of weeks with them.

They did everything possible to keep her busy.

Marcus and Kevin had a blast being together; they did not have the slightest clue what happened.

On the weekend, they went to the amusement park, and they had an enjoyable time; they rode the rides, and had fun meeting the characters, and most of all, the kids had a great time in the park.

Sunday evening, she attended a basketball game in which her brother Josh, played. She was shouting and cheering him on. She always enjoyed going to his games when they were younger.

The following days, she and Katy spent lots of time together shopping, dining, and enjoying other activities.

Sunday morning, her mood was somber, because she was going back to Texas in the afternoon.

Her mom and Donald picked her up from the airport and swung by Jacob, and Laurie's, to check on them.

They each encouraged each other and promised to keep praying for one another.

After another week at home, Cindy finally went back to work.

Her co-workers welcomed her back, and those that had not seen her or had spoken to her since the tragedy, offered their condolences and sympathy.

Everyone was mindful of her grief and tried their best not to pile up any more unnecessary stress upon her.

Later that evening, when she got home, she discussed with her mom again, about selling the house, and moving to an apartment.

"For one," she said, "it would be too much of a burden to pay that huge mortgage, and secondly, too much of a hassle going to and from work, from here, and I would not want to transfer from my job."

"You could keep the house; I will help you with the mortgage." Her mom said

"I am worried about you staying by yourself in an apartment."

"Mom, I will buy a smaller home later, but for now an apartment will do. I will ask Johanna to move back with me, she is like my younger sister, and she is familiar with Marcus, and the only reason she left, and went back home, is because I moved in with you."

Cindy pitched the idea to Johanna, and asked her to let her know as soon as she could so she could find an apartment.

The next day, Johanna called her and said she would come and live with her whenever she was ready.

After a month, Cindy had the house on the market and moved into an apartment, not too far from where the house was located; she would still be close to her mom and her job.

Johanna moved in with her and said she would register to start school at the community college in the fall.

She said she would schedule her classes, so that she would still be available to drop off and pick up Marcus from school.

Cindy told Johanna she would pay her every month for taking care of Marcus; she also bought her a good used car so she could get around.

Cindy tried ignoring her anniversary the day it came up, but she happened to go to the closet to retrieve an item, when she noticed an item they had in their room the night of the wedding.

And she broke down and wept bitterly until Johanna consoled and comforted her.

And that was Cindy's life pattern for the next few months; she cried often especially when a particular date came up that reminded her of an activity they celebrated together.

She called Mark's parents and told them that she was coming over to pick up Happy, who had been at their home since the tragedy, but they were not in favor of giving her up, they said, it helped them heal.

"Laurie, that is the reason I would like my dog; it will help me, and definitely Marcus, because he is so fond of the dog."

After the conversation quickly turned into an argument, and headed towards hostility, Cindy hung up the phone, but said she would pick up her dog on the weekend.

As the days went by, Cindy learned to live without Mark, and she accepted the fact that he was gone.

She was slowly moving on and making plans for her and Marcus's future.

During the next few months, she organized her finances and she took care of her affairs.

She donated some of Mark's clothing and items to charity, and to his friends.

She got a buyer for the house, so she sold most of the items that were in there, and the rest she put into a storage facility.

It was hectic for a few months, but with the help of others, she managed.

Chapter EIGHTY-THREE

THE LONG-AWAITED DAY OF July 16th arrived; Cindy woke up early that day and went to the courtroom, where she sat at the front, because she wanted Chris to see her face and look at her throughout the trial.

The courtroom was packed with the locals, who had come to show their support for her, and they wanted to see what would happen to this man.

Cindy was accompanied by her mother and Mark's parents, and some of her friends.

The trial was not expected to last too long because there was so much compelling evidence against the accuser.

The procedure went on for three days; during that time, the accuser admitted to shooting Mark and said he did not mean to do it, but the situation went out of hand, and that he was sorry, and apologized to Cindy and her family.

At the end of the third day, the case was turned over to the jury for deliberation.

By the end of the fourth day, they came out with a verdict.

"Guilty on all counts," was the verdict.

The courtroom erupted with joy, as they claimed that justice had been served.

Cindy cried because she was relieved, and that was one more step that would help her heal, and she knew that Mark's killer would not be roaming the streets to commit another senseless crime

The Judge instructed that he be remanded in custody and be brought back on August 3rd for sentencing.

Cindy, Karen, and her in-laws, also Katy, who was there to give support, were elated with the decision.

"Thank you, Lord, for giving us justice for Mark's death." Cindy said, as she sobbed.

Karen, and the others gathered around her and the parents, and supported them and encouraged them.

Cindy said to Katy, "it was a bitter- sweet decision;" she was happy he was being held accountable for his actions, but it was painful because she was still without Mark.

"I hope the Judge gives him the maximum sentence," Katy said, "he deserves to be treated like the criminal that he is."

"I will be there at the sentencing, I can't wait to find out how long the Judge put that killer away for," Cindy expressed.

On their way home, the small group stopped at the restaurant around the corner close to her apartment and enjoyed a meal and celebrated the verdict.

"I am thankful to have a friend and sister like you, and I really appreciate you taking a day from your job, and coming to support me, and to spend the weekend with me."

"For you Cindy, I would do anything, you are the friend everyone desires to have. I love you dearly." Katy said.

"The feelings are mutual," replied Cindy.

It was a weekend where they did not do much outside of the apartment but spent most of the time inside with the boys.

Cindy hated to see Katy leave on Sunday evening, but she knew she had to because she had her own affairs to take care of.

"Johanna, this is Marcus first birthday without his dad and that hurts," Cindy said to her, "who ever thought, that he would be so young without a father?"

On sentencing day, Karen picked up Cindy, and they went to the courthouse where a crowd was already gathered.

Inside, tension was high, as the people did not know what to expect, especially with this Judge who had a reputation of being lenient. During the trial, he was very stern with the prosecutors, but many observed that he was mild with the defense team.

The Judge ordered that the convicted accuser be brought in, and he promised a speedy sentencing.

Chris locked his eyes with Cindy then quickly turned his head to avoid making any further contact with her.

Judge Mathews asked everyone to be seated and to be quiet; he gave a small speech and then read the counts and the punishment allowed by law and then he gave the sentence.

"I hereby sentence you, Chris Rogbert, according to the power given to me, to a life in prison, without the possibility of parole, for the death of Mark Jackrose."

Cindy let out a great sigh of relief. "Thank you, Lord, thank you," she said.

And most of the people in the courtroom felt the same way; they were pleased with the sentencing.

Karen said to her daughter, "at least he won't be out there anymore to harm anyone."

"Mom, I am so happy; at least I know Mark's death did not happen in vain, and his killer's life has ended too, though in a different way."

"As this chapter closes in your life, let's hope that better things are on the horizon for you."

"I hope so, mom, I really hope so."

"My child, God is able to see you through, you just have to trust him from here onwards."

"Being a regular at church, would help a lot, there would be plenty of support in this area."

"Mom, can we speak about that sometime later? I can't address this now."

"Okay, okay, it is your call."

Karen dropped her daughter at her apartment and continued to her house.

Chapter *EIGHTY-FOUR*

THE WEEKS THAT FOLLOWED, Cindy went into a deep depression, with lots of mood swings.

Her birthday came and went in September, almost un-noticed; she did not care, and did not want to celebrate it.

Then came thanksgiving, and to her it meant nothing, but another day. She declined all invitations and stayed home alone and pitied herself.

Marcus spent thanksgiving, and the rest of the week with his Grandma Karen, while Johanna went home to be with her family for the holiday.

And this pattern continued with Cindy; she did not feel the need to socialize.

She scheduled herself to work on Christmas day, so she would not have to and socialize with family and friends.

At work, many noticed the change in her demeanor, and the change in her attitude towards her work, but they knew what she had been through, so they sympathized with her.

A couple of her good friends at work tried to encourage her to move on and told her to ease away from the past and concentrate on the handsome young son that she had to guide to a great life.

Katy, and Liz, her two best friends, refused to let her get down on herself, they kept encouraging her, and always tried to lift her spirit, but sometimes their efforts came up short.

Her mom told her that she was still young, and she still had lots of years ahead, once God permits it, so she should move on, she also told her that Mark would like for her to go on with her life.

For the next two years, nothing dramatic happened in her life, apart from falling away from Mark's parents, after they had some bitter arguments, some finger pointing, and a few misunderstandings, but otherwise, life was on the upside for her, and she made some progress with her attitude and self-esteem.

Besides spending time on the phone with her best friends, Katy and Liz, she and her friend Junie spent a great deal of time on the phone.

She loved talking to him and felt comfortable telling him things that she knew were safe with him.

She trusted him and knew that he always had her best interest at heart.

He never disrespected her and he continued to encourage her in the things he knew were profitable for her.

She also helped him in his business whenever she had the opportunity to do so.

His wife became concerned about their relationship, but he assured her that they were just good friends who supported each other.

Chapter *EIGHTY-FIVE*

THE WEEKEND FOLLOWING HER 33rd birthday, Cindy went to work with Junie on Saturday, her off day.

About 11:15am a young man walked into the clinic; he was tall and good looking. He caught Cindy's eye and she was curious to know who he was.

She purposely went into the room where he was with Dr. King, to ask a question, which could have waited later, but that was just her scheme to get his attention.

Junie introduced her to his patient.

"This is John, he is here to get his annual checkup, and John, this is my friend and co-worker, Nurse Cindy."

He stretched out his hand and said, "nice to meet you."

After she left the room, John asked Junie so many questions about Cindy.

"She is a wonderful person, and frankly, I would not encourage her to be anywhere close to you, you playboy, right now that would be the worst thing that could happen to her is to get hurt in a relationship."

"Buddy, relax, I was just saying how pretty she is, and it would be nice to have her as a friend, but I guess, you are her protector."

"Glad you recognized that, and I will protect her from you."

"I thought we were buddies?"

"Yes, we are, that is why I am saying these things, because I know you, and I know your reputation."

"People change Junie, especially when they find the right person."

"I have been hearing that from you for a while now, but it is a broken record, your promises are just those broken promises."

At the end of the day's work, before they shut down the clinic, Cindy asked Junie a few questions about John.

"Interested in him?"

"Not really, just curious."

"Be careful, because curiosity kills the cat, so be careful, because I saw you exchange numbers, but I am trusting that you would be wise and diligent, and you would make the right decisions."

"He has been my friend and patient, for a long time. He is a professor at the University down at Senhouse."

"Don't worry my friend, I will be careful."

That night, John called Cindy and asked if she would go out to dinner with him?

She accepted and arranged to go out with him on Friday evening.

He picked her up around 7:10pm and took her to one of those fancy and expensive restaurants in downtown, Houston.

He was a perfect gentleman, opened the car door for her, pulled her chair out for her at the table, and waited for her to place her order before he placed his.

The food was delicious and the service was great. They had a great conversation during dinner, and they got to know more about each other.

On the way back to her apartment, John brought up conversations that were not appropriate, they were not what Cindy wanted to hear, and she quickly shut them down.

He walked her to her apartment, and said, "have a good night," then he tried to give her a peck on the lips, but Cindy was having none of that.

He left disappointed, but had he behaved like he did at the restaurant, he would have had another date with her, but because of his behavior, and attitude at the end of their date, she decided not to go out with him again.

The next day she called Junie, and told him, what happened with her date with John.

And he said, "I am glad that you figured him out, and you extinguished the flame before it got to be a huge fire."

Cindy slowly started to go out with the friends that she and Mark used to go out with, she was surely starting to enjoy her life again.

She attended most of Marcus's activities, such as soccer and basketball.

Liz and Shawn were happy to hear that Cindy planned to come to New York for the Christmas.

Going to New York this time was much different because there was no Mark to accompany them, but she still planned to have a great time because she loved New York.

She was so happy that Mark took pictures on their last visit to New York.

Cindy kept saying to herself, "I wonder if Mark knew that he was going to leave this world, because certain things he did and said, and his behavior not too long before his death was unusual, but again, I will never know."

It was nice seeing Shawn and Liz and Jessie, Liz's younger brother, who came from Florida to spend Christmas with them.

They had a great time in New York, aside from the void that was in their lives; they made the best of the moments they got to spend together, and after Mark's death, they promised not to take anyone for granted.

Johanna and Jessie spent the time getting to know each other, and they developed a nice friendship during their time in New York.

Cindy came back to Texas rejuvenated, and ready to take on the world, but that joyful spirit did not last long, because the anniversary of Mark's funeral had her feeling down again, but this time it was less painful than the previous years.

John suddenly called and asked her if she would accompany him to a concert.

She quickly turned him down. She asked him why he had not called until now.

He came up with a million excuses, but she did not believe any of them, and she told him she would not venture anywhere with him, and that she was totally disappointed in him.

It was that time again in Texas, summertime, heat and more heat, which had Cindy, Johanna, and Marcus, spending many weekends when she was not working, or had something significant to do, in Galveston.

Marcus was now grown to the point where he understood, not fully, but enough about death, to know that his dad was killed and would not be coming back to them.

He always loved the water and spent a good deal of his time in the water, whenever they went to Galveston.

Chapter EIGHTY-SIX

FOR HER 34TH BIRTHDAY, Cindy, Marcus and Johanna, went to spend the weekend in San Antonio. This time she had more opportunities to move around the city because Marcus was much bigger now, and it made it easier to move around.

They enjoyed boat rides in the nights and went to the coolest restaurants. Cindy enjoyed the weekend to the fullest and was in the best of moods.

It was an enjoyable weekend, and she had a pleasant and quiet birthday celebration.

Work on Monday, her co-workers had a small get together planned for her birthday; she was surprised, but thankful, and she enjoyed the small celebration.

On her way home that evening, Cindy felt her vehicle driving awkwardly, so she pulled to the shoulder of the highway, and examined her vehicle, and realized that her driver's side front tire was very low, and leaking air, so she got back into her vehicle, and turned on her hazard lights, then checked the trunk of the car to check to see if the spare tire was in tack.

She picked up her phone but did not know who she could call to come and assist her.

She thought about calling Sam, Mark's friend, but she felt uneasy doing that. "You know what? I will call one of the tow trucks to come and take my vehicle to the tire shop."

Just as she was about to call the number of the tow company, which was located a couple blocks from her apartment, a vehicle pulled up behind her vehicle.

A handsome young man got out of the vehicle and said, "hi, my name is Peter."

"I'm Cindy."

"I saw your vehicle blinkers on, and you standing at the back of your vehicle with your trunk open, I figured this is a damsel in distress, so I stopped to see if I can be of assistance to you."

"Well thanks, Peter for your consideration, your help is really needed," and she said laughing, "I am not a damsel, but a widow."

"Widow? Too young to be a widow."

"Anyway, I would appreciate it if you would change this tire for me, please."

"Sure, not a problem."

It took him less than no time to remove and replace the other tire on the vehicle.

"Here you go," he said.

"Thank you so much Peter, you were heaven sent."

And the two spoke for a short while and exchanged numbers; he watched her drive away, before he went on his way.

Roughly around 7:10pm, Peter called.

"Hi Cindy, this is Peter."

"Hi, I did not expect to hear from you so soon."

"I just wanted to know that you had made it home safely."

"Thanks for following up, so was nice of you to do. Again, thanks for your help."

"Tell me, are you always that nice to people, or just me, because you saw my vulnerability and you decided to take the opportunity to win me over?"

"Ouch, you don't have to be so harsh, I try to be good to everyone I come across, because you never know when you are going to need someone to help you."

"Sorry, I did not mean to be that blunt, but it is me, not you, I am in that frame of mind lately."

"I know it is kind of soon, and you barely know me, but I would love to take you out to lunch or dinner, whenever you want?"

"Peter, you said all the right things before you asked. It is really kind of soon, and like you said, I don't really know you, why would I chance going anywhere alone with you?"

"You know what Cindy? Forget that I asked you out, and just to let you know, I am not a criminal, I was just trying to get to know you better."

"Sorry you took it that way, but that was not what I was implying, and I sure would love to go to lunch with you."

"I am off Saturday, is this a good time for you?"

"Sure, is 1: pm, okay with you? Any preference?"

"That is fine Peter, I am okay with whatever place you choose."

"What time do I pick you up?"

"You don't have to pick me up, I will drive, and meet you there."

Cindy made it to the Sealake Seafood restaurant about 12:55pm, and there was Peter waiting for her.

He came out to meet her and walked her to their table.

Being the gentleman that he was, he pulled out her chair and waited until she was seated before he took his seat.

"Let me say thank you for accepting my invitation, and before we go any further, let me say how beautiful you look."

"Oh thank, you, and you don't look too bad yourself," she laughed.

"Check out the menu, the appetizers look enticing, which one do you care for?'

"I am good, thanks."

After the waitress brought their drinks, they placed their order for their meal.

While waiting, they chatted and tried to find out more about each other.

"I did not ask, but I am assuming that you are a nurse?"

"Yes, I am, I know you saw me in uniform, so that should have given you the idea."

"Exactly, my next question is, where are you working?"

" I am in the medical center." She replied

"Is that all you are going to say?"

"For now, yeah."

"What about you?'

"I work at OBC Energy company, I am a chemical engineer."

"I am 35 years old, never been married nor do I have any kids."

"No, something is wrong, someone as handsome as you and well educated, with such a great job is free and single?"

"Thanks for the compliment, but some men can be picky too, besides, I have been in a few relationships, but they were not what I was looking for."

"What are you looking for?" she asked

"Love in exchange for love."

Then the waitress brought their food.

"Looks good," Cindy said.

"Hope you enjoy it," he said to her.

"Looks like you come here a lot?'

"What made you say that?" he asked her.

"It is obvious, because all the workers in here know you. Is this where you bring all your girlfriends?" she asked laughing.

"I am a regular in here, I love the food, and that is what a bachelor does. I have been here with a couple of ladies, but most of the time, I come here by myself. This is my kitchen." He said jokingly.

"Are you a good cook?' he asked her

"I think I could hold my own, but again, it is those who tasted my cooking, that gave me the confidence."

"Will I ever get to judge your cooking?"

"We will see, time will tell."

"At least, that gives me hope." He replied.

"Hmmm, I don't really know…but.

"What are you trying to ask? Cindy asked Peter.

"It could be sensitive, that is why it bothers me to ask."

"Please go ahead and ask, if I feel it is an appropriate question, I will answer, if not I won't.

"You said that you are a widow, and you look very young, what happened to your husband?"

Cindy dropped her head and looked away for a short while.

"Did I say something wrong?" he asked, "I did not mean to make you feel sad in any way."

"My husband was killed."

And she remained quiet for a little while, and when she was about to shed a tear, she got up and went to the lady's room.

She came back a few minutes later, sat for a short while, and asked if they could leave.

"Sure, sure, let me take care of this, and we will be on our way."

"Peter, I am sorry that our lunch ended in this way, but the memory of my husband's death is so painful, and I am still trying to cope without him.

"My mistake, I sure will be more sensitive next time, that is if you go out with me again."

"I will go out with you again, at least I owe you that much. So far you are awesome, and I enjoy your company."

"Glad you feel that way, and the feelings are mutual."

On their way home, they stopped at the ice-cream parlor and sat and ate a couple scoops of ice-cream, before they said bye, and went their separate ways.

Cindy was pleased with the lunch date, and she was impressed with Peter and she liked him.

She made a few stops, before making it back to her apartment.

She quickly called Katy, and told her about meeting Peter, and of their lunch date.

"Girl, give me details, is he cute? Does he have money?" And she just kept going.

"Oh yeah, he is cute, you should know me by now, I don't know too much about him yet, but the basic things, like his work, and he is not married, and other small details, but everything will come in time."

"Get on the ball, get details," she said jokingly, "but seriously, I just want you to be happy, and I want you to be very careful, don't go into any relationship right now with feelings, but make sure your heart is in it, and make sure you will get someone that won't break your heart."

"Thanks sis, for the advice, but I will be careful."

"Now I want you to do something for me."

"Anything for you. What is my assignment?" she said jokingly.

"I want you to call OBC Energy Company and ask for Peter Latrine. I need to know if he is really working there, and if he is an engineer like he said."

"I am on it first thing Monday morning."

"Thank you, I am puzzled by all these positives in his life, yet he does not have a wife, a girlfriend, or any children, something does not add up, yet he is so friendly and well mannered, but I will be observing him."

"Great, that is the way to go. You do not want to get hurt at this junction in your life."

"Katie, I will call you back, he is calling right now, I will keep you updated."

"Talk to you Cindy, be careful."

"Hello Peter, nice to hear from you."

"Oh, I was just checking to make sure that you are okay."

"Thanks for checking, but why wouldn't I be, okay?

"I did not mean it that way."

"How did you mean it?'

"Okay my bad, wrong choice of words, let me start again, how are you doing?"

"I am doing okay, sorry for being difficult, but I did not want you to think that because I am a young widow, that I am desperate."

"Oh no, no, that is the furthest thing from my mind. I don't know you enough, for me to come up with a conclusion like this. And if I came across in this manner, I am very sorry."

"It is okay, no harm done."

"So, what are you doing this wonderful Saturday night?" he asked.

"Actually, I am relaxing watching a movie before I go to bed."

"And you? I am surprised that you are not in a club, or at a bar with your friends."

"All of the above sounds good, but I am not a club person, I only do that occasionally. And friends, sometimes I keep them at bay, I don't want to hear the same things being repeated."

"You must be thinking that I'm weird, eh?

"Not really, everyone is different, and honestly, I like your style."

"I am not a club person either, I was not brought up that way."

"Talking about restaurant, do you want to do dinner with me tomorrow night?"

"Sounds nice, but I will pass this time, but will take a rain check, I hope you don't mind?"

"That is okay, just let me know when you are available, and we will go."

"Thanks, Cindy, for your time, and you enjoy the rest of the night."

"You too Peter, have a great night, and I will talk to you again, soon."

After they hung up, Cindy wondered if she was being too stern with Peter, was she coming across as a miserable person?

She called Katy and told her what transpired during her call with Peter, and how she felt.

"Great, you need to send a message to him that you are a strong and independent woman, but at the same time, you don't want him to think that you are an obnoxious person, someone very difficult to get along with."

"Yeah, I know, I know, but at the same time, I don't want to present myself as a desperate person, a piece of meat on a platter waiting to be devoured."

They spoke for a good while, before they realized it way past time for bed.

The next morning, her phone rang about 9:30am, it was her mom, asking if she was attending church today?

"Not today mom, I went to bed late last night, and I need to catch up on some sleep."

"That is not good Cindy, you have to make an effort to attend church when you are off from work and you need to raise that boy going to church."

"Mom, I will eventually, but right now, I am not ready to socialize with church folks."

"Cindy, I can't believe you just said that to me, what's going on?'

"Mom, it is nothing, I just need time."

They talked and argued for a little while longer, then her mom concluded, that it was her life, and she was free to do as she pleased, but she just wanted her to remember, she was brought up going to church and how disappointed she was with her decision.

The following few weeks, Cindy tried to be on the quiet side, just followed her regular routine, work, home, spent time with Marcus, and talked to her regular circle, and sometimes Peter.

Thanksgiving was to be held at Karen's; it was her turn to host.

Cindy invited Peter to come over, and she did not mention it to anybody, but Katy.

Katy and her confided in each other, they kept things between them, they had a close relationship.

Chapter EIGHTY-SEVEN

KATY DID THE RESEARCH that Cindy instructed her to do, and found out, that all that Peter said was true.

It was a little bit chilly that Thursday morning, but it warmed up as the day went on.

Cindy, Katy, and Liz, the three Forevers, helped Karen with the cooking, and as a result, the food was ready on time.

Jacob, and Laurie, were the last of the guest to arrive, they came in and greeted Karen and the others, but coldly said hi to Cindy, because they were not on the best of terms. Marcus was the one who had them communicating with each other.

Laurie did not always favor Cindy for her son, Jacob was the one who liked her, and thought that his son had made a wise choice. Laurie went as far as blaming Cindy for Mark's death, said she was partially responsible.

Cindy did not pay any attention to her and her theory.

After they had gathered around the table, and were preparing to say grace, the doorbell rang.

Cindy knew who it was and went to answer the door.

"Please come in" she said politely, and she gave him a hug, and led him into the house to meet the rest of the folks.

First person, she introduced him to was Karen.

"Mom, meet my friend Peter, I invited him to have thanksgiving with us."

"Hi Peter, welcome to my home."

"Thanks, Karen, and nice to meet you."

"A friend of Cindy is a friend of the family, make yourself at home."

Then Cindy motioned to Katy, who was coming from the room, and heading to the table, to come over.

"This is Peter," she said, smiling.

"I am Katy, Cindy's twin sister, nice meeting you."

"Cindy, you did not tell me that you had a twin sister?"

"We are not twins by birth, but by association."

She is married to my brother, whom you will meet soon.

They walked over to the side where he was, and Cindy said, "this is my brother Joshua."

"Hi Joshua, I am Peter."

"Josh, we will speak later, after things quiets down, let me introduce him to David and the others."

She said to all that were at the table, "this is my friend Peter," and they introduced themselves.

Donald led them in prayer, and then they dove into the massive food collaboration that was on the table, and it was served buffet style, so everyone could eat as much as they desired.

Laurie did not take much food, she said she had lost her appetite, and remarked to her husband, that she believed, Cindy had this man while she was with Mark.

He dismissed that opinion quickly, and said that could not be right, because Mark had been dead for a while, and as far as he could tell, these two had just met, that is why she was introducing him to her family.

Plus, he said, it has been a long time since Mark's death, and she is entitled to move on with her life.

That upset Laurie, even more, and accused him of not being on her side, and that he did not care for their son like she did.

The others in the meanwhile, were having fun, and some of them made it their business to talk about Cindy, and her man friend.

There was a certain group, that made it a habit, to speak about someone or people, during this time, it had become a tradition, a nasty tradition, and this year, Cindy was the topic to talk about.

Peter quickly became attached to Cindy's brothers, and he joined the guys, as the gravitated towards the television to watch the football game.

The younger ladies navigated to the game room and enjoyed watching the kids play while they chatted about many things, especially, men, and they watched a couple movies.

"Cindy, you were so right with your description, this guy is a hunk, now he really has me suspicious of him."

"Katie, now you understand, what I said to you, I am either blessed or cursed with an imposter, because good things just don't come dropping into your laps, without you having to struggle to obtain it."

"Struggle? Not you, with your beauty, you could attract any man to you." Katie said with a smile.

"Flattering me won't get you anywhere, what do you want from me?" she said laughing, "but keep the compliments coming, I don't mind."

"Funny, but you know it's true."

Then Cindy left and went to speak to her mom.

"So, you have been dating, and you can't even trust me or your brothers to let us know? I am just saying that, because if something would happen to you, God forbid, we would like to be in the light, not the darkness."

"Mom, I met this guy about two months ago, we went out a couple of times, he is a nice guy, but I am not ready to commit to a relationship, unless I am 100% sure that this is the guy for me, but for now we are just dating."

"Dear, I just want you to be careful, and if he is the one for you, I don't want you comparing him to Mark, because you won't find another Mark."

"Is he from around here?"

"No, he came from one of those small towns outside of Beaumont."

"He moved to the Houston area, after he graduated from college, to work with one of the oil companies."

"So, he is a decent guy, with a good career, that is a good step."

"Mom, you know me better than that, I would not be with someone that has no ambition."

Not too long after their conversation, Cindy went to speak with her brothers. Peter quickly made a point to speak with Karen.

The two conversed for at least 15 minutes.

Karen drilled him, but he took it all in stride, because he realized just what a close-knit family they were.

The gathering slowly dwindled, and just the immediate family and Peter were left.

They all helped in clearing the table and tidying up the kitchen before they sat down to relax for a while.

Then Peter and Cindy had to leave.

"It was my pleasure meeting you, you have such a nice family, and I really do appreciate the hospitality that was shown to me, hopefully, I will continue to see you in the future."

"We enjoyed having you," Karen replied, "and like you said, hopefully we will continue to see each other if things go well."

The brothers were in unison with the same sentiments.

"What are your plans for Saturday night?" Peter asked Cindy's brothers.

"No plans," Josh answered.

"What about coming over to my place, we could watch the basketball games, and chill."

"How come you never invited me to your home, and here comes my brothers and they are invited?"

"I am not inviting just them, I am inviting you, the ladies too."

Peter walked Cindy to her vehicle and said he would call her later.

Ten minutes after she left, Peter called to see if she had made it home.

"Thanks for checking on me, and I hope you made it home safely too."

"Yes, I did, not too long ago."

"That means, you are not too far from me." She replied.

"Actually, I am about 10 minutes from the Medical Center, not sure how far I am from you since I don't know where you are living."

"I am living at the Broken Woods apartments, at the corner of Greenlane and Harold drive."

"Thanks, Cindy, for finally letting me into your life, even though you are doing it a little by little, but better slowly than never."

Then he said, "I am living at the Brooksville condominiums in the Pecan Ville area."

Joshua and the rest of the family gave their views and opinions about Peter, and they were mostly favorable.

Although they questioned, his being a bachelor, never being married and no kids, he had a well-rounded life, one that was successful.

And Karen pondered that thought in her heart.

Apart from this, the brothers and Katy loved him.

Saturday evening, they left the house about 7pm, and stopped at Cindy's apartment to pick her up, since she wanted to ride with them.

They arrived at Peter's place about 7:35pm, they waited at the gate for Peter to buzz them in.

The area was well kept, and from the looks of the place, you knew it was expensive to live there.

Peter's condo was located towards the middle of the complex.

They parked in his visitors' spots, which were in front of his condo.

Peter had a two-bedroom condo, and the visitors were so impressed to see how clean and how well kept and organized it was.

"Peter, are you truthful that you live alone, and you don't have anyone else in your life?" Cindy asked him jokingly.

"I am certain," he replied, "why?"

"Because your condo says otherwise. No bachelor can keep an apartment or condo so neat, clean, and well put together like this."

"Thanks for the compliment, but this is who I am. My mom, who left us a few years ago, and my father who divorced my mom, when I was about to graduate high school, taught me to appreciate what I have been blessed with, and to take nothing for granted, so I adopted that advice from them, and try to live that way."

They ordered a couple pizzas and some other snacks, and sat to watch the game.

Shortly after the game, they had to leave because most of them had to travel the next day.

Joshua's game was on Tuesday in Dallas, so he planned to leave early Monday morning to join his teammates, while his wife and son, would head back to Florida on Wednesday.

They left Peter's place with a good impression of him, and the brothers gave their sister the approval, to be with Peter.

"Like I said, we are just dating, where it leads to, time will tell; I like him and love his attitude, but we will see."

They walked Cindy and Johanna, along with Marcus to the apartment, made sure that they were safe, then left for home.

Cindy called Peter as soon as she settled down.

"Hi Peter, just letting you know that we are home safe, and to say that I am very thankful for your hospitality this evening. You were a good host."

"Oh, thank you, but the pleasure was all mine to have you and your family spending quality time with me, what more can I ask?"

I am hoping that is not a one time treat but would be a routine occurrence.

Cindy and Peter spent the next hour and a half on the phone, and tackled different subjects, including Marcus.

After that phone call, Cindy realized how much in love she was with Peter, but she still wanted to take it slowly and did not want him to know right now how deeply in love she was with him.

Chapter EIGHTY-EIGHT

PETER ASKED HER TO spend Christmas day with him, but she declined the invitation because she was scheduled to work.

Peter was disappointed, but not discouraged; he was the type of person who pursues what he desired, so he thought of another plan.

He found out what time she was scheduled to go to lunch, and he planned around that.

He bought a lovely bouquet of beautiful roses and went to the hospital where she worked. He showed up at the front desk, and inquired about her, told them who he was, and was directed to the area where she worked.

He approached the nurse's station and asked to see Cindy; he was asked to wait while she was contacted.

He sat in the waiting area with his back towards the nurse's station.

She came in and asked for the person who was here to see her.

They pointed to the guy who was sitting on the chair looking out of the window.

She approached the person, and said, "hello," and Peter turned around with the bouquet of flowers in his hands, and he handed them to her.

She was so shocked to see him, and wondered why he had come?

"Would you go to lunch with me since you can't come to my home?"

She blushed, and looked around to see if anyone was watching, then she caught the nurses staring in her direction.

She said, "sure, my lunch is scheduled for 1pm. There is a great cafeteria at the end of the building."

"That is alright with me, just want to be with you for Christmas."

As they passed by the nurses' station, she could hear them whispering, and heard some of the remarks they made, which were complimentary remarks about Peter.

They sat in the corner near the window that overlooked the water fountain.

And he said, "the food is good, but the company is much better, thanks for having lunch with me."

"Had I said no, would you have given up?"

"You are getting to know me better; I would just think of something else to do."

Cindy was so impressed that Peter would go to that length to spend time with her; that just warmed her heart more towards him, and she was falling deeper in love with him.

"When she came back to the nurses' area, she was met with all types of questions and opinions.

Charlene, her friend, asked, "is this the new beau in your life?"

"Yes, he is," Cindy replied.

"He is so cute, what a body, where does he work out? I need to go there," Charlene said jokingly.

"Stay away from my baby," Cindy said, and gave a big laugh.

The other nurses gave her a thumbs up, and told her that her boyfriend was handsome.

Someone said, "you sure know how to pick them," she was referring to Mark.

Cindy felt uneasy when she heard that, because her mind flashed back to Mark, and she fought hard to keep her emotions under control.

She left work earlier than scheduled, with the permission from her manager, because she wanted to spend some quality time with Marcus for Christmas.

They had planned on opening their gifts the day after, but since she came home early, they opened them on Christmas day.

It was a bittersweet day for her, she found a great guy, someone who cared for her, but it was difficult for her because she remembered an awesome guy, the one who was the love of her life, the one who knew and understood her better than anyone else, and the person who was an awesome father to her one and only son.

And Marcus did not make it any easier for her, he kept saying that he missed his dad and wished that he was there.

She asked him if he wanted to go to his grandparents tomorrow, to spend the day with them, and he quickly said no, and that he did not want to be over there.

She had planned to tell him about Peter, but then realized that this was not the time because he was in a sad mood, and bringing up a man that would be there instead of his dad would not be a good idea.

Cindy said, "to him, he would see a replacement for his dad, but to me, Mark can never be replaced and will be a part of my life forever."

At that moment, she had a flash back, and it got to her, and she reached out and hugged Marcus as tightly as she could, and said to him, "your mama will always be here for you, I won't leave you, I will be here."

Then she rested her head on top of his and cried.

It was a solemn moment for her, it came out of nowhere, a few hours ago, she was all smiles, and excited about a new man in her life, and now she was debating whether she needed any man in her life at all.

They went back to the original plan, to open their gifts, on the next day, in the morning.

After a few minutes with Johanna, and Marcus, Cindy went to bed, feeling very sad, she cried herself to sleep.

During that period, Peter called her phone numerous times, but could not reach her being with concern, he called Joshua, who called his mom to find out what was going on.

Karen told him that she was okay, she was just tired and was not in the best mood because she missed Mark, and went to sleep early.

He related the message to Peter, who felt better after receiving the information.

She woke up late in the morning, because it was her day off.

Johanna had prepared breakfast, so right after they ate, they opened gifts.

Marcus was excited because he loved the gifts that he received, especially the basketball hoop that he received from Joshua.

Cindy did not hear from Peter so she called him to find out what was going on.

"Hi Cindy, what's going on?" he asked.

"What do you mean, 'what's going on?' Are you not supposed to ask how I'm doing?"

"Sorry, how are you doing? The reason that I asked what's going on is because since you left yesterday, I haven't heard from you. I had to call your family to find out if you were okay."

"You did? You mean, you went to all that trouble to find out about me?'

"Yes, because I was deeply concerned."

"I went to bed early last night; I was not in the best of moods, so I did what I normally do when I am depressed, I sleep."

"After such a wonderful afternoon that we had, well, I wondered how you could be in a bad mood?

"Is it something I did or said yesterday?"

"Peter, this had nothing to do with you. It was all me, and I am sorry if I had you worried, and, I did not say that I was in a bad mood, I said, I was not in the best of moods."

"You know what? Let's drop this, and move on, but in the future, I would be grateful if you could give me a call and let me know that you are okay before hitting the sack."

"Going forward, I promise that I will do that."

"What are you doing today, care to join me?"

"Sorry, I have to decline; I already made plans to spend some quality time with Marcus; I promised to take him to the mall and other activities."

"We could make it a three-man team; I would be glad to join you all."

"Great, but no, I don't want to have to explain to Marcus who you are right now, I was planning on doing that after the season was over, besides, I have not had some quality time with him for a while, therefore I took time off to do that. Understand?"

"Sure, I am hoping in the near future, we will do that together."

"That is my hope too."

After they hung up, Cindy felt bad for him because she could hear the dejection in his voice, but she did not regret making that decision.

Cindy called her mom to see how she was doing, not anticipating that she was going to get a lecture.

"My dear, I am doing fine, couldn't be better, you see when you have Jesus as the mainstay in your life, you will be at peace.

Are you at peace, My dear?"

"Mom I am, but I just called to find out how you were doing, that's all."

"I know that Cindy, but I am just letting you know, that I am okay, as long as Christ is the captain of my ship, because he always steers me to the right places, and at the right time, he knows the ocean, so I am safe in his hands."

"How are things with you and Peter?'

"Mom, so far, it is going well, he treats me well, and he is interested in my life and Marcus's life."

"Great," she replied.

"Please tell me, does he go to church? Have you invited him to church? But again, how can you invite him,

When are you not going yourself?"

"Mom, we just started the relationship; that will come with time."

"He might be great now because he is trying to win your heart, but once that happens, he will change, because he is not a God-fearing man, and therefore, his love might not be genuine. I am just looking out for you, my daughter."

"Mom, thanks for your concern, I know of couples that lasted for a long time together, and never been at church, so you, see? There is love outside of church."

"They did not turn their backs on God, it is different for those that knew God and turned their backs on him."

"Mom let's change the subject. Marcus told me that he is going by granny next week, did you know that?"

"No, he did not tell me, but I guess he is just as crazy as his mama," hahaha.

"Funny, I am just fine, and am in the best frame of mind."

"Anyway, I will talk with you later, say hello to your husband."

"Why don't you talk to him, or call him, every now and then?"

"Mom, I am happy with the way the relationship is, so let's just leave it at that, okay?"

"Okay, I will speak with you later."

The next few days, Cindy spent some quality time with Marcus. They enjoyed each other's company, and they bonded tighter than they were before.

Cindy was satisfied that she did set that time aside for her son, she always cherished the moments that they shared together.

Cindy told Marcus about Peter, she took the time and explained to him about the relationship that she and Peter had and told him that he would not be replacing his dad but would be a part of their lives.

Chapter *EIGHTY-NINE*

Sunday afternoon, she was relaxing in her bedroom, when her phone rang, and it was Katy,

"Cindy, are you looking at the news?"

"No, I am here relaxing."

"Turn on your television and look at the breaking news!"

Cindy quickly turned on the television and saw a policeman leading Kirk away in handcuffs and a huge crowd gathered in the square.

"What's going on?" She asked Katy.

"He has been arrested for rape; he has allegedly raped a cheer-leader from the team cheer leading squad."

"I have been praying for this day to come for so long, and finally, my prayer has been answered; I hope he rots in prison." She said, as she sobbed.

"I am with you sister, that dirty old man, his day has arrived, and he shall pay for what he did to you."

"See? From being one of the basketball stars in the country to now a jailbird, and ultimately, a prisoner."

"And I hope other women come forward, because I am pretty sure, you two, are not the only ones."

"Kate, I am so thankful, and I really appreciate you, someone else would have spilled the information, especially, when the person you loved so much, asked for the information, and you withheld it from him, because of our relationship, that is incredible, you barely find that level of loyalty anywhere. I love you sis."

"Same here sis, and I am so glad they caught this rapist, this will give you a little bit of comfort and satisfaction."

They spoke for another hour, before Cindy said bye, and went to prepare for her upcoming day's work.

Cindy and Peter spent a lot of time together, in the next few months that followed, they travelled, attended certain activities, and dined out on numerous occasions.

Their relationship grew stronger as time went along, they trusted, and loved each other more fervently, as the relationship matured.

Peter introduced Cindy to his brother Greg, and his sister Stephanie, who were living in their small town outside of Beaumont.

Peter tried to convince Cindy to move in with him, but he was not successful.

She told him frankly, that this would not happen until they got married, and that was her stand on this subject, and she did not back down.

Chapter *Chapter* NINETY

PETER, CINDY, JOHANNA, AND Marcus, almost got into an accident on their way to Dallas to her sister Jennifer's wedding.

Without a warning, an eighteen-wheeler swung in front of them, and forced them off the road.

Peter managed to steer the car away from the wall that was ahead of them.

He slightly touched it and damaged his vehicle on the rear side of the driver's side.

"Thank you, Lord, this could have been so much worse than we experienced, only your mercies spared us."

They all sat there shaking in their seats, as they tried to digest what had just happened.

Eventually, they made it to Dallas, and were happy to check into the hotel.

It was a lovely wedding, and Cindy was happy that she was able to attend.

Her sister was thrilled to see her, because it had been a while since they had seen each other; the last time was at Mark's funeral.

Jennifer was happy to see her nephew, and to meet Peter and Johanna.

They made it back to Houston around 7:30pm on Sunday evening.

They spent a couple of hours at Peter's condo before he took them to their apartment.

Later, they spoke on the phone, and during their conversation, she found out that his birthday would be in a couple of weeks, June 29th, she planned to have a surprised birthday celebration for him.

She planned and organized with a few of his friends, and his brother and sister to celebrate his birthday on Saturday, which was a day after his birthday.

She went back and forth to the location, to make sure everything was in place, and ready.

With her charm and smarts, she was able to get him to go to the location without any suspicion.

He was shocked and surprised to see the welcome and birthday cheers he received when he opened the door; he had no clue this was planned for him. Seeing his brother and sister there was the biggest surprise to him.

He hugged and thanked Cindy for her thoughtfulness and for caring enough to go to that length to celebrate his birthday.

"I can't remember, or if ever, that I had a birthday celebration," and he was a little bit emotional.

"Thanks to Cindy, and to everyone who made this possible."

"Thanks brother, and you my sister, for making the trip here to celebrate with us."

"Okay, let the party begin."

And without further delay, the party was in high speed. The food was plentiful, and the drinks were in abundance, as the DJ kept the music coming, so the dancing continued, and yes, the noise level went up some notches.

The party lasted until about 2:am, and by 3:am, everyone had left, and the place was cleaned, and the furniture was rearranged, and everything back in order.

On their way home, Peter told Cindy that this was his best birthday yet and could not wait to see what the future held.

"Should I drop Johanna off at the apartment, and you could come and spend the rest of the night at my place?"

"Not a good idea Peter, I would not consider leaving Johanna alone in the apartment to spend the night at your place. There will be lots of nights at your place in the future."

"Sorry, I just wanted to spend some more time with you."

"You could come to my place since Marcus is with his granny, and I know Johanna would stay in her room."

Peter was beyond happy when she said that and quickly accepted her proposal.

They had a wonderful intimate time; at first it was difficult for Cindy, because for the first time, she was intimate in bed with a man that was not Mark, and in her mind, she was comparing him to Mark, and she accepted it, but it was not as enjoyable as Mark.

Peter left about 5:am, before the neighbors could be nosey. He was so excited about what had taken place, and could not believe that the day and night had gone so great.

He called a few minutes later, to let her know that he had made it home safely.

Cindy sat up in her bed, feeling guilty for what had just happened, because she had promised not to go to bed with Peter until he said 'I do,' she did not want him to lose interest in her, but she failed on her promise, and now her biggest fear was whether he would stay or go, now that he had gotten what he desired.

But for the next few weeks, nothing changed negatively; as matter of fact, he was even nicer than before, and that gave her hope that everything would be alright.

He helped her put together a small party for Marcus's birthday.

They held it at Karen's house, with a few of Marcus classmate, and some other friends.

It lasted until about 7:pm, because the next day was a working day.

As Cindy's birthday approached, Peter thought about ways he could outdo Cindy on her birthday celebration.

He wanted her birthday to be the best that she ever had, then it struck him he would take her to Las Vegas for the weekend.

One week before her birthday, he told her about his plan to take her somewhere special. He asked her to talk with her mom, so Marcus and Johanna could spend the weekend at her house.

"Hi, Johanna, you have a choice to stay with my mom or you could go home, because I will be gone beginning on Friday for the entire weekend."

Johanna decided to stay at Karen is for the weekend.

Cindy felt good about her decision because Marcus loved being around her; she was like a big sister to him.

Karen called Cindy when she found out from Marcus that his mom was going on a trip, and that he was coming over to her house, and asked her if that was true.

After Cindy confirmed it, she asked her, where are you going?

"I am not sure mom; it is a surprise birthday trip from Peter."

"I do not like that. So many things are happening, at least I need to know where you are going to be in case I must reach you."

"Mom, you have my phone number, we will always be in touch, you know how much Marcus means to me, I will always call to check on him."

"I will not be at ease until I know where you will be at."

"As soon as I finds out, I will let you know, but for now, I am just going to wait on my surprise."

Chapter NINETY-ONE

CINDY DID NOT FIND out until Friday at the Las Vegas airport. The flight was continuing to Portland, Oregon, and the things he said to her, made her believe that was where they were going.

When they landed in Las Vegas, and the people were disembarking, he sat there until the last person passed by, then he stood up, and said, "get your bag, we are getting off here."

They grabbed their carry-on bags and got off the plane, then to the baggage area to collect their small bag.

Following that, they went to the rental counter to rent a car; when Cindy saw that, she said to him, "I thought we were taking a taxi to the hotel?"

"No, I always drive when I come here."

"That means, you are familiar with the roads, right?"

"Yes, I am, don't be scared, I got this."

They made it to the hotel about 8:30pm, and he parked the rental in the garage, then walked to the front desk to check in.

Instantly, the front desk clerk recognized Peter.

"Hi Peter," she said, "it's been a while since you have been here, say a year and a half, right?"

"Hi Janet, how are you doing? I see your memory is spot on, but I am glad to be back."

While he was chatting and checking in, Cindy excused herself, and went to the lady's room; she could have waited until they got to their room, but she wanted to call her mom privately.

"Mom, I am in Las Vegas, I will be back on Sunday." And she gave her the hotel name and promised to call her later to give her the room number.

"Vegas?" her mom replied, "are you crazy?"

"Mom, I will call you later, I can't discuss this right now."

She made it back to the front desk where Peter was still chatting with Janet.

They went up to their room which was very nice and expensive.

"You came here quite often?" Cindy questioned him.

"A few times, yes," Peter answered.

"So this is where you brought all your past girlfriends?"

"You are making it sound like I had a ton of girlfriends, but yes, I came here with a couple girlfriends."

"I know, because you are well known around here, even some of the maids, know you, must have been a great guest."

"Cindy, let's not mess up this weekend, what was done in the past, is just that, the past, so please, let's enjoy your birthday celebration to the fullest."

Cindy agreed but kept all these things in her heart.

After they showered, they dressed up, and went to have some dinner in one of his favorite restaurants on the Vegas strip, which was a few minutes from where they were.

Cindy was impressed, with what she saw so far, from the airport to the hotel, and now the strip, she was very impressed.

When they had finished eating, Peter said, "we are not going to waste any moment on this strip, would you like to go see one of these shows tonight?"

"Oh yeah, definitely, I have heard so much about Vegas and the shows, I can't believe that I am actually here, and about to go to one of the shows, amazing."

Peter gave her a list of the shows that were on that night, so she could make a choice of the one she wanted to see.

She chose one of the Cirque de soleil shows.

She was amazed by the awe-inspiring entertainers, with all these colors, and costumes, and the highly skilled performers.

After the show ended, Peter decided that they were going to spend a few hours at the casino.

"Casino?" oh, no, my mom would be so angry with me if she knew that I went to the casino. She is totally against gambling; it's against her religious beliefs, and I kind of agree with her."

"Well, mom is not here, and besides, how is she going to find out? I don't see a spy here, do you?"

"No, but my conscience would bother me."

"Cindy, this is a new experience for you, that opportunity might not come for you again, you may, or may not come back here again, so it's up to you, the decision is yours, you are grown enough to make your own decisions."

"You know what? You are right, I am going to enjoy this week-end."

From that moment, she loosened up and was ready to have fun.

They played a few games, won and lost a few times before they called it a night.

It was a short walk back to their hotel; they walked hand in hand under the bright lights, enjoying the scenery, as they strolled along.

As they were on the top floor, their view from their room was breathtaking.

They sat at the edge of the bed and gazed out of their balcony, and took in the scenery, and looked at the busy strip below.

They were so tired from the travelling, and from the other activities that they attended, that it did not take them long to fall asleep.

Peter woke up, while she was still sleeping, and went downstairs, into one of the restaurants, and picked up breakfast and brought it back to the room.

While he was downstairs, Cindy woke up, and she called her mom and gave her more details, of where they were, and the number to reach her, if she could not get her on her phone.

She inquired of her boy and assured her that she was having a great time, and that everything was okay.

When they had finished eating, they took a few items, and went to their next adventure, the air tour.

They were picked up from the hotel and taken to the location where the flight was to take off.

"Wow, this is amazing," Cindy said to Peter, as they were treated with up close views of above and below the Grand Canyon rim.

They saw great landscapes, the dam and a lake, all the while being educated about what they were seeing.

It was an eye-opening experience for Cindy, this being her first time experiencing something like this, unlike Peter, who had seen this many times.

The whole adventure took about 3 hours, so they were back in their room about 4pm.

They rested for a while, had room service, then left later in that evening to enjoy a few more activities.

Scared, but finally convinced by Peter, she agreed to go on the high roller.

She did not regret listening to him, because this was a breath-taking ride, on the world's highest observation wheel. She got to the pinnacle point, which was about 550 feet high, and she looked down at the strip, and the view was magnificent.

After that, though she would have loved to check out other activities, but she was too tired, and just wanted to be in her hotel room.

"What a day and night", she said to Peter, "I enjoyed every bit of it, thanks for a great birthday."

"I am so glad that you are enjoying your birthday, you deserve every bit of happiness that comes your way."

The two love birds showered, then relocated to the jacuzzi, (which were only installed in the most expensive rooms), then the fun began.

They eventually made it to the bed, where their passion went wild, and they engaged in passionate intimacy.

They had promised from their last sexual encounter, that next time they would protect themselves to avoid pregnancy, because they wanted to plan for that, but in the heat of their passion, they forgot about their promise, and had intercourse naturally.

As soon as they had done climaxing, Cindy hit Peter a couple of small slaps on his back and was furious, and said, "you were supposed to wear protection and you did not."

"We both forgot, we were engaged in the present, and followed our desires, and forgot about the future, and that was what happened."

Cindy laid on the bed and panicked; she was hoping that nothing happened in the area of pregnancy.

"Cheer up Cindy, you will be okay, nothing happened."

They continued chatting as Peter stroked his hand through her hair, until she slowly gave way to sleep.

The alarm went off at 9:am, they quickly got off the bed, showered, dressed, and they went downstairs to check out, then left for the airport.

They turned in the rental, checked in, and waited to board their flight to Houston.

"How was your weekend?" he asked

"One of the most entertaining in my life, I will never forget it.

He was happy to hear that, but he was a little bit disappointed, he wanted to hear her say, one of the most romantic of her life, but he was happy that she had a great time.

Chapter NINETY-TWO

IT WAS A SMOOTH flight back to Texas. They left their vehicle in the park and fly area, so they did not have to wait on someone to pick them up.

They stopped at Karen's for a short while to pick up Johanna and Marcus, then Peter dropped them off at the apartment, before continuing to his place.

He called a few minutes later to let her know that he was home. She always wanted that confirmation, because since Mark's tragedy, she remained paranoid.

She had put in for the Monday off, so she rested and did not wake up until about 11.30am, ate a light breakfast, called Peter, then went back to bed.

She woke up when Johanna and Marcus came home.

Later in the evening, she spoke to her mom, and as expected, her mom was not thrilled about her trip to Las Vegas.

But she made it clear to her mom that she knew what she was doing, and she handled everything, the way it was supposed to be handled.

The next day at work, her friends were eager to hear of her weekend happenings, they knew that it was her birthday, and they saw previously, how awesome her boyfriend treated her, so they were expecting to hear about something special.

When she told them that she went to Las Vegas, they did not believe it, because they knew her, and what she believed, but when she told them of the places that she went, and the things that she did, they believed her.

"Sarah, one of her best friends on the job, came up to her, and asked her for details.

But she told her a lot of the details of the regular stuff, but of the private moments, she kept to herself.

She was not going to tell Katy that she had gone to Vegas, but because her mom told Joshua, she had to tell Katy.

She explained to her that it was a surprise, and she did not know until they made it to Vegas, and then she went into details about her trip

Yet Cindy was worried, she was praying that she did not get pregnant over the weekend.

She knew it would be a bad image to portray in her circle because she knew what people would say and the reproach that would be coming her way.

She went through it with Mark, and it was terrible, and hurtful, and vowed not to go through that again, and here she was, not sure if she was in the same predicament again.

The next few weeks were rather quiet; it was just the regular routine.

She saw Peter a few times but spoke to him daily, and their love grew.

She never thought she would love like that again after Mark, but Peter came close.

She was not one that was too intrigued with jewelry, but Peter bought her a pair of gold earrings and a beautiful bracelet, and she was elated.

And because she was not a person who went out often, she wondered where she would wear them, said to herself, thanksgiving is about a week away, and it would be at Shawn's house, in one of her favorite cities, New York, and that would be a swell time to show off her eye-catching jewelry.

They made it to New York on Tuesday night, and went to Shawn's place, though Peter wanted to stay at a hotel, but Cindy was against it.

She explained that Shawn and Liz insisted that they stay at their house, and she did not want to disappoint them, so she obliged, and furthermore, Shawn and Liz always stayed at her home when they came to the Houston area.

Karen and Donald checked into a hotel that was very close to Shawn's house, which was very convenient.

Jacob and Laurie, Mark's parents, did not attend, they stated that they were not fans of flying, but most of the folks did not believe that.

Thanksgiving Day, Shawn's house was buzzing with excitement, as they participated in the thanksgiving celebration.

As planned, Cindy displayed her jewelry, and she received numerous compliments concerning her jewelry.

And she was proud to establish that she received them, from her Beau, Peter.

They loved the way Peter was treating Cindy, and they let him know that he was appreciated, but Karen, her mom, was not convinced that Peter was genuine, and was very skeptical of him, besides saying that to her daughter, she did not say anything to anyone else, but kept her feelings to herself.

They admitted that they had a wonderful weekend and vowed to be in attendance the next year.

The flight back to Texas was bumpy, and frightening, because of some bad weather they encountered, when they left New York, but besides that, the flight was okay, and they landed in Houston safely.

On Tuesday, Cindy wore her jewelry to work, which brought about several compliments, and comments, mostly positive, though there were a few, who had a few negative things to say.

Chapter NINETY-THREE

On the third Saturday in October, Peter and Cindy, went to Florida to surprise Joshua during one of his home basketball games. He noticed them during the first quarter of the game, and was shocked to see them there, anyway, he had a great game, and they had lots of fun at the game.

Cindy and Peter had a wonderful weekend, she enjoyed being around Katy, as usual, and she and Peter spent quality time together, and they roamed the town at night.

Peter was still negligent, and Cindy careless when they were intimate again, Cindy was banking on being in her safe space and would be safe.

But unfortunately for them, this turned out to be false safety, because 7 weeks had passed, and Cindy was yet to have a period, and she was extremely worried, although she said, it might be just her mind playing tricks on her, because she believed that she was safe.

She informed Peter about the situation, and he responded, without enthusiasm, that he would not be happy if she was, he was hoping that she was not pregnant.

"Peter, that would be bad for me; my company does not encourage having children out of wedlock.

I think they have a policy in reference to that, but I don't think it has ever been enforced, but I am still concerned."

"I love my job and would hate to be out of a job because of that."

Peter remained quiet, and looked distant, like he was contemplating something, then he said, "if this is the case, do we have any other alternatives?"

"Like what?" she asked.

"If you are pregnant, do we have to…you know...

"You know what?" Cindy interrupted.

"I mean keep the pregnancy?" Peter said.

"If you are talking about abortion, forget about it pal, because there is no way that I am going to abort this child, if there is a child."

And Cindy was furious with Peter for even thinking like that.

"I thought you would be excited about having a child with me, but now I know. Thanks"

"Cindy, that is not what I meant, I am thinking of you and your job, and other stuff; sorry if it came out that way, of course, I would be happy to have a child with you."

Cindy did not say anything after that, and picked up her bag, and said "I'm heading home."

"Bye, I will talk to you later," and she left his place and went home.

Cindy made an appointment to see her doctor.

Doctor James was happy to see Cindy again, and after a brief conversation, began examining her, and did some blood work and ran some tests.

And as she already suspected but just wanted confirmation, she was pregnant.

Cindy was 7 weeks pregnant.

At that moment, she was troubled, was not sure what to do. She was not eager to tell Peter, because she was not pleased with him from their previous conversation concerning the situation, and she did not want to tell anyone else about it until she had decided what path she would take, that is apart from abortion.

She called Peter and told him the outcome of the visit to the doctor, and what was ahead for her.

"Oh Cindy, I will be there for you, we will go through this to-gether, what is your next step?"

"I don't know, let me think about it," and she hung up the phone, and went to her bed, and cried herself to sleep.

The next day Peter called her while she was at work and asked if they could have dinner at his place.

Cindy agreed; she was hoping that they would iron out details concerning their situation.

It was a beautiful Friday evening; it was a cool night. Cindy went home to her apartment to check on Johanna and Marcus, then she freshened up, and went over to Peter's place.

Peter came home early from work and ordered dinner from the seafood restaurant that was around the corner from his complex, he kept it warm and ready for when she arrived.

They sat at the table and enjoyed the meal, as they chatted about work and other issues, not mentioning their situation.

When they had finished dinner, they went to the bedroom, and sat at the edge of the bed, and watched television.

"How do you feel being pregnant?"

"Same as the other time, the only difference, this time I am not sure of my path going forward."

"What do you mean? We will be okay; we will be a family."

"Family? Are you going to marry me?" Cindy questioned him.

Peter paused, and then stumbled for words.

"I always wanted to marry you, but not like this, I wanted to have the whole hoopla that goes with marriage, like the engagement, lots of invitations, and a huge ceremony, you know what I mean?"

"Yes, I know what you mean, you are stalling, but you should have thought about all these things before you got intimate with me,"

"You know what? Forget about this marriage thing, I think, I will be better by myself."

"Not so easily, my dear, I loved you before, I love you now, and we are in this together, if that is what it takes to keep us together, that is what it will be."

"Cindy, my darling, do you want to marry me?"

"I would love to say yes, but not when it looks like I am forcing you into that, and that is not what I want, because your heart is far from marrying me for me."

"You could not be any further from the truth, I always wanted you to be my wife, and was hoping that would happen soon."

"Let me sleep on it tonight, and I will let you know tomorrow."

After they spent two more hours with each other, Cindy said it was time to leave.

"Can you just stay the night, seeing it is already late?"

"I thought we went through that already? If there was no one at my apartment, I surely would have stayed the night, but I can't leave them alone."

Peter followed Cindy home, and made sure that she was inside her apartment before he drove back to his place.

He called later to let her know that he was home safe.

She sat on her bed, and so many thoughts went through her mind.

"Am I doing the right thing by marrying Peter? Do I want to be a single mom raising two kids? And most importantly, does Peter really love me?"

And she wrestled with these thoughts going through her mind, after pondering it, she concluded, that she would marry him.

She woke up early that Saturday morning, and she prepared breakfast, and after they had eaten, she called Peter to give him an answer.

Peter was barely awake, he stayed up watching a movie, so he slept in late.

"Pete, I will swing by your place about 1:pm, do you want me to pick up some food at the restaurant?"

"You could if you feel like it, I am not too hungry, I had a big breakfast."

She arrived at his place about 1:30pm, and there he was, well prepared, he had two glasses, and a bowl fill with ice, and a bottle of champagne on the table.

"What is the occasion?' she asked him.

"We are celebrating our baby conception."

"You confused me. One time you are very low in energy concerning my pregnancy, next moment, you are riding high above the clouds with excitement, hard to figure."

"I know how you feel, but I thought about it, and I realized that it is a blessing to be able to have a child, and I am thankful for the blessing.

They ate the food Cindy brought, and they toasted to their unborn baby, and drank some champagne to celebrate that.

As they sat on the couch, Cindy said, "Peter, I would like to be your wife, so my answer is yes, I will marry you."

"Thanks babe, let's make it happen."

"I am sorry that you desired a big wedding, with all the guests, and glitter and thrills, I would love that for you too, but I am not willing to go through all that stress, neither do I want to put this baby through that stress."

"We can have a small wedding, and later when we are settled, we can have a big celebration."

"Thanks, Pete, for seeing things the way I saw it. Also, I would love to get that done as quickly as possible."

"We could go to the justice of peace in Galveston, and have it done." Peter said.

"I was thinking more of a small ceremony at my church. A few members from your family and mine and a few friends, that is all."

"Cindy, I can't do that church thing, I am not ready for that yet."

"Even it is for this one time, you can make an exception, I would hate to tell my folks, to join me at a Justice of peace, not that there is anything wrong with the Justice of Peace, but I would appreciate if it would be in a church."

"Think about it and let me know as soon as possible."

"Okay, I will let you know."

Cindy had barely made it home, when Peter called, and said, for this one time, he would make an exception, but I am letting you know that this going to church won't be a habitual thing when we get married."

"I will start working on the details, but first, we need to set a date."

"I have vacation starting on Monday the 22nd, which is about 3 weeks away,' he said.

"What about the 20th? "It is the Saturday before your vacation."

"Saturday the 20th, it is."

Chapter *NINETY-FOUR*

Now Cindy was in a predicament, she did not know how to approach her mom, with these two items. First the marriage, then the baby.

She knew what she was going up against, but she decided to deal with it now, and let the chips fall where they may.

She dialed her mom, she knew what her mom was going to say, but she still wanted to give her the opportunity to say it.

"Hi mom, how are you doing today?"

"Your mom is doing okay, thank my Lord for that, are Marcus and Johanna doing, okay?" also, how is your life going with your man friend?"

"Mom don't say it like that, he is the man that I am about to spend the rest of my life with; as a matter of fact, we are planning get married this month, on the 20th.

"What? What is going on? What is the rush? You just met this guy barely a year ago, no, don't tell me you are pregnant?"

Cindy took a long pause before she answered,

"Oh, I get it, this is what this is about, you are trying to cover up this pregnancy, by getting married, so it would look like as soon as you got married, you became with child. You could fool men and people around you, but you can't fool God."

Cindy expected that response from her mom, so she prepared herself to receive the lecture.

"How far are you?"

"Mom, let's deal with the wedding, then we can deal with the pregnancy later."

"It is going to be a small wedding, just family and a handful of friends.

"I have been through a big wedding before, and I don't want to go through that hassle again."

"Is it going to be in the church?"

"I hope so, I have not spoken to the pastor yet, I will be calling him, as soon as I am done talking to you."

"Anyway, I hope things work out good for you, you have my blessings, although, this isn't what I envisioned for you when you were growing up. But you will always have my love."

"Mom, I have to go, I will call you soon and don't tell anyone, I want to be the one to tell them"

After she got off the phone, Cindy called the pastor to make arrangement for him to perform the wedding ceremony, and to find out the availability of the church that Saturday.

It turned out that all things fell into place, and she was booked for that date.

Cindy was exhausted, but she still had to spend a few minutes with Marcus, before he went to bed, so she put everything else on hold for the next day and attended to Marcus.

She woke Sunday morning, and had Johanna prepare Marcus's outfit, then they had breakfast, before they left for church.

Her mom, also Mark's mom, were surprised to see her there.

After service was over, and they had picked up Marcus from kid's church, they came over to greet Karen and the others.

"What a surprise?" Karen exclaimed, "and you could have told me last night that you were coming."

"Mom, I don't have to tell you everything, besides, I love surprises."

Then she went over to Mark's parents and greeted them.

The reception from Laurie was still cold, but she expected that, and she did not let that phase her, as always, Jacob was happy to see her.

They were happy to see Marcus and asked Cindy when would he be coming to spend some time with them?

Cindy said he would soon, but she would call and notify them when the time came for him to come over.

Cindy followed her mom to her house, she knew she would get food to eat, because her mom's custom was to get up early on Sundays, and cook before she left for service.

She spent the day there, talking on the phone with Katy, and Liz. She invited them to the wedding, after apologizing for the short notice.

They both decided to attend, which did not surprise her, because they were true friends.

Later she called Junie, to invite him.

And he said, "are you serious? Who is this guy? I did not know you were even dating?"

"He is a wonderful man, he treats me good, and he loves me dearly, and he just can't wait to marry me."

"Sounds good that he cares for you, and I am hoping and praying that things will work out for you."

"Thanks Junie, coming from you, it means a lot to me."

She also called Mario her friend to check on him.

Mario had moved on, and was in a serious relationship, he had his heart set on Cindy, but when she defined their relationship, he was disappointed and turned his interests elsewhere.

After a few more calls, she told Johanna to pack up as it was time to head home.

At work the next day, she went to see Ms. Joseph and invited her to her wedding, she also told her good friend Sarah, and invited her and her boyfriend Dave.

The next few weeks were hectic, trying to get everything ready for the wedding day.

Both Katy and Liz came in on the Wednesday before so they could help her with the wedding.

On Friday, the day before the wedding, David, Shawn, Lisa, and Kellie, also Peter's siblings, Greg, and Stephanie made it into town.

It was an early morning wedding, the ceremony went along smoothly and quickly, and they were now husband and wife.

There was a small reception that followed at Peter's condo complex at the club house.

The reception lasted for about 4 hours, before everyone dispersed.

Most of the guests had left by Sunday evening.

Cindy moved her things that she wouldn't be in need of immediately to a storeroom.

Her lease was scheduled to end at the end of the month; she had 10 days left on there.

Cindy and the rest of them, moved into Peter's place; Cindy knew it was a risk having Johanna, move in with them, because of Peter, not that she did not trust him, but the temptation would be there, but she said she would have eyes wide open, and she would put in deterrents.

She had asked her to move back with her parents, but Peter insisted that she stay. He said Marcus needs her, and she would be a big help with him.

Chapter *NINETY- FIVE*

Two MONTHS AFTER SHE got married, Cindy revealed that she was pregnant, and since she did not carry a big baby bump, no one except her mom and Katy knew it happened before she got married.

Peter and Cindy's relationship strengthened daily, he spent a lot of time with her, he would come from work and would rub her stomach and would speak to the baby oftentimes.

Cindy was so pleased with the way Peter was treating her and the baby, and the way he took care of Marcus, like he was his own, and even her mother was starting to doubt herself, and wondered if he was the real deal.

Peter said that they should sell the condo and buy a house, Cindy agreed, and they started the process of looking for one.

She asked him, if they could get one in the same area where she had her previous one, because of the proximity to her job.

But there was a new development that was next to her previous area, so they decided to look in there instead.

The Latrine family was in their new house by the end of April, and got the condo sold, a month after.

They prepared the baby's room, bought the baby's crib, and other items that the baby would need.

They knew the baby was due at the end of June, or the early part of July, but they had others believing that it was due in September.

She told her manager at work, the same information, and submitted her request for maternity leave, for that period.

She and her family, and friends were at the house, Sunday, July 9th, having a small pool party, it was humid, and hot.

They were having lots of fun, when suddenly, Cindy felt a contraction, she called Peter, who was grilling, and he quickly came to find out what she needed, she told him about the contraction, and right away, he knew that she was in labor.

He called Johanna and told her that Cindy was having her baby, and they were leaving for the hospital.

"Please inform the guests, better yet tell Karen, and let het address that, and you take care of Marcus, and other things, we will keep you up to date.

And they left for the hospital.

"On their way, Peter called Dr James, who then gave the instructions that he needed to follow.

They arrived at the hospital around 6:25pm, and were escorted to the delivery area, where the nurses took over from there.

She was moved into a room, where her vitals were taken, and where she was examined, to see how much she had dilated,

The contractions came more frequently, and stronger.

Peter was panicky, because he had never been in that position before. He tried speaking gently to her, which she responded okay, but each time a contraction came, she snapped at him, and grabbed and squeezed his hand tightly, and he was, "what is this for?"

And she said, "shut up, it is your fault that I am in pain, ouch," as another contraction came through.

He started to get emotional and was asked to wait in the waiting room.

The doctor came in, and had move to the delivery room, so she could have the baby.

And within 10 minutes, she had the baby, a beautiful baby girl.

They allowed her to hold the baby for a few minutes, but then took the baby from her, and told her that the baby had to be placed in the Nicu area, because she had jaundice.

Cindy was heartbroken, but as a nurse, she knew that was not the worst of conditions, she knew that the baby would not be going home with her now.

And as expected, she left the hospital after two days, without her baby girl.

It was difficult for her, but with the support of her husband and mother, she was able to cope with the situation.

Most of her friends, and co-workers, believed that she had a pre-mature baby, because she made them believe that her child was due in September.

After 3 weeks in the hospital, her baby girl was allowed to go home.

"Welcome home, Nicole," Cindy joyfully said, "we were waiting diligently for you, meet your brother Marcus, and you adopted big sister Johanna, and of course, the troublemaker, the one who caused this in the first place, your daddy, Peter."

The celebration continued, as Karen came over to meet her grandchild.

Katy, Liz, and some of her friends called to congratulate her and Peter.

Peter spent so much time in Nicole's room, kept adding more decorations daily, he was so proud to be a daddy, and it showed.

After a week since Nicole had been home, Cindy said, to Peter, "we have to dedicate this baby next Sunday, I have contacted the Pastor, and had it arranged."

"You did what? How come you did not run this by me before you did that? And what is that anyway?"

"I did not run this by you because I thought that would be okay, because that is the normal, and customary thing to do."

"When a baby is born, it is a spiritual thing to do, to present that child to God, who gave that child life, and has allowed us to have that child. We must ask for His guidance for that child to be able to navigate in this world,"

"You mean, you were never dedicated or christened as a child?"

"Sorry, but I was never into all that stuff, that is why I said, church was not my biggest thrill."

"That is hard to believe, seeing you grew up in a small town, where church is a big community thing."

Peter was not interested in listening to church stuff, and declined to attend, so she stopped trying to convince him.

"With or without you, my baby and I will be going to church on Sunday, and there will be a ceremony, where she will be dedicated."

Cindy was troubled by the reaction of Peter and started wondering if her mom was right in the remarks she made.

Sunday morning, the day of the ceremony, Cindy had Johanna prepare Marcus for church, as she took care of Nicole and herself, and to her surprise, she saw Peter dressing up, and she asked him, "Where are you off to?"

"This is the last time I am going to church with you," he said, "I am not comfortable going there."

"Thanks for coming, it means a lot to me." Cindy exclaimed.

The service was great, so was the ceremony, there were 7 babies that were dedicated that day.

Peter whispered to Cindy, "my Nicole is the cutest among them, hands down."

"Yes, she is cute," Replied Cindy.

The ceremony went on swiftly and quickly; the Pastor took each child individually, and as he came to Cindy, he took Nicole from her and prayed to God on behalf of this child, and then proceeded to pray for the parents.

He rested one hand on Cindy and the other on Peter and prayed for them.

That made Peter so uncomfortable and he could not wait for this ceremony to be over with.

After the ceremony, they met with Karen for a short time, before they returned to their home.

On their way home, Cindy looked at Peter, and said to him, "thanks for coming to stand on behalf of your daughter, I really appreciated that."

"Church is not my thing, but I am glad that I went , I was not comfortable with the Preacher laying his hands on me, but I guess, it was okay.'

"What is it about church that you do not like?" Cindy questioned him.

"I had some bad experiences with church folks, and therefore, I decided not to have anything to do with church folks, and church people."

"Supposing I had told you when we just started dating about my church background, would you had continued to date me?"

"Probably I would, probably I would not, I don't know, but I am glad that I did stay with you."

Cindy herself was not a regular church goer; that changed when she attended college. She said her earlier years were dictated by her mom and she was forced to go.

They stopped at an Italian restaurant to have lunch and they received so many compliments on Nicole because of her beauty and the way she was dressed.

Peter was just beaming with pride; he loved the compliments that were coming their way and was in no rush to leave the restaurant.

Finally, they made it home; Cindy was happy because her shoes were killing her, they were too tight and too high. She quickly placed them in the closet and got into some more relaxing clothes and shoes.

They relaxed for the remainder of the day. They both spent time on the phones with their friends.

Cindy spoke to Katie about Mark's parents, and told her how nasty Laurie was towards her and that she cared less how she felt.

Marcus used to spend at least a weekend a month with them, but since his mom and grandmom were at it constantly, his time with them was cut down drastically.

The latter part of the evening found Peter absorbed with Sunday night football, and paid little attention to the rest of them, so Cindy took that time to converse with Johanna.

They spoke to each other, but were always in a hurry, but this night she took the time to really have a good conversation.

She said to her, "Jo, since your graduation in May from the Community College, I have not gotten the chance to at least throw a little celebration for you; why don't we do that 2 Saturdays from now, if that is okay with you?"

"Oh sure, I would love that," Johanna replied.

"Okay, it is on, invite your friends, and let me know how you want this planned."

"I thought you were going to continue working toward your bachelor's degree"

"Yes, I am, but with the baby, and all that is happening now, I thought I would hold back and start in January instead."

"I was not aware of that, thank you so much for your consideration. By the way, how are things going with you and Jessie?"

"We are doing okay, things are steady between us, but I told him, I want to get my degree first before I can consider a totally committed relationship."

"Good for you, I am very proud of you."

They continued with their conversation a little while longer before preparing for bed.

Chapter NINETY-SIX

CINDY SPENT MOST OF her time off work, bonding with her daughter, she gave most of her attention to her.

Her birthday came and went, with no big flare, because she chose not to make it a big issue, she was too occupied with Nicole to care about birthday celebration. She gave God thanks and praised him for another great year and asked him for an even better upcoming year.

Her maternity period ended, and it was time to go back to work.

It was the second Monday in October, and she woke up feeling very depressed and sad, because she was leaving her daughter, to go back to work.

This was a very difficult time for her; with Marcus it was hard, but nothing compared to the way she was feeling now.

At work she was very quiet throughout the day; Sarah, her friend, asked her if everything was okay with her and with her family, but she told her everything was fine, and explained to her, the way she was feeling because of having to come to work and leave her daughter home.

Eventually, she got through the day and rushed home; she was so happy to see her daughter.

"Jo, I know you probably got tired of me calling to check up on Nicole, but I am sorry, I couldn't help it, and you know I trust you, but one day, you will understand when you have a child of your own."

"Don't' worry Cindy, I do understand." Johanna replied.

This happened throughout the week, but every day it got better, until the weekend came, and the anxiety was abated.

On Saturday, Peter and Cindy went to the bank to open a joint checking account; they had been doing everything like they were not married, and other than the house, they had nothing else showing a joint relationship.

They wanted this checking account to used as a means of paying certain bills and to be used for other miscellaneous items.

They said they would sit sometime later and discuss their finances.

In the meantime, they were planning a great thanksgiving, their first as a married couple, and they were nominated to be the host this year, so they planned on making it grand.

They were anxious to have people come over to their new home, to meet their new baby, and to have fun.

As was the custom, Katie and Liz, came in early in the week to spend time with Cindy, and to assist her in cooking, although this year, it would be less cooking, because Peter planned to have most of the food catered.

He said Cindy did not need the stress put on her this year, especially, she just had a baby.

He was well prepared, with a variety of food and meat; he had baked and smoked turkeys.

They had lots of drinks, and this time, there was lots of alcohol, because that was who Peter was, he loved his drinks, and he catered for his friends, even though, Cindy was not pleased with it, there was nothing she could do to stop him.

They gathered on Thursday as traditionally done, and the turn-out was great, because this year, Peter invited some of his friends and family.

The atmosphere this year was different, but good, there was more excitement, more mingling, and less segregating.

Katy and Liz were so excited to meet little Nicole, Cindy told them how pretty she was, so they were eager to meet her.

And they were not disappointed, because to them, Nicole was even more beautiful than Cindy described her.

The guys, as they did every year, ignored the ladies, and stuck to the television and the football games, while the younger ladies congregated in the bedroom to talk about their husbands, boy-friends, and anything that they could get a laugh of.

These activities continued until the evening time; by 8:00, most of the guests had left and those who remained were the people that were spending the weekend with the Latrine's.

They stayed up late into the night playing games, watching tele-vision, and just socializing.

The next day, they went to the mall, and other shopping venues. This took most of their time. On the way back to the house, they stopped at an ice-cream shop to have a few scoops of ice-cream.

The guys played dominoes, watched games on the television, and joked around throughout the night. The ladies had fun in their own ways.

Sunday afternoon, Katie and her son left for Florida, and Shawn and Liz left for New York.

"I had a good thanksgiving, I enjoyed your family, and your friends' company, it was a really cool vibe." Peter told Cindy.

"Glad you did, I am fortunate and blessed to have these people in my life, had it not been for them, I don't know how I would have fared during the crisis periods I went through the last few years."

The next hour, they just sat and talked.

During that time, Cindy received a phone call from Junie. She could tell from Peter's face that he was not happy about it.

When she hung up, he asked, "Who was that?"

"My friend, Dr. King. He was just checking on me."

"He kind of does that real often," he said disgustedly.

"That's what friend do, they check up on each other, is that a problem?"

"Not really, I am just saying that he calls quite often."

Cindy did not respond, because she saw where this conversation was heading and she wanted no part of it.

After a few more minutes, they went to the bedroom, and there was tension in there, but Cindy quickly dismissed it, she went to bed and went to sleep.

In the morning, they greeted each other as usual, but was light on the conversation.

As the week proceeded, the relationship slowly restored to normal.

The next few weeks, they planned for their anniversary, and for Christmas at the same time, since Christmas was a few days away from their anniversary.

For their anniversary, Peter suggested going back to Las Vegas, but Cindy quickly extinguished that suggestion.

"How can we go and have fun in Las Vegas and leave a six-month-old child with Johanna? I don't think this is a good suggestion," she emphasized.

"Sorry, I did not look at it this way, any other suggestion?"

"We don't have to go anywhere, we could go out to a fancy restaurant, and spend some quality time in the town together; we will have lots of anniversaries to come where we could go somewhere far."

"Agreed, I know this restaurant downtown, that is top notch, I know you will like it, trust me on this one. I will call and make a reservation." Peter concluded.

After spending valuable time with Marcus and Nicole, Cindy prepared for her dinner date with her husband.

"Honey, how should I dress?"

"It is a top-notch restaurant, so dress to impress, I don't mean churchie, but not too formal, neither too casual. The very elite of the city eat there."

Cindy was impressed when she got to the restaurant, she had no idea, that they had this type of restaurant in the city.

The view from the top was amazing, you could see the beauty of the city in the night. The restaurant was perched high on a top floor of the building.

They sat at a table that was outside of the main dining area, it was secluded, yet opened enough, where they could enjoy the great view.

"This is amazing, my dear, good taste, I love the ambiance around here."

"Glad you like it, I can't wait till you get to taste the food, I know you will like it."

They brought the food, and Cindy was eager to taste it, so she could find out what her husband was talking about.

And she was not disappointed. The food was enjoyable and delicious.

"You were right, it sure tasted good, and the presentation was remarkable, the only issue I have with it, is that the portions are very small."

"You are too greedy" and he laughed at her, "it appeared small, but it is filling."

"For you, yes, but not for me. I love a fair amount of food for the big sum of money that we are going to pay, this place is not cheap."

They spent another hour at the restaurant, then they went up town to the waterfall wall to have a few pictures taken.

They made it home right before midnight.

"I had a great night, I couldn't ask for anything more, thank you." Cindy said thankfully.

"You are my heartbeat, and I would do anything to keep my heart beating, I love you." Peter said lovingly.

"I love you too, and I am so happy we found each other."

They went to their bedroom and had some passionate time together with no worry about pregnancy, because Cindy was now on the pill.

They were both off the next day, so they did not have to worry about waking up early.

The next few days would be Christmas, and fortunately for them, they had done all their Christmas preparations and shopping already, so they avoided the hassle of being out there shopping.

Christmas day, Donald and Karen came over, to bring their gifts, and to spend some time with the family.

Cindy baked her Christmas ham and cooked a variety of dishes for the family, and for her invited guests, Sarah and her now husband.

Following lunch, they gathered around the Christmas tree, passed out gifts and opened them.

Christmas day went by quickly, came and gone like a blur, the entire season went by quickly.

Chapter NINETY-SEVEN

PETER AND CINDY'S, LOVE grew, and they cherished their family; they did a lot of things together, as one unit, the two of them embraced the phase, "two shall become one." They started thinking alike and behaved more alike than ever before.

They made the family a priority over everything else and tried not to let any petty thing come between them, and they remained committed to each other.

Cindy wanted the entire family to make going to church a habitual occurrence, but she could not get her husband to agree to that, and after much trying, she gave up on him attending.

That affected her negatively, and instead of him following her to church, she started sliding away from church herself; it was no longer a regular thing, but an occasional occurrence.

Her mother spoke to her about it, and she resisted the admonishments and the advice she gave.

Karen told her, that all was rosy now, but it would change because this guy was leading her away from God, and how was she expected to be at peace?

Cindy tried to please her husband constantly, and in so doing, she alienated many that were close to her.

But going into her third year of marriage, things started to change negatively.

One of the protocols that they had established between them, after they got married, was to have one day a week, where they would get away from the family and everything else, and to go to dinner, or some other activity, for at least one hour.

For three weeks in a row, he was not able to keep that commitment, and when she approached him and questioned him about it, he became furious, and gave excuses that made no sense at all.

Friday afternoon, Cindy left work, and on her way home, she stopped at the grocery store to pick up a few items that she needed. She reached home about 45 minutes later than usual. Upon arrival, she noticed Peter sorting out some clothes, like someone that was about to go out, and before she could say anything to him, he told her that he and Steve, his buddy, and some other guys, were going bowling.

"How come you did not tell me?" she asked him

"I am telling you now. I did not know until late this afternoon."

"Yeah right, you usually call me at work and inform me of what is happening, I really do not believe you." Cindy said angrily.

"I am not going to argue with you." And he walked away.

She heard him in the shower and realized that he was not going to change his mind and that he was going.

While in the shower, his phone rang, and the name that popped up on the screen, was Courtney. She quickly scribbled the number on a piece of a paper and placed it in a drawer in the kitchen.

And she said to herself, "I don't believe this is happening to me, I can't go through this again, I am hoping that I am wrong about my suspicion."

"As soon as he came out of the shower, Cindy asked him, 'who is Courtney?"

He staggered for a minute, then he collected himself, and said, "an old high school friend."

"How come you never mention her before?" How come she is calling you at this present time? Is she going bowling too?"

"Why? Did you go through my phone? Anyway, I saw her recently and we renewed our friendship, that is all."

"I did not go through your phone, it rang, and it was sitting right there on the bed, even Nicole could read the name that was showing on the screen."

"Anyway, it is nothing, I will be back in a couple of hours."

Cindy was tempted to call Courtney, but she resisted the notion, she thought it might cause more harm than good.

Steve, Peter's buddy, told him that he was messing up, "why do you want to mess up a great relationship like this?"

"Courtney," he said, "is trouble, she will chew you up and spit you out, that is what she does. Take it from me, I have seen her victims."

"Hey, buddy, I am not going to mess up, I love my wife, I don't want a relationship with her."

"My brother, that is how is starts, she is cunning she will work her way into you, and before you realize it, you will be trapped; stay away from this woman, that is all I am going to say on that."

Peter came home about 11:00, and he smelled like someone who had been drinking.

"How was it? "Cindy asked gently.

"Lots of fun, we had a good time."

"I know you drink, but not to get drunk. What happened to-night that caused you to be drunk?"

"I am not drunk, I am fine."

"You could fool me."

Peter went into the bedroom took off his shoes, and lay across the bed, and in an instant, he was snoring away.

Cindy sat on the couch in the living room and hoped and prayed this was not going to be habitual but just a one in a while thing.

When he woke up in the morning, he realized what happened; he walked into the living room, and saw his wife lying on the couch, because of his drunkenness.

When Cindy woke up, she was upset, she checked on her children, and conversed with Johanna, but barely said anything to Peter.

He apologized for what happened, and shamefully went back to the bedroom.

Peter tried to be nice during the week, even bought her some expensive chocolate; he tried to win back her affection. He spent lots of time with Nicole and took Marcus out for ice-cream twice during the week, all this to get her forgiveness.

Cindy slowly accepted his way of saying that he was sorry, and forgave him, although, she was still troubled by his friendship with Courtney.

"If it was an old friend he met, and there was nothing going on, why did he hide it from me?" she wondered.

She promised to keep her eyes and ears open and would monitor him closely, but secretly.

The following months were almost normal, as before, they were back to doing their routine stuff together and demonstrated their love to each other.

On Peter's birthday, after all the activities of the day were over, Peter and Cindy laid on the bed, and were engaged in conversation, when Peter asked Cindy, "when are we having another baby?"

"I thought when we came together as a couple, we said we were only going to have one child. What possessed you to want to have another?"

"Because I was hoping that we would try for a boy, I need someone to carry my name."

"That is not a reasonable way of thinking, who guarantees us that we will get a boy, we are not God. Who says we won't have another girl, second time around?"

"Well, we won't know until we try," Peter replied.

"Not going to happen," Cindy exclaimed, by the way, we already have two children, a boy and a girl, so what is the issue?"

"Because Marcus is not my son, not my flesh and blood, I need someone to carry my name."

"What did you just say? I can't believe what I am hearing." And Cindy burst into tears, and got up from the bed, and stormed out into the living room. She was sobbing so hard, that Johanna and Marcus came to see what was going on.

Then Peter came out of the bedroom, and tried to hug her, and said, "I am sorry, I did not mean it that way, it came out wrong."

Cindy brushed away his hands, and said, "I have nothing to say to you."

She wanted to talk to someone so badly, but because she had alienated her loved ones from her, for the sake of Peter, she did not know who to call.

Her best bet was Katy, she knew regardless of how she isolated herself from Katy, she would still be there for her, if needed.

And she was not prepared to hear her mom saying, I told you so.

That night she slept on the couch, refusing to sleep in the same bed with Peter.

In the morning, she got up and prepared breakfast, and laid it on the table and sat there and waited on the others to join.

And to her surprise, Peter came and sat down with the others, and sat there like nothing had happened. She said to herself, "what a guy, heartless."

This was one of the quietest times they had at the table. The tension was so high that it made everyone feel uncomfortable.

After breakfast, Peter left for the gym, they barely said anything between them.

"Man, what happened?" his buddy Steve asked

"What you mean what happened?"

"You are always last one here, I mean always late, and here you are today, ahead of those guys."

"Buddy, I had a situation at home, and had to leave earlier than normal.

"What did you mess up now?"

"Cindy and I were having a casual conversation, which led to a discussion about having another child, and to cut it short, I told her Marcus was not my biological son, and that I wanted a son of my own and that did not sit well with her."

"Of course, what did you expect? How could you say something like that to your wife? Those are hurtful words, not what she expected to hear."

"Don't get me wrong. I know where you are coming from, but you should have used skillful ways in trying to convince her, but this, end of the road my brother, unless something miraculous happens."

"Listen Steve, the other guys don't need to know that. cool?"

"I get it, this is your issue, and you have my support. By the way, how is Courtney?"

"Hey, lay off this, now is not the time to bring that up."

"My bad, brother, I apologize. Come on, let's get to work."

Meanwhile at home, Cindy had a hard time dealing with that comment.

She finally worked up the courage to pick up the phone, and call Katy, she knew, if there was one person that would listen to her, it would be Katy.

"Hello, what a surprise, it has been a long time, but as always, I am always happy to hear from you, my dear, how are you doing?"

"First of all. Let me say that I am very sorry, that I have pulled away and isolated myself from you and the others. I miss our tight relationship."

"Healthwise, all of the family are doing good, but mentally, I am a wreck."

"Oh no, what is going on?"

And Cindy explained to her the situation between Peter and herself.

"Peter said what? I thought that guy loved you, and your family?"

"After this he came back and said he was sorry, but I don't believe him; he said what was in his heart, and it is very hard for me to trust him again."

"He had Josh and I fooled; we thought that he was a good guy, but if this is how he is thinking he is a jerk. Sorry to say that about your husband, but this is the way I feel right now."

"It is okay to feel that way, I can understand, also. I am losing trust in him," and she also told her about the incident with Courtney.

"Never expected to hear these things about him, but people change, or show their true colors as time goes by, but you will survive this, I know you, and I will be there for you."

"Don't tell Joshua about this, I don't want it to get to my mother, or to go anywhere else from here."

"You should know me better than that; if you say it is for my ears only, that is how it is going to be."

"Thanks, Katie, I know that I can count on you, and I promise you, that I will not neglect you like I did in the past, we are sisters forever regardless of what happens."

"I know sis, I love you forever, too."

Cindy felt better, and relieved, after speaking to Katy, she then turned her attention to her sister Johanna, and to her two children.

Peter came back from the gym, with a bouquet of red roses in his hand, and handed them to Cindy, apologizing as he gave them to her.

The card attached to the flowers read, "I don't know what I was thinking, but I am sorry, I love you."

Cindy took the flowers, and said thank you, and she put the flowers on top of the dining table.

She tried her best to portray that it was just a misunderstanding, so that the children would not be troubled by what was happening, but Marcus was now older, knew something was wrong, but had no idea, that he was involved.

Despite what happened, Cindy felt obligated to Peter, and did not want to do anything that would end their marriage.

Peter, for the next few months, was the nicest guy on the planet, and treated Cindy with the outmost respect, and care.

But he kept his friendship with Courtney close, he just did it more secretly and discreetly.

It didn't matter how hard he tried to be loving to Cindy, nor how much he tried to be a devoted husband, that close friendship with Courtney affected his total commitment to Cindy and the family.

First, it started affecting their finances. He deposited less into their joint account that they had set up to pay the bills, and Cindy recognized that, and questioned him about it.

"Are not the bills still getting paid? As a matter of fact, from here on, I will pay all the bills and you don't have to set funds aside for that."

"You used to help with other things in the house apart from the general bills, but now you won't contribute to simple basic things like groceries and other items. I must purchase and supply all the basics, and necessary needs in this house; you don't help in purchasing clothes, or other items for your daughter."

"You should not be complaining; you make lots of money, these basic things are not putting a strain on you."

"That is not the point. We are a team, well so I thought, and I don't think it is fair that I have to contribute to all the needs of the house, while I don't know what you do with your money, as a matter of fact, I don't even know how much money you make, I don't know anything about your finances; you refuse to sit with me to discuss our finances. You prepare our annual taxes at year's end, and you don't provide me with a copy, you just let me know what we are getting back or paying back, you think this is right for a married couple?"

"It looks like you are all worked up about money issues, why don't you leave this alone? The bills are being paid."

Cindy had nothing else to say on that issue, in one sense, she was happy that she had not combined her finances with Peter, because he was not trustworthy.

She knew that she was sound financially, and she was able to stand on her own apart from him.

She had money set aside for Marcus from his dad's life insurance, and she had money put aside in case of an emergency.

Also, she had set up an account on behalf of her daughter, in case anything happened to her, she would be taken care of.

Cindy decided, from here on, that she was just going to provide him with basic husband needs, like cooking, laundry, and so on, but emotionally, she was not going to be attached to him.

The affection was destroyed from his actions and she was going to live with that.

"I know he was a loving and genuine guy, but I believed that ended once Courtney came into the picture, that changed everything."

She decided, she needed to know about Courtney. She got the number that she had put in the drawer, and contemplated calling Courtney, to talk to her, but after considering it, she did not.

But things only got worse, after each passing month, and Cindy was looking for answers. The only person she could talk to was Katy, and she was tired of bothering her with her problems. She did not want to tell her mom because she knew what she would say. The only other person she had confidence in telling her problems to was Junie, but the last time they spoke, she hung up on him because he told her that he believed she had made a mistake by marrying Peter.

He told her that, "anyone who wanted nothing to do with God was a bad person to hook up with," and she became angry with him for saying that.

Now, she wished she could talk to him, but was too proud to tell him that he was right, so she refused to call him.

Chapter NINETY-EIGHT

CINDY WAS WILLING TO live with Peter and his faults, and said she would be tolerant of Courtney being in the picture because she wanted to save her marriage, for her pride and for her children's sake.

But Peter got worse, he became more deliberate in his actions, he kept coming home later and later after work, he would not even give an excuse for his lateness.

This became unbearable to Cindy; she was tired of crying herself to sleep at night, so she decided to find out more about Courtney.

Sarah her co-worker; and good friend, her husband is a detective, so she spoke to them about what was happening with her husband and Courtney.

She told them she had no proof, but was just suspicious, and asked Dave for his help in tracking her husband to see if he was involved with Courtney.

"Sarah, please let this stay with the three of us."

"You know I will Cindy," Sarah assured her.

Cindy continued to be a good wife to Peter, hoping that he would return to the person that he was when she fell in love with him.

Dave called Cindy and asked her to meet him at Ossie's restaurant during her lunch time.

Cindy did not know what to expect as she went to meet Dave at the restaurant.

Dave revealed to Cindy that her husband and Courtney, like she suspected, had a steady romantic relationship, and not just friends, like he claimed.

He provided her the pictures and information, that verified his findings. What got to her the most was the picture and information of her husband and Courtney at the hotel.

She froze, she could barely talk, as he provided verified proof of the affair.

She got up, and made it to the bathroom, and cried sorely, then she sat on the toilet and just gazed at the ceiling as she continued to cry.

When she came out, Dave said he was just about to send a waitress in there to see if she was okay.

He tried to comfort her, and gave her some advice on what to do, or not do.

That afternoon, Cindy could hardly wait to get home.

Sarah came to the nurses' station, and knowing what happened, tried to cheer her up, in funny little ways.

She reached home and immediately called Katy, and told her what she found out, and how hurt she was.

"I am about to call this Courtney lady and give her a piece of my mind."

"Cindy, please, don't do anything in the heat of the moment, sit down and relax, and later on, we will come up with the best solution for the situation."

"I know what you are saying, but I am not going to say anything negative to her, I am just going to find out from her if she knows that Peter is a married man."

As soon as she got off the phone with Katy, she dialed Courtney's number, and she told her who she was, and asked her if she knew Peter? But Courtney said she was not going to give information to someone she didn't know. But then she thought about it and answered Cindy.

Courtney figured this was the best opportunity to introduce herself as the mistress of Peter. She was the type that loves drama.

"And by the way, Peter is right here, do you want to talk to him?' she asked, and she laughed sarcastically.

About an hour after her encounter with Courtney, Peter came home.

He stormed into the bedroom, furious, and shouted at Cindy, and asked her, "why did you call Courtney, and ask all those questions, didn't I tell you that we were just friends?"

"Friends? Friends don't hug in such a fashion, friends don't do lunch like they were husband and wife, or boyfriend and girlfriend, and friends, don't go to hotels, and she went to the drawer and brought the pictures out and placed them in front of him.

He lost it. She was ironing her uniform for work and he came up to her and grabbed at her, and took a swing at her, but missed, he then took the hot iron from her hand and stuck it to her side. She screamed in pain, as the hot iron sizzled through her clothes and her skin, as the scent of burning clothes, and flesh filled the air.

As she screamed, Marcus and his little sister came running to the room to find out what was happening to their mom.

Peter dropped the iron, and took his keys and rushed out of the door.

Marcus held his sister's hand and came to his mother's aid.

He cried when he saw the injury to his mother's side. He did what his mother told him to do, in assisting her to ease the pain.

He asked if he should call granny, or the police, but she told him no, but instructed him to get a few pieces of ice, and to get the Vicks vapor rub from the medicine cabinet, and they did together what needed to be done to take care of the injury.

It still hurt a lot, but it was better than when it just happened, and the pain slowly subsided, as the ointment took effect.

"Mama, why did he do that to you? Why is he so mean?" Marcus asked as he cried.

"Son, it is okay, your mama will be fine, I will be okay in a while."

"Don't tell Sister Johanna anything about that, you will make her cry, okay?"

"Yes, mom, I won't"

She sent them back to their rooms, but she was concerned with their state of mind, after witnessing, such a heinous act.

Johanna came in and asked, "did you burn something in here? I smelled it as soon as I entered the door."

"Yep, I did, but everything is okay, it was all my fault, I think I should open the window for a few minutes to let the scent out."

Not too long after that, Peter came in, and he acted like nothing ever happened. He said hello to Johanna and glanced at Cindy and just walked into the bedroom.

Meanwhile, Marcus laid on his bed, and just could not sleep because the episode that he witnessed, kept playing over and over in his head.

Johanna found it strange, that Marcus was still up, and not wanting to sleep. She questioned him, but he gave her no answers. She believed that he experienced some stressful situation, when he was with his friends earlier in the day.

Cindy sat in the rocking chair that was in the bedroom and cried until she fell asleep.

Peter slept on the bed and paid no attention to Cindy; he had no remorse for what he did.

The next day, Johanna asked for a sit down with Cindy.

Peter had left for work and Cindy had the day off.

They talked about different things, and they talked about the kids, before Johanna said to Cindy, "I think I should move out and move on."

"Why? What made you want to do that? Did something bad happen?"

"Nothing bad happened, I just think that at my age and since I have finished school, I think I should give you and your husband some space."

"Jo, let us be honest with each other, tell me the truth, did Peter say anything to you?"

"No, he did not, but I can tell that all is not well with you two and I don't want to be the cause of it."

"Jo, I trust you, and I am hoping that what I am about to tell you won't leave this room, deal?"

"Oh Cindy, you know that you can trust me. You did in the past, why would you think that I would change now?"

"Peter has an outside relationship with a lady name Courtney, and that has led to his bad behavior lately. He has changed drastically, and he treats me badly."

"When I met him, he was such a gentleman. I never thought he could have changed that much."

"Cindy, I am going to be honest with you. Peter has always been like that; he disguised his ways so carefully, that you could not and did not detect all his bad ways."

"If Peter was so good, as handsome as he was, who had everything going for him, do you think he would have been available? With no wife, no girlfriend, because he could not commit to one. Think on these things."

"Girl, you sound like my mom, that is exactly what she said, but I ignored her, but now I am paying for it."

"You see why I am in no rush to get married with Jessie? I love him, but he must prove himself to me, not that he won't change after we get married, some men do change, but at least, I knew him for a while, and hope it will be different."

"Jo, you have been so reserved, and you try not get involve in other people affairs, but girl, you are wise beyond your age."

"Anyway Jo, you can't leave, I want you to stay, because honestly, I am scared; I'm afraid what Peter might do when he knows that there is no adult in the house, I would be at his mercy."

"I understand all this, but what makes you think he won't hurt both of us? Because I would be a witness to his criminal activities?"

"Our chances are better, if we are together, and besides, the children are glued to you, they would be lost without you."

"I don't know, let me think about it, and I will let you know."

"See?"

"What happened? You are badly injured, you need to visit the doctor, you need to go to the emergency room."

"Peter did that because I contacted Courtney to find out what was going on. He took the hot iron that I was using to iron my uniform and burned me. I lied to you, the scent that you smelled was my clothes and skin."

"Did you call the police? Did you tell your mother or brothers?"

"No, I did not, and I do not want you to contact them, I don't want them getting involved, I am fine now."

"No, you are not. This will get infected, and you could end up in the hospital, you are a nurse, you should know better. We are going to the doctor, no one will know."

"I don't want to get him in trouble, he will only make it worse for me."

"Okay, if you don't want to go to the police, at least let us go to the doctor, if you don't want to do it for you, do it for your children, you need to be there for them."

"I will go because you are very convincible and you will not take no for an answer."

They drove to the other side of town, to the opposite side of her job. She would be devastated if someone from her job would have seen her.

Cindy went to the emergency room while Johanna stayed in the vehicle with the children.

The nurse asked her how it happened?

She did not want the police involved, so she came up with a lame excuse. The nurse sensed that she was not telling the truth, but there was nothing she could do about it.

After about an hour, she was out and joined the others in the car.

"That was not too bad, right?"

"No, it was not, thanks, I am so glad the day that you came into my life."

"So, tell me, are you going to leave this guy? He is going to hurt you badly, if you don't."

"I can't, I have the children, and it is complicated."

"You could if you wanted to. I am very concerned for you."

Chapter NINETY-NINE

THE MONTHS THAT FOLLOWED, Peter and Cindy, lived in the house like roommates. Cindy shouldered the burden of the bills.

For the second year in a row, Peter did not attend the annual thanksgiving dinner tradition that they had, and when the family inquired about him, Cindy came up with an excuse for him not attending.

Everyone knew that she was not telling the truth because her excuse made no sense.

One thing was certain, Cindy was glad to be there, she was yearning to see Katy, and to give her details of what had transpired since their last major conversation.

After she listened to all that Cindy had to say, Katie advised Cindy to leave this guy. She told her if she did not want to divorce him she would at least separate from him, for her own good.

But Cindy was not in favor of this advice, and said she would give him a chance to change. She was hoping that the relationship with Courtney was just a fling and he would come to his senses and come home.

Katy felt sorry for her; she realized that she was being naïve.

The thanksgiving weekend was great, as usual, and they went through the same routine, as usual. The person who enjoyed it the most was Cindy, because she had cut off ties with most people, so she was happy to reconnect with them, even it was just for the weekend.

The group from Texas made it back from Florida safely on Sunday evening.

Upon arrival at the house, Cindy realized that her vehicle was not there in the garage, but Peter's vehicle was. She quickly called him to find out why her vehicle was not there.

He said, he had issues with his car and could not get it to start.

Cindy took his keys and went into the garage and tried starting his car, and with no hesitation, it started on the first try, so she knew that he was lying.

But what got to Cindy was a message she heard on the answering machine and it was from Courtney.

It said, "hi Peter, are you still coming to the thanksgiving dinner? I am waiting, please let me know." Then she said, oops, I just saw you pulling in, ignore this message."

Cindy knew that Courtney did this on purpose to get to her, and to put a wider gap between her and her husband relationship.

She was also furious that Peter would give this woman their home phone number, which they had agreed would be used only for family members and close friends.

She was fuming with rage until she got a headache.

"Relax Cindy," Johana said, "she is doing that to get to you, don't fall for that, ignore this woman, your real issue is with your husband."

Then she measured her blood pressure, which was extremely high, and thus the cause of the headache. She brought medication to her and made sure she took one before she left for her room.

Because of all the stress Peter had been putting her through, Cindy's health deteriorated steadily.

Johanna encouraged her to tell her mom, what was going on, but she refused.

Peter came home late that night, and said, "your vehicle is in the garage, and for the record, it is still in one piece." And he was not happy because she called him about it.

Cindy turned on the answering machine and played the message and turned up the volume so he could hear it.

After it was done playing, he looked at her, with eyes blazing, waiting to hear, what she was going to say, but Cindy held her peace and went to her children's room, to check on them, because she could hear that they were not sleeping.

After she got them to fall asleep, she went to her bedroom and then went to bed.

This is the reason Cindy did not get off the pills; even though she and Peter were not intimate anymore, she did not trust him.

As she laid next to him (which Katy and Johanna told her she should not do) he suddenly felt the need to be intimate; she told him no, she was not having sex of any kind with him, not the way, he had been treating her, and besides, she didn't know what his health status was since he been having other relationships.

He became irate, and said, "you will, whether you want to or not, I am still your husband, and you can't deny me my pleasures."

And she refused to willingly give up herself to him, but he, being stronger than her, wrestled with her until she could no longer put-up resistance.

Johanna heard all the commotions and she heard her crying, so she went to the bathroom, and turned the faucet as strong as it opened, hoping to send a message to him, that she heard what he was doing, and that she was a witness; she knew that was a risk, but she was willing to take it.

That did work; he instantly stopped his assault, and got up and went to the bathroom, while Cindy laid on the bed, her pillow soaked with tears, as she stared at the ceiling.

He came back from the bathroom and went to sleep.

She got up, to take a shower and cried the whole time she was bathing.

Many thoughts rushed through her mind, some were thoughts of retaliation, while some were thoughts of giving up. She was hurting, and did not know what to do, but she knew something had to be done.

The following day at work, Sarah approached her and told her, "I need to talk to you, and yes, we are going to have a sit down at lunch time, I am not taking no for an answer."

They met up at 1:15 at the cafeteria, and as soon as they sat down, Sarah asked Cindy, "what is going on? Everyone is noticing a big change in you, not just work, but your physique. You are now way skinnier than you know who. You have taken her place as the skinniest one, and that is not good, because it is not a good skinny.

Cindy emotionally emptied herself to Sarah, and told her all that she had been through, and to conclude the conversation, she showed her side where she had been burned.

"Oh no, this can't be, we have to get the authorities involved, did you tell your mother or brothers?"

"No, I did not, and I don't want them involved, please, don't say anything to anyone, I am pleading with you, I don't want to die, I want to be there for my children; he is vicious."

"Yes, I understand that, but if you don't get help, and if you don't stop him, you will die anyway. I can't leave you in this state, I must do something. I am sorry, I must break my promise. I must do something.

"Please, Sarah, please leave it alone, it will get better, I promise, and don't tell Dave, he is part of the law, and I don't want the law involved. They don't enforce the law until something happens, and by then I would be dead, so for my sake, and my children's sake, just let it be, I will figure a way out."

"No, you won't, and it will not get better for you, probably for him, but not for you." And with that said, Sarah went to the bathroom and cried. She could not believe that her friend was in this situation and that her hands were tied, where she could not get help.

She wanted to tell Dave so badly, so they could make Courtney's life miserable, but she had to keep her promise to Cindy, but she didn't know how long she could keep it, because if she continued to keep deteriorating, she would have to do something, before it would be too late, yet she wanted Cindy to keep trusting her.

Chapter ONE HUNDRED

CINDY WAS LIVING IN pain and false hope, because as the months went by, the abuse became more frequent and more vicious, and Cindy's health was headed downward.

She was living in fear, scared of her husband, and worried about her children.

She wanted to leave, but she was scared to death and she wondered what her family and friends would say, so she opted to stay.

She was having a conversation with Peter, when he said something that annoyed her, and she replied to him, but before she could finish her sentence, she felt a stinging blow to her face, that knocked her off her feet, and before too long, the swelling began.

Marcus who was about to turn 17, ran to his mom's defense.

"I am going to deal with you man, I am tired of you hurting my mom, I am going to hurt you, and he was headed to the kitchen, but his mom grabbed him, and held on to him, and tried to cool him down to avoid the situation from escalating.

Cindy took an icepack and held it to her face to prevent it from swelling any bigger, and for the swelling to go down.

Peter took his keys and stormed out of the house; immediately after he left, Johanna came home from visiting her parents.

She immediately noticed the swelling of Cindy's face, and the icepack, that she held, and asked her, "What happened to your face?

Before she could answer, Marcus said, "Peter, struck my mom in her face; I wanted to hurt him, but my mom stopped me."

"Markie, I know you meant well, I know you wanted to defend your mother, but even though you are much bigger than what your age says, you are still not able to fight this jerk, he is much stronger than you. Understand?"

"Cindy, this has to stop, you can't go on living like this, you can't sustain all the abuse, you will break down, sooner or later, and you know what, I am going to do something about it, I am going to call Dr. King, and let him know what is going on, he is one of your most trusted friends, and he will get this resolved, for sure. Peter will be in jail."

"Oh no, don't do that, he will definitely kill me now, because he has falsely accused me of being with Junie, and he will use that as an excuse to do what he wants to do."

"Anyway, someone needs to know what's happening, you need help, and if I don't do something, and God forbid, something should happen to you, I will not forgive myself for not doing something when I had the chance to."

Chapter ONE HUNDRED-ONE

MARCUS HAD A GAME at a school close to his grandma's house and he asked his mom if he could stay at Grannies house for the night; it was Friday, and the basketball game would be over a little bit late.

She agreed and told him to be careful.

Marcus was the star on the high school team, and he was being watched by college scouts because he was talented.

Karen was happy to have her grandson home for the night, she always enjoyed his and his sister's company.

After taking a shower and preparing for bed, Marcus sat with his granny and they began to converse,

"How is your mom, Nicole, Johanna, and Peter doing?" she asked

"They are doing okay. I started taking lessons for my driver's license," he said.

Karen knew right away that something was wrong, because he switched the topic too quickly, because he did not want to talk about something.

"Marcus, you need to tell me the truth, you can and should tell Granny what is going on; don't hide things from me."

"Granny, if I tell you, my mom will get into more trouble, Peter will beat her again."

"Beat her? Peter is beating my daughter? Is he crazy? Is he putting his hands on my daughter?'

And Marcus expounded on the details of all that had been going on in the house, he did not know everything, but gave her a pretty good idea of what was going on.

Karen was upset and called Cindy.

"Hi mom, how are you? Did Marcus make it home safely? I called him a few minutes ago but did not get him."

"He made it home okay, I guess when you called, he was in the shower, I thought he had called you back, check your phone, also I heard him speaking to Johanna.'

"Cindy, I am furious, and very upset."

"Why mom?"

"Because of you. Marcus told me what was going on with you, and the treatment that you have been receiving under the hands of Peter.

Is Peter home?"

"No mom, he is not, plus, I did not want you to get involved, it would only make matters worse."

"Well, if you are so stupid to see that this man is going to kill you, I am not, and I am going to fix this, I am not going to stand by and watch it happen, a matter of fact, I am about to call your brothers to inform them of all that is going on."

"Mom, I told you to leave this alone, and don't get my brothers involved; it will only get worse."

"They are your brothers, who care about you greatly." And then Karen hung up.

She called Joshua who is the calmer of the brothers.

"Hi mom, what is going on? You usually don't call this late at night, unless it is something very important'

"It is Cindy."

"Is she okay?" Joshua asked, somewhat panicky.

"She is not in any accident, or nothing of this sort, but she is being beaten, very regularly by her husband, I mean black eyes, and scars over her body, and she has been hiding these things from us. Marcus is the one who just revealed this to me, after I questioned him."

"I called her, and she is defending him because she is afraid of him."

"I called you first, because I know David can act crazy sometimes, and things could go south in a hurry, but you are the one with the cooler head and will handle it better."

"This guy is crazy; did he lose his mind? I am about to call him right now; I will call you back."

"Joshua, your sister said don't get involved; it will only get worse."

"Yes, it will get worse for him." And he hung up.

"Katy, you know this guy is beating my sister? Is he crazy? Who does he think he is?"

Katy did not know what to say. If she told him that she knew, there were no excuses that would justify her actions, and if he found out that she knew all along, that could spell trouble for their relationship.

But Katy decided to be true to Cindy, and said nothing, especially now that they had discovered what was happening.

He called Cindy. At first, she did not pick up because she had an idea why he was calling, so he called back again; she hesitated for a moment because Peter was there, but she realized, he would just keep calling if she didn't answer, so she did.

"Hi Josh, what is up?"

"I have just finished speaking with mom, and she filled me on with what is going on with you. Is Peter there?" he asked, and she hesitated to answer, so he said, "let me talk to him."

"I don't think that's a good idea."

Joshua did not say anything back to her but hung up the phone. She knew that he was furious.

"What is up that Joshua, if it is Joshua, is calling you this late at night? I think it is your doctor friend, and you are using your brother to try to get this past me."

Cindy was afraid, she knew that he was just about to go bonkers, but just after he demanded to see her phone, his phone rang, and it was Joshua. He had just saved her unknowingly.

"Hello Joshua," he answered, "what's up bro? it has been a while."

"Peter, this is not a social call, I am furious, I was told that you have been abusing and beating my sister, man I am disappointed in you, I had the outmost respect for you, that was the last thing I expected to hear, and that dummy sister of mine, went through all this abused without saying anything? I am angrier with her."

"Let me say it clearly and very simply; stop putting your hands on my sister, that is all I am going to say."

"Man, I don't know who you have been speaking to, but I don't abuse your sister."

"Okay, I hope you got my message." Joshua said, and he hung up.

"I am feeling sorry for Cindy, she's a wonderful person and she does not deserve this; I thought she had found the right guy who would make her life happy, no one saw this coming."

I spoke to him, and I know for sure he got my message.

Joshua called his mom and told her everything would be okay.

Meanwhile, back at Cindy's, it was more tumultuous, the only difference was he yelled, and hailed accusations, and insults at her, but did not put his hands on her.

Johanna felt better. She heard some of the conversations between them, and realized that Joshua had intervened, and that prevented him from striking her.

Marcus came home in the morning, and was greeted with a big hug from Johanna, and she told him, he had saved his mom's life.

And he explained to her how he told granny.

Peter, on his way out of the door, looked at Marcus with a stern angry look, and murmured something underneath his breath, as he walked away.

"Marcus, why did you tell granny about my business? I did not want them involved."

"I know mom, but I can't stay here and watch you being abused by this no-good man. If I did not tell her, I would have hurt this man."

Cindy was happy that he did tell her mom because she knew that he would not put his hands on her again because he knew her brother meant what he said and he respected her brother.

After speaking to Marcus, she realized that he did not know about Courtney and that was why her mom did not mention it to her, and she wanted to keep it that way.

Later in the afternoon, her mom called and they spoke for a while. Her mom wanted to know what caused him to be so upset that he kept putting his hands on her, but Cindy just kept on making excuses for him and took most of the blame.

Peter spent less time at home since his talk with Joshua. He spent a lot of time with Courtney, and no longer did it in secret. He was seen in public, openly embracing Courtney, and showed no concern of being seen.

They lived in a small development, and most people knew each other; he knew eventually her family or friends would find out about Courtney, but that did not bother him at all.

Courtney lived about 10 minutes away in the Green Garden subdivision located at St. Mary's Avenue.

It did not bother Courtney that Peter was married and had a family, she was just about herself, she saw his weaknesses and she capitalized on them; she knew he had a great job and would be able to supply her needs because she presumed that he had money.

Chapter ONE HUNDRED-TWO

CINDY WAS EMBARRASSED BY a co-worker that never cared for her. When Cindy approached her concerning a situation that she had not taken care of, she responded by saying to Cindy, in the company of the other co-workers, "you can't control your husband who is out there having an affair publicly, but here you are wanting to push me around?"

Cindy was shocked that this was known among the nurses, and no one said anything to her about it, but spoke behind her back.

She went to Ms. Joseph and told her what happened and asked for the rest of the day off because she was not feeling well.

Ms. Joseph said, "the nurse will be disciplined. You know, you just can't come and say to me, I am not feeling well and just want to leave; you are the head nurse, you have to be a good example for the other nurses."

Cindy left Ms. Joseph's office, dejected and upset that Ms. Joseph would look at her in that way.

She worked for another hour before she collapsed in the waiting area when she went to speak with a patient.

It was a chaotic scene, the nurses were going back and forth, and they were very concerned about her health, and the seriousness of the situation. Ms. Joseph came out of her office, when she heard the commotion coming from the outside of her office. "What is happening?" she asked, and when she saw the panic that was on their faces, she knew something was wrong.

"Cindy, she has passed out, and she has been rushed to the E.R."

Ms. Joseph felt weak as she heard the news, and sat on the nearest chair she could find; she had dismissed Cindy's request because she did not believe her. She wished she had dealt with her differently.

Cindy was in a diabetic coma, and the prognosis was not good.

An attempt to contact her husband was made but he could not be reached, so they called her mother to relate the news.

Her mom contacted Cindy's brothers to let them know what had happened; she also told Joshua that they tried to reach Peter, but they could not find him.

Joshua called Peter and told him what was going on, but he did not sound too concerned, but said, he would be heading to the hospital.

Joshua did not know about Courtney and did not know that she was the root of all these problems.

Karen made it to the hospital as quickly as she could, and went to the emergency area to inquire about her daughter.

The nurses told her that Cindy was in a diabetic coma, and that the doctor would be out shortly to give her the details.

She sat in the waiting area, hoping that the doctor would be out soon.

While she sat there, Peter showed up; he was not in a concerned mode, neither did he looked like he was worried.

"Hi Karen," he said, and he went to the nurses' desk to find out more about Cindy's condition.

Sarah and a few other nurses were also in the waiting room, hoping to hear good news from the doctor.

Sarah came to Karen and encouraged her; she told her that Cindy was a fighter, and she was sure Cindy would come out of that okay, and said to her, don't give up on her.

"I know my child, and I believe my God will bring her back to health, there is nothing that he can't do, we just must believe.

Sarah loved Karen's spirit and words of encouragement, which also helped to strengthen her.

The doctor came out and said to Karen and Peter, "she is still in a coma, but I saw signs that made me believe she would recover."

"Oh, praise God," Karen exclaimed, "he is in charge, and she will be okay."

That was not the news Peter was hoping for; he thought that the situation would lead to his freedom, without having to do something drastic, and furthermore, he had his sights on the life insurance.

"You don't look too excited about the great news the doctor gave, what is going on?" Karen demanded

"I am happy and everything is fine, and nothing is going on."

And he said, "I will be back," and he left.

"No wonder my daughter is in a coma if this is the type of treatment she has been getting from this man; she thought she was strong, but this abuse was too much."

Sarah said to Karen, "the affair with Courtney really got to Cindy."

"Courtney who?"

"Whoops," Sarah thought she knew about Courtney.

"I thought you knew about the relationship Peter has with this lady named Courtney."

"Cindy hides everything from me, it took her son Marcus to tell me about the abuse that she was going through, but Courtney? That is news to me, and I would bet, this is what is causing all the problems."

"How long has this been going on?"

"It has been a while; this is what started the deterioration of their marriage."

"I wished she had told me, or her brothers and maybe this would not have gone so far and been so critical?"

While Karen was speaking, Johanna and Cindy's children showed up.

"Grandma, how is my mom doing?" Marcus asked.

"The doctor said she should recover, and we are praying that she will make a complete recovery."

"Can I go in to see her?"

"We have to wait on the doctor to give the okay to do that."

Not too long after she said that the doctor appeared again.

"Good news, your daughter has just opened her eyes, and is also talking."

"You can go in to see her, but I recommend not more than three at a time, and the nurse will monitor everything, including the time limit to spend in there,"

"Thanks, so much doctor, appreciate it." Karen said to him.

Karen, Marcus, and Sarah went in first.

Cindy smiled when she saw them but was still weak and pale.

"Hi," she said, in a weak voice.

Marcus sat on the bed, and hugged his mom, and said to her, "you dare don't do that again, you understand? You scared me to death."

And the others in the room said, "yes, don't do that again."

Then Karen asked her, "how are you feeling?"

"Mom, I am feeling better, I had no idea what happened, all I remember...."

And Karen stopped her, "save your energy, we can go over that later, but for now, you need to relax, and rest as much as you can. We will take care of things at home, and whatever else that needs to be done, okay?"

"I did not know that you were diabetic, I would have warned you about stress, and other situations that effect it, but I had no idea."

"Mom, neither did I, high blood pressure, yes, but diabetes, had no idea that I had it."

"The doctor said my sugar level was dangerously low, and had I not been in the hospital, he was not sure if I would have made it."

"Guys, I am so sorry to have put you through this."

Karen chimed in, "don't worry about that now, you are here, alive and doing better, and for that we are grateful."

"Now just concentrate on getting better, and within no time, you will be out of here." Sarah told her.

"Where is my Nicole?"

"She is in the waiting room, she will be in as soon as we leave, and we are doing that now, take care, and we will see you soon, we love you." And Karen ushered the others out.

"Mommy, mommy," Nicole came in crying.

"Hi Nics," mommy is so glad to see you, how are you doing?"

"Mom, what is wrong? When are you coming home?"

"Mommy will be home soon."

"Okay guys, say bye to your mommy, we have to let her get some rest, so she can come home quickly," and Johanna said bye, as she and Nicole left the room.

As they were about to leave the waiting room, Peter showed up, and asked the nurse to go in to visit his wife.

She told him that she was sorry, but it was time for her to rest, but since he is the husband, she would allow him not more than 3 minutes in there, and she would have to accompany him.

He did not like that idea, and fussed about it, but she stuck to her words, and told him, this is the only choice he had, did he want to go in or not?

He reluctantly went in the room.

"Hi Cindy, how are you doing?" he asked.

Cindy did not reply, she did not open her eyes, and laid there like she could not hear him.

The nurse was appalled by his actions. He did not sound like someone that was concerned about a loved one that was in a state of critical health.

He stood away from the bed, did not hold her hand, or show any loving gestures towards her. What a loser, thought the nurse.

She quickly ushered him out of the room, as soon as his 3 minutes were up, and hoped that he did show up here again.

He glanced at Karen and the others and walked by, without saying a word.

Karen asked Johanna, if she and the children would like to stay at her house, until Cindy was released from the hospital, but Johanna told her that they would be okay.

They left the hospital and went home.

Karen stayed with them for a little while, just to make sure that they were okay.

She could not resist the opportunity to question Peter about his affair with Courtney.

"How could you do this to my daughter?" she asked him.

"Lady, stay out of this, this has nothing to do with you."

"Of course, it has everything to do with me, this is my daughter, and I will stand up for her, if she can't stand for herself."

He just mumbled something and went to the bedroom.

Karen left after a few more minutes; she immediately called Joshua and told him all that she had learned from Sarah while she was at the hospital.

He was very upset and suggested that Cindy leave the house and move in with her until she was stable.

Karen was fearful for Cindy's life because so many abuse victims die from not being properly protected. The law can only go to an extent, but so many times they are not enforced.

Karen visited Cindy again the following day, and learned from Cindy that the doctor said she could go home tomorrow.

She welcomed the news, and hoped that this was a good sign of good things to come.

Chapter ONE HUNDRED-THREE

BRIGHT AND EARLY FRIDAY morning, Karen picked up Cindy from the hospital, and took her home; she tried convincing Cindy to come and stay with her until she was strong enough, and completely healed, but Cindy declined the invitation and said she would be fine at her home.

Karen was tempted to bring up Courtney but realized this was not the time for that and she did not want to put her through any stress, especially now.

"It is so nice to be home," Cindy said, as she made it into the house.

She received the warmest greetings from her children and Johanna.

"Jo, I want to thank you so much, for being there for my children, you are more than a cousin to me, you are my sister, my friend, and I promise you, I will never forget all that you have done for me."

After breakfast, Cindy went to rest. Her phone kept ringing constantly, so Johanna turned it off, so she could get a good peaceful rest.

She then left to go to the pharmacy to pick up Cindy's medication.

She was now instructed to take insulin because she had diabetes.

She returned home and kept the insulin in her bedroom, thinking that Peter might do something evil with it.

Joshua had spoken to Peter after his mom told him about Courtney.

He threatened him and promised him that he would make life very difficult from here on.

Peter changed a little bit since Joshua spoke to him; he was more subdued, and showed a little more interest in the family

That made Cindy suspicious and she wondered what scheme he was trying to implement, and promised to watch him like a hawk.

Again, she understood that Joshua had spoken to him, at length, so she knew that was why he was suddenly acting differently, but still, she was not going to let her guard down.

Cindy went back to work; she been away since the day she passed out; she wished she had more time to stay home with her children, but she had used up all her short-term disability.

They were happy to see her back to work, but more so to see her looking healthier.

"Girl, we missed you, things were different while you were gone, we are happy that you are back, we needed you."

"Thanks, Emma, "I missed you too, and I am happy to be back."

Ms. Joseph came out and asked her to come to her office.

Cindy wondered what this was about, what had happened since she been gone.

"Close the door and have a seat. First, how are you feeling?"

"I am doing good."

"Let me apologize for the way I handled our conversation the last time we spoke.

You told me that you were not feeling well, and I did not take you at your word, and then this happened, so I am truly sorry."

Ms. Joseph, I can't remember having a conversation before I was hospitalized, but whatever it was, that is in the past and I just want to forget whatever it was, and look forward to today and beyond."

"I am all for that, no hesitation here," Ms. Joseph said, feeling relief, because of how the conversation went.

"You must be doing something good with your staff, because they missed you, and prayed that you would be okay."

"I try to do my best with them and give everyone respect; I expect them to respect me, and I try to make things more enjoyable for them."

"That is all, but before you go, let me say to you, please take care of yourself, look after you first, then you will be profitable to others."

She took these words to heart and promised she would take care of herself.

Sarah vowed to be a watchman over her; she planned to keep an eye on her to assured she would follow the doctor's advice.

They went to lunch on Friday and Sarah tried her best not to mention Peter or anything or anyone associated to him.

Cindy mentioned that she saw a slight change in Peter lately, but Sarah cautioned her, not be fooled by that.

Sarah knew the real reason why he had changed and was debating whether to tell her or not.

Sarah called Dave when Cindy went to the bathroom, and asked him if she should tell Cindy about what he had told her.

He said she should, at least she would not be blindsided and fall into a deeper spot than she was in now.

Continuing their lunch, Sarah said, "Cindy, the reason Peter is being so nice and acting different is because he is on the rebound.

Dave found out that Courtney is also involved with someone else, and Peter can't handle that, he has withdrawn from her a lot, and that is why he is trying to come back to you."

"I am sorry about that, I did not mean to spring this on you like that, but as I promised, I will be looking out for your interest, so there is no way I could allow this guy to use you again."

"Thank you so much for telling me, if you did not tell me, and I found out that you knew, I would be upset with you, but you don't have to worry about me, I have decided not to fall victim to Peter, again, whether I love him or not, I won't let that cloud my judgement."

"I am going to play the game with him, and see what I get out of him; for instance, get him to pay some of the bills, I could welcome that, but my dear, my eyes will be wide open to see and observe things."

Things improved between Peter and Cindy, he treated her much differently, than he had a few months ago, and even asked to contribute to the needs of the house.

Although she said she would not fall into his trap again, she had a soft spot in her heart for him and let her guard down somewhat.

When her mom learned that Cindy and Peter were a couple again and was treating him as if nothing happened, she got upset, and wondered what type of child she had raised. She said she knew she taught her about forgiveness, but she did not teach her to be stupid, because she was sure that guy was playing her, because he could not have changed automatically like this.

None of her family members, nor any of her friends, trusted Peter, and they warned her constantly, about letting herself get suckered again.

But Cindy kept saying she was doing this for her daughter, she was willing to forgive him because she wanted her daughter to have a relationship with him.

Her mom tried to speak some sense into her, but she took no heed.

Karen said to Donald, "I always knew that my daughter was a stubborn person, ever since she was little, but her stubbornness did not bring her anything good, and here she is doing it again, and I just know, it will not end well."

Peter warmed himself back slowly into her life, and did this at the expense of her family and friends. He tried to keep her away from them, because he did not want them to convince her to leave him, and he did not want her to find out from them that his relationship with Courtney was on the rocky side.

Johanna hated Peter with a passion, she did not like the way he treated Cindy, and, because he twice made advances at her, but she shut him down, and handled him without any damage being done.

She did not tell Cindy, because she took care of it, and she did not know how Cindy might have received it, because that was during the time when she thought, that he could do nothing wrong.

Johanna had planned to get married to Jessie, but three years ago, she called off their relationship, when she found out about something hurtful he had done to her. She then vowed to be single forever.

Cindy was so comfortable with the environment at home lately that she planned on celebrating her 43rd birthday with a small party, mainly with Peter and his friends, because none of her family members wanted to be there.

Chapter ONE HUNDRED-FOUR

MARCUS GRADUATED IN MAY, but because of all that was happening with the family, the unstableness, and the turmoil, they only attended the ceremony, but they did not have a celebration.

He got a full scholarship to attend college in Waco Texas, he was one of the top basketball recruits in the country, he had many choices, but chose to stay in the State where he could be close to his mom.

In the Middle of August, Cindy planned a late celebration for his graduation, and to celebrate his leaving for college.

She reserved the subdivision community center for the bash.

The turnout was massive, mostly teenagers, and young adults, most of them were his buddies.

Also, his uncles, David, Joshua and Shawn, and their families came to celebrate with him.

Peter had shown up for a short while before he made his exit through the back door, because he realized he was not welcome among their midst.

The big bash was a success, there were no major incidents, just a few small glitches. The teenagers behaved better than expected, and they had a lot of fun.

It was a hard chore to clean up after this big bash, but with the help of the family and friends, the place was cleaned and organized in no time.

Many who came to the party were happy to see Cindy; she had withdrawn herself from most of them and only kept in touch with Katy regularly, and every now and then, would contact Liz, but they knew what was going on, and they were praying for her freedom.

When Peter left the party he went home and started watching a move; he said to himself that his relationship with Cindy was not going to work because none of her family members and friends did not like him.

He picked up the phone and called Courtney hoping that she would answer because they had broken up in an ugly way.

"Hi dear," she answered, "I'm so glad you called, I was tempted to call you a couple weeks ago, but I was not sure how I would have been received, so I hesitated, and besides, I did not want to come between you and your wife again."

"Honey you should have called; my wife and I are not in the best of places, and besides, I missed you so much. Are you still seeing that guy?'

"No, I broke up with that loser, he was nothing like you, complete opposite. After being with him, now I know for sure, what a good man you are."

But this was Courtney, she always had a plan in mind, and this time was no different.

She wanted back in Peter's life, but this time she wanted to be his wife. She wanted her name on all his assets, especially his bank accounts. She knew a lot about his finances, because he flaunted his information in front of her all the time, to impress her, so she knew that he was on good standing,

"When can I see you again Courts?"

"You can now, if you wish, I am here alone"

"I will be there in a few minutes."

"Where is wifie?"

"She is too busy for me now, see you in a bit."

He cranked up his vehicle and hastily headed to Courtney's place.

He barely drove 3 miles before he was pulled over by a policeman, who was parked and waiting to stop those who broke the speed limit.

Peter came up with a couple of excuses, but none of them prevented the policeman from giving him a ticket.

When Courtney did not hear from him, she assumed that he had issues with his wife that prevented him from coming to her.

She decided to call him anyway, to find out what was happening.

"Hi babe, you won't believe what just happened?"

"Yeah, your wife took your keys, and you can't get out."

"Funny. I got a ticket on my way to your house. The policeman said I was speeding, which I debated with him, but it didn't help. I will be there shortly."

"Sorry to hear about the ticket, I know you were anxious to come over to sweetness, but you did not have to get into trouble to do that." And she laughed.

"You think this is funny? It is all your fault."

During their time together, Courtney emphasized to Peter, that she did not want to be a second fiddle to anyone anymore, she wanted to be someone's wife, and if it could not be him, she would love to know, so she could find a husband.

But Peter begged and pleaded with her to give him some time, so he could sort things out.

Peter made it back home and Cindy was up waiting on him.

"What happened? When you disappeared from the party, I was worried something had happened to you. I called but you didn't answer."

"After not being appreciated at the party, I left and went for a drive to free up my mind."

Peter planned on staying close to Cindy, until he was sure of Courtney's commitment. He was using Cindy as a backup in case it did not work out again with Courtney.

All of Cindy's people were upset with her, because of her withdrawal from them, and her loyalty to Peter.

Marcus left for college, but before he did, he told his mom exactly what was on his mind, and it was not pleasant, he was very upset with her, he never thought she would do that to them again.

Peter was not worried about Cindy making it financially, he knew besides her job, Marcus was destined to play professional basketball, and he would always take care of his mother, so he did not feel obliged to support her financially, the little that he was doing now, was just to stay in good standing with her.

On Monday, Peter went to the phone company, and he got a new phone, with a new number, and requested that everything be done online, he wanted no paperwork.

He blocked Courtney's number from his regular phone, so he wouldn't receive any calls from her, but he gave her his new number, and told her he had gotten a new phone, and his number had changed.

She did not believe him, she knew the game, and how it was played, but she went along with it.

The restoration of the secret relationship with Courtney continued for a while without being detected by Cindy, because she thought everything was going well between her and Peter, and that he had changed.

Until that morning.

Cindy was looking for a few documents that she needed to take with her to Nicole's yearly doctor appointment. While searching through the archive of papers, and other items that were in the bottom drawer, she came across a cell phone.

She turned it on, and realized that it was an active phone, and that it belonged to Peter. She quickly noted the number and placed it back where she found it.

Peter came out from the shower and had no idea that she had discovered his secret.

Her plan was not to confront him until she had spoken to Dave, and had received all the information about the phone, and what was going on, so until then, it was business as usual.

Now she knew for sure that what Sarah had told her about his issue with Courtney was true.

She realized that he did not care, did not love her, and everything he did was just pretense.

Cindy told Sarah, and she contacted Dave to see what he could find about the phone.

It did not take long, for Dave to give her the evidence, that Peter was using the phone to communicate with Courtney.

Cindy was more disappointed, than hurt; she had hoped that he had changed, and that they were working to mend their marriage, but she knew now that it was truly over.

Peter still put up a front, he portrayed himself as a loving husband, and pretended to be a good father to Nicole, but all along he had a plan.

Chapter *ONE HUNDRED-FIVE*

On Valentine's Day, before they both left for work, they got into a heated argument; it got so bad that Cindy's blood pressure went dangerously high.

She immediately felt bad and told Peter that she was feeling bad; the room was spinning before her eyes, and she crumbled to her feet. She motioned to him to get her medicine from the medicine cabinet, but instead, he mumbled something, and then left her right there, and left for work.

Fortunately, for Cindy, as soon as he left, Johanna came in from her workout at the gym,

She shouted Cindy's name hoping that she had not left yet for work. She wanted to say a quick hello to her, as they kept missing each other in passing.

She glanced in the garage, to see Cindy's vehicle there, yet she was not answering.

Johanna began to panic, and prayed that Cindy had just overslept, and that it was not a bad situation.

She quickly ran into Cindy's bedroom, and saw her sitting on the floor, barely conscious.

Johanna dashed to the medicine cabinet, and took the smelling substance, along with her high blood medicine, and rushed back to her.

She splashed some of the substance in her face, which helped a bit, and then she took her pressure reading, which was way above the normal.

Cindy could hardly talk, she tried to, but her words were not clear, just senseless.

Johanna gave her the pills, and then just hugged her, and began crying, but after a while, the medicine kicked in, and Cindy was able to speak clearly.

"What happened? And why am I still here and not at work?" she asked Johanna.

Johanna explained to her what happened and chastised her for not taking her medication.

Cindy told her she usually does before leaving for work, but she could remember arguing with Peter, and felt bad, and asked him to hand her the medicine from the cabinet, and he refused to, and that is all she remembered.

"I thank God for you again, you are like an angel assigned to me; had you not showed up the time that you did, it would have ended up bad for me."

"Sis, God has a way of working out things, and by now, you should have realized that"

"I can't believe that Peter left me here to die, and just walked away."

"We have been warning you, but you are very stubborn, and you failed to listen to our warnings, but instead, you have pushed everyone away from you."

"Why are you still standing with me, when everyone else is not?"

"Because I live with you, and felt, that I could not walk away from you, not at this stage in your life. I am the lifeline that you still have, and if I should cut it off, you will drown.

"Come here, give me a hug."

Cindy called Ms. Joseph, and told her that she was running late, because she had a health emergency.

"Thanks for letting me know, and I will see you when you get here, take care of yourself."

Sarah called, "are you okay? I called earlier when I saw you did not show up, and I know that is not like you, I was worried that you had encountered some trouble."

"I saw your call, but I had just left the house, and knew I would see you soon. Sorry about that, but everything is okay, I should be there shortly."

When she got there, one of the nurses said to her, "a Valentine morning surprise? Could not wait until after work?"

"Yeah right, I told you before that I replaced the lock, and hid the keys; I couldn't remember where I hid them."

"Hahaha, you are so funny, I am so glad to see that you have rediscovered your great sense of humor."

After a great day at work, Cindy went home and was happy to see Johanna and Nicole in the kitchen preparing dinner.

"We know how much this day means to you, so we are preparing you a Valentine's dinner. We are here for you; we will help you celebrate."

Cindy knew Johanna was referring to her anniversary with Mark. She was thankful to them and enjoyed the meal they prepared.

Then the phone rang. It was Katy and Liz, who teamed up together to talk to her.

Cindy had been ignoring, them because she did not want to hear what they had to say in reference to Peter, but this time, she was happy to hear from them.

"Hello, sisters, I'm happy to hear your voices." She said.

For a moment, they were shocked, but tried not to dampen the moment.

"We feel the same way," Katy replied.

"We just want to wish you a happy Valentine's Day, we know how much it means to you," they said.

"My daughter and Johanna teamed up to cook me dinner; that touched my heart. It was extra delicious because of the hands that prepared it."

"Your daughter is a chip off the old block, very loving and caring, like her mother." Liz said.

The friends spoke for a long time, they tried not to mention anything about Peter, but in their conversation, something came up that brought up his name, so they elaborated on it, and in so doing, Liz found out a few things that she had no idea that Cindy went through, and then Liz said to Cindy,

"I hate to talk about that kind of relationship, but I am scared for you," and she started crying.

"My aunt was in the same position as you are right now, we all warned her and asked her to get out while she could, but she chose to stay in that abusive relationship, claimed that she was doing it for her three kids, but two weeks before I left for college, it happened, he snapped, and took her life.

That is why I am telling you, my dearest friend, to get out while you can, because he will not change for the better. I am saying that with love."

Cindy thanked her for the advice, and thanked them for calling, and promised to stay in touch, then she hung up.

Peter did not come home after work, and she knew that he was with Courtney.

She went into her bedroom, showered, then sat on the rocking chair in the corner of the room.

As she reflected on her life, she concluded that she needed to move on with her life, and she needed to be happy again, even if it meant getting Peter out of her life.

"But again," she said, "I made a promise to myself that I was not going to get divorced, because I made a vow, and I intend to keep it."

She sat there confused, she was in the crossroads, one led to move on without him, and the other led to stay, no matter what, and she was not sure which one to choose.

She sat there and thought about Mark, she remembered their wedding night, and she wished that he was still here.

The more she thought about it, the sadder she became, until she was overwhelmed with emotion and burst into tears.

She fell asleep in the chair, being very sad.

Peter came in and saw her sitting there, and he thought to himself that she stayed up waiting for him, and he did not show up, because he was with Courtney.

He even felt a little bit of compassion for her, especially after the terrible and insensitive thing he did to her that morning. He was relieved that he did not get a call from the hospital or elsewhere concerning her, although, he had wished something bad would have happened, and he would not held liable for the outcome, but for now, he was okay that it ended well.

In the morning, before he left for work, he apologized and said how sorry he was for what transpired yesterday.

Cindy did not know what to make of this, she did not know if she believed him, or whether he was genuine, or just playing with her emotions and her heart.

Cindy said, "this man is vicious, not only is he abusing me physically, but also mentally, he plays with my emotions, I hate that."

Chapter ONE HUNDRED-SIX

THE MONTHS THAT FOLLOWED, he was on his best behavior, he was almost flawless in his ways.

Cindy thought, deja vu, trouble with him and Courtney again, but she said, this time, she was not going to fall into the same trap again.

She confronted him and asked him about the secret phone he had, which he used to contact Courtney

He was shocked that she knew about it, and that he got caught, he became defensive, and furious, and shouted, at the top of his lungs.

Johanna was at her part time job, so the only other person in the house was Nicole, she had just celebrated her 12th birthday.

"What are you doing sneaking in my things?"

"I was not sneaking in your stuff, I just happened to come across the phone when I was looking for Nicole's documents for her doctor's visit."

"So, you mean, all this time you have been getting into my phone and meddling in my business, and violating my privacy?"

Cindy decided to stand up to Peter. She made up her mind, that if today was the day, he took her out, so be it, but she was determined to stand up against him.

"What privacy?" she said, "it is more like secrecy, and sneaky as a rat, you just got caught, so you are upset."

"Here you are, playing nice guy, trying to convince me that you had changed, but you were not telling the truth."

"Woman, I am a grown man, and I don't have to tell you anything, neither do I have to hide anything from you, I do as I please."

"Then why hide it? You deceiver."

That response infuriated him even more, and the curse words were coming out of his mouth in abundance.

All that time, their daughter was in her room, listening and crying.

"The only reason you are here now is because Courtney kicked you to the curb, she loved your money, but preferred another honey."

"No one kicked me to the curb, I am free to come and go, whenever I want."

"Yeah, you are free to come here, but you can't go over there now, not at this minute, someone else is there, instead of you."

"So, you have become a stalker now? Are you following me around?"

"Why would I waste my precious time following a worthless person like you?"

That response got underneath his skin, he took up a picture that was right next to him, and tossed it at her, she managed to get out of the way, as it smashed against the wall next to her."

"I am that same worthless person that you are married to."

"Yep, I know, when we met, you had integrity, but since you went hooked up with Courtney your integrity and character disappeared, and I mean quickly, now here you are of no value"

"Listen woman, I don't have to stay here and listen to your garbage."

"Where would you go? You can't go to her place, so you must stay here and hear what I have to say."

"What possessed you to give up your family, and go out there and cheat? I gave you my all, I sacrificed for your happiness, I treated you with respect, whatever you wanted, I gave to you, what happened?"

"Sometimes a man needs change, I reached that point, where I needed something else."

"I guessed that you could not keep that something else, or that something else did not want you anymore? Now what?"

"You think you know it all? You always thought you were smarter and better than everyone else, but you are not."

"You are the only person who think this of me, the people around me will tell you something different, and since I hooked up with you, all you did was try to compete with me, instead of embracing me for who I was, and helping us grow together as a couple."

Then Peter responded, "You think that you are a saint? I know you used to mess around, you thought you were fooling me?"

"Man, you get a life, you are so guilty and embarrassed that you are just making up stuff, you know well if I was messing around, you would not have waited until now to say that; you would have raised the roof.

Cheating was not part of my lifestyle, even when you gave me a reason to do so, I did not, because this is not who I am.

You should have been happy with me, but you traded my love for garbage."

"Here you go again, putting down someone else, calling people garbage."

"I did not call anybody garbage, I am referring to the relationship, but you're so bent on defending your mistress, that you can't see reality."

Cindy felt good getting these things off her chest, she wanted to do that a long time ago, but she was scared he would hurt her badly, so she held her peace, but now she was letting it out.

The words that she said, got his attention, and he called Cindy all kinds of derogatory names, and accused her of things that never happened.

She responded, by saying, "you are big grown-up man, acting like a kindergarten child, come on, be a man."

"You think you are more educated than me? You can't walk in my shoes."

"You're sure right, I can't, and don't want to walk in these shoes, too messy. Your shoes are gutless, can't seem to hold on or stick to anything of substance, and had it not been for me, you would just keep sliding, all over the place.

"Woman, you are nothing, you are a piece of

"You don't need to say it, because that is all that comes out of your mouth, don't you realize that your daughter is in the room listening, and hearing all this foul language?"

"My daughter? This child is not my daughter, I am not the father."

"What? Are you freaking crazy? I can't believe you just said that."

"Yes, I did say that; you were cheating with this doctor guy, and got pregnant, and having me thinking she was my child."

"You piece of garbage, good for nothing, son of a gun, you are standing here, and disclaiming your child, and accusing me of cheating?"

Cindy began to cry, and she got very angry.

"I wish, with all my heart, that you were not her father, she would not have a loser like you listed as a father."

"No wonder, you molested her and pretended like it was an accident; you thought I did not know? You old dog. I did not say anything to you, because I knew you would deny it, and hate her, but I should have reported it, and let them lock you up, you bastard."

And she came up to him, and said, "you disgust me, you are worse than I thought, what did I ever see in you? I can't believe you just said this. This is hurting me to the core."

And she touched him, and before she knew it, he slapped her in the face, and pushed her away from him.

In the meantime, Nicole their daughter, picked up the phone, and called the emergency number, that her mom had taught her to call, if there was something bad happening.

"Hello," the operator answered, "who is this? and what is your emergency?"

"My dad is hitting my mommy."

The operator recognized that this was a voice of a child, so she needed to comfort her, while she obtained the information.

"What is your name?" she asked her.

"Nicole."

"How old are you, Nicole?"

"I am 12 years old."

"Is this your mama's house?"

"Yes, my mama is on the floor, and she has blood."

"Where is the blood?"

"On her head. Please help my mom," and she was crying uncontrollably.

"Where is your daddy?"

"He is standing over by my mommy."

"We are coming to take care of your mommy; we will be right there."

At the moment that she was talking to Nicole, she heard the sirens approaching the area.

"Nicole, you did well, thank you for helping your mama. Take care, and your mama will be okay, bye Nicole."

"Bye."

The police arrived, and knocked on the door, and identified themselves.

Peter opened the door, and with his hands lifted, as instructed, he ushered them in.

One officer questioned Peter, while the other attended to Cindy.

He checked for a pulse and found one. She was unconscious, she had been knocked out cold, because her head slammed against the edge of the couch, when she fell from the push.

At the same time, the paramedics arrived, and took over from the police officer.

They took her vitals, and said, she needed to be transported to the hospital immediately.

Johanna had just come back from her shift.

"What is going on?" she asked the policeman, what is wrong with Cindy?"

"Who are you?" the policeman asked her, "are you a member of the family?"

After he verified who she was, he gave her the details, of what he was told that happened.

"Where is Nicole?" she asked.

She went to her room and saw her hiding behind the door, while she cried, continually.

"Nicky" she said, "come here, baby," and she cradled her in her arms, and comforted her. What happened baby?"

"Mom and dad were talking loud at each other, then dad hit her and pushed her, and she fell and was bleeding."

The version Peter gave them was different. He said they were playing, and she slipped and fell, and hit her head on the edge of the couch.

Peter was taken to the police station for further questioning.

After they questioned the daughter, who was the only witness to the incident, they determined that her story was credible enough to warrant holding Peter for assault.

Johanna called Karen and told her what had happened.

Karen as expected, was very angry. She was tired of going to the emergency room to visit her daughter. She was more upset with her daughter than she was with anybody else, because her daughter refused to take the advice of those who cared for her welfare. Yet as a mother, she was fearful, when she heard the news.

She stopped at Cindy's house, and picked up Johanna, and Nicole, and went to the hospital.

Upon arrival, they met Cindy up and alert in a room. She had her head bandaged, where she received the gash from the fall.

"How are you?" Karen asked, noticeably upset.

"I am doing okay, just a little bit lightheaded."

The doctor came and said, "she was lucky, a little lower close to her temple, and she might not be here talking to you all."

"Anyway, I am going to keep her here overnight for further observance."

"I can't believe that you are here again, because of your refusal to cut ties with this man, what is it going to take Cindy, for you to listen? The next time, yes I said it, as long as you are with this man, there will be a next time, and then you might not be that fortunate, and I don't want to come and see you in another place."

"That is what you are wishing?"

"Child, stop being so argumentative, you know exactly what I meant. You better get your act together before it is too late."

"Are you going to press charges against that good for nothing man?"

"It was so traumatizing for this young child to see and hear all of the ugly violence, now she is in need of counseling

"You know that Peter told the police that you all were playing, and you slipped and hit your head. Is that so?"

Cindy did not answer, and that just triggered more anger from her mom.

"What does this guy have over you? What threat has he made that has you so afraid?" Karen asked.

"Mom, I am fine, and I will deal with it, when I get out of here."

"Come on Johanna, and Nicole, let us get out of here."

"Mom, can I stay with you?"

"Sorry, Nicks, this is a hospital, and it is not allowed, but mommy will be home tomorrow; in the meantime, Aunt Johanna will be there for you."

Peter bonded out from the jail and was told charges could still be filed against him, if his wife decided to do so.

From the jailhouse, he went to his house, collected a few things, and moved to Courtney's place.

She was the one who bailed him out, and advised him to come and stay with her, until everything was ironed out at his house,

Chapter ONE HUNDRED-SEVEN

CINDY CAME HOME TO the news that Peter had moved in with Courtney.

She was happy that he went, because she would not have to deal with him anymore, but she was angry, because he ended up at Courtney's house, she thought Courtney had won, and hated that.

The policemen visited Cindy to get her version of what happened, and to find out, if she would file charges.

She allowed them in the house and sat down with them.

"Madam, can you tell us what happened?"

"Well…we were," and she stopped, she remembered the call she received earlier in the morning, threatening her and Nicole, so she was hesitant, to say exactly what happened.

"We were playing, and then started talking, which led to an argument, then I touched him, and that was the last I remembered."

"Do you want to file charges against him? This way, you can have protection from him, he would not be able to come close to you."

"Officer, can I think about it?"

Johanna chimed in, "time? What time? You have been going through this abuse regularly, and now you get the chance to nail this bastard, and you are saying let me think about it? Cindy, I can't understand you, what is wrong with you?"

"Peter has moved on to another place of residence, no harm done, I just want to move on."

"Well, I can't force you, but if you change your mind, here is my card, give me a call, or you could go to the station and file your case."

"Thanks, Officer Hank."

After the police left, Nicole came up to her mommy, and said, "Mommy, why did you lie to the policeman? I saw daddy hit you, and he pushed you."

"Yes, you are making your daughter be a liar, because she gave a different story than what you gave, shame on you, Cindy." Johanna was furious.

"Nicks, I am sorry, but mommy had to do this to protect you, I will explain it to you one of these days."

An hour after the policemen left, Karen called to see how Cindy was doing.

"Hi Jo, I called your phone instead of Cindy, in case she was resting, is she doing better?"

"Mom, she is sitting right here, I am mad at her. The police officers were here to get her statement, and they asked her if she would file charges against Peter, and she did not."

"Hand over the phone to her."

"Cindy, honestly, tell me what is going on? Why are you reluctant to have Peter disciplined for what he has done to you?"

"Mom, are you not the one that brought me up that I should forgive others who have wronged me?"

"Yes, I did, but I did not teach you to stay in harm's way, because you feel you have to forgive someone."

"You can forgive someone, but you don't encourage someone to be evil, and to do bad things, when that person needs to be corrected, and be responsible for his or her actions."

"You should not hold hatred in your heart towards him, but he must pay for his actions."

"Mom, I will think about it."

Then someone else was calling on the other line; and it was Marcus, so she hung up to talk to her son.

"Hi son, how are you doing?"

"I should be asking you that, because the news I got about you is troubling, tell me, what is really going on?"

"Everything is okay now, I just had an incident with Peter, but that is all over now, everything has been taken care of."

"Mom, should I come home, and take care of this guy, once and for all?"

"Son, that is the last thing I would recommend for you to do, as a matter of fact, you should not even be talking like that, that is not Christ like. You are about to enter the professional world of basketball; I would not want you to jeopardize that."

"Mom, I hate to see this keep happening to you, and it is bothering me, and I won't be at peace, until I know that devil is out of your life for good."

"Sometimes, I have flashbacks of the things that you went through with this man.

I remember so many times, he would come home drunk, and just beat up on you, and you would not cry, or say anything, because you did not want us to know what was happening, but mom we knew, we were crying all the time, but we just could not do anything to help, but we were aware.

I remember seeing him punch you so hard in your stomach, that you crumbled to your knees, that image still burns in my mind, and I will never forget it, and for the life of me, I don't know how you are still with this man."

"Son, I went through all this, for you and later Nicole. I was constantly threatened by him, saying he would hurt you, if I left, and I know he would have. The man I was with before his affair, is not the same man. He changed when the affair began.

At first, he treated you like his own, and then came Nicole, and I thought we had a great family, but as he changed, he also changed towards you, and pretended to love Nicole.

I gave my all to him, and he took it for granted, I gave him my heart, and he tore it apart."

"Son, I did not mean to pour all this on you, but since you asked, I just felt that I had to tell you; I have been carrying these burdens for so long; it's a heavy load to carry, and I can't do that anymore. He made me alienate my family and friends, there was hardly anyone I could talk to, besides Jo, and sometimes Katy, and even then, I did not want to tell them, because I thought I was being a burden to them, especially when I was not doing the things that they told me to do."

Johanna was right there listening, and said, "Cindy, why didn't you tell me all these things? We would have figured out a way; I wished that you had told me."

"Mom, feel free to talk to me, get it off your chest, I am free now, I have the time."

"I was talking to Katy on the phone and was telling her about Peter. I told her how Peter was treating me so badly, and how much I missed your father, and that same instant, he came in, but I did not hear when he came into the house, neither when he came into the bedroom, and he stood there, and listened to me, as soon as I got off the phone, he attacked me so viciously."

Cindy began crying as the memories of that attack came back to her, and that was too much for Johanna, she started crying too, and poor Nicole join them and cried, meanwhile, Marcus was sobbing very hard on the phone.

And Cindy continued amidst the tears. "You probably can recall that I stayed home for two days from work, and I called in and told my manager that I was sick, and told her something about my stomach. Well honestly, I was sick, because I was in pain, I could barely move, all my body hurt then.

Son, I know I should not be saying that to you, but I swear, if I had had a gun in the house, I would have killed that man, and faced whatever the outcome would have been, not that I am telling you that it is okay to do that, I am just saying, at the time, that's how great the pain was, but let me emphasize to you violence does not pay.

I also told you not to hate anybody, but let me confess to you, I hate this man with such a passion, unlike the love for your father. Two extremes.

I hope God will grant me the opportunity to forgive him one day, but for now, it is not happening.

Oh, how I missed your dad, why did he have to go? Why has he left me in this vulnerable state?"

"Mom, I miss him too, I wished he was here to watch me play ball."

"It had gotten so bad for me, nobody knows, but I thought of ending it, but I remembered you and Nicole, I could not fathom you living in this world, without a father, or mother, and my mom always says it is not God's will for us to decide who should live or who should die, so I had to make the sacrifice and bear the pain.

"Imagine that? With all the money he said that he has, and is making, I had no proof of that, because he hid all this information from me, so I had no knowledge of his finances.

At year's end, he did the taxes, but here is what got to me; Peter took a check of mines forged my signature and wrote a check to himself for five thousand dollars.

When I confronted him, and said I was going to report it to the police, he promised, that me and my children would end up in a mess, and it would seem like an accident, because he knew what to do."

"Mom. That is enough, I can't take more of this, and you still think I should do nothing?"

"Exactly my son, God will take care of Peter, believe me, he will."

"I came that close to leaving you all when I felt sick, but God knew that I still wanted to be here for you, so he spared my life, and to Him, I am so grateful."

"So, mom, you said all this, let me ask you, are you still going to stay with this man?"

"Marcus, I am not sure, he has moved on, let's wait and see what happens."

"Okay mom, I will talk to you later, I have to go to practice."

"Bye son, and take care, will talk to you soon."

On the other side of town, Peter and Courtney were going through their issues.

Courtney told Peter the only way they were going to live together was if they were married.

She had her own agenda and was money hungry.

Peter knew his choices were to either divorce Cindy and marry Courtney, or beg Cindy to move back home.

Peter went to work, and throughout the day, he scrutinized the options that were before him, and by the end of the day, he had made up his mind.

He came home, and said, "Courtney, I have come to a conclusion, I will divorce my wife and will marry you."

"Oh Peter, that is great news, you make me feel so good inside, best thing you could do, now we can have a great life together."

"I think so too, because I do love you."

She did not respond with 'I love you too,' but rather, "how soon will that be?"

"I am going to start on the process today," he assured her.

Johanna had a different perspective of Cindy after she listened to her on the call with her son. She did not know that Cindy had all those issues that were weighing her down so heavily, and she apologized to her for the extra pressure she added on.

Back at work, Cindy had to deal with the rumors that circulated around her, she expected it, and she was prepared to deal with it.

And she knew that there would be some that sympathized with her, while there would be others who would blame her for the mishaps that she went through.

Chapter ONE HUNDRED-EIGHT

THE MONTHS THAT FOLLOWED were not the brightest for Cindy, she experienced loneliness like she never felt before.

Although she had promised to get close to her family and friends again, she did not keep that promise, and now that she needed them, she was too ashamed to reach out to them.

She was going through a very rough period in her life; she was very depressed.

Her mom, who had been her main support, was not interfering in her life anymore, because she felt that she let Peter off the hook when she refused to have him charged for his actions.

She said she couldn't stomach watching her daughter's life rapidly fading away.

She opted instead to stay away, and she diligently prayed for her daily, and hoped that she would come to her senses, and make the right decisions.

Karen thought about her daughter every minute of every day; she worried about her, and she was fearful that the next call she received would be the dreadful call.

She never thought in her wildest dreams, that Cindy would end up in the situation that she was in. It bothered her so much that it affected her health.

She offered her daughter help so many times, but her daughter turned down the help, so there was nothing left for her to do, but to watch from the sideline, and watch her beloved daughter waste her life away.

And she was right, Cindy was wasting away, she had lost a lot of weight, and the stress was showing in her face.

Cindy isolated herself from the world.

She went to work, but barely interacted with anyone, except for work issues.

Cindy even avoided Sarah her rock, because she did not want to get any more advice.

At home, she was mostly quiet and spent a little time with Nicole, but spent most of the time in her bedroom, only coming out late in the evening to spend a few minutes with them, before she retreated to her room.

Johanna was very concerned about her, and it broke her heart to see how miserable, her sister was, and what bothered her, is that she did not know how to help her because Cindy had built a wall around her.

Johanna knew that she needed help, but she did not know where to turn, she was losing Cindy, and that was happening quickly, she did not know who to turn to for help, but she knew something had to be done, and it had to be quick.

She thought of her friend, Dr. King, but she knew he had just lost his wife in a horrific traffic accident, and besides, Cindy had shunned him the last time they communicated, and was not sure if he would care to reconnect with her now.

Johanna was also concern with Nicole's welfare, because the bond she had with her mother was not as strong as it used to be because of her mom's mental state.

It got worse, Cindy received some bad news, although her mom and others thought of it as good news, and the answer to their prayers.

She received a hand delivered envelope from Peter's lawyer, and inside were divorce papers.

Cindy freaked out, 'what?" she said, "divorce? I am not getting a divorce."

As she let out a loud scream of anguish, her daughter came running, "mom, what's wrong? Are you okay?" and she held on to her, as they both cried.

Johanna came and comforted her, and said, "it will be okay, we will get through this."

Cindy sat on the chair for almost 10 minutes, without saying anything, but just stared at the ceiling.

Then she said, "Jo, why me? Why? What have I ever done wrong that would merit the punishment that I am going through?

It's been like this most of my life. I only experienced short seasons of happiness, which were usually cancelled by long, hard, painful seasons of sorrow upon sorrow.

When will I get a break?"

"Cindy, you have to look elsewhere for help."

"Elsewhere like where? I can't see anyone who can help me?"

"GOD can."

"God?"

"Where was God when my mom and dad divorced, and my brothers and I were left to struggle? Where was he when I was bullied at school, and almost dropped out? You said He can help, why didn't he help me?"

"Cindy, did you ever ask him?"

"I went to church with my mom, we prayed, she always prayed for us, but yet, all these bad things still happened to me."

At that moment, her phone rang, and on the other end was Peter.

"Did you get the divorce papers?" he asked.

"You bastard, I can't believe you are doing this? You are a low life, piece of crap."

"Don't you want to get rid of this piece of crap? Now is your chance, sign the documents."

"I said I would not, but you know what? You are right for once, I will sign it, and get rid of this stinking rubbish, pure garbage." And she hung up on him.

"You did the right thing, Johanna said to her, let garbage go where it belongs, to the trash bin."

Cindy laughed, "you're right, he is going to the trash bin, the bin and the trash deserve each other."

Cindy hugged her daughter, and sobbed and said to her, it was the biggest mistake I ever made in my life, when I gave you this man as a father, I wish that I had never met him, I hate myself for doing that, I do."

"Mom, if you did not meet him, I would not be here."

"That is not what I meant baby; I mean I should not have married him."

"Mom, he said that he was not my father."

"Nicks, I am sorry that you heard all those things, but from my heart to yours, he is your father, I have never cheated on this man, or any of my relationships, your mama is not that type of person.

I hate him more than ever for saying that you are the cause why he got married to me.

He said he was not ready to get married, but because I got pregnant, he was forced to marry me.

"Nicks, mommy is tired, and I need to rest, Aunty Johanna will stay up with you a little bit, I will see you when I wake up."

Cindy went into her bedroom, laid on the bed, but just could not sleep.

She was so depressed that she felt it down in her bones.

And the more she thought of the state of her life, she became more depressed.

She said, "I have never owned a gun, and thank God, I don't, because if I did, I might be committing a horrible thing about now. Here I am miserable, and he is out there having fun, that bugs me."

She wrestled with so many ideas, most of them destructive ideas.

She eventually fell asleep and did not wake up until the next day.

That pattern continued for months, and her depression got worse by the day.

Cindy kept slacking off in taking her medications, especially her insulin, despite the continued efforts of Johanna, reminding her daily to take them.

She was not consistent in taking her blood pressure medication regularly, which often led to her having very close calls for strokes, and heart problems, because her pressure sometimes got danger-ously high.

The environmental at work, did not help her either; her co-workers talked about her often, and she had become a byword of most of them.

And it got worse, she found out that Peter and Courtney had gotten married a few days ago.

Cindy did not take this news well.

She went home and was not in the best of moods.

After briefly talking to Johanna and Nicole, she opened a bottle of wine that she had in the wine cabinet and isolated herself in her bedroom.

Cindy was not one that used illegal drugs, nor consumed alco-hol, but the pressure from all that she was going through, especial-ly the news that she just received about Peter's wedding, put her over the edge, and she decided to drink the alcohol for relief.

Bad idea: the alcohol and her medications did not collaborate well together, so instead of relief, she got more pain.

Her anxiety level went up higher, and she went into a deep, deep depression, and started crying.

She acted like a crazy person as she went around the bedroom, and anything she saw that reminded her of Peter, she either tore it, or broke it, as she continued to scream in agony, so much so that her daughter and Johanna were extremely scared that she was having a mental breakdown.

Johanna rushed to the room, fearing that she might get hit with the flying objects that were being hurled around; she covered her face and yelled to get Cindy's attention.

Then she ran up to her, embraced her, and helped calmed her down, as they both sobbed together.

Cindy called in sick, for a couple of days, and as her situation worsened, she refused to take her medication, regardless of how much Johanna and Nicole pleaded with her.

Johanna called Karen, and told her what was going on, and the state that Cindy was in.

Karen advised Johanna to put the blood pressure pills in a glass of water, and after they had dissolved, offer or entice her to drink it.

Johanna did just what she was instructed to do, and after much pleading, she was able to get her to drink the water.

This helped in normalizing her blood pressure, which would prevent a stroke or heart attack, but the biggest problem she had, was the diabetes, and she was hesitant to take the insulin.

Cindy finally answered Karen, and to Karen's surprise, she was listening, and was not arguing with her, like she had been doing lately, but spoke in a quiet soft voice, like someone that had given up and was submissive.

Anyway, Karen was able to get her to take the insulin.

These episodes of missing work, refusing medications, and being in a depressed mood, continued on a regular basis, until it finally reached a breaking point.

Her boss called her into her office, and informed her, that she was placing her on probation, and would have one month to get her act together in order to meet the performance level, that was required for the job, if not, she would have to release her from her job.

Cindy was angry with her for doing that and claimed that everyone was against her.

She reached the point where she was so bitter against everyone, and thought that no one had her back, no one had her best interest in mind, although she was the one who isolated them, because of her Peter.

Peter still had some of his items in the house, and Cindy took everything of his she could find, and placed them next to the garbage can, to be collected by the garbage truck.

That is when Johanna knew that she was getting over him, she could tell that she had made up her mind.

Cindy called Ms. Joseph and requested a leave of absence for the next six months.

Ms. Joseph informed her that this request could not be negotiated via telephone but must be done in office.

Cindy agreed, but informed Ms. Joseph that she was sick and would not be able to come to work for the next two days.

Ms. Joseph was trying her best to be lenient with Cindy, and was trying her best to help keep her job, because she cared for Cindy, and knew what she was going through. She knew who she was when she first started to work with her. She watched her changed into the person she now was, from the darling that she used to be. She felt compassion for her and was trying to help her any way she could, but she knew certain policies would not allow her to help the way she wanted.

Chapter *ONE HUNDRED-NINE*

JOHANNA WAS ABOUT AN hour, from making it home from her shift, so Cindy was alone at home with her daughter Nicole. She went into her room and spent some precious time with her, she tried to explain to her what she was going through, and as she kissed her, and was leaving her room, Nicole asked her, "mom, why are you not talking to grandma?"

"My dear, I do talk to her, but not as often as I used to; things have changed between us, she has given up on me, everyone has given up on me, and mommy is alone and lonely. Your mama is hurting badly.

"Where are you hurting mom?"

"Your mom is hurting inside, my heart is broken, your mom has no joy left inside of her, and your mommy does not know where to turn, or who to turn to."

"Mommy I will pray for you."

"Thanks, dear, but even God has given up on me."

"No, mommy, grandma said that God never give up on us."

"Okay, mommy will speak with God; you watch your programs until Johanna comes, then we will have our dinner. Mommy loves you a whole lot, love you forever, see you in a while."

Cindy went into her bedroom, but did not close the door, and she sat on her bed, and said,

"When I was a teenager, I remembered my mom quoted Mathew chapter 11 verses 28 through 30, which says, come unto you, if you labor and are bowed down because of a heavy load, and I will give you rest.

Take your yoke and put it upon me, and learn from me, because I am meek, and lowly in heart, and if you do these things, you will find rest for your soul.

You also said that your yoke is easy, and your burden is light. Well, my God, this is what I am looking for, to get rid of this heavy burden, and to get a lighter burden.

"So, God, if you are there, I need to talk to you. I have heard that you can help me, so I am coming to you for help.

First, Lord, why have you neglected me? Since I was a small girl to now, you have ignored me.

I remember, crying and asking you, to keep my daddy from leaving my mom, and he still left. Why did you let him leave? Why did I have to grow up without him? Then Lord, you took him away from me forever, why Lord? He was the best person in my life, why did you take him away? I have been hurting ever since, I am still missing him.

Lord, where were you when I was being raped, and was crying for help? You abandoned me, Lord. I went through this alone, this was one of the darkest days of my life, and because of that day, I had to give up my first child, this is hurting me to this day, when

I remember the trauma that I went through at the clinic, I hate myself even more.

Lord, I know you are probably saying that I am complaining, but my mom and my daughter, and Johanna, said I could talk to you, so I am here talking to you, Lord.

My life is just full of mishaps and pain, and tragedy, one after the other.

Mark was a good guy, the love of my life, and you took him away from me too, and Lord, why didn't you stop me from giving my heart to this horrible man Peter?

He has abused me beyond explanation, he has done terrible things in the bedroom, where no one could see, that I have not told anybody, because they were too horrific, but Lord you knew, why didn't you stop him? For instance, when he threw water on me on the bed, while I was sleeping, I could have gotten sick and die.

And because of these things, I am here crying to you, because I am hurting, my heart is broken in so many pieces, this heavy load that I am carrying, I can't carry it anymore, I really can't.

Peter, Lord, has done more harm, and caused more pain in my life, than all my misfortunes put together.

I thought that he was the one for me, but how I was wrong, at first, he was like a godsent, but now I realize, that he was the devil in disguise.

I gave him my all, but he betrayed me. You might be asking why I am telling you all this? But Lord, these things have led me to where I am today.

Again, why did he have to go to someone else? I thought my love was enough for him, but I was wrong.

Lord, I wish that you had stopped me from falling in love with him, now I would not be so angry, and full of wrath.

God, I know, I am fussing, but I'm sorry, I must get it off my chest, for I am dying with pain of a broken heart.

My friends said time will help the pain, and it won't be that severe, but, honestly, it hurts more because the evidence is still there, and when I am alone, the episodes of all my traumatic experiences, play in my head.

If it were not for my kids, I am sure Peter would be dead, I know that is wrong, but that is how I felt then, and honestly, I still wish that he was dead.

I am confessing, I hate this man with a passion, and if I see him again, I don't know what I would do.

Presently God, I don't like anybody, because humans have failed me.

God, I know this is a long prayer, and some of it might not make any sense, and I am still shedding tears, and crying my heart out, but I must empty out myself, I have come to the end of my rope, I can't go on anymore.

My mom and friends say that you can help me, so I am here for that help, but if you choose not to help me, I am okay with that too.

Please take care of my boy, and my beautiful girl, watch over them, and please Lord, don't let them go through in their lives, the things that I went through. Lord always reminds them that I loved them.

As I come to the end of the journey, I don't know what else to say, but I am scared, but I think this is for the best, only if you say otherwise, and save me, this is it."

Cindy, said, I can't do it, I can't take my life, I can't go out like this, this is wrong. My mom always taught us to let God do his work, don't take his job from him.

But the pain is unbearable, I can't continue like this, my life is meaningless.

And she struggled back and forth with the decision.

Then she concluded that she was not going to do it.

She got up from the bed, and opened the door, and was about to go into the living room, when she felt a sharp pain in her chest, she grabbed on to her left side of her chest and collapsed to the floor. She was having a heart attack; her blood pressure had gone extremely high.

Johanna came home from work, and as was her custom she went to say hi to Nicole, then they went to say hello to Cindy.

They saw Cindy sprawled on the floor, barely moving.

Johanna rushed to her and checked her pulse, and fortunately there was one.

Johanna panicked and for a moment, she froze.

But when Nicole shouted mommy, she snapped out of it, then took her phone, and called 911 emergency.

They instructed her what to do until the paramedics got here.

At first Cindy mumbled something, then slipped into unconsciousness, and laid there motionless.

Johanna kept checking her pulse, and that was what gave her a little hope, each time she found that she had one.

She called Karen and told her what happened. Karen screamed, and hung up, not waiting for details, she headed for Cindy's house.

The paramedics were there in no time, they checked her vitals and immediately loaded her in the ambulance and took her to the hospital.

Johanna called Katy, and told her about Cindy, and asked her to relay the information to Joshua.

"How serious is it" she asked while sobbing bitterly.

"It does not look good," Johanna replied, "only a miracle from God can save her now."

Johanna also called David and Liz, to tell them what was going on."

In less than no time, Karen was at the door knocking.

"Where is she?" she asked.

"You just missed them, they have taken her to the hospital, I think they said that she has suffered a heart attack.

Johanna also called Dr. King, and told him what had just happened, and she told him where she was taken to, he then thanked her for the information, and promised to visit her as soon as it was possible for him to do so. This was also the hospital, where he worked.

She called Sarah, one of her best friends and co-worker, and shared the news with her.

She was hesitant to call Marcus, because she did not know how to tell him, but eventually, she did.

She took Nicole, and went to the hospital, which was a few miles down the road, from the house.

As they were driving, she and Nicole kept praying, crying, and hoping, that God would save Cindy, and bring her back to them.

Karen was at the emergency room waiting area, anxious to hear from the doctor.

Not too long after that, Sarah and Nancy, her co-workers, joined them at the hospital. They were vigorously praying and were hoping for the best news.

Dr. King came to the waiting room to see who was there; he introduced himself to those that had not met him before, and he spoke to Karen and Johanna, and told them that he was going in the room right now, and he would let them know as quickly as possible what her condition was.

Dr. King, on his way to the room, met with Dr. Ramphart, who gave him an update, and what her prognosis was.

And he said to him, "it does not look good."

Dr. King, asked him, if he could address the family, since he was familiar with them, which he agreed to.

But before he went out to them, he went to Cindy's bedside, to talk to her, hoping that she would be able to hear him.

He said to her, "I know you are in there, and you are not going to leave us, I have prayed for you, and I believe God heard my prayer, and will give you back to us."

"I am here, and will be here until you wake up, so you better come out of this quickly, there are so many here waiting to welcome you back."

After he said that, he went out to tell the others what was going on.

Chapter ONE HUNDRED-TEN

"Cindy has suffered massive heart failure, and a slight stroke; the prognosis is not good; it would take a miracle to bring her back, and even then, she might be incapacitated, which is the medical perspective, but when I spoke to God, I got a different response. She will come back to us, and will come back healthy, but it is going to take a lot of work."

"Who is going to join me and believe? Keep on praying and watch the Mighty hands of GOD go to work. Those of you that are skeptical, you will be disappointed, because my GOD is able."

Karen was shocked, to hear the doctor speaking like this, she did not know that he had accepted Christ and become a Christian.

All this happened after his wife was killed in an auto accident.

He had two choices after the accident, either to get angry at God, or to get to know God, and he chose the latter. Since then, he said that his life had been peaceful and satisfying.

Day two came, and Cindy had no change in her condition, which caused some anxiety with her family and friends, especially to Marcus, her son.

The doctor was trying to find out when she had taken her pills last, because he said, it looked like her pressure was extremely high for a long time, and when she got angry, her heart went to the max that it could handle, then gave up.

Joshua and Katy came in that evening, after he was granted a medical release from his team. Also, David made it in that night.

And the atmosphere in the waiting room was solemn, as they continued to pray for her recovery.

But with every passing day, their hope diminished, because Cindy did not improve, but the pillars of the group, Junie and Karen, remained hopeful, and kept on believing.

On day five, Dr. King begged and persuaded Dr. Ramphart to try a procedure that he had developed a couple of years back, when he was faced with a similar situation. Although he did not get to perform the procedure because the patient died before he had a chance to try it, he was still confident, that it would make a difference.

Dr. Ramphart knew that he was taking a risk, but he said, in the condition that she was in, it could only get better, not worse, so why not?

Dr. King tried his experiment and waited to see what the result would be.

For the five days that Cindy was at the hospital, the doctor said, she literally died three times and came back, that is how hard she was fighting, and how much prayer that was being sent up to God, on her behalf.

Dr. King asked his mother -in -law to stay with his daughter for the next few nights, while he stayed at the hospital.

He stayed at Cindy's bedside, together with Marcus, during the nights.

From the day he tried the experiment, nothing new happened, but he was not giving up hope, neither was he giving up on Cindy.

Every night he spoke to her, even though she did not respond; he believed that she was hearing him, so he spoke sweet words to her.

In the daytime she was blessed to have one of the sweetest nurses take care of her.

Nurse Kim had always been committed to her patients; she always went the extra mile to ensure their happiness.

She was a devoted Christian, and would encourage her patients, as much as possible, to stay strong, and point them to the King of hope, who is God.

She monitored Cindy regularly to see if she was making progress.

On her break, she would come in, and she would read to her, hoping that she was hearing her, and at the end of her visit, she would finish with a prayer.

On day seven, when the group had left for the evening, Junie, after his shift, went home, and freshened up, but came back to be at her side.

He met Marcus there who was tired, and sleepy, but he was committed to being there for his mom.

Junie and he conversed, and they would say good things to Cindy because they wanted her to know how special she was.

They arranged a sleep schedule, so they could both get some rest.

Around 1:am in the morning, Junie shook Marcus, 'look!" he excitedly said, and Marcus jumped up from the sleep, and noticed that his mom had moved her fingers.

He started crying because he was so happy and realized that there was hope that she might come out of this.

Junie quietly took the fingers that she was moving and squeezed them, hoping that she would squeeze them back, but disappointedly, she did not respond. He was not discouraged, but to the contrary, he was excited, because he saw a glimpse of hope.

They paid close attention to her during the remainder of the night, but nothing unusual happened.

In the morning, they were anxious to share with the others the good news.

"Karen, something excited happened last night, Cindy moved her fingers for a good minute, and I saw a slight movement on the screen, Karen, there is hope."

"Hallelujah, thank you Jesus," Karen responded, and a few drops of tears trickled down her face.

And as the others came to their daily visits, she told them the updated news.

Dr. Ramphart could not believe what he was hearing, and said, "I was told to inform the family that they would have to say goodbye, because she could only be kept for two more days, but this is great news, plans will have to be changed."

During the nighttime, Marcus swore to Junie that he saw his mom open her eyes for a quick second, but Junie said it might be his imagination, although he believed it could have happened.

The next day, Dr. Ramphart could not believe what he was seeing; Cindy's blood pressure was trending upwards, a few days ago she had no pressure, and she was assisted by the machine to do everything, but he could see that she was trying to do things on her own; she was making progress without the help of the machine.

After he did what he needed to do, he went out to her mother, and said to her, "I have some good news," and he explained to her what had happened.

And Karen being a nurse, knew that things were heading in the right direction.

"I am keeping her on the machine, just to be on the safe side; I will discuss it with Dr. King when he comes in, and we will decide what needs to be done from there. But don't stop praying, she is not out of the woods yet."

"Yes, we will keep on talking to God, we will be praising him for what he has done, and what He is doing, and what He will continue to do. Amen"

Junie came in and was told the great news.

He was very joyful and praised God for his goodness.

He quickly went to her room, there he met Katy comforting and encouraging Cindy.

He checked a few details on the monitor and was very much encouraged by what he observed.

He told Katy, "Looks like our girl is starting to turn the corner to a road of recovery, but we still have to be cautious, and continue praying."

Throughout the night, her condition remained steady, her pressure did not drop, though he wished it would increase a little bit more, but he knew it would with time.

Her heart was getting stronger, which was a wonderful sign that she was recovering.

On day 14, about 8:15pm, Cindy opened her eyes, and those that were in the room were so excited, but had to be cautioned, to keep it quiet, because there were other patients, that needed the quietness.

Also, they could not startle Cindy, so most of them went outside of the room to express their joy.

Cindy continued to get better, but it was a slow process, and those who were anxious to see her be completely recovered, knew that it would require patience on their parts, and they had to give her their full support.

Chapter ONE HUNDRED-ELEVEN

AFTER 6 WEEKS OF hospitalization, she was moved to rehabilitation to continue with the recovery process.

Junie spent almost all his free time at the rehab place; he had determined to help her make a full recovery.

Cindy progressed steadily, her memory was slowly returning to where she recognized certain things, her speech was getting clearer, she was able to put more words together, and make better sentences.

One thing that got better during her recovery process, was the control of her diabetes.

She did not need all the insulin that she used to get before her incident, but the amount that she needed now, the nurses were able to administer regularly, and timely.

And Junie said this pattern must continue even if she makes a full recovery, and he would see to it, that it happened.

Junie arranged with the management of the facility, so he could take daily walks with Cindy, to help speed up her recovery.

They started with a few steps, for a few minutes, and gradually they became small walks, for a longer period.

Junie and Cindy spent a lot of time together, because he wanted to be there for her, as much as possible.

On one of their walks, Cindy asked Junie, "who are you? Are we related?"

"I am your friend, I am a doctor, who wants to see you get better."

Junie was disappointed that she did not know who he was, but he understood the reason why.

After thinking of it, he was happy that she did not recognize him, this way, they would develop a new friendship, and all the bad things that happened in the past, would be behind them.

But that theory was not going to work for too much longer, because she was recovering much quicker than they anticipated.

Her memory was getting sharper, and she was remembering more things daily.

When Johanna came to visit her, she said to her, "you look familiar, what is your name?"

"I am Johanna, I am your cousin, and your friend." And she stopped at that, she did not want to overload her brain, and make it more difficult for her. At least she gave her, a bit of information that she could digest.

Chapter ONE HUNDRED-TWELVE

WITHIN A YEAR AND some months of being at the rehab center, Cindy had made a considerable amount of recovering, her memory was returning, although it had a long way to go before it could get to where it was before the crisis. She remembered her children, also Johanna, and other members of her family.

She was not completely healed, but she was good enough to leave the rehab center, and to finish her recovery process at home.

Cindy did not remember too much about what happened before her incident, but she remembered praying to God, and asking for help, and thought that He did not care, and had given up on her.

But now, with most of her memory back, she realized how wrong she was, and that He gave her an opportunity at life again, and she owed everything to Him.

Cindy met with Dr. Ramphart, after setting up an appointment with him. She needed some questions to be answered, and to find out about her path going forward.

"Hi Cindy, it is such a pleasure to see you, I am so glad I can say that because you died on me three times, and had it not been for God's mercy, and for Him to allow this young doctor into your life to save you, I don't know what the outcome would have been."

"I don't think I have seen anyone as concerned for an individual like he was."

"He was willing to try or do almost anything that would bring you back from near death."

"He came up with a procedure that had never been used on any other patient before; I was reluctant to let him try it on you, but I thought nothing worse could happen, and after his pleading, I allowed it, and because of it, here you are."

"Who was this doctor, is it Dr. King?"

"Yes, he is the one who saved your life."

Cindy was wondering why did he not mention that to her? Why was he being so humbled?

From the time she opened her eyes, he had been there. She was now wondering if there was history between the two of them.

Later that evening, when Junie came to her place, she sat with him for a while and as they were conversing, she asked him questions about himself, to see if she could remember if there was a special connection between them.

Since she could not get what she wanted from him, from just plainly conversing, she asked him directly.

"Dr. King, what was the relationship between the two of us before my memory was affected?"

"It is a long story, not sure if we should get into that right now."

"Okay, just give a little bit of information each time we are together, and I might just get to put the pieces together.

"You were a student nurse, and you came to my clinic to do your clinical, and from there we became friends.

I was interested in being with you, but you were with someone else; I thought you were on the road to getting married, so I moved on, only to find out that you had ended the relationship with that guy, but did not tell me until it was too late; by then I was with someone else and had moved on."

"That is enough for now; that is a lot to digest, you will receive the rest of the story as time goes by."

"Doc, this is good to know."

"Call me Junie, that is what friends call me."

"Who else can give me information about you?"

"Best people, Katy and Johanna, I guarantee you that they will give an honest account of my life, and my relationship with you, up to the day you went to the hospital.

The next year and a half, Cindy learned a lot about her past, and of people that were part of her past.

Some things and people, she remembered vividly, and some she remembered vaguely.

Cindy's life had changed drastically, since the incident, she was happy, just like when she was living her life with Mark.

She was told about Peter, and the type of person he was, but her friends did not go into details, in order to avoid her thinking too much about it.

And she said, she wanted to move forward and not dwell in the past.

Soon Cindy had made almost a complete recovery, except for a few minor issues; she was healthy and most of her memory was restored.

Chapter ONE HUNDRED-THIRTEEN

PETER'S MARRIAGE TO COURTNEY lasted for two and a half years.

She cheated on him and had a steady relationship with a guy name Walter.

Courtney divorced Peter, took the majority of his assets, and got married to Walter.

Peter suffered a major stroke because of what Courtney did. Since Peter had no one to go to, after his stay at the hospital, he was placed in a home for the disabled, and has been there since.

Cindy went back into nursing and was hired at the hospital where her mom had worked.

Cindy and her mom were knitted together again, just like a blanket. They spent a lot of time together.

She and Junie got closer and became real good friends, just like when they first met, only difference now, they were both single.

Cindy and Nicole had developed a great relationship, not just mother and daughter, but they treated each other like best friends.

She was very proud of Nicole and vowed to protect her at all costs.

It had been a while since they had done any celebrating, so Karen, along with Katy, Liz, and Johanna, set up a celebration for Cindy upcoming birthday, which was two months away.

They would also plan to celebrate Marcus' achievement of being drafted to the professional basketball league. He was fortunate to be drafted by a team in Florida, where his Uncle Joshua was the assistant coach.

He was so excited to play the game he loved and to be compensated for it, also knowing that he would be able to assist his mom whenever the need arose, that warmed his heart.

What a bash it was, there was so much love shown and the family and friends were just happy to be together.

Cindy gave a heartfelt speech which brought some people to tears. She thanked everyone who helped during her years of convalescence, and particularly, those that were there for her in the darkest days of her life.

But most of all, she thanked God for coming through for her, even after she lambasted Him for not helping her during the various crises in her life. She made a public apology to him She wanted everyone to know how wrong she was, and how right He was. She considered herself blessed to be surrounded by such amazing family and friends, even when she drove them away from her, they remained committed to her.

Then she said, "Oh doctor King, what more can I say, because of you, I am standing here today.

God has used you to bring me back to life, and for that, I will be forever grateful. You are the greatest hero in my life, thank you so much. You are a special man."

And not to make it any easier on the emotions, Marcus expressed his love for his mother and thanked everyone that was there for him during the hard time of his life, he vowed to give back and to always remember where he came from.

It was a celebration full of tears, but also filled with laughter; it was a roller coaster of emotions.

Cindy said she was ready to live life to the fullest, she decided to view the hurts and turmoil as learning experiences and to put them behind her.

Cindy was home Sunday afternoon with Johanna and Nicole; they were just relaxing, when her phone rang.

"Hi, is this Cindy?" the person asked.

"Yes, I am, how can I help you, and who are you?"

"I am Tammy, and I am calling from I Care Home for the aged and disable. I am calling to let you know that Peter Latrine has passed away, and your daughter Nicole was listed as his only family member, and next of kin.

So, it is our policy to always notify the next of kin in the death of their loved one.

Since there is no one to claim his body, the government will take the responsibility for his burial. Sorry about your loss, also, he left a letter addressed to Nicole, this we will mail to you."

Cindy related the information to Johanna, and said to Nicole, "your father has passed away, but before he did, he left instructions to contact you when he passed."

"Mom, I thought he said that he was not my father?"

"Pay no attention to that my child, he was your father, your mommy did not cheat on him because I am not that type of person, I will always be true to whoever I am with. Anyway, this is behind us now, the way he lived, led to his demise, and sadly, there is no one mourning for him."

Johanna remembered that Cindy always used to say, God will take care of Peter and would judge him according to the things that he did, and she said to herself, "she was so right, as he lived, so he died, miserable."

Then Cindy said, "as the year is coming to an end, it looks like all my misfortunes, tragedy, and hurts, are going with it, and I hope that this approaching year, will be filled with joyful events, and a life of happiness.'

Cindy received the letter in the mail from the Home for the Aged and Disabled; inside the envelope, was the letter to Nicole.

Peter acknowledged his mistakes and asked for Cindy's forgiveness, and regretted all the evil things he did to her.

He asked Nicole to forgive him for saying that he was not her father, and hurting her so badly, he said, she is, and will always be his daughter, and that he was sorry that she did not hear him say it, but he loved her, and hoped she would find the compassion in her heart to forgive him.

He said that he had left her his life insurance of $300,000, because she was his beneficiary, nobody knew about it, and a secret investment, valued over $100,000, he had at one of the financial investment companies.

He left instructions, for her to obtain them.

Cindy could not believe it, but she knew he was a sneaky guy, so she was not surprised.

Nicole was very happy about the money, but very sad, that he had to wait until he was dying, to express his love for her, and that hurt her very much.

Cindy called Karen and told her the news about Peter and of his request.

Karen, though she was glad that he was forever out of her daughter's life, felt sorry for him, the way his life ended was heart breaking.

Then she said, "the decisions you make in life will determine how your life will be lived."

Chapter ONE HUNDRED-FOURTEEN

Sunday morning, Cindy was the first one up and ready to go to church. Since she had recovered from her illness, with the help of Junie, she had made church a great part of her life, she had given and committed her life to God.

Donald, and Karen drove over to Cindy's house, and they rode in one vehicle, the minivan.

They were happy to see Junie waiting for them when they got there.

Since Junie's wife death, he has been faithful and steadfast in his walk with God.

He used every opportunity in his practice to tell others about God's love, and of His promises.

After the service was over the family along with Doctor King, went to the Mediterranean restaurant on Grigg street to have lunch.

They sat at the table that was on the porch to avoid the inside crowd.

While waiting for their food, Doctor King said, "I have received word that I have been recognized by the Board of Medical Doctors, for the procedure that I performed on you, Cindy, that ended up saving your life. And to that, I say, "to GOD be the glory, great and mighty things He has done.

I plan to have this procedure patented as soon as possible, and to name the procedure Cindy's option."

"Congratulations are in order Dr. King, and I wish for even greater things for you in the future.'

"Thanks, Karen. Cindy was the one who pushed me into using it, so she deserves some of the credit. I did not want to see her die, so I tried all that I knew to save her."

"You are so humble, and that makes you who you are, I am so happy, and blessed, to call you, my friend.

"Thanks Cindy, the feelings are mutual."

After enjoying their meal, they went to their various homes.

That night, before going to sleep, Cindy knelt before her bed, and spoke to God. She said, "Oh GOD, I am not worthy to come before you this night, but please allow me to.

First, I want to thank you for sparing my life, because I was told, that I left my body three times, on the hospital bed, and you sent me back each time, because I did not want to die, despite all that I said, and I was not ready spiritually, I probably might have gone to a place that would be away from you, but you gave me one more chance to make it right with you.

"Thank you, Lord, thank you."

"I have been through some rough things in my life, things that were too much for me to handle, some were painful and hurtful, that sometimes I wished that I would be like a bird, where I could just fly away, far from everyone and everything, and go somewhere deserted, and just be at rest, and then I would find peace."

"Lord, I thought of doing it my own way and finding a way to exit this world, but I realized that was not the way to do it, because that is not my call to make."

"So, Father, as I kneel before you this night, I just want to thank you for all your goodness to me."

"I want to say how sorry I am for blaming you for the things that I went through in my life."

"Father, in time like these, I just wanted to blame someone for my mishaps, and Father, I made you my first choice, I am so sorry,"

Then Cindy lifted her hands in the air and praised God, as she cried loudly because of the passion she felt for God.

Johanna and Nicole simultaneously came out of their rooms and came rushing to Cindy's room, hoping that she had not fallen into that depression mode again.

But when they got to the room, there she was thanking, and praising God.

Cindy said, "thank you Lord for the rugged and steep mountains you helped me climb; if my mountains had been smooth, I would have had nothing to grip, that would have gotten me to the top."

"I remember when I was growing up, my mother told us about a character in the bible called Peter, she said it came from the book of Mathew, chapter 9, verses 26-33. She said, he was walking on the water going towards you, and when he looked around him, he saw the big waves, he saw all his problems, his issues, his pain, and his hurt, and he took his eyes off of you, and concentrated on the things that were causing him to sink, and he was sinking fast, and he called out to you, and you reached out to him, and saved him."

"Dear God, this was me, that was my life, instead of coming to you, I looked at all my problems and hurt. I looked at the waves that were about to crash over me and thought I could handle all these things on my own, and although I was sinking, my stubbornness still prevent me from calling to you for help, but when I was almost gone, you still reached out and saved me."

"Father, I realized the God that you are, even though we take our eyes from you, and look at our problems, and we are about to perish, you, out of your love for us, would still reach out and save us."

"Thank you, Lord."

"Now I just want to close my prayer by thanking you for all the blessings that you have bestowed upon me, if I should name them all, it would take me forever, but allow me to mention a few.

First, I want to thank you for the blessing of life, Father, I took it for granted, and almost lost it, but how thankful I am that you allowed me to have it back, I love you, Lord."

"My family, how grateful I am to have such a wonderful family, a wonderful son, who is so dear to me, and a beautiful daughter, who is precious to me."

"I pray God, that I will be there for them, and to advise them on choosing your path the best road in life."

"Mothers are extra special, and the one you blessed me with, what a blessing, thank you for her, Lord, continue to lead, and guide her, my dear Lord."

"I thank you for fathers who love you and raise their children to trust you."

"And lastly Lord, I want to thank you for close loved ones, family members, especially my dearest brothers, and special cousin Johanna, I don't know where I would be without her."

"Yes Lord, Junie, my doctor, he is so special to me, always has been, and I care for him just as much. Jesus, I had promised myself never to be in another relationship, but my heart yearns to be with this man, Lord please guide me."

"The future is in your hands, and you know and see everything, so it does not matter how much I love this man, and how I much I feel for him, if it is not going to work out, and if I must go through a painful relationship again, don't let me go into this relationship."

Please God, give me signs that are either for it or against it, please let me know.

Now I am going to end with the prayer that I was taught, since I was a kid, and took it for granted all these years.

Our Father, who art in heaven, hallowed be your name, your kingdom come, your will be done on earth as it is in heaven, give us this day our daily bread, and forgive us our trespasses, as we forgive those who trespass against us, and lead us not into temptation, but deliver us from evil, for thine is the kingdom, and the power, and the glory, for ever and ever, amen.

P.S Lord

Please help me to forgive others, for this is a hard thing for me to do, especially what I have been through, makes it difficult for me to do, but if you can forgive me, I should do the same to others, and move on."

Cindy opened her eyes, and saw Johanna, and Nicole kneeling on the other side of the bed.

She said, "thank you Lord Jesus, thank you."

And they got up from their knees and did a group hug with some tears in between.

The next day Cindy went to work feeling so free in her spirit, she was feeling good physically, and emotionally, she had soundness of mind, and she was in a good place mentally.

And this change was reflected in her work, and with her relationships, especially with her family, and close friends.

On Saturday, she and her mother spent the day together. They went to the mall and did a little bit of shopping, they went to get manicured, and pedicured while they were out there.

On their way home, Karen asked Cindy, "how do you feel about Dr. King?"

"He is a good man." She replied

"I mean, are you attracted to him?" Karen explained.

"Mom honestly?"

"Yes honestly," Karen said.

"I am very much attracted to him, from the first time I met him when we were younger, and I would not mind, if I spend the rest of my life with him, but I am fearful to have my heart broken again, I don't think I would survive this time."

"You know Cindy, this has been on my mind constantly, and I did not know why, so I prayed earnestly about it, and the response I got, is that it was His will that you two be together, so that is why I asked you the question to see if your answer was in alignment with the answer I got."

They agreed that it was meant to be, so they just had to wait on God for his leadership.

Following service on Sunday, Junie invited the group to have lunch with him.

They followed him for about fourteen miles to 6th street and Lagoon, which was on the other side of town, because right at that intersection, was the restaurant where they had their first lunch date.

"Hi Doc, "Brittany greeted him, "it has been a long time since you have been here, and this young lady, didn't I see you here before? It has been a while, but your face still hasn't changed, still pretty."

"Yes, you probably did, but it has been a long time since we came by." Junie said.

"Come, I will personally walk you to your table, Doc, you have always been a good customer."

"An owner like you leaves no choice, but to be a good customer." Junie replied.

After having their appetizer placed on the table, they proceeded in placing their orders for their main course.

After which Junie excused himself and went to the restroom.

Then he sneaked into the kitchen area, and spoke to the waitress who took their orders, and assigned to their table.

He gave her an elegant engagement ring and asked her to place it on Cindy's plate, but to make sure that it was hidden that it would not be noticed instantly but placed where she would recognize it when she started eating.

He then went back to his seat and waited for the food.

"Are you okay, Doc? The ladies almost sent me to see what was going on with you in there, they wanted to make sure that you were not kidnapped or had abandoned us and made it out through the backdoor."

"Funny, you are a funny family. I had to check all my pennies, to make sure there were enough to pay the bill, especially after that big meal I saw Cindy order.

"Hahaha, you've got jokes, my meal was the least expensive of the bunch," Cindy joked.

Not too long after this exchange, the waitress came with Donald and Karen's food, shortly followed by Johanna and Nicole's, and lastly, she brought Junie and Cindy's.

Karen said grace, and they began immediately to eat, like they were starving.

A few moments after they started eating, Cindy uncovered the small container which was supposed to contain the sauce for her steak; when she gasped, she said, "Oh my gosh."

Then everyone paid attention to her. In this little container, was a sparkling heavy carat diamond ring.

Immediately, Dr. King came and knelt before her on one knee, and said gently, "Cindy, my dear, would you spend the rest of your life with me? Will you marry me?"

Cindy sat there bewildered, for a moment then stood up and shouted "yes, yes, yes."

Junie flew up from his knee, and embraced and kissed her, and said "thank you, Jesus."

Everyone stop eating, because they were so excited and they congratulated Junie and Cindy.

Also joining the celebration were Brittany, and Susan the waitress.

They presented the newly engaged couple with a special bottle of wine, compliments of the restaurant crew.

They asked that their food be place into takeaway containers, Junie paid the bill, and then thanked Brittany and her staff for their excellence service.

When they made it outside to the parking lot, Junie said, "Cindy Is riding with me, for I have made plans, in case she said yes, and since she did, my plans stand. If she had said no, I would have been devastated, but I would have allowed her to go home with you all.

"See you a little bit later."

"Be careful and enjoy your planned activities." Karen cautioned.

Marcus' team was in Dallas, and was scheduled to play at 8:30 pm. He called Cindy and told her he would swing by the next morning to visit her before he made it back to Florida.

Cindy was looking forward to his visit, she requested the day off from work, so she could spend some time with him.

She was so surprised, when Junie told her he was taking her to the house, so she could get ready, for an overnight trip.

They got all the things that they would need for the trip and drove to the airport.

The flight was a short one, and Cindy did not realize what was going on until they landed in Dallas, then she started to connect the dots.

They checked into the hotel which was a few minutes from the basketball arena.

They made it to the game early enough, where they surprised Marcus before he started to warm up.

"Mom," he said, "what are you doing here? I did not know you were coming?" he said in disbelief, "but I am so happy to see you."

Then he greeted Dr. King whom he loves and respected very much.

Cindy grabbed his hands in such a manner, that her bling would be noticed by him.

"Wow," he said, you got engaged? When did this happened?"

"A few hours ago, Junie surprised me and brought me here to see you play."

Marcus hugged Junie, and said, "thank you, sir, for caring for my mom, and being there for her. I will never forget your goodness towards her."

Cindy called Johanna and told her that they were in Dallas at Marcus' game and would spend the night in Dallas, and would be home in the morning.

Marcus had a great game, he performed well, and his team won the game.

After the game, they spoke for a while, then went to dinner.

Following that Marcus went to his hotel and Junie and Cindy did likewise.

Cindy was not worried about being alone in a hotel room with Junie, because she knew what kind of person he was, and would respect her wishes.

Junie sat next to Cindy on the bed, and said, "I never thought this day would have been possible, after we both moved with our lives, and had families of our own, that I would have been given another chance to be with you. Now you are going to be my wife, God is good. He works in miraculous ways."

"I have not stopped blaming myself, for not telling you sooner how I felt, that episode ate me up immensely, that is, until I came across Mark, which helped me to move on, but I always cared about you, and was happy when you got married to your lovely wife, and you were blessed with a wonderful daughter. I knew then that we were both happy, and nothing else needed to be done, but to cherish our great friendship.

"After Jessica died in that terrible auto accident, I went into a dark place, I did not want to see or talk to anybody, but you, but I could not, because you had shut me out."

"I am sorry that I did that, you know what I was going through, which was not a good excuse, for not being there for a friend, although if you had let Johanna know what happened, I would have reached out to you."

"I am so thankful for my daughter Rachel, who helped me heal from the pain of the tragedy, and by the way, she gave her blessing to our relationship."

"Give her my love next time you speak to her; I would like to meet her soon."

"I am so happy that Johanna called me, and informed me of your situation, I was very sad and concerned about your condition, but I was happy to reconnect with you, and told myself, if you made it through, I would never leave your side again.

When I came to the hospital and saw your condition, and read the doctor's report, and when I spoke to the doctor, I knew that it would take a miracle to bring you back to life, and back to me, but I did not give up hope, because I knew, if anyone could bring you back, it would be God, so I prayed nonstop, and I thank him for making you well again, even when there was no sign of that being a reality."

"I am glad that you prayed," Cindy said, "because I know without a doubt, prayer works. I prayed in my own way before I slipped into that place, and God did not look at me, and my rambling, but demonstrated His love, and saved me from death."

"After I saw signs, that God was answering my prayers, along with others, I stuck to your side, I wanted to be there when you opened your eyes, which I believed you would, and look into your eyes, and let you know that I would be there for you."

"And now that we are here, it is a testament to your faith, and trust in God, believing that I would wake up from this calamity, and be made completely well again. I am grateful to have a person like you in my life.

I love you, Junie, and I am praying we will be together forever."

"My dear Cindy, you can count on that, I plan to be at your side, no matter what, I want to give you joy and want to make you happy like never before."

They stayed up a little bit longer, before they called it a night, and went to sleep.

Their flight back to Houston was just a few minutes apart from Marcus, so they landed in Houston at almost the same time.

They picked up their vehicle and Junie dropped off Cindy and Marcus, then continued to his place.

Marcus spent a few hours with his mom and sister Nicole, he remained low key, because he did not want the public to know that he was there, because he did not want them storming his mom's place. He went and checked on his grandma before he left for Florida.

Chapter ONE HUNDRED-FIFTEEN

JUNIE AND CINDY CHOSE June 15th for their wedding, and they were busy planning for that date. They planned to have an average size wedding of about 50 guests, which would be mostly family, and friends. After they had reviewed and organized their guest list, they settled on 65 people in all.

Because of their busy schedule, they turned over the planning to a wedding planner and asked Johanna to be an overseer of the entire process.

One of the most anticipated weeks of their lives had finally arrived, and Junie and Cindy were beyond excited, but also nervous.

Katy and Liz came in early in the week, so they could support and help Cindy through this special occasion.

It was a hectic Saturday morning for Junie and Cindy; they were busy making sure that all things were in place for the wedding ceremony and reception.

The ceremony started on time and proceeded according to the agenda.

Pastor Steve made sure that everything went according to plan.

He performed his part up to the vows and asked the couple to say their vows to each other because that is what they wanted.

"Cindy my love, our lives as one begin today, and I promise you, as of today, I am going to love you more than I ever did before, I will love you as I love myself, and will forever be by your side, through it all, whether it be laughter, or sadness, great health or sickness, whatever the situation, I will be there. What I am saying is that you are stuck with me, until death do us part.

You are not only beautiful on the outside, but you are honestly an angel inside, you are so selfless, that is why you attract so many around you. I love you so much Cindy."

"Junie, I am so fortunate and blessed to have such a Godly man like you to be my companion for the rest of my life, I am so thankful to the Lord, that he allowed us to reconnect, and to have this forever love for each other. I will be at your side, a strong support to lift you up whenever you need lifting, or someone to lean on. I love you from the depths of my heart, and I promise to love you, until death, do us part."

"Such great vows," said Pastor, "and I have prayed that these vows will be kept."

He continued with the remainder of the ceremony, and everything went flawless, then he came to the proclamation, and said, "upon the power invested in me by the State of Texas, I now pronounce you, Kevin Junior King, and Samantha Cindy Gregaben, husband and wife, you may kiss your bride."

A burst of laughter erupted in the church, as Junie embraced Cindy, and kissed her, and would not stop, until the Pastor joked, "I have another assignment."

The ceremony ended, and they were now officially husband and wife, they gathered outside with the bridal party, and took pictures, and the family and friends gave their blessings and showered them with congratulatory messages and best wishes.

They left for the reception hall, where there were a few people who had not made it to the church.

The master of ceremonies, James had the party swinging; he had everything under control.

The food was excellent and there was a wide variety of drinks.

Their first dance together as a married couple was spectacular.

"Wow, you surprise me I did not expect you to be such a good dancer, you are very light on your feet, and the moves, it looks like you have been practicing," Cindy remarked.

"My dear, this is natural, I was born with dancing feet, and this is just one of the many splendid surprises you will encounter."

"I can hardly wait," Cindy jokingly replied.

After a couple hours of mingling and having fun with family and friends, the couple said goodbye, and exited the location and to the hotel on the Westheimer Parkway, where they would be spending the night.

In their hotel room, Junie said to Cindy, "I never thought in my wildest dreams, after all had fallen apart after we met, that this day and night would have been possible, but let me tell you dear, that I am so thankful that it is a reality, and not a dream.'

"To be honest, Junie, I had made up my mind, that I would not be a wife anymore in my life. I had the best man and the worst man in my life. The latter left such a bitter taste in my mouth, that I concluded, never to marry again."

"Then here comes Junie, my knight in shining armor, you are impossible to resist.

"And here I am secure in your strong loving arms."

After a night of fun, and knowing each other for the first time, the two lovers went to bed, because they were to fly out Sunday evening to Italy, for a week and a half, for their honeymoon.

After church service, Donald and Karen went to Cindy's house to spend time with them and to drive them to the airport.

The flight from Houston to Italy took almost 12 hours, which during that time they slept for about 10 hours.

The hotel that they booked, was about 5 minutes from Peretola airport, so they had a short ride to the hotel.

They were tired from jet lag, and their bodies had to adjust to the time difference, so because of these factors, they rested and slept most of the day.

In the nighttime, they went one block from the hotel to a popular restaurant to have dinner and made it back to the hotel about 9:30 pm.

Before they left Houston, they set a clause to their honeymoon vacation, "no hold back nights", and Junie was set on keeping this clause, and to extract every bit of honey that was in that comb.

In the daytime, they visited different attractions, such as Bardini Gardens, the Leaning tower of Pisa Cirque Terre, and some others.

Nighttime, as mentioned before, was set aside for their passionate time.

During their stay in Italy, they also visited Venice, and were very impressed with the city.

They also took some time to visit Rome, the Vatican, and other historical sites.

They had a great honeymoon and enjoyed their stay in Italy.

They made it back to Houston on Wednesday morning, and just like they did in Italy, they rested on their return to Houston.

Junie decided to spend the last weekend with Cindy at the house, because they had decided that she would move into Junie's house.

Cindy was hesitant at first, because she did not want to be in that influential neighborhood, but after having a reasonable discussion, she gave in, and agreed to move to Junie's house, which was now her house too.

Cindy and Junie agreed to let Johanna stay in Cindy's house, which was paid off.

Johanna had met, and was in a relationship with a fire fighter, that she met at the gym.

Johanna promised to take care of the house and showered the couple with her gratitude.

Nicole did not want to change her school, since she only had as short time left before graduation, and did not want to leave her friends. She wanted to stay with Johanna, but Cindy did not go for that, and told her, "Honey, life moves forward, never backward, love the true friends that you already have, but look forward to make new friends, who knows to what height they could get you to go? And you might be a blessing to some of them."

Cindy's words got through to Nicole, and she agreed to change school.

It was an emotional last weekend for Cindy at her house. It was not easy turning it over to Johanna, and moving to Junie's, but she knew, that this was something she had to do.

Chapter ONE HUNDRED-SIXTEEN

SUNDAY NIGHT, ABOUT 8:PM, Junie and Cindy arrived at Junie's residence for the first time as a wedded couple, they were going to live together for the first time, unlike her previous marriages, where she lived with her prospective husbands, before being married.

As soon as they got in, Junie took Cindy's hand, and led her to the study, and asked that they kneel together, and said, "we are going to start this process of living together as one, with the ultimate blessing of God.

Then he began to pray.

He thanked God first for them being in the best of health and thanked Him for the wonders He did in Cindy's full recovery.

He asked God to give them wisdom, as they were about to embark on a new journey together.

"Lord," he said, "I haven't the slightest clue what is going to happen tomorrow, but I am positive that you know, what I am asking is that you lead us as a couple into the future, to love and to embrace each other, and to make each other better, as an individual, and to make us better as a couple.

Father, we both went through a past that we both eager to move on from, we are two broken, people, but we know who you are, and we can't wait to see what you will do to these broken lives, as you put the pieces back together, to reflect who you are.

Take our hearts, and hands, and lead us unto the right path, for your name's sake, be our shepherd, and lead us wherever it pleases you, in Jesus Precious, and Holy name, we pray, Amen."

And Cindy said, "Amen", and JITA.

"JITA?" what is that?" Junie asked.

Cindy smiled, and said graciously,

J, Jesus

I, Is

T The

A, Answer

Junie laughed and said "Amen."

As time went by, the two of them continued to grow more and more in love, and stayed true to God, and flourished in their relationship.

ABOUT THE AUTHOR

Osmond Constance lived in Dominica and the US Virgin Islands, now lives in Houston, Texas, with his wife, daughter and Leyla the cute family dog.

BOOKS BY OSMOND CONSTANCE
The Verdict
God Simple Poems to You
The Storm That Formed the Human Rainbow

Lightning Source UK Ltd.
Milton Keynes UK
UKHW020813121222
413794UK00015B/808